Out of Nippon

"*Stay*, Nikki," Toshikazu laughed. His face was twisted in a smile of joy, almost feral in its intensity. His white poplin jacket—soaked in blood—was wrapped round his left hand. "Stay with me," he repeated. "*Die* with me." His teeth were red with blood.

Horror convulsed her stomach. She shied back from him. For the first time she saw where she was. Not the narrow alleyways of Shinjuku as she'd expected. They were in the halls of the Nagara Building's executive floors. Soft carpet was underfoot, and the walls were hung with expensive works of art, but piles of garbage filled the corners. In the shifting half-light, she saw the red eyes of a rat watching her.

"*Die* with me, Nikki."

Torg
The Possibility Wars

The Near Now ... Later today, early tomorrow, sometime next week, the world began to end.

They came from other realities, raiders joined together to steal the awesome energy of Earth's possibilities. They have brought with them their own realities, creating areas where rules of nature are radically different — turning huge portions of the Earth into *someplace else*.

At first it seemed that Japan, the Land of the Rising Sun, was unaffected. The borders of the island nation were surrounded by dark clouds and stormy weather, but, otherwise, the country seemed the same.

But it soon became apparent to those who could see that something was *wrong* in Nippon. Powerful megacorporations grew into existence almost overnight, and they absorbed much of corporate Japan. New technological breakthroughs happened frequently, but the spiritual side of Japan, its heart and soul, was shrinking.

But standing between Japan, and Earth, and total victory for the evil *High Lords*™ are the *Storm Knights*™, men and women who have weathered the raging storms of change and continue to fight off the invaders.

TORG

The Possibility Wars™

created by Greg Gorden and Bill Slavicsek

Out of Nippon

by Nigel Findley

WEST
END
BOOKS®

OUT OF NIPPON
A West End Games Book/September 1992

All Rights Reserved.
Copyright © 1992 by West End Games.

First Printing: September, 1992.
Printed in the United States of America.

0 9 8 7 6 5 4 3 2 1

Library of Congress Catalog Card Number: 92-81085
ISBN: 0-87431-345-7

Cover Art by John Paul Genzo

Graphic Design by Stephen Crane

Edited by Ed Stark

West End Games
RR 3 Box 2345
Honesdale, PA 18431

Chapter One

Night in downtown Tokyo was a surrealistic vision, Nikki Carlson thought for the thousandth time. The tall corporate headquarters buildings that surrounded her were ziggurats of light reaching into the sky, impressionistic sculptures created by artists who used glowing gems as their medium. Anti-collision lights on V/STOL jump-jets threaded their ways between the buildings, or drifted above them, like harsh and brilliant stars that had taken to wandering free of the firmament. And below, the wide streets of the Marunouchi district were rivers of light, even this late at night; Tokyo seemed to be a city that never really slept.

In crystal-clear air, the view would have been magical enough. But the night *wasn't* clear. Tokyo, and the whole of Japan, or so she'd heard, was covered by a thin mist that never really cleared. Meteorologists on NHK, the national broadcasting system, described the mist as a "minor climatic aberration," no doubt caused by the upheavals that were occurring elsewhere in the world. Nikki wasn't sure that she quite believed that.

She *thought* that the mists had first cloaked Tokyo *before* the face of the world had started to change, but she wasn't certain.

She shrugged. It didn't really matter. The mist was here, and it made the night *more* than magical. The closer or brighter lights flared into rainbow-hued halos, while those in the middle distance were softened and diffused. What was even more beautiful, Nikki thought, was the way the mist seemed to pick up the lights of the city until the air itself glowed, shading to a shimmering mother-of-pearl hue directly above. It was like being in a water-color painted by a master.

Nikki rested her forehead against the cool glass of the window and looked down. From here, on the tenth floor, the mist made it difficult to make out individual cars as they cruised down Etai-dori, the street on which this building was situated. Further down Etai-dori was the glass monolith that was the Kanawa Corporation building, two hundred and fifty meters high, sixty-plus stories, the great steel K mounted on its sharply-sloping roof facing the open sky. The Kanawa edifice dwarfed the buildings around it, just the way that Kanawa Corporation dwarfed the corporations those buildings represented.

In a country that sometimes seemed to be run by the large corporations, Kanawa was the premier *megacorporation*. Nikki remembered seeing a program on NHK that itemized some of the major organizations directly owned by Kanawa. In some ways, the size of the list, and what it implied about the pervasiveness of Kanawa's influence, was frightening. Back in the States, people had often joked about corporations like General Foods indirectly owning everything that was worth owning ... or, at least, they had joked about that before the upheavals, what the Japanese oh-so-politely called Kawaru, "the Change." Here in Japan the jokes about global ownership weren't funny.

One of the few companies that Kanawa *didn't* own seemed to be the one that Nikki worked for, Nagara Corporation. An incredibly successful research company, Nagara apparently had sufficient financial clout, and sufficient investor confidence on the Nikkei Stock Market, to fight off not one but two hostile takeover attempts by an outfit that was generally suspected to be a front for Kanawa. The independence of Nagara, particularly when threatened by an opponent the size of Kanawa, gave Nikki a strong sense of pride.

Which was amusing, she had to admit. Nagara was in no way "her" company, and she had little enough reason to feel any loyalty toward it. She was far removed from the rarified heights of the corporate pyramid where such matters were conducted, almost as far as the cooks and others who usually worked in the cafeteria where she now stood. Further, she wasn't even fully accepted by the people with whom she worked on a daily basis. *After all*, she thought wryly, *how could I be?* Nikki Carlson was an American and a woman, two strikes against her in xenophobic and chauvinistic Japan.

Despite that, though, she *did* enjoy working for Nagara. When she'd arrived in Japan, newly graduated from Berkeley with a degree in genetics, her intention had been to find work that would support her at a basic level for five or six months while she learned something about the country. After half a year or so of working, she'd planned to spend whatever money she'd saved to travel around Japan, and maybe elsewhere in Asia. Then she'd intended to return to America and decide whether to enroll in graduate school or try her luck in the work force with only a Bachelor of Science degree.

But things never work out the way you think they will, do they? Nikki mused. She'd hoped to get a job teaching English, a thriving business in Tokyo. Or maybe she'd be lucky enough to track down some modelling jobs. (After all, she was tall and blonde, with bright blue eyes, which made her very "marketable" in the modelling industry. Despite the anti-Western bias shown by Japanese culture, there was a great demand for people with a "stereotypical" Western appearance in the print and TV advertizing industry.) Nikki hadn't come to Japan seeking a career, so a big income wasn't an issue. All she wanted was enough to live on, with hopefully some savings left over for travel.

It was sheer luck, "Fate," her mother would have called it, that Nikki was practicing her Japanese by reading the *Tokyo Shimbun* newspaper as she ate a frugal dinner in a little back-alley *yakitori* bar. The ad was in the "Careers" section, which Nikki didn't usually bother to read, and she'd certainly have skimmed over it if it hadn't been written in both Japanese and English.

A research company called Nagara Corporation was looking for lab technicians, the ad had stated. Requirements included a bachelor's degree in biochemistry, genetics, or a related discipline, and hands-on experience with automated genetic analysis equipment. Nikki read the ad with amazement: it could almost have been written specifically for her. Her personal experience with genetic analyzers wasn't extensive. But the latest generation of the computerized machines had just come onto the market, the lab in which she'd worked at Berkeley had been the "beta test" site for one such product, so there wouldn't be many people with *more* experience, or so she figured.

Nikki had thought through her options as she'd finished off her glass of *Sapporo* beer. As she'd found out over the past week, the demand for English teachers wasn't anywhere near as great as she'd expected. And, while there *was* a demand for models, she'd come to realize it would take time to make the contacts she'd need to break into that industry. Money was becoming an issue, which meant that she couldn't afford that time. She had to find a job *soon*. She could probably have found work as a cocktail waitress, she'd figured, making barely enough money to live on and spending much of her time avoiding the wandering hands of drunk Japanese *sararimen* ... But here was something in her own specialty; this was the kind of job she'd been thinking of applying for when she eventually returned to the States. She'd be crazy if she didn't apply for it, no matter how unlikely it was that she'd get it.

She'd checked the address on the ad. The normal procedure would have been to send in her resume and wait for them to contact her. But what the hell? Her trip to Japan was supposed to be a learning experience, wasn't it? And applying for a job in person, without even a letter or a phone call first, something she'd never have had the courage to do at home, was certainly that ...

The address had turned out to be the Nagara Building, a forty-story block in the Marunouchi district, only a couple of blocks from the Marunouchi Central Station. Although definitely a large building in its own right, the bronze-glass tower had seemed to fade almost into insignificance in comparison to the Kanawa monolith two blocks away, half as tall again as the structure in front of which Nikki had stood. The Nagara logo, a representation of an origami crane, surrounded by a circle of stars, had been inlaid into the marble lobby floor in what looked like gold, she recalled.

Afterward, Nikki found herself unable to remember any real details of the interview process. There were vague recollections of a series of managers, all male, all Japanese, asking her questions about her background, her experience, her goals, even her hobbies and interests. And then she remembered being led through gleamingly clean labs, where white-coated technicians were working with computerized analysis equipment that made the "cutting edge" gear she'd used at Berkeley look like it belonged in a museum. Finally, she remembered meeting a hard-faced man in his late thirties, whose name she hadn't caught at the time, who offered her a firm handshake and brusquely welcomed her to the Genetic Research Division of Nagara Corporation. It was only later that she'd learned the man was Agatamori Eichiro, Eichiro-san, the senior manager in charge of the division for which she now worked.

Nikki moved back from the window with a smile. Nagara was a pretty damn good place to work, it had turned out. There was no doubt that the company did much more than the vast majority of American companies to take care of their employees. Housing, security, sometimes even cradle-to-grave medical coverage …

And amenities like this cafeteria, she added mentally, looking around her. She well knew that the price of food in Japan had been rising steeply over the last couple of years, in large part due to the takeover of agricultural land by the corporations. The cost of rice had almost doubled in the three years since Nikki had arrived in Japan, and when you looked at what it cost to buy a good steak … No wonder the *burakumin*, the poor and homeless, like the ones who managed (somehow) to subsist in the middle of the city, were finding it ever harder to eke out an existence.

The cost of food wasn't much of an issue for those lucky enough to work for Nagara and other corporations like it, though. The *sararimen*, and sarari*women*, she carefully appended, employed by Nagara could eat at this cafeteria and others like it, and buy much of the food they needed for their families from stores at special "corporate rates." The price of food, here and in the "approved" stores, was kept artificially low for Nagara employees. *Ridiculously* low: Nikki could buy a steak sandwich in the cafeteria for 680¥, or a little under five dollars at the current rate of exchange, while in the restaurants of Marunouchi it would have cost her almost *five times* that sum. Japanese-style food, *yakitori*, perhaps, or *bento* box lunches, cost even less. (*Predictable*, Nikki thought. Western visitors to Japan quickly found that they paid a very solid premium for trying to emulate the lifestyle they had at home.) Understandably, Nikki cooked many of her meals with food purchased under the "corporate plan" and ate most of the rest at the cafeteria. She was so much of a regular, and always made a point to be polite to the serving staff, that she thought she'd started to see a thawing in their icy impassiveness.

Even the location of the cafeteria reflected the attention the corporation paid to its employees. In just about any American facility, the employee cafeteria would have been in the basement, or maybe in a lowly outbuilding, while the higher floors of the office block would be reserved for *important* things like managers' offices. Here? The cafeteria was in one corner of the tenth floor, with two entire walls made up of windows, and high enough to provide an excellent view. It was an interesting choice, and a good one, Nikki thought. The cafeteria gave all the *shaikujin*, the devoted employees, a wonderful view of the heart of Tokyo, and the sense that they were part of something very great and very important. It told them that they held a significant place in the cosmos that was Japan.

The cafeteria was closed now, of course. Like most of the corporate skyscrapers around it, the Nagara headquarters worked on a semi-official day of seven in the morning to five or six in the evening. Enough employees worked late frequently enough to warrant running dinner service until nine at night. After that, all but the most dedicated sararimen were on their way home, or maybe boozing it up at the *Tengu*, a chain of restaurants and bars that had a franchise location only two hundred meters from the Nagara building. By twelve-thirty, Nikki checked her watch; *Twelve-forty-five*, she corrected herself — the place was always deserted.

Almost deserted. That was the one thing she could take "issue" with about her work. She simply *loved* her job. (How often had she heard that statement, spoken in a sarcastic tone? But in her case it was true.) She'd quickly realized she had a knack for using the some-times-temperamental automated analyzers; she often thought it was almost as if they "understood" each other, she and the machines. Because of the two strikes already against her — female and *gaijin* (foreigner) — it had taken her supervisors some time to recognize this. But when they did — thanks, in fact, to Nikki pulling her direct boss's fat out of a really big fire of his own creation — she had to admit that they moved fast. More than a few noses were put out of joint when she was transferred to another department within the Genetic Research Division, and put in charge of a workgroup — designated Group Five — that included people who had considerably more formal training and seniority than she. In most cases, she smoothed the ruffled feathers not through any feats of diplomacy, but simply by being good, damn good, at what she did. *And*, she told herself, *that's one thing that everyone here recognizes and admires:* competence.

So in most areas, her job was as close to perfect as she could imagine. The only sore point was the hours. It wasn't that her bosses were slavedrivers, keeping her here until well after midnight. No, it was only the laws of physics and chemistry that were dictatorial. (*And who do I appeal those to?* she wondered with a grin.) There were certain chemical processes used in genetic analysis that simply took one hell of a long time. Even though they didn't always have to be "baby-sat" from start to finish, there *did* have to be people around at initiation and completion ... whenever completion might happen to be. And Nikki was a good enough workgroup leader to know not to ask her colleagues to do something she wouldn't do herself. What this meant was that, all to often, Nikki found herself in her basement lab either hours before most people would be waking up, or hours after most had left for the day.

"No, no, no, how many times do I have to tell you? The breakfast line-up doesn't start for another five hours."

With a broad smile, Nikki turned at the amused voice behind her. "Breakfast?" she asked in mock surprise. "You mean I'm late for dinner?"

The young Japanese man who faced her shook his head in feigned disgust. "*Gaijin*," he sighed. "When will you become civilized, Carrson-*san*?" Nikki chuckled at the way he mispronounced her name, aping the difficulty which many of her colleagues had, or pretended to have, with the R-L combination. "I thought I'd find you here," he added.

Nikki nodded. "I like it here, Toshikazu. It's a good place to think."

"Yes," Toshikazu Kasigi agreed. (Strictly speaking, his name was Kasigi Toshikazu, in Japan, the family name came first. But, as a matter of convenience, most Japanese put their given name first, in the Western fashion.) "No interruptions ..." Toshikazu grinned wryly, "... *most* of the time."

"The sequences are ready?" It was Nikki's turn to sigh. "Ah, well, no rest for the wicked."

Nikki looked Toshikazu over as she followed him out of the cafeteria toward the elevators. He wasn't tall, he stood an inch or two shorter than Nikki's five-foot-nine, but there was something about his slender, well-proportioned build that made her feel he was taller. He was about Nikki's age, about twenty-four, she thought, with a smooth, unlined face that seemed to settle naturally into a wry smile, and dark eyes that flashed with humor. (Nikki remembered with scorn the Westerners who'd told her that all Japanese look alike. *Idiots.* Although the differences might show up in different features, Japanese faces were as distinct as American faces ... to anyone who made the effort to actually *look*.) He moved easily, gracefully, almost, with an economy of effort that made her wonder whether he practiced any of the martial arts in his spare time.

She knew next to nothing about Toshikazu's life outside work, she realized. She knew a lot about *him*, his hopes and fears, his attitudes about science, and about the social problems facing his country, that kind of thing, but, she was somewhat surprised to note, he'd never talked about his day-to-day life. Where did he live? Was he married? (She didn't think so; no ring.) What did he do with his time? She found it intensely interesting that she knew so little, and, honestly, didn't really *worry* that she knew so little, about a close friend.

Because Toshikazu *was* a friend, by far her closest friend in Japan, perhaps her *only* one, she admitted a little uncomfortably, and had become one of the brightest parts of her job. A geneticist by training, like her, he had a much better grasp of the actual biochemistry behind what they were doing, and was much more familiar than she was with the theoretical breakthroughs on which the automated analyzers were based. When she'd realized this, she'd felt acutely uncomfortable. But for his part, Toshikazu seemed to have no qualms over being in a workgroup led by someone who was his academic inferior. (When she'd eventually broached the subject with him, he'd just shrugged and said, "I've read the books. But all the books in the world aren't going to give me the rapport with the machines that you have." She'd never raised the topic again.)

Apart from Nikki and Toshikazu, the other members of Group Five were in their forties and fifties — all males, technicians who'd risen as far as their talents would take them, and had been forced to face the fact that they'd never hold positions more senior than those they currently had. The age difference added the third strike against Nikki as far as they were concerned. How could they respect a female *gaijin* who was fifteen or more years their junior? The fact that they were the only two close in age brought Nikki and Toshikazu even closer.

She hadn't completely realized that there was a friendship building up until she'd noticed how often Toshikazu was "coincidentally" turning out to have the duty when she was staying particularly late. Since that time, they'd frequently talked over coffee or meals, and shared jokes around the lab — the butts of which were often the other humorless members of the workgroup.

I bet they think we're lovers, Toshikazu and I, Nikki thought with a smile. She was sure the same thought had occurred to Toshikazu. On occasion, he'd made some double entendre remarks that were guaranteed to get the others thinking. *Prying minds want to know. Let them wonder*.

As it was, they were only friends. Not that Nikki hadn't wondered about the possibilities of the alternative. She just wasn't comfortable initiating something that might eventually break up their friendship and their work relationship. *Ah, well*, she told herself, *if it's supposed to happen it'll happen*.

The call light next to the elevator came on as she and Toshikazu came within a yard of the door. Something to do with the identification badges all Nagara employees had to wear, she figured. The badge was about the same size and thickness as a credit card, with a three-dimensional holographic photograph of the wearer — *a neat trick, that*, she thought. It wouldn't be too hard to build a tiny microchip into the card, she figured, designed to broadcast the wearer's identity to sensors in the area. The only time she knew it actually did something was when it automatically called the elevator — convenient sometimes, particularly when her arms were full, but hardly worth the effort and cost of setting up the system. Presumably it must have some security function, like opening certain doors only for authorized personnel, but it never affected her day-to-day life one way or another. Putting it on her lapel before she entered the building in the morning was just one more ingrained ritual.

As they waited for the elevator to arrive, Nikki heard a footfall on the polished floor behind her. She turned quickly.

It was one of the corporate security guards. A big man, wearing semi-rigid body armor, in the blue-trimmed white color scheme of Nagara, with the symbol of the *origami* crane on the shoulders. The surface of the armor was shaped into the contours of over-developed muscles — in much the same way that Roman-style leather breastplates were, Nikki recalled — adding considerably to the guard's intimidating presence. His mirror-finished helmet visor was down, totally concealing his features. When Nikki looked into his face, all she could see was a curved and distorted reflection of herself and Toshikazu.

On impulse, Nikki flashed him a smile. No response, none at all. *Might as well smile at a statue*, she thought. Or one of the security robots she sometimes saw cruising the basement hallways late at night. The guard watched them impassively, his hand resting near the large pistol on his hip, until they'd stepped into the elevator and the door had closed behind her.

"I don't even think they're human," Nikki muttered as the elevator started down. "Why do we need them

anyway? They just scare the hell out of people."
Toshikazu shrugged. "It's not like Nagara's a bank,"
she went on, "there's nothing here to steal."

"I suppose the people at Tomita Technologies
thought the same thing," he said quietly, naming a
company that Nikki remembered from the news.
Tomita was a small electronics company based in the
Akihabara district of Tokyo. During a weekday evening,
a week or so ago, unidentified gunmen had broken
into the Tomita facilities. They'd ranged freely through
the building, killing anyone who got in their way, and
stealing the back-up tapes from the company's mainframe computer, before planting enough explosives to
blow the computer system into shrapnel.

Tomita Technologies effectively ceased to exist. The
best of the company's engineers and designers were
hired away by Zamftech Computers, while the rest
drifted away to other employers. The owner and CEO
of the company, Ryuki Tomita, had been found dead in
his home two days ago. (He'd committed suicide in the
traditional manner, Nikki recalled with a shudder.
Seppuku: he'd sliced his belly open with a large knife.)
The official conclusion by the police was that the attack
had been the action of "wreckers," according to Tokyo
urban folklore, vandals dedicated to the destruction of
the happy and productive Japanese corporate way of
life, and hence the ultimate traitors to society.

"Are you expecting wreckers here?" Nikki asked
sarcastically.

Toshikazu snorted his derision. "Wreckers. *Garbage*."

Nikki nodded in agreement. It was obvious to both
of them that the people who'd attacked Tomita Technologies had something more on their minds than just
interfering with the Japanese way of life. (*Maybe
Zamftech Computers had something to do with it*, Nikki
had speculated at the time. *They were the ones to gain
most by it.*) There was no doubt about it: neither she nor

Toshikazu believed in wreckers.

But most people did, she knew — or *pretended* to believe. The corporations and even the government pushed the "wreckers" story hard. *And why not?* she asked herself. *Wreckers are a convenient fiction.*

It was good to have Toshikazu to talk to about things like this, she realized. Everybody else in Group Five — in fact, everyone else she ever talked to — seemed to fully accept the "party line." Only Toshikazu seemed interested in making the effort to think things through for himself. She poked him gently in the ribs. "Are you sure you're from around here?" she asked with a smile.

He chuckled. "I'm that obvious, am I?" Then he grew serious. "Maybe I should be careful about that," he added quietly. "We have an old proverb in Japan, 'The nail that sticks up gets hammered down.'"

* * *

In atmosphere, the lab that Nikki called "hers" was effectively the direct opposite of the cafeteria. Buried in the Nagara building's first sub-basement level, out of necessity it had no windows. Its walls and its low ceiling were the spotless white of an operating room, intensifying the almost-painful glare of the overhead lights. The temperature was decidedly chilly — about 14° C, or 57° F — and the humidity was kept so close to zero that when she'd started working here Nikki had been plagued by nosebleeds. She knew well why temperature and humidity were important — some of the automated analyzers were as sensitive to environmental conditions as old-style mainframe computers — but the uncomfortably cold and dry air constantly communicated the idea that the "comfort" of the machines was more vital than her own comfort. Well, there was nothing she could do about it except wear warmer clothes.

The lab looked like a cross between a computer room and a chemistry lab. One half of the large room was taken up with marble-topped workbenches, all of them covered with an array of tangled tubes, flasks and retorts that might have been constructed by a mad glassblower. The other half was devoted to the analyzers: two rows of spotless white machines about the size of refrigerators laid down on their sides. The polished metal cases were totally featureless. The sockets into which technicians inserted the small glass vials containing the samples to be analyzed were concealed by access ports, and all the machines were controlled and monitored remotely, using a single control terminal that looked like a standard office microcomputer.

As soon as they'd returned from the cafeteria, Toshikazu had settled himself down in front of the control terminal and begun tapping away on the keyboard. Now he leaned back and stretched luxuriously. "Okay," he said, "that's got it." He hit a final key, and the screen filled with a complex graph.

Nikki leaned over his shoulder for a closer look. She reached out and touched a particularly high peak on the graph. "That's the lysine peak, right?" she asked. Toshikazu nodded. "Then what's *that*?" She indicated another peak, next to the first and almost as high.

He shrugged. "It's not lysine," he pointed out. "Not quite."

Nikki straightened up, rubbing her eyes. Her head felt like it was stuffed with cotton wool. *Too many late nights*, she told herself. "So this protein isn't going to do the job?" she asked.

"Not a chance," Toshikazu replied firmly. "There's enough of this almost-lysine that it's just not going to fold right."

Nikki nodded. That sounded as though it made sense. Lysine was an amino acid, one of the major "building blocks" of proteins and enzymes, complex substances that all living cells used to control the vital chemical reactions that kept them alive. When the amino acids that made up the protein were strung together in the right order, attractions and repulsions between the individual molecules would cause the protein to fold up on itself in a very specific way, forming a particular three-dimensional shape that was characteristic of the specific protein involved. This three-dimensional shape had a great deal to do with the chemical activity of the protein. A protein that wasn't the right shape simply wouldn't do what it was supposed to do.

And this protein that they'd been analyzing had something wrong with it. In many places along its length, where there should have been a molecule of lysine, there was something else, a molecule that was something like lysine but, as Toshikazu said, not quite. Since this almost-lysine had different chemical properties, it wouldn't exhibit quite the same attractions and repulsions as real lysine. Which meant that the protein wouldn't fold up on itself exactly the right way, and would form a different three-dimensional shape. Which, in turn, meant that this protein wouldn't work the way it was supposed to. Nikki guessed that any cell depending on this abnormal version of the protein simply wouldn't be able to function and would die.

Nikki felt Toshikazu's eyes on her, and shook herself free of her thoughts. *He's better at the theoretical side than I am*, she reminded herself. *He'll have already figured this out.* "So it's non-functional?"

"Totally." Toshikazu grinned. "The guys next door have blown it again."

The guys next door. That was *another* thing that bothered Nikki a little about her job, she had to admit. "Next door" was the so-called Special Projects lab, a secure area that nobody in her department was authorized to enter. The "company line" was that the Special

Projects group was working on a special initiative that had to be protected against industrial espionage. It seemed that all Nagara employees, apart from her and Toshikazu, of course, accepted this without question, and showed not one iota of curiosity about what was going on in the secure area.

Nikki, more than anyone else perhaps, had reason to wonder what the Special Projects lab was up to, but also had the most background on which to make educated guesses. As it turned out, the major responsibility of her workgroup was to analyze material transferred to them by the Special Projects group. Sometimes it was a sample of DNA, other times — like tonight — a protein. Some of the time, Nikki's group was tasked to determine something specific about the sample — such as the molecular weight — which made analysis easy. More often, however, she was given no guidance at all, no hint as to what the Special Projects people were looking for, and instructed to carry out an exhaustive analysis. That was the case with tonight's processing run: Special Projects hadn't told her anything about the sample — *not even that it was a protein, for heaven's sakes*, she groused — and instructed to find out everything she could about it.

When she completed her analyses, she simply turned the information back over to Special Projects, and that was the last she ever heard about it. No feedback as to the accuracy or quality of her analysis; no thanks or commendations; nothing. On one occasion — and only one — she'd asked her supervisor where her group's analyses went and what would be done with them. To her surprise, the response to her idle curiosity was a harsh dressing down, and an official reprimand inserted into her personnel record. (*Just like I'm in the army*, she thought.)

Nikki knew some of the people who worked in Special Projects, not strictly true; she knew *of* them and could recognize them by sight, but she didn't *know* them on any personal level. They kept themselves very much apart from the other research personnel, rarely eating in the staff cafeteria, and when they did staying in a tight, closed grouping away from everyone else. They were arrogant — even more arrogant than the other senior researchers — and wouldn't even deign to respond when Nikki said "good morning" to them in the hallway. *They're the elite*, she told herself, *or at least they think they are*. She sighed. Maybe it was just another facet of security.

That made her smile. *Security*. She wondered how the big bosses would react if they learned how much she'd figured out about what happened in Special Projects. *Probably have an aneurysm*, she told herself with a grin.

It wasn't that difficult, really. Just about anyone in Group Five, and probably others, could have figured out just as much. Of course, nobody else but she and Toshikazu had the necessary curiosity or interest. It was just a matter of picking up little clues here and there and putting them together, just like in a detective novel.

The first clue was that Nikki was initially asked to analyze mainly pure genetic material — DNA. Recently, however, most of the samples sent over from Special Projects were proteins. At first, the DNA samples were just plain *wrong*. There was always some major anomaly, something significant enough that the DNA simply couldn't have functioned in a living creature. With time, however, the size and the importance of the anomalies had decreased. Finally, most of the DNA samples seemed to be totally functional — or *potentially* so, at least.

At about this point the samples switched mainly to proteins, which are chemicals that are coded for by the DNA. At first, the proteins Nikki's workgroup received were as non-functional as the initial DNA samples. But then, with time, the anomalies in the proteins had become smaller and smaller until the last couple of samples — apart from today's disaster — were almost normal in structure and function.

Nikki could draw only one conclusion from all of this. The Special Projects lab was working on some kind of new technique for genetic engineering. Initially, the technique had been so undependable that they couldn't accurately or consistently create functional DNA. With experience, however, they refined the system until the DNA worked the way they wanted it to. Then they took the next step, testing the proteins coded for by the DNA they'd created. A much more precise way of checking for small errors than directly analyzing the DNA itself, the protein analyses had shown up errors in the original genetic code. But the errors in the proteins were becoming less and less serious, which implied that the Special Projects researchers were finally getting a real handle on their new technique.

So what did that imply about the Special Projects lab itself? Most genetic engineering — particularly anything to do with animals, and *particularly* anything new and experimental — gets done in specially secure labs. "Secure" in this case meant some kind of containment, not to keep potential industrial spies out, but to keep any potential mistakes in. They'd use, Nikki figured, something called P3 containment: a combination of hermetically-sealed rooms, airlocks, filters and sterilization techniques that should keep *anything* from getting out into the environment.

And just what were they engineering? Nikki didn't know. Some things were obvious: the proteins she was analyzing didn't come from bacteria, and she didn't think they came from plants. Animals, then — but not from primates, like the great apes or mankind; she'd have recognized them immediately.

So the Special Projects lab was using a new — and probably radically different — technique to genetically engineer animals of some kind. When Nikki had been at university, people were talking about the possibility of engineering pigs or cows so that they'd gain weight much faster than normal, without the use of steroids or other potentially harmful drugs, so that farmers could bring them to market much faster. But that talk was just speculation; nobody expected it to happen within the next five or more years. Could that be what Special Projects was working on? A more efficient beef cow? Considering the shrinking amount of land available to farms, a project like this made a lot of sense in Japan. And, considering the market situation, if Nagara could bring this off, the corporation could make billions.

With that in mind, Nikki could understand the need for security, to at least *some* degree. Industrial espionage *did* happen in Japan. (From some of the stories she'd heard on the grapevine, it seemed to rival *sumo* as the national sport ...) But didn't her bosses realize that the heavy-handed way they handled things *prompted* people to dig into what was happening? (*Or some people, at least*, she amended.)

Ah, well, she told herself, *management's not my concern. That's why we hire bosses.* "So how are we going to write this one up?" she asked Toshikazu. "'Protein non-functional due to faulty tertiary structure?'"

After a moment, Toshikazu nodded. "Sounds good to me. Append the full analysis?"

"As usual." Nikki grinned. "So they'll know we're earning our money."

Toshikazu opened his mouth to reply ... and the lab rang like a gong. The floor jolted once, hard, under Nikki's feet, forcing her to grab onto the analyzer next to her to keep her feet. The overhead lights flickered and cut out.

Luckily the darkness didn't last long, not long enough for Nikki to panic. Emergency lights, mounted in the corners of the room, cut in. The lab equipment cast alien shadows under the oblique illumination.

The floor was steady after that single impact: no aftershocks or tremors. Nikki shook her head to clear it. Her head hurt as though a giant had slapped her simultaneously on both ears.

Toshikazu was looking at her in shock. "Earthquake ..." She said, her voice sounding muffled in her own ears. *What else could it be?* part of her mind asked. *Japan's on the Pacific Ring of Fire, after all ...*

But Toshikazu was shaking his head as he got to his feet. "No earthquake. Explosion," he told her. "Next door."

"Next ...?" she started, but he didn't wait to hear her out. He was already on his way out the door.

She followed him into the hallway. The overhead lights were out here, too, and only half of the emergency lights seemed to be working. *Explosion? What the hell could have happened?* she asked herself. She stopped in her tracks for a moment — *maybe running towards an explosion in a P3 containment lab isn't such a good idea* — but Toshikazu hadn't slackened his pace, and she couldn't very well let her friend go on alone. She hurried to catch up.

The corridor ended at a large powered sliding door marked with the international icon meaning "Do Not Enter." Beneath that were the *kanji* characters for "Authorized Personnel Only." The entire door and the frame around it were painted black, making the red icon and lettering stand out in harsh contrast. Beyond here was the Special Projects area, strictly off limits to the members of Nikki's department. To ensure that, the door was always locked, and could only opened by inserting a valid identification card into a reader slot beside the door and punching a multi- digit code into the associated keypad.

That was the way it normally worked. But what about in an emergency? Nikki couldn't believe that the designers wouldn't have anticipated some kind of disaster. She walked closer to the control keypad. Yes, there was a single key that was flashing red. An emergency release?

She glanced over at Toshikazu, her expression a question. He was looking at the keypad too. He shrugged and nodded. *What have I got to lose?* She reached out and pressed the flashing key.

The door slid back silently, and acrid smoke rolled out into the hallway. Instantly, Nikki's eyes began to water. The smoke caught in her throat. *Toxic?* she asked herself. *Probably not.* In any case, she didn't know where to begin looking for gas masks.

Toshikazu's eyes were streaming too, but he stopped only long enough to pull a cloth handkerchief from his pocket and hold it over his mouth and nose, before heading on. Nikki hesitated again. *Dammit*, she swore to herself, *fools rush in. Why not wait for security to handle it?*

She knew the answer, of course. The Special Projects team worked late as often as Group Five did, maybe more often. That meant the odds were good there were people in there, maybe trapped, maybe injured, maybe dying. Toshikazu couldn't just leave them to their fate, and neither could she. She searched her pockets for a handkerchief. Nothing. She grabbed the lapel of her white labcoat and folded it over her mouth. *Not good, but better than nothing.*

With the security door open, the smoke was thinning out, but it still cut visibility down to a couple of meters. Toshikazu was a dark shape ahead of her.

She caught up with him when he stopped at a T-intersection in the hallway. She looked left and right. The smoke seemed thicker to the left. She grabbed his arm, almost dragged him after her. "This way," she told him needlessly.

There was another security door ahead, like the one they'd passed through except that this one was open. She'd guessed right, Nikki saw at once, the smoke was coming from this direction. Almost subliminally, she heard sharp cracks from ahead. *Small secondary explosions?* part of her mind speculated. The smoke seemed to be thinner near the floor, so she moved forward in a crouch.

The door opened into a lab very much like Nikki's own. The same marble-topped benches, the same medusa's-heads of tubing and electronics. Only the double rows of genetic analyzers were missing. She looked around quickly. *Nobody here. Good.* To her right was another doorway, the security door again standing open. She glanced back to make sure that Toshikazu was still with her, then hurried through it.

Another lab, similar to the first … Except that this one looked like a bomb had gone off it in. (*Which might not be too far wrong,* she told herself.) Small fires were burning everywhere, pouring the acrid smoke into the air, cutting visibility to almost nothing. The floor was blackened and buckled, and the acoustic tile of the ceiling had collapsed. Light fixtures hung by exposed cables, their plastic fittings melting in the flames.

Without thinking, Nikki took a step forward, then stopped as something crunched under her feet. She looked down. It was broken glass. *Broken? Almost powdered,* she told herself. The blast from the explosion must have broken every bit of glassware in the place.

She felt Toshikazu's presence beside her. "What the hell happened here?" she asked him.

He shrugged. "There's nothing we use that could cause an explosion like that."

There were more of the sharp cracks that Nikki had heard earlier. What *were* they? she asked herself. Secondary explosions? But the fire was *here* …

Toshikazu grabbed her arm, hard enough to hurt. She turned to tell him to let go.

And then she saw her friend was pointing, to the left of the door. She spun in the direction he was indicating.

The air left her lungs in a gasp of surprise. A fluke air current had thinned the smoke so that they could see to the far side of the lab. Instead of the familiar white panelling, the entire wall seemed to be made out of glass. *No, not glass*, part of Nikki's mind amended, *something stronger or it would have been blown out by the explosion*. On the other side of the transparent barrier was yet another lab. She recognized its layout at once. Fume hoods, acrylic "glove boxes," sealed enclosures with remote manipulators like the arms of dismembered robots. A P3 containment lab, it couldn't be anything else. For an instant she congratulated herself on having guessed right.

But only for an instant. Then horror took over. The P3 lab was ablaze, too. The room beyond the glass wall was filled with billowing black smoke, shot through with red tongues of flame. Not just the small, isolated fires of this room; the entire lab was an inferno.

And, worst of all, there were figures moving in the smoke. She couldn't make them out clearly, *Thank God I can't*, she thought, but they were definitely there. Human shapes thrashing in the thick smoke. Choking, dying …

She tried to run forward, but Toshikazu's firm grip on her arm held her back. "No," he told her quietly, "it's no use."

She pulled against his grip once, then stopped. What did she think she was going to do anyway? Smash the glass-like wall that had resisted an explosion? And then what: rush into a compromised P3 lab? *If there's P3 containment, it's there for a reason.*

"What do we do?" she wailed.

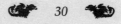

Toshikazu didn't have time to answer. Sharp cracks sounded to their right, followed by a man's scream of agony. Both of them spun towards the sounds.

For the first time, Nikki realized what she was hearing. *Shots! But what …? Wreckers?*

Something whip-cracked past her ear, slammed into the wall behind her. Beside her, Toshikazu flung himself to the floor. "Get down," he hissed. "Nikki, get down."

But she stood frozen. There was another burst of gunshots, then figures moved in the smoke at the far end of the lab. Someone emerged.

Black-clad, head to toe, only the area around his eyes was visible. A *ninja*? Nikki's shocked brain guessed. But no, the dark figure didn't match the images of the semi-mythical assassins that she'd seen in books and on the movie screen. The clothes weren't the simple garments of light cotton that she associated with ninjas. This man wore a black jumpsuit, covered with pouches and pockets closed with velcro. Three small spheres, not much larger than golf balls, hung from a bandolier that crossed his chest. (*Grenades*?) On his head he wore a tight-fitting black ski mask, not the wrapped cloth of a ninja. The eyes that looked at her were cold and hard — western, not oriental.

It took only an instant for her brain to register these details. Then she saw the weapon in the man's hand. Something like a pistol, not large but somehow more dangerous for its small size. The barrel was pointing directly between her eyes.

She wanted to say something, to plead with the black-clad man for her life. But the words were frozen in her throat. An ice-cold hand seemed to squeeze her heart. *I'm going to die.* Time seemed to slow down around her, almost like a movie run in slow motion. She watched, unable to move, as the man tightened his grip on the small weapon. His finger touched the trigger, began to tighten …

"Sergei, no." The voice that echoed through the room had the snap of command. Involuntarily, Nikki turned toward the voice.

Another figure emerged from the smoke. Another man, wearing the same black coveralls, carrying a similar weapon. But this one didn't have his ski mask on. His face was hard, finely-chiseled, with steel-grey eyes. His short blond hair was matted with blood. "No," he snapped again. "Cover them."

The first man, the one called Sergei, hesitated. Nikki could feel his desire to pull the trigger, to blow her head off. His eyes told her how he viewed her: as nothing but an obstacle, to be eliminated in the most expedient manner. For an instant, Nikki felt the dreadful certainty that he'd fire anyway.

But then discipline took over. He lowered the weapon from its aiming point between her eyes. The weapon still pointed at her, was still ready to cut her in two. But the gunman was no longer right on the verge of using it. "Move away," he growled. "Against the wall, both of you."

Unable to take her eyes from her would-be killer, Nikki backed away. Broken glass crunched under her feet. In her peripheral vision, she could see Toshikazu climbing to his feet and moving with her.

Three more figures emerged from the smoke, black shapes seeming to coalesce out of the black billows. One was hobbling painfully, a bloody wound visible on one thigh. The second was helping his wounded comrade. Despite the distractions, both had their weapons — submachine guns, Nikki decided at last — held ready. Both guns tracked over to Nikki and Toshikazu, probably an instinctive reaction, before the owners realized that the one named Sergei had things well in hand.

The third figure — the "eyes behind" — was walking backwards, eyes and gun barrel scanning over the smoke. Nikki wondered what good that did; she could see nothing through the black clouds.

But the rear guard obviously could. He triggered a short burst from his weapon, the flat drumming much quieter than Nikki would have expected. A hoarse yell of pain echoed from the depths of the smoke, followed by two deeper-throated, booming discharges. Bullets smashed marble chips from the top of a lab table, and ricocheted off with piercing whines. Toshikazu dropped to the floor once more, again trying to drag Nikki down with him. This time she didn't resist, crouching down below the level of the tables. *For all the cover it gives us*, she thought.

Now Nikki could see movement in the smoke. Something lurched forward — a white figure, hugely muscled. It took her a moment to recognize it: a Nagara Corporation security guard in his body armor. A massive gun in the guard's hand boomed twice. The black-clad rear guard cried out in pain and fell, but still managed to keep his weapon lined up on its target. He squeezed off another burst.

Nikki could see the bullets slamming into the guard's broad chest, shattering the rigid armor and driving through into the flesh beneath. Blood burst out, spattering across the white armor. Falling back under the impact of the burst, the guard pumped another big bullet into the ceiling.

And then all the black-garbed raiders were firing into the smoke as they backed toward the door. The one who'd been felled by the guard's shot was trying to struggle to his feet. Even though she couldn't see his face, she could see his agony in every movement. His left arm hung limply, as lifeless as a slab of meat, and blood pooled on the floor, but still he kept firing as he struggled.

There were more white shapes in the smoke, and

she could see the muzzle flashes of the guards' weapons. Bullets slammed into the floor and walls, and the air was filled with screaming ricochets. The raiders continued their fighting withdrawal, keeping up a murderous rate of fire. Nikki saw a guard's mirrored face shield shatter under the impact of a well-aimed burst. She was thankful the man collapsed backward into the smoke before she could see what the bullets must have done to his face. Another screamed and jackknifed forward as shots pulverized his stomach armor.

Nikki's mind was a swirl of emotions: horror and fear, mostly, but with disturbing subtones. The black figures — were they wreckers? That they were enemies of Nagara was beyond doubt; did that mean they were *her* enemies? Sergei had wanted to cut her down, but the blond man — the leader, he had to be — had called him off. That had to mean something. Nikki disliked and feared the white-armored Nagara security guards, but to see them shot down like this ... that was something different.

And then the was the wounded raider, still struggling to join his fellows. She could almost *feel* his pain, and his determination seemed to resonate through her nervous system. Was he an enemy? Maybe, but still ... Without really being aware of it, she raised her head for a better view. *Will he make it?*

"Keep your fool head *down!*" It was the blond leader again. So fast that Nikki hardly saw him move, he was beside his wounded comrade, almost dragging the lurching figure back toward the door. Both continued to pump fire into the smoke.

There was still movement in there, and the shooting continued. But it seemed to Nikki to be blind. The guards were hanging back in the smoke, she thought, using it as cover. *How many casualties have they taken?* she suddenly wondered. Three that she'd seen, probably more. *That might be enough to teach even those arrogant bastards a little caution.*

All the raiders but the leader and the badly-wounded one were out of the lab. For a moment, those last two were framed in the doorway that led into the other lab. Then, with a final long burst of gunfire, they were gone. For a few moments there was silence, so heavy as to seem almost tangible. But then the guards opened fire again from the cover of the smoke.

What the hell was that *all about?* Nikki asked herself. She began to stand, but Toshikazu dragged her roughly down again. "We're not safe yet," he hissed.

As if on cue, security guards burst from the smoke, five of them, weapons blazing, a reckless charge at enemies who weren't there any more. The guards hesitated for a moment, looking around wildly. For a moment, Nikki had the overpowering urge to yell, "They went thataway!" She choked back a laugh. Hysteria, her mind warned.

Four of the guards rushed through the door into the other lab. One moved slowly toward where Nikki and Toshikazu crouched. The guard's gun was levelled at them, and Nikki could tell from the way the barrel vibrated that he had a death-grip on the butt. Why? part of her brain wondered. *Fear? Anger? Blood-lust?* A ball of ice seemed to materialize in her stomach. *Any one of those could be reason enough to kill us.* "We're friends," she gasped out.

The guard's gun swung, and for the second time in as many minutes she was staring down the muzzle of a weapon. Again she was frozen in place, incapable of any movement. In the guard's curved faceplate, she could see a distorted image of her own face, her mouth gaping in horror.

"*Iie, iie!*" Toshikazu leapt to his feet beside her. He was clutching his Nagara identification badge, the plastic square that all employees had to wear at all times, holding the lapel of his lab coat out toward the guard. All the while he was yelling in Japanese, much too fast for Nikki to make any sense of what he was saying. Catching on quickly, she grabbed her own ID badge, almost tearing it off her coat in her haste.

For a moment nobody moved. Then, with a grunt that could have been relief or disgust, the guard lowered his pistol. He looked over his shoulder and barked something to several more armor-clad guards who were cautiously emerging from the smoke. They nodded, and took off in pursuit of the raiders.

"Come with me," the guard told them in brusque Japanese. "Someone will deal with you."

That doesn't sound reassuring, Nikki thought, but decided against making any remark. The guard gestured with his weapon, not *quite* pointing it at them, and they walked ahead of him the way his colleagues had gone. Nikki turned back, trying to get another look into the containment lab. But the smoke had closed back over the transparent wall, blocking her view.

She looked over at Toshikazu. Her friend's face was pale, and there was a sheen of sweat on his high forehead. But after a moment his familiar smile reappeared. "Remind me that I'm working too many late nights," he whispered to her.

Chapter Two

The musical chiming of the alarm brought Nikki to sudden consciousness. With a groan, she rolled over and hit the OFF button on the clock beside the bed, then just lay for a few moments, staring up at the ceiling. The sheets and blankets were wrapped around her like loose, damp ropes, soaked with her own sweat.

Nikki usually hated the chiming of the alarm, wishing for just a few more minutes of uninterrupted sleep. Not today. This morning, the alarm was a welcome relief, an escape from the dreams that had pursued her all night. Dreams of fire and smoke, gunfire and torn bodies, blood and screams. Her head felt as though it was full of cotton wool, and her mouth tasted like dead things. She rubbed her eyes, tried to moisten dry lips with a tongue that felt like sandpaper.

God, she thought, *and I used to* wish *that something exciting would happen to me*. As she reached for the glass of water on the bedside table, she was a little surprised to note that her hand wasn't shaking. She took a sip of the tepid water, swilled it around in her mouth. The dry tissue of her tongue and cheeks seemed to absorb the water like a sponge. *Maybe boredom isn't that bad.*

She glanced at the clock. Eleven in the morning. That meant she'd had, what, about five hours of sleep. Normally that was more than enough to see her through the day, as long as she didn't make a habit of it. But today she felt as drained and fuzzy-headed as if she'd just closed her eyes. *Well, I suppose that makes sense,* she thought. *It's not as if my sleep was restful.* She took another mouthful of water, then sat up and ran a hand through her dishevelled hair.

Did they get out alive, she found herself wondering, *those* wreckers *or whoever they were?* She shook her head at the thought. How could she have mixed emotions on the matter, she asked herself. The raiders had attacked *her* corporation — well, not really her corporation, but the one that employed her, and that was almost the same. They'd killed the scientists in the Special Projects lab, hadn't they? (She shut her eyes, tried to suppress a mental image of the figures thrashing and dying in the fire and smoke of the containment lab.) They'd killed the security guards, shot them dead for trying to do their job.

But they didn't *kill you, did they?* The thought came unbidden from some secret part of her mind. The one called Sergei had wanted to, but the blond leader had ordered him to leave her and Toshikazu alive. *Why?*

The Nagara security chief, a harsh, scar-faced man that everybody called Yamato-san, had asked that again and again during the interminable questioning that had followed the raid. The guards had led Nikki and Toshikazu up from the basement to the ground-floor security office, where they'd been questioned — *interrogated*, she corrected — for almost five hours. Alone and then together, they'd had to repeat over and over again just what had happened — sometimes to stone-faced security personnel, sometimes into a tape recorder, and once in front of a video camera. At the time, Nikki had found herself wondering when she'd be hooked up to a lie detector. But then she'd realized that a corporation as sophisticated as Nagara probably didn't need anything as primitive as a polygraph. (*A voice stress analyzer,* she guessed, *maybe built into the tape recorder. They wouldn't have missed a trick like that.*) Yamato-san had sat in several of the questioning sessions, occasionally dropping in queries of his own.

And those queries had all come back to one point: Why had the "wreckers" left her and Toshikazu alive? She didn't have an answer, of course, and she could sense the security chief's frustration and anger at her repeated response of "I don't know." At one time anger had flared within her, and she'd drawn breath to demand whether Yamato thought she was involved somehow. But then she'd looked into Yamato's icily furious eyes. The words had died on her lips, and the anger burning in her chest had been extinguished by cold fear. *They couldn't suspect* that, *could they?*

Of course they could, another part of her brain had answered. Suspicion of betrayal seemed to be part of the Japanese psyche. (*Had it always been like that?* she wondered. She didn't think so, but she couldn't be sure when the change had occurred.)

So she'd had no good answer for Yamato-*san* — not one she wanted to tell him. She had some ideas — speculations, more like wild guesses really — but she felt no urge to share them with him.

Why *had* the raiders let them live? It was almost as if the attackers had specific targets — the Special Projects lab, and the scientists who worked there. The security guards were killed mainly because they were trying to kill the raiders. And Nikki and Toshikazu? They were innocent bystanders — not the targets of the raid, and noncombatants. Would wreckers have acted that way? Not the ones who'd assaulted Tomita Technologies. There, anyone unfortunate enough to encounter the raiders was brutally slaughtered. These raiders were different. They weren't slow to deal death if it was warranted — according to their criteria — but they were selective as to their victims. *Interesting*.

She'd kept those thoughts, unfocused as they were, to herself. Eventually, the security guards — even Yamato-*san* — had seemed to tire of the interrogation. She knew that her story and Toshikazu's matched on all points — they were both telling the truth, after all — and the guards had eventually had to accept the fact. It was almost six in the morning when they'd been released, with a final harsh injunction not to talk to anyone about what had happened. As they'd left the security office together, Toshikazu had taken her hand and given it a reassuring squeeze, and then they'd gone their separate ways. Nikki had taken a bus home to her apartment, and collapsed into bed. And then the nightmares had come.

She climbed from bed and padded into the bathroom. A splash of cold water on her face helped clear her head a little. From the cabinet she took a tube of extra-strength aspirin, and poured one out onto her palm — then hesitated and added a second. Her mouth was still dry when she tried to swallow them, and even a whole glass of water didn't stop them from sticking uncomfortably in the back of her throat. She looked at herself in the mirror, saw the dark circles under her blood-shot eyes. *Don't I look a treat?* she thought. *People will think I spent the night in a* sake *shop.* She glanced back through the bathroom door at the bed. What she really needed was more sleep. Why not just call in sick? *But more sleep probably means more dreams*, she thought with a chill. She didn't need that. With a sigh, she started readying herself to face the day.

As she dressed, she considered turning on the radio to see if she could catch some news. Normally she had the radio on while she ate breakfast, tuned to the Voice of America. When she'd first moved to Japan, she'd always listened to the local radio stations, to practice her Japanese. But with time she'd noticed that the news those stations reported was always local in character, always focussed on events within Japan, or even solely within Tokyo itself. There was rarely anything from the world outside, and almost nothing about what was going on in the United States. And when there was news from the States, it was always about something that related somehow to Japan and Japanese interests: grain or wood shipments, or new trade agreements between the two nations. Never anything about what Nikki considered important — like the chaos that was wracking California and the whole west coast.

That was when she'd tuned her radio to the Voice of America. Originally intended for American servicemen overseas, she thought she'd remembered reading, the Voice had now become the best source of news for American civilians abroad. Originating from the new national capital of Houston, the Voice was beamed to several of the few communications satellites that still functioned, and broadcast throughout the world. Presumably, anywhere around the globe that Americans had radios — *and where radios still work*, she mentally added — they could tune in to the Voice and keep up to date on what was going on back at home. A few years ago, Nikki would never have thought that she'd become one of those so tied to the States that they couldn't live without American news. But now, with the upheavals all over the world, she found it very reassuring to be able to hear frank reports on what was going on.

It still amazed her, but the local Japanese radio stations, and even the national TV network, NHK, never had anything substantive to say about what the Voice of America called the Possibility Wars. Sure, sometimes NHK or the others would make some coy remark about *Kawaru* — "the Change" — having some negative impact on international trade, or something like that, but that was it. *Again, nothing that didn't relate directly to Japanese interests*, Nikki thought. For the hundredth time, she wondered how Japan seemed to have avoided the chaos that was wracking the rest of the world.

Nobody seemed to know how it had happened; or, if they did, Voice of America wasn't sharing the knowledge. All that Nikki knew was that, almost two years ago now, what the world thought of as reality began to change. The upheavals were as massive as they were disorienting. Physical laws seemed to change on an immense scale, over huge regions of the world. And even in those changes there was little sense of consistency. In some parts of the globe, strange technologies that might have come directly from 1930s-vintage pulp fiction worked reliably; in others, virtually nothing more technically advanced than a pair of scissors or a crossbow would function.

It wasn't only the physical laws that had changed, Nikki knew. Societies altered, seemingly overnight, and even individuals underwent horrifying changes, or so claimed the Voice of America. At first, Nikki had discounted what she'd been hearing, trying desperately to believe that she was listening to an elaborate and grotesque practical joke. But there was no way she could close her mind for long to what was happening. Nobody could continue a hoax for so long. She had to face the facts. Parts of Southeast Asia had become a realm of nightmares become real. Dinosaurs and sentient lizards hunted the east coast and around the Great Lakes, much of the west coast, and parts of the Canadian north. Dragons flew the skies of the British Isles, while Viking raiders sailed the North Sea. France and much of Western Europe had become a cruel and twisted techno-theocracy. And a reborn Egyptian empire, unlike that imagined by any pharaoh, was striving to extend its influence throughout the Middle East, reinforced by weapons based on science that, by all the physical laws that Nikki had studied, simply shouldn't work.

Some areas hadn't been affected — at least not obviously. Japan, for one. Russia and the newly-independent countries that had once made up the Soviet Union. China. Australia and India. South Africa. So far, those regions had suffered little directly — although, of course, few escaped the effects as neighbors, allies and trade partners underwent *Kawaru*.

Many of the regions that *had* undergone the Change were fighting back, struggling to defeat the strange forces that were attempting to alter the world beyond recognition. That struggle was what the Voice of America called the Possibility Wars. (*Why "Possibility?"* Nikki wondered again. The word seemed to have some immense significance, but one that was beyond her understanding.)

Here she was in her safe little corporate-subsidized apartment, with her corporate-supplied computer system — light-years better than anything she could possibly have owned at home — and her sophisticated home entertainment system. It would be easy enough to keep her focus on the here and now, and pretend that nothing outside these walls — or this city, or this country — had any real significance. That, she thought, was what the vast majority of her colleagues seemed satisfied doing. But, although turning her back on the rest of the world would have its comforts, there was no way she could do that. Even if the Possibility Wars didn't directly affect her, she still felt it was her … well, her *duty*, in a way, to learn what she could about how her home, and the rest of the world, was faring.

But not this morning, she told herself firmly. She was too tired, too stressed to worry about crises half a world away. *Enough chaos right here and now without looking for it elsewhere.*

* * *

It was almost eleven forty-five when Nikki finally walked into the Nagara Building lobby — almost *four hours* after the official start of the business day. There were advantages to coming in this late, of course — *on top of getting at least* some *sleep.* She'd missed the playing of the corporate anthem — a particularly brash and bombastic thing with lots of blaring trumpets and clashing cymbals — over the building's public address system, an eight-thirty ritual. She also didn't have to weather the accusing looks she always received for not attending the semi-official morning calisthenics class. (*Company anthems, and group calisthenics.* She still found the concepts rather amusing. When she'd first come to this country, she'd known that Japanese corporations had their own ideas of how things were done, but knowing and experiencing them first-hand were two different things.)

As she crossed the lobby to the elevator, she saw two of the white-armored security guards. They were standing a few meters apart against the back wall, facing the main doors. For a moment, Nikki was puzzled. Normally there were no armored guards in the lobby. There *were* two guards always stationed at the reception desk — they were in their accustomed places today, she noticed — but what she thought of as the "stormtroopers" never came into the public areas during the business day. *As if Nagara's embarrassed that they exist, or as if the corporation doesn't want to scare casual visitors,* she thought. Today, though, there were *two,* just hanging around casually as if they had no better place to be.

But then she looked at the guards again. Although they were just standing there, there was little casual about them. What she'd first thought was a relaxed posture *wasn't*; their stance was poised, like a karate master, ready to move in any direction at an instant's notice. Their right hands, seeming just to hang casually at their sides, were centimeters away from the butts of their sidearms. And their helmets, with their mirrored visors down, were scanning back and forth ceaselessly. She felt a chill on the nape of her neck as she realized that their positions in the lobby were just as purposeful as their stance. *From where they're standing, they have perfect line of sight — and line of* fire *— to everywhere in the lobby,* she understood. And there was no risk of either one getting in the other's line of fire should anything happen. They were taking the events of last night very seriously. *As well they should,* another part of her brain added.

She suddenly realized that she'd come to a complete halt in the middle of the lobby, and was staring at the guards. Both their helmets had turned toward her, and she could almost feel their cold and steady eyes boring into her through their mirrored faceplates. With an effort, she forced herself to move. She could still feel their eyes on her back as she waited for the elevator to arrive in response to her security badge, an unpleasant sensation like someone brushing the back of her neck with a feather. The feeling faded only when she'd stepped into the elevator and the doors had closed on her.

She shook her head to banish the lingering discomfort she felt. *They weren't watching me, not me* as *me,* she told herself. *They only cared about me as someone in the area they were supposed to guard.* Of course that was it. But still she couldn't shake the feeling that they'd known who she was, and were giving her their complete attention.

The elevator reached the first sub-basement level, and the doors opened. As she stepped out into the corridor, Nikki found herself stopping again. *Something's missing* ... It took her a moment to realize what part of her mind was expecting. *No smoke in the air.* Of course not, the building's air conditioning would have scrubbed every trace of the acrid smoke from the air. *And* — she glanced at the white floor — *no blood stains.* The last time she'd passed here, on the way to the security office for her interrogation, there'd been smudges and streaks of dark red, blood from the wounded raiders, and from the guards who'd been after them. (*Did they make it?* she found herself wondering again, then ruthlessly forced the thought from her mind.) She shook her head again to clear it, and headed for her lab.

The other members of Group Five were already there, of course, busily at work. Omi was sitting at the control terminal; Ito and Toshima had one of the automated analyzers open, and were making delicate adjustments to its interior; Matsukara and Zakoji were preparing another sample for analysis; and Bojo was reading a report as it came off the printer. They all looked up as she walked in, eyes and face expressionless. Then, as one, they looked away and went back to their work.

What the hell was that *about?* Nikki wondered. Sure, she'd never been on the best of terms, socially, with her colleagues, but normally they'd at least offer her a polite *"Konichi-wa"* when she arrived in the morning. She looked around for Toshikazu.

At least *he* gave her a warm smile, from over at the far lab table where he was handling a pipette with his usual economy of motion. She walked over to him and asked, "What's going on?"

He shrugged, apparently unperturbed. "Perhaps they got out of the wrong side of the bed this morning." His voice was casual — *purposely* casual, Nikki thought. "Why don't you check your e-mail?" he suggested.

"What do you …?" she started to ask, then shut her mouth. *Something's going on here, and I don't like it.* She nodded. "I'll do that," she told him, forcing her voice into the same casual tone he'd used. "Talk to you later?"

He nodded. *Count on it*, his expression seemed to say.

She shrugged and walked over to her "office." Not an office really, just a couple of six-foot-high dividers attached to the wall, forming a three-sided cubicle around her desk. She set her attache case down on the floor, shrugged into her knee-length labcoat, and settled herself in the chair. She hit a key on the computer keyboard, and the Nagara Corporation logo appeared on the screen. Quickly she logged onto the system, and brought up the corporate electronic mail program.

Her eyebrows raised in surprise. There were the usual array of messages in her in-box — scheduling queries, requisitions, and the other day-to-day matters she had to handle as a workgroup leader — but with them was something out of the ordinary. A general-broadcast message, issued by the office of Nagara's Chief Executive Officer, Kubota-san, sent to every employee of the corporation. Ignoring the other messages, she cursored down to that entry and hit the key to display the full text on her screen.

As she read through it, her eyebrows rose even further, and she sat back in her chair. *That isn't right*, she thought, *that isn't right at all.* She scanned the message again, paying more attention to her translation to make sure she picked up on every nuance of the language.

To all Nagara employees, it read. *Last night at approximately one A.M., Nagara Corporation became the victim of a heinous act of sabotage. A group of a dozen wreckers entered the building, by means that have yet to be established, and inflicted damage upon Nagara's Special Projects*

department. *This damage, although not serious, was wide-
spread, impacting the Special Projects department's ability
to perform its vital work. It is believed that the wreckers'
target was the department's computer system, which contains all the data that the group has collected over the past
months.*

*It is my honor to report to you that this attempt was foiled
by the quick and heroic actions of Nagara Security personnel. At great risk to themselves, they succeeded in driving the
wreckers away before any damage could be done to the
computer system. Following their standing orders to put the
safety of Nagara employees and equipment as the highest
priority, the security personnel were unable to prevent the
wreckers from escaping, presumably by the same route by
which they gained access to the building. I am glad to report
that there were no fatalities or serious injuries, either among
the Special Projects workers or the security personnel.*

*It grieves me to have to add that there is strong evidence
that the wreckers received help from within this corporation
— either in the form of information, or as direct aid. Nagara
Security is currently following up on the clues left behind by
these traitors to the corporation, and I am confident that they
will be brought to justice in the immediate future.*

*In the meantime, loyal Nagara employees should not find
themselves inconvenienced by the investigation, or by the
heightened level of security which our personnel have been
forced to adopt. I am confident that the perpetrators will soon
be identified, and that tranquility will soon return to this
corporation.*

Nikki rubbed at her temples — the dull headache
she'd felt on waking was back — and began to re-read
the message yet again. *That's* not *right*. There were at
least three, maybe more, fallacies — *no, out-and-out lies!*
— in Kubota-*san*'s e-mail message. She ticked them off
mentally.

One: The damage to the Special Projects lab was
anything but "not serious" — the whole lab was de-

stroyed. (A chilling image of figures thrashing in the flames and the smoke flashed through her mind, before she forcibly suppressed it.)

Two: The Special Projects lab didn't process its data on the central corporate computer system, as did Nikki's workgroup and all the other labs in the building. They had their own, stand-alone system ... which was located *in* the Special Projects lab itself. There was no way that system could have survived.

Three: "No fatalities or serious injuries." *Like hell!* Nikki had seen several security guards badly wounded. And the one who'd taken a burst of submachine gun fire through his visor: *You can't tell me that someone can shrug that off and be back at work the next morning.*

Maybe four: The raiders weren't stereotypical "wreckers."

And those comments about help from inside Nagara — that just doesn't make sense. She'd seen nothing that indicated the raiders had to have inside help; she just didn't believe it.

But everybody else would. The thought sprung unbidden to mind. *All the loyal little Nagara employees — they're going to believe everything that Kubota-san says.*

She suddenly felt cold. Was that why the other members of her workgroup had looked at her strangely? They'd have read Kubota's message, first thing when they came in at eight o'clock, *and* they'd have believed it. And they all knew that she'd been in the lab late last night, even if they hadn't heard all the details of what had happened. They couldn't think that she ...

But they *could*, she realized, they *could* think that she'd been involved. They didn't like her, and it was always easier to distrust someone who was disliked. Add to that the fact that distrust and fear of betrayal — paranoia, almost — seemed somehow to have become ingrained into Japanese society. *And* add the fact that she was a *gaijin*, something not quite human.

"So, you read it?"

She turned at the quiet voice. Toshikazu was standing in the "doorway" to her cubicle. "Yes," she started, "I …" It took her a moment to realize that Toshikazu was speaking English. She knew he was as fluent as a native speaker, but they always spoke Japanese when they were together, largely to give her a chance to practice. Instinctively, she glanced around to see if any of the others were listening, but the cubicle walls blocked her view. She didn't think anybody else spoke English, but she didn't know for sure. With a shrug, she forced that thought from her mind. *Now* I'm *being paranoid.*

"Yes," she repeated, "I read it. But it's all wrong."

Toshikazu grinned. "Of course it is," he agreed. "They couldn't very well admit that Special Projects is *gone* — maybe with all their data." She nodded. He, too, had realized what the fire in the lab probably meant for the computer system. "After all," he went on, "it probably weakens Nagara's position in the market, the loss of whatever it was they were doing next door. And you never admit weakness; it's just an invitation for a hostile takeover. Just like you never admit that a bunch of scruffy wreckers can kill your security guards. It shakes the confidence of the good little workers in the great and protective corporation." His grin faded. "You read the piece about the inside help?"

She nodded, and gestured with a chin — a movement that encompassed everyone outside the cubicle. "They think it was me," she said flatly.

Slowly he nodded. His expression was calm, but she could see his concern for her in his eyes. "Probably," he agreed, "but it doesn't matter. The people who matter — Yamato, Eichiro, and Kubota himself — they all know there was no inside help. They know you're not involved."

"Then why say *that*?" She pointed at the screen.

He shrugged. "*Pour encouragez les autres*, perhaps?" he suggested. "To keep everybody on edge, and watching? That's going to help security" — he grimaced, as if he'd tasted something bitter — "even though it will be hard on everyone's nerves."

"But that's paranoid."

Toshikazu's wry grin was back. "Of course. Paranoia is a tool."

His grin was infectious, and she found herself smiling back, despite the knot of tension that still sat in her stomach. "Is that another old Japanese proverb?"

He looked surprised. "That? No, that's Toshikazu's First Law of Corporate Behavior." He laid a hand gently on Nikki's shoulder, a gesture that surprised her — he rarely touched her, or anyone. "Don't worry, my friend," he told her reassuringly, "this will all blow over. It always does."

* * *

Toshikazu's probably right, she found herself thinking later in the day, *I just wish it'd blow over* now.

Her work usually engrossed and excited her; today it was a chore. The fact that the dull headache, and the leaden feeling in her body, had stayed with her didn't help. But what really got to her was the others in her workgroup. She could swear she felt their eyes on her, watching her anytime she turned her back on them — *As though they expect me to conjure up a bunch of wreckers out of thin air*, she thought angrily. When she gave them instructions or asked them questions, they were always coldly precise in their responses — never anything that she could label impolite, but it was obvious there was no love lost between them.

At first this morning, she'd thought that the destruction of the Special Projects lab would mean that Group Five wouldn't have much to do. After all, the majority of their work revolved around the samples that were sent in from next door for analysis. *And they won't be sending anything for awhile,* she thought, *if they ever do again.* To her surprise, however, she found that there was still a lot of work that had to be done. Mainly administrative work, but also genetic analysis on other projects in which other groups — not members of the Special Projects department — were engaged. According to her group's mandate, the Special Projects analyses were the highest priority, which meant that the other work kept getting bumped out of the schedule. Now that there was nothing to pre-empt it, she realized how much of a backlog there actually was. She sighed. *And I'd been hoping for an easy day.*

By four o'clock she was exhausted. Her headache was still there — it was getting worse, in fact — and she felt as burned out as if she'd put in a sixteen hour day. Finally, however, the work load slackened enough for her to slow down, at least for a few minutes. She returned to her cubicle, enjoying the respite from the constant looks from her colleagues that she thought were growing more and more accusatory. *Or am I just tired?* she asked herself. She sat down at her computer terminal and logged on.

Her job at Nagara had turned out to be even more of a learning experience than she'd expected. Constantly pushed to stay up to date on everything Group Five was working on, she was continuously gaining new insights into how the advanced automated analyzers could be used to their best effect. When she returned to the States, she realized, she'd be a real prize, in demand by any company that was working on similar projects … but only if she remembered what she'd learned in Japan. To that end, she'd started keeping a journal, recording any major insights, ideas or questions that came up during the work day. Already she thought that some of the concepts she'd come up with — real blue-sky ideas that didn't fit into Nagara's way of working — might be worth serious money if she could only develop them in a suitable environment. At first she'd kept the journal file in her normal computer directory, in clear text. But then after a while, she'd created another directory — a personal one that only she had access to — and she'd used a password program to encrypt the file. Every time she accessed the journal and had to enter her password, she felt a little embarrassed — *I'm getting as paranoid as everyone else around here,* she told herself — but maybe Toshikazu was right: maybe paranoia *was* a tool.

The journal had two uses, she'd found. One was to record new insights; the other was to motivate and encourage her. When she was feeling flat, she found that reading through the journal and seeing just how far she'd progressed really cheered her up. It was for that second reason that she keyed in the command to access her personal directory.

To her surprise, instead of displaying a listing of the files in the directory, the computer beeped. A terse message — DIRECTORY LOCKED — flashed on the screen.

Nikki frowned. *That's never happened before.* A computer glitch, maybe? She typed in the command again.

Another beep. DIRECTORY LOCKED. *Dammit.* She tried again.

Beep. DIRECTORY LOCKED.

Again. *Beep.* DIRECTORY LOCKED.

With a muttered curse, she typed in a command for the terminal to run a self-diagnostic. *Maybe the explosion last night did something. Or maybe the raiders did something to the main system.* But that didn't make sense. She'd been using the computer all day without the slightest sign of a problem.

The self-diagnostic finished its run, and the screen filled with *kanji* characters. Tracing each line of the

 53

screen with a finger, she carefully read through the report. Then she sat back, puzzled. According to the diagnostic program, nothing was wrong with the terminal, or with the central system. *One last time.* She entered the command to access the directory.

Beep. DIRECTORY LOCKED.

"God*damn* it!" She glared at the screen in frustrated anger.

"Problems?"

She turned. Toshikazu was standing behind her. For a moment her anger spilled over onto him — *he moves so quietly, why doesn't he ever knock?* — but then she forced herself to speak calmly. "Computer glitch," she told him shortly. "I can't get into my directory."

He gestured toward the terminal. "May I?"

"Be my guest." She stood up, offering him her chair.

He settled himself before the keyboard and looked over the text on the screen. "Did you run a diagnostic?" he asked, then answered himself, "Yes you did." He scrolled the display back so he could read the report. "Hmm," he mused, "no computer problem. Maybe ..." His voice trailed off.

"Maybe what?"

He didn't answer her directly, just typed in a complex command. Even looking over his shoulder, Nikki couldn't see exactly what he did, so fast did his fingers move. *He's much better at this than I am,* she reminded herself.

Again the screen filled with *kanji* characters. Now it was Toshikazu's turn to sit back and stare at the terminal in puzzlement.

"What?" she asked again.

Toshikazu didn't reply at once. When he turned the chair to face her, his face was carefully schooled into expressionlessness. "Your directory has been locked out," he said carefully. "You no longer have access rights to the directory, either read or write."

"*What?*" she demanded, glaring at the screen again. "It's not a glitch?"

He shook his head. "It's no glitch," he said quietly. "The system operator did this. At" — he pointed to a line on the screen — "at about seven o'clock this morning."

"What? *Why?*"

Toshikazu shrugged. From the look on his face, Nikki was sure that he had some idea. But she knew Toshikazu well enough to realize that he didn't like speculating without enough to go on, and wouldn't tell her anything until he was sure.

She nodded abruptly. "I'll handle this." She reached for the telephone.

And was surprised as he laid a hand on her wrist. His touch was gentle but firm, and she could as easily have lifted the entire desk as pick up the phone with his hand there. She looked at him in mixed exasperation and surprise. *I didn't know he was that strong*, part of her mind reflected.

His face was still calm — *deliberately so*, she thought — but she could see something in his eyes. Behind that placid face, his mind was racing. "Do what you must," he told her quietly. "But tread carefully, my friend." And with that cryptic comment, he removed his hand, stood up and left her cubicle.

She watched him go in complete bewilderment. For a moment she considered following him, demanding that he tell her what she meant. But then she discarded the idea. *He's my friend,* she told herself, *he's doing what he thinks best.* She shook her head in baffled anger. *I'll talk to him about this later.* First, though, she had to get to the bottom of this locked directory. She picked up the phone and punched in the extension for the Management Information Systems department, the group that oversaw the computer system for the entire corporation.

"*Mushi mushi?*" She didn't recognize the voice that answered the phone, and honestly didn't care who it was.

"My personal directory is locked out," Nikki snapped. "Nikki Carlson, employee number 21488762. Remove the lock."

There was a moment of silence on the other end of the phone. Nikki knew she'd spoken harshly, using a form of address that was more direct than polite, verging on a direct order. She knew that the people in MIS thought themselves important, managing as they did the computer system for the entire corporation, and were used to being addressed very politely. But at the moment she was too angry to waste time playing along with anyone's delusions of grandeur.

The man on the phone hissed softly through his teeth, a sound of anger and insult, but she didn't care. "I will check," the man said coldly. "Hold, please." Before she could say anything, she heard a click, and the earphone was filled with the music — slightly discordant to her Western ears — of *koto* and *samisen*. *He'll probably leave me on hold all day*, she fumed silently to herself.

But it was less than half a minute later that the cold voice came back on the line. "There is no lock on your directory," the man said flatly.

Nikki stared at the phone in disbelief. Anger flared hot in her chest. "I said the directory is locked," she almost snarled into the phone. "I know when a directory is locked, believe me. *Un*lock it. *Now*."

"So sorry, Carrson-*san*," the man said, his voice so polite as to be condescending. "There is no lock. Perhaps you forgot your password, *neh*?"

Nikki gripped the handpiece so hard that the tendons in her forearm ached. She wanted to swear at this … this drone. But she knew that wouldn't help. She forced herself to speak calmly and coldly. "You are wrong," she told him, "you have made a mistake." *Words calculated to infuriate any Japanese corporator*, she knew. "Connect me with Suganama-*san*." The man on the phone hesitated. "You know Suganama-*san*?" she asked, as sweetly as she could manage. "The manager of MIS? Your boss?"

"Suganama-*san* is busy …" For the first time the voice was a little hesitant. *You didn't know I knew your boss, did you?* she thought with a grim smile. *Now you think maybe you've gone a little too far.*

"Suganama-*san* will take my call," she told him quietly. "Tell him I'm waiting." There was another click, and the music returned.

Nikki breathed deeply, trying to flush the anger out of her system. *Petty*, she chided herself, *yelling at somebody who's probably got nothing to do with what's going on, then scaring the hell out of him. But I want my bloody directory unlocked …*

There was a soft click from the phone, and the music was stilled. A warm voice, old but still strong, sounded in her ear. "Good day, Miss Carrson," Hiroyo Suganama said carefully, in that short phrase exhausting the entire extent of his English. With obvious relief, he lapsed back into Japanese. "I understand you have a problem?"

In her mind Nikki pictured Hiroyo Suganama sitting at his desk. An old man, older than Nagara's official retirement age of sixty-five — *which means he's got serious pull with the Board of Directors*, she thought. He was a big man, his bulk showing that he'd been physically powerful in his youth. Even though time had taken its toll on his body, she knew his mind was still rapier-quick — she'd once heard another MIS employee make a telling comment about Suganama: "He's forgotten more about computers than the rest of us will ever know." Even though his official position in the Nagara hierarchy was about equal to division manager—about equal to her own superior, Agatamori Eichiro — his age, and his personal reputation, ensured that even people well up the scale from Eichiro treated him with careful respect.

She'd met Suganama early on in her tenure at Nagara, and — to the surprise of both of them — they'd got on well. She found him to be a grandfatherly kind of man, much warmer than any other senior manager she'd met. He in turn seemed to look on her almost as a daughter or granddaughter — someone whose career he could follow with pride, and assist where he honorably could — even though she was a *gaijin*. Although not truly a friend — they met and spoke only rarely — she considered him to be something of a mentor.

"*Konichi-wa*, Suganama-*san*," she said politely. (Despite their relationship she'd never used his first name, and probably never would.) "Yes. Yes, I do have a problem." Quickly she repeated what she'd told the first man. "But he said there was no lock," she concluded.

"Mmmm." Suganama was silent for a moment. Then he spoke quietly — hesitantly, for the first time since Nikki had known him. "There *is* a lock, Miss Carrson. Its emplacement was requested by Yamato-san. You know Yamato-*san*?"

The security chief. Nikki ground her teeth as she remembered the morning's interrogation, but kept her voice as emotionless as she could. "Yes, I know Yamato-*san*."

"Then I am very much afraid you must ask him concerning its removal, Miss Carrson. I am sorry."

"There is nothing to apologize for, Suganama-*san*," she said. "Thank you. *Domo arrigato gozaimas*." She broke the connection before he could say anything else — a breach of etiquette, but she just didn't really give a damn at the moment.

She was mad — *Mad as a wet cat*, as her mother

would have said. Immediately she keyed in the number for the security office, punching the keys almost hard enough to break the plastic phone.

"*Mushi mushi*?" Another drone, it could just as well have been the same one from the voice. But the tone this time was different, even more arrogant and cold. A voice that went perfectly with Corporate Security.

"This is Nikki Carlson, employee number 21488762," she repeated. "You put a lock on my personal directory, and I want it removed."

"Hold." A click, followed by *samisen* music. *Not even an attempt at politeness this time*, she thought.

The wait was even shorter this time. "There is no lock on your directory," the voice said with no preamble. "An error, no doubt. *Try* again." And the phone went dead in her hand.

She slammed the handset down on the cradle with a muttered curse. *Try again?* Then she hesitated. *Why not?* She hammered in the command to access the directory …

And a file listing filled the screen. Nikki stared at it in disbelief. The lock was gone. What did that mean?

What it means, she thought after a moment, *is that security put the lock on, then removed it when I made a noise about it.* She grinned mirthlessly. The security drone on the phone had been telling the strict and literal truth, she realized. When he told her there was no lock, he'd already removed it. She laughed, a dry bark with no humor in it. *You know you're losing it when getting told the truth ticks you off …*

She leaned back in her chair, tried to force herself to relax. *Okay, she thought, so security locked out my personal directory.* Why? A few wild possibilities passed through her mind, but none of them made much sense. *Not to the way I think*, she mused, *but how about them?* She'd often thought that some of the things Corporate Security did made little sense. Maybe the logical thing to do was to bring in someone who had a better feeling for what made Japanese corporations tick …

She stood, and went to the doorway of her cubicle. "Toshikazu," she called quietly, "could you come here, please?"

Toshikazu looked up from where he was working alongside Bojo at one of the analyzers. He nodded quickly, issued a few curt instructions to Bojo, and waited for the older man to nod his understanding. Then he hurried over toward Nikki, wiping his hands dry on his labcoat. "Problem solved?" he asked quietly, in English, as he reached her.

It took Nikki a serious effort of will not to glance around at the others. In a way, she didn't have to: she could feel their eyes on her. "I think we should check the supplies," she suggested, also in English.

Toshikazu's eyebrows rose a minuscule degree, but his voice contained no emotion. "Perhaps a good idea," he agreed. He stepped aside and gestured for her to lead the way. (*Always polite*, Nikki thought with a grin.)

As they crossed the lab toward the door, the others watched them. Or, more probably, watched *her*, Nikki reflected. They must have overheard her phone conversations. What conclusions had they drawn? *Nothing good*, she decided. She was tempted to snap at them, tell them to get back to what they were supposed to be doing. But she knew that if she broke and showed weakness now, it would be pure hell regaining their respect after this was all over. *If it was* ever *all over*, the thought came unbidden, but she crushed it ruthlessly.

The supply room was across the hallway from Nikki's lab, a small room filled with shelving units, the shelves themselves packed with boxes of supplies and bottles of reagents. The room was slightly refrigerated to maximize the useful life of the chemicals, but even so it was marginally warmer than the lab itself.

Nikki held the door open while Toshikazu joined

her inside, then shut it behind him. She glanced around the bare white walls and ceiling. *Bugged*? She shook her head in disgust at her own thought. *That's too paranoid*, she told herself.

"What has happened?" Toshikazu asked, again in English.

Keeping to the same language, she gave him a quick run-down of the last half-hours events. She watched his eyes as she spoke, looking for some indication that he understood what was going on. But his face remained as unchanging as a statue's. "And when I logged back on, the lock was gone," she concluded at last. "What the *hell* is going on here?"

Toshikazu was silent for a moment in thought. His gaze was expressionless. '*The eyes are windows to the soul*,' she thought, *but he's closed the drapes*. What *was* going on?

Finally he spoke. "There are several possibilities," he said slowly. "Perhaps they wished to search for any personal correspondence you might have on the system, or maybe phone or address lists. They would be interested in anything that shed some light on your thoughts and your motivations." He hesitated, then added, "*And* your loyalties." He paused again, as though about to say something else, but then he simply shrugged wordlessly.

Nikki looked into his eyes. There was something there; she could see he was thinking something he hadn't yet put into words. *Why*?

"We're friends, Toshikazu?" she asked quietly, then went on without waiting for an answer. "Then why are you holding something back?" He glanced away from her scrutiny, and for the first time she saw emotion in his face: shame. "I know you think you're helping me," she continued gently, "but I don't want to be kept in the dark. What is it you're not telling me? What is it you know?"

He was silent again, and she could almost feel his racing thoughts. After a dozen heartbeats, his eyes again met hers, and this time they were clear. "Know?" he mused softly. "I *know* nothing; I just suspect."

"Then why won't you share your suspicions?"

He shrugged, as though uncomfortable putting it into words. "These are security matters," he began, his voice bleak. "In security matters, sometimes it is best to be ignorant of what they may be after, or of what they may be planning. If you are innocent, you have no need to know — that's what people say. If you *do* know, even if you *are* innocent, you will certainly react to the knowledge. And if you *do* react, how will the security forces interpret that reaction? They will be searching for anything out of the ordinary, and you will have just given them what they are looking for."

Nikki snorted. "That's ridiculous," she told him flatly. "You're saying the best thing to do is bury my head in the sand. That's not going to help."

Toshikazu shrugged again. "Perhaps," he said, although from his voice she knew he wasn't convinced. "Perhaps you may be right." His wry grin returned. "'The nail that sticks up gets hammered down.' Maybe I take that *too* seriously, now."

"So what should I do now?"

"I suggest you look through the directory for anything out of the ordinary," he answered immediately. "Are there any missing files? Are any files missing data?"

"I'll do that." She gave Toshikazu a warm smile. "Thank you," she said softly. "You're a good friend."

"I hope so," he said earnestly.

* * *

Nikki typed in the now-familiar computer command to access her private directory, almost expecting to find it locked again. But there was no beep, no

DIRECTORY LOCKED message. Obediently, the computer filled the terminal screen with a listing of all the files in the directory.

There were about forty of them, more than enough to fill a single screen. At first she'd only kept her work journal in this directory. But with time, she'd filled it out with more and more files. Letters to friends at home, written on coffee breaks and run off on the laser printer late at night when only Toshikazu was around. (Fortunately, the computer was "bilingual" in that it could handle both English letters and *kanji* characters. All of her personal files were in English.) Address and phone records. Personal to-do lists. Records for her personal accounting, and lists of financial and career goals. It had taken her a while to feel comfortable with using the computer system as a personal resource, but as soon as she'd started she couldn't understand how she'd ever functioned without it. Now she had to scan through all those files. *I can't remember half of what should be there*, she thought. *How will I know if something's missing?* But even though she thought it was futile, she pressed on.

It was at the bottom of the file list that she found it: a file name that didn't look immediately familiar. Not that it was too different from the files around it — files with names like MOTHER.LET, SAMANTHA.LET, STEVE.LET, and TO-DO.NOT. *STORM.LET*, it was called. Most of the others she remembered, or she could at least guess what they contained from the names she'd chosen at the time. But not STORM.LET. Puzzled, she hit the function key that would display the contents of the file on the screen.

The computer beeped and flashed a message on the status line at the top of the screen — ENTER PASSWORD (STORM.LET):

Encrypted, she thought. The only time the computer asked for a password before opening a file was if the

 63

person who'd created the file had encrypted it for secrecy and locked it out. Without the password, the file would appear as unintelligible garbage, if the person trying to view it could even get it to display at all. Nikki rarely encrypted her personal files. Only letters dealing with particularly personal or emotional issues, and her work journal, were locked. It was more a reflex than anything, about akin to hiding a diary in a desk drawer rather than leaving it out in the open — and not much more useful, when it came down to it. She always used the same password for any files she happened to lock, something she knew she'd have no trouble remembering: *NLMC*, for Nikki Louise Mary Carlson. She knew that anybody who was serious about cracking into her files would include that as one of their first guesses; the primary rule of computer security was always to use a password that had no obvious connection with anything that anyone else knew about you. Locking a file with her own initials — it was basically useless, other than as a trick to make herself less uncomfortable about leaving intensely personal matter on the corporate computer system.

At least I don't have to worry about not remembering the password. She typed in the letters NLMC and hit the Enter key.

Beep. INVALID PASSWORD, the terminal displayed.

What? Maybe she'd mis-keyed it: "NMLC" instead of "NLMC," maybe. She tried again.

Again the beep, again INVALID PASSWORD. STORM.LET remained encrypted and locked.

Nikki gnawed at her lower lip with her front teeth. Something was very wrong. Something *continued* to be very wrong. "Toshikazu," she called, pitching her voice just loudly enough to be heard outside the cubicle.

He was there immediately, almost as if he'd been

waiting for her summons. "Yes, Nikki?" She pointed to the file listing on the screen. "Something missing?" he asked, now speaking in English.

Nikki kept her voice low. "Something *added*," she corrected him. "This one, here." She indicated the offending entry in the listing.

"Not yours?" Toshikazu's voice held something more than surprise, Nikki thought, but his face was once more expressionless. (*That should tell me something*, she mused, *when he goes stone-faced he's holding something back*.) "What is in it?"

"Not mine," she confirmed. "And it's locked and encrypted."

"Truly?" That had shocked him, Nikki could tell. "Delete it, Nikki. Get rid of it. Now."

"I want to see what's in it," she told him, keeping her voice as calm as she could, free of the anger she felt. "Somebody's trying to screw me over. Can you decrypt it for me?"

"No, I can't. Not in time."

It was Nikki's turn to feel shock. A cold ball of ice was in the pit of her stomach. "In time for what?"

Toshikazu pointed at the large digital clock on the wall of the lab. The red digits read 4:51. "At five o'clock every day, the MIS department backs up the entire memory of the computer onto magnetic tape."

"So what?"

Toshikazu pitched his voice even lower, until it was barely more than a whisper. "Nikki," he said, "somebody created that file, locked it so you could never read it — I assume they hoped you would never try — and placed it in your directory. We can only assume they intend it to be found, by *somebody*. I think that would be very bad. Disastrous."

She stared at him. Her mind was racing. "Are you saying ...?"

He cut her off. "I beg forgiveness," he whispered

urgently, "I advised you badly earlier. You were right, I was in error — ignorance is not safety." He pointed to the file listing on the screen. "Delete that file. If you obliterate it before MIS performs their backup, nobody can prove that it was ever there. If you wait ..."

He didn't have to complete the thought; Nikki knew where he was headed. *If it's still there when the backup's run, there's permanent proof that it was there.* Whatever it is. It made sense, but ... "It's locked, Toshikazu," she reminded him. "I can't delete it without the password."

"*Kusotare*," he swore quietly. "Forgive me, I thought ... allow me."

Nikki rolled her chair out of the way, and Toshikazu crouched at the keyboard. As before, she tried to watch over his shoulder — watch and learn — but he worked too fast.

It wasn't easy. From what she knew of the computer's operating system architecture, it should have been impossible. Repeatedly, the computer beeped its refusal to follow the typed commands, echoed by Toshikazu's growled Japanese oaths. She looked up at the digital clock — 4:57. *Beep.*

Toshikazu mumbled in anger to himself as the computer again refused to execute his commands. Watching over his shoulder, she saw him clear the screen and start again.

The clock read 4:58. Even though she still didn't really understand exactly what was going on, Toshikazu's urgency was contagious. She shifted uncomfortably from foot to foot, hating the forced inaction. *I should be doing something to help,* she told herself. But there wasn't anything she could do, she realized with a sick, sinking feeling in her belly. Toshikazu was already way beyond her understanding of the system and her capabilities, off somewhere in some uncharted territory of computer arcana.

Beep. It was 4:59. She found herself worrying at a corner of a broken thumbnail with her front teeth. With an effort, she forced both hands to her sides. Once more she looked over Toshikazu's shoulder.

It took her a moment to understand what she was seeing. Toshikazu had hacked his way deep into the operating system of the computer system, deeper than even the system operator could normally go. Instead of issuing the normal type of operating system commands — like COPY or DELETE — her friend was writing short assembly-language routines on the fly, tiny programs to take direct control of the system's hardware, bypassing the operating system's structure of checks and balances, control and security. *How can anybody work so fast?* she found herself wondering. Toshikazu's fingers were moving so quickly as to seem almost a blur. She was overcome with amazement at her friend's skill.

Even so, he wasn't going to make it, she realized. The thought carried with it no real fear, just a sense of resignation and fatalism.

But then it was over. Toshikazu was sitting back in her chair, breathing deeply, as if trying to clear his body of fatigue poisons built up over the course of a marathon run. He stretched his arms, worked his shoulders to release their tension. On the screen there was no evidence of his deep penetration into the system — just the file listing of Nikki's personal directory. She leaned closer. Yes, STORM.LET was gone.

The computer beeped, then its small speaker played a tinny rendition of the first phrase from the corporate anthem — the normal indication that the system-wide backup had begun. She glanced up at the digital clock. It was 5:00.

Gently, she laid a hand on Toshikazu's shoulder. He looked up at her, a sheen of sweat on his forehead. He gave her a tired smile. "A little too close for comfort, I think," he murmured.

"Thank you," she began, "I ..." But then she trailed off, not knowing what to say. But Toshikazu's smile just grew broader, and she realized that words weren't necessary. *You don't have to thank close friends*, she thought, *if it's important, they know*. She squeezed his shoulder. Toshikazu reached up and rested his own hand on hers. His palm was cool and smooth. With surprise, she felt a sudden warmth grow in her chest, spreading down to her stomach.

Toshikazu must have sensed the change, maybe seen it in her eyes, because he removed his hand from hers and pushed the chair back from the computer. When he stood up, his smile was still there, but it was more formal, as though he'd tightened his control over himself. But there was still warmth in his eyes, she saw. *He felt the same thing I did*, she told herself. *What was it?* Part of her mind thought she knew what it might be. *But now* certainly *isn't the time for that*. And that, she realized, was why Toshikazu had withdrawn — at least partially — behind his armor of Japanese politeness. We'll talk about this later, she promised herself. For the moment, though, there were more pressing things to discuss.

"*Domo arrigato gozaimas*, Toshikazu Kasigi," she said formally, bowing slightly from the hips in the Japanese manner. "I am in your debt." Before he could respond, she took a deep breath and continued quietly, "You said earlier that somebody created that file and put it in my directory — and they locked it, so I couldn't delete it. So that it would be found?"

Toshikazu's smile faded and he nodded. "So I speculate."

"So that would mean ..." Her mind shied back from the obvious conclusion, but she forced herself to face the fear. "So that would mean somebody's trying to link me with last night."

Toshikazu nodded again, slowly. He glanced around him, as if afraid of eavesdroppers, and lowered his voice even further. Nikki had to lean close to him to pick out his words. "I have heard through sources," Toshikazu said in English, "that Eichiro-san has suffered great loss of face from the events of last night. To use one of your more pungent American phrases, 'his balls are in a vice.'" Nikki grinned at the way the idiom sounded coming from Toshikazu's lips. But her smile quickly faded in the face of her friend's seriousness.

"The Special Projects lab was very important to Nagara's future," Toshikazu continued. "*Exceptionally* important. Pivotal, in fact. It was Eichiro-san's project, his instigation, his responsibility. And now it is gone. It looks exceptionally bad on Eichiro-san's record that the 'wreckers' managed to penetrate the security that he had established around the lab. The success of the raid is, to the Board's way of thinking, his responsibility and his shame." He hesitated, fixed Nikki with his dark eyes. "How much less shameful would his failure seem if it were to be proven that Eichiro-san had been betrayed from within …?" He let his voice trail off.

Nikki nodded slowly. It made a horrible kind of sense, taking into account what she knew about the paranoia that flowed like a subterranean river through Japanese corporate culture. "A frame, then?" she asked.

Toshikazu inclined his head. "Perhaps."

She waited for her friend to say more, but he held his peace. *That's right*, she thought, *he doesn't like speculating without enough data to go on.* "So what do you think I should do?" she asked.

He was silent for a few more seconds, then shrugged. "I would suggest nothing," he said at last. "The manufactured evidence is gone, the only person who has any record of it being there is the one who planted it. If you react in any way, you risk stirring up the suspicions of those the evidence was supposed to convince. I think the best course — the only course — is to carry on as though nothing had happened."

She snorted. "Just play dumb?" she demanded.

He shrugged again. "What else would you do?" he asked. "Accuse Eichiro-*san* of trying to frame you? Take your case to Kubota-*san* in the executive penthouse? The evidence is gone, it would be your word against that of Eichiro-*san*, and you are …"

"A *gaijin*," Nikki cut in, "I know."

"I was going to say 'a relatively junior technician,'" Toshikazu continued mildly. "What else would you do? Resign, and storm off in high dudgeon? That would just convince everyone that you were guilty, and you would find it difficult gaining further employment anywhere in Japan."

Nikki sighed. She recognized the truth in what Toshikazu was saying. But …

"It is difficult, I know," Toshikazu said quietly, seeming to read her mind. "But you have little choice but to keep your guard up, and stay aware of what happens around you."

He's right, she admitted with another resigned sigh. Impulsively, she reached out and squeezed his arm. "Keep my guard up," she echoed. "That goes for you too."

He nodded, for the first time his face showing an expression of worry.

* * *

The tenth floor cafeteria was crowded, now, filled with the dull hubbub of multiple muted conversation. *Quite different from the last time I saw it*, Nikki thought as she walked into the large room. The large windows looked out onto noontime Tokyo. A pale, watery sun shone through the familiar light mist, glinting palely off the great steel K atop the Kanawa Building, further down Etai-dori. Nikki looked around. The other mem-

bers of her workgroup were sitting at a table near the
automated cash-desks, heads bowed together as if in
deep conversation. For a moment she perversely considered joining them, just to see them stop their conversation, to feel their discomfort. But then she put the
idea aside as petty, unworthy. *And it would be just as
uncomfortable for me, anyway*, she admitted to herself.
She glanced around again. There was Toshikazu, sitting alone at a table near one of the great windows.
Their eyes met, and the young man smiled warmly at
her. She saw the bowl of *soba* noodles on the table in
front of her, and her stomach growled. Flashing
Toshikazu a quick smile and a wink, she joined the
lineup in front of the serving counters.

She was feeling much better today. A good night's
sleep — interrupted only occasionally by nightmares
— had made a huge difference in the way her body felt,
and in her entire outlook on the world. Memories of the
mysterious locked file, and Toshikazu's struggles to
erase it, still rankled, still filled her with profound
unease. But today her determination, her resolution,
were back. So somebody was trying to manipulate her,
was that it? She might follow Toshikazu's advice, to act
normally, but — by God — if she found any more
evidence of some kind of Machiavellian machinations
trying to ensnare her, she wasn't going to just sit back
fatalistically and accept her fate. She was going to *fight*.

From the large serving counters she selected a large
bowl of soba noodles in a light *miso*-style broth. For desert
she picked out a perfect, unblemished pear-apple, swathed
in a mesh of elastic white plastic foam. She inserted her
corporate credit card into the automated cash-desk's slot,
and waited while the system deducted the 475¥ cost of
her meal. Then she took her tray and crossed the large
room to join Toshikazu at his table.

He greeted her with a companionable smile, but
was too busy with his noodles to say anything. She

settled herself down in the plastic-backed chair. Carefully she took the thin wooden chopsticks from their paper sheath, separated them with a dry snick, and rubbed them gently together to remove the rough edges. The noodles were cooked perfectly, she found, soft but not boiled to sogginess.

Out of the corner of her eye she saw a familiar face at a nearby table. She turned.

It was a large-framed man with a face the texture of weathered leather and a full shock of white hair: Hiroyo Suganama, the MIS director. *I should thank him for yesterday*, Nikki thought. But it wouldn't be polite to interrupt the man's meal, she knew. Oh, well, she'd catch him on the way out.

She and Toshikazu ate without speaking, both enjoying the companionable silence. Throughout the meal, Nikki turned occasionally, trying to catch Suganama's eye, ready to give him a warm smile. But the old man kept his eyes down, concentrating on the two sticks of *yakitori* on his plate. At one time, for just an instant, she thought she felt the man's eyes on her, but when she turned to look, he was again busy with his food. The moment bothered her a little. Was Suganama ignoring her, for some reason? Then she shook the thought off. *Paranoid thinking again*, she told herself.

When Nikki and Toshikazu had finished their meal, they stacked their empty trays in the middle of the table for the staff to take away. "I'll see you in a moment," she told Toshikazu, "I want to talk to a friend." Toshikazu nodded good-naturedly. A smile on her face, Nikki started toward Suganama.

The white-haired man looked up. For an instant their eyes met. Suganama's face flushed suddenly, and he looked quickly away. Hurriedly, he put his chopsticks down on his plate next to the unfinished *yakitori*. Then, looking for all the world like someone who'd just remembered an important appointment, he bolted to his feet. As Nikki watched, stunned, he turned his back on her, and strode across the room and out the door, disappearing around the corner into the hallway.

Nikki stood, dumbfounded. Then she felt a presence at her elbow. She turned, unsurprised to find Toshikazu standing beside her. Expressionlessly, he was watching the door through which Suganama had vanished. "What was that all about?" she asked quietly.

Toshikazu shook his head. "I don't know," he replied in Japanese. "But I'll find out for you, if you like. Suganama-*san* is ... an old friend of the family, you might say. I'll see you down in the lab."

Nikki watched him stride out the same door the MIS director had used. She shook her head in befuddlement. Toshikazu had never mentioned that he knew such an august personage as Suganama. *But then, he never talks about his family*, she remembered. It didn't really matter anyway. Suganama's behavior was much more puzzling than Toshikazu's family connections. Why had the old man — her mentor, as she liked to think — avoided her so pointedly? Something was definitely happening, and the fact that she didn't understand it made it feel infinitely worse.

Chapter Three

The rest of Nikki's workgroup were back at work when she returned to the lab. They glanced up when she entered, but the speed with which they looked back to their work just reinforced the fact that they were ignoring her. Anger warred with confusion in her chest, a churning knot of emotion, as she crossed the lab to her cubicle. *Maybe I should just resign,* she thought grimly. *So what if I don't work anywhere else in Japan? I could get a job in any research lab in America.* She slumped down in her desk chair.

But quitting isn't really an option, is it? she asked herself. She'd always prided herself on her tenacity, her ability to stick with any course she'd chosen and see it through to its conclusion. It was her "way."

It seemed like only a couple of minutes later that she took a momentary break, but according to the digital clock on the wall she'd been working for almost half an hour. She stood up, stretched, and looked out into the lab from the door of her cubicle. Toshikazu still wasn't back, she noticed with some surprise. What was he talking to Suganama about that would take half an hour? *Oh, well, she thought, maybe Suganama-san knows what's behind all this intrigue crap.* She turned to go back into her cubicle, but movement at the lab door caught her eye.

The door had swung back, and two white-armored Security "stormtroopers" strode in. Behind them she saw two others with their backs to her, flanking the doorway. *What the hell is this?* she asked herself.

The two guards strode directly toward her, the members of Group Five looking up in their wake and staring at their armored backs. Stopping in front of her, they both bowed millimetrically. The one on the right flipped up his mirrored faceplate. His eyes were the grey of cold steel.

"Carrson-*san*," the guard said, "Eichiro-*san* invites you to speak with him. Would you care to accompany us?"

It wasn't an order, not quite. She *could*, by all rights, refuse — effectively upping the ante, and seeing how the guards would respond. For a moment she considered doing just that, but then decided against it. *What good will it do to make a scene? If Eichiro wants to see me, he'll order me up to his office — if not now, then later. Why not go with dignity?*

Those thoughts had flashed through Nikki's mind in a split second, hardly long enough for the guards to note the hesitation. She forced her face into an expressionless mask, and returned the guards' bows with a slight nod. "I accept Eichiro-*san*'s kind offer of hospitality," she said coolly, using the mode of speech that one would use to a trusted servant, and pitching her voice so the others in her workgroup could hear her. "You will escort me to him at once."

The guard's brow furrowed slightly in ill-concealed anger. Without overstepping the bounds of Japanese propriety, Nikki had, by her phrasing, verbally "demoted" them to the status of underlings providing a service. She kept her face totally expressionless, but inside she was smiling. *Even a small victory's a victory*, she told herself. Without glancing back — simply assuming that the guards would follow her — she strode to the door. As she passed, the other lab workers looked at her, and shot veiled "I told you so" glances back and forth among themselves, but she kept her gaze straight ahead, ignoring them.

She stepped out into the hallway where the two other guards stood, only now glancing back to see the first two following her. It was hard to maintain the imperious manner she'd assumed. Inside she was scared — scared and worried. If Toshikazu was right about Eichiro losing serious face over the attack by the "wreckers," what was this meeting going to be about?

Without speaking, the four armored guards formed up in a square formation with Nikki in the center. Then they started for the elevator.

* * *

Agatamori Eichiro's office was on the thirty-eighth floor of the Nagara Building, only two floors below the penthouse floor devoted entirely to the corporation's Chief Executive Officer, Kubota-san, and his personal staff. The office itself looked roughly north, toward where the trees that surrounded the Imperial Palace could be seen over the intervening buildings. Nikki was conscious of the view for only a second, before her full attention was captured by the man sitting behind the large teak desk.

Eichiro-*san* was a hard-looking man in his late thirties, with a strong, heavy jaw and a mouth that seemed to naturally settle into a frown of aloof displeasure. His black hair was cut in the latest Tokyo style — short, almost spiked, on top, but at the back and sides touching the collar of his dark, impeccably tailored suit. Nikki had initially met him when she'd been going through the hiring process on first joining Nagara. In fact, it was Eichiro, as senior manager of the Genetic Research Division, who had so brusquely welcomed her to the Nagara fold. At that time, it had been the man's eyes that she'd most noticed. Dark and hard, they looked, as cold as the glass eye of the stuffed panther she'd seen in the Tokyo National History Museum. Cold, but alive too, always moving as though their owner was noticing everything, and glinting with a sharp understanding — and sometimes a grim amusement — about all that surrounded him. Those eyes didn't seem quite human, she'd thought at the time.

And now those eyes were fixed on her, as she stood before Eichiro's desk. The four security guards had escorted Nikki to the thirty-ninth floor, to an anteroom warded by a drone-like assistant. Hardly looking up from his desk, the drone had pressed a button, and the door into the inner office had swung open. This whole scene had been played out without anyone — the escorts, the drone, or Nikki herself — saying a word. Obviously everyone knew who she was and why she was there.

As the door opened, Nikki had taken another deep breath to try to still the fear that churned in her belly. Then, keeping her back straight and her face expressionless, she'd stepped forward into Eichiro's office, leaving her armored escort in the outer office. The door had closed behind her with a metallic click that had a sense of finality about it.

Eichiro looked her up and down wordlessly. His thick forefinger, banded with a heavy gold ring, tapped — seemingly idly — at the teak desk. He glanced to his right, to the other man in the office sitting in one of the comfortable visitor chairs set around the desk. It was Iwao Yamato, the security chief. The chill in Nikki's belly grew in intensity. As the two men — both very powerful within the structure of Nagara — glared at her, she felt the urge to back away, to hide somewhere.

But she schooled her face to immobility, hoping her eyes didn't give away her fear. She bowed to Eichiro. *"Konichi-wa*, Eichiro-*san*," she said. "Yamato-*san*," she added, repeating the bow, but not quite so deeply. "You sent for me?"

The division manager regarded her in silence for a few more seconds, his perpetual frown deepening marginally. Then he nodded sharply. "Thank you for accepting my invitation," he said, a hint of irony tingeing his voice. *He's enjoying this*, Nikki realized with a shock. Eichiro indicated a chair situated directly in front of his desk, but about six feet back, set apart from the rest of the office's furniture. "Please be seated."

Nikki settled herself into the comfortable chair, tried to relax as much as she could. She could feel a cold prickling along her hairline — *the start of a cold sweat, maybe?*

"We have some questions to ask you," Eichiro told her flatly. "If you answer truthfully and completely, all will be well for you." He turned to the security chief and nodded.

"Thank you, Eichiro-*san*." Yamato stood, strolled slowly around to the front of the manager's desk. All the while, he was regarding Nikki with a mix of curiosity and distaste — the expression of someone examining a particularly noxious specimen of spider in a museum case. Nikki was sure Yamato's expression and his pacing were an act, designed to unsettle her. (*And it's working*, she had to admit.) The situation seemed somehow familiar, but she couldn't put her finger on it immediately.

Then it came to her. This was all like a scene out of a courtroom drama — the accused called to the witness stand, with the prosecuting attorney pacing in front of her like a caged tiger, while the judge watches calmly from behind his desk. For a moment she felt a nervous laugh bubbling in her throat. *This is just too theatrical*, she told herself. But then she looked at the faces of Eichiro and Yamato. They were dead serious about this. *I'm on trial here*. Her skin felt cold all over.

Yamato stopped directly in front of her, fixed her with a cold gaze. "Miss Carlson," he began, taking great effort to pronounce the name correctly, "we would like you to tell us about your friends." His voice was calm, reasonable — a drastic contrast to the hostility of his expression.

Nikki glanced over at Eichiro. He was leaning back in his chair, half-closed eyes regarding her over steepled fingers. His body language spoke of boredom, but she could see the glint of his eyes under the drooping lids. She knew he was paying close attention.

She returned her concentration to Yamato. "What friends do you mean?" she asked — although as she said it, she had the horrible intuition that she already knew.

Yamato smiled — or tried to. His tight cheeks and tensed jaw turned the expression into a grimace. "Come, Miss Carlson," he said lightly, "don't waste our time. We know of your connection with the wreckers. We just want to hear the confirmation from your own lips."

And there it was, what Nikki had been both dreading and expecting. Anger mixed with fear in her chest, fire and ice. "There's no connection," she said sharply. "I don't know who they were. They've got nothing to do with me."

Yamato shrugged. "So you say." He paused for a moment. When he continued, his voice was even softer, silky-smooth. "You listen to the Voice of America radio station, don't you, Miss Carlson?"

Nikki was taken aback. *How the hell do they know that?* She listened to the radio only at home, never at work. *Are they bugging my apartment?* "Yes," she snapped, "if it's any of your business what I listen to at home."

The security chief nodded slowly. "Yes, I see," he mused. "It's interesting, Miss Carlson. We have found that there are frequently broadcasts on the Voice of America that seem to be in error. The business reports sometimes discuss companies that simply don't exist. Have you ever noticed that?" He hurried on before Nikki had a chance to answer. "This fascinated us, so we had various experts analyze these 'errors' for any content they may have other than the obvious. Do you know what we found?" Again, he gave Nikki no time to respond. "We found that those 'errors' are actually coded messages, directed to covert groups operating within Japan. And who else could these covert groups be but the wreckers who threaten our society?" He turned to Nikki again, his rictus-like smile back on his face. "And you listen to the Voice of America, do you, Miss Carlson? How interesting." Yamato glanced at Eichiro, maybe checking to see if his point had made any impact on the senior manager. But Eichiro-*san* gave no sign of even having heard, although his hard eyes were still fixed on Nikki.

Pure anger flared in Nikki's chest. "So I listen to the Voice of America," she snapped. "So *what*? Maybe there *are* messages, I don't know. But they're not directed to me."

The two Japanese men were watching her coldly. *Emotion won't help me*, she realized. With an effort, she forced herself into a semblance of calm. She settled back in her chair, crossed her legs. "Whether or not I listen to the radio is totally irrelevant," she stated flatly.

Yamato shrugged. "Perhaps." He paused for a moment, then started on a new tack. "When you applied for employment here at Nagara Corporation, you applied to no other corporation, before or after. Isn't that true?"

Nikki nodded. "That's true," she confirmed.

"Interesting," Yamato mused. "Of all the advertisements in the newspapers and elsewhere describing positions similar to yours, you chose to apply for only the one with Nagara."

"I didn't *read* any of the other advertisements," Nikki shot back. "Yours was the only one in English and Japanese."

But Yamato went on as though he hadn't heard her. "Interesting," he repeated. "One might conclude that it might somehow serve you in the future to be part of the corporate structure at Nagara. Perhaps that's why you came to Japan in the first place, *neh*? To infiltrate our corporation?"

Nikki's control slipped. "That's *paranoid*!" she snapped.

Yamato's eyebrows rose in an expression of feigned surprise. "Paranoid, Miss Carlson? Not so. Paranoids falsely believe that enemies surround them. The events of two nights ago *prove* that our enemies exist, wouldn't you agree?"

"I've worked here for years," she shot back. "Am I going to invest years of my life just to be involved in one incident?"

Yamato shrugged again. "Why not?" he asked rhetorically. "When one is firmly dedicated to a goal, how much of a sacrifice is a few years?"

"This is *ridiculous*!" She started to rise. "I don't have to sit here and listen to these insinuations ..."

Eichiro's calm voice froze her in her seat. "I submit that you do, Miss Carlson," he said quietly. "We are trying to get to the bottom of a disturbing situation, and we ask your cooperation. Perhaps Yamato-*san* is somewhat" — he hesitated, seeking the right word — "somewhat *zealous* in making his points, but they are points that must be made. And when he is finished, we would like to hear your answers to them. If you are unwilling to cooperate, one must wonder exactly *why*. Do you understand me, Miss Carlson?"

Nikki ground her teeth. *I understand you, alright*, she thought *Stay around and listen to this crap, or you'll decide I'm guilty here and now.* "I understand," she grated, her voice harsh through tight lips.

Eichiro nodded his thanks to Nikki — an insulting and condescending gesture, she thought — and glanced at Yamato to continue.

Yamato bowed slightly, and indicated the multi-line phone on Eichiro's desk. "With your permission, Eichiro-*san* ...?" At Eichiro's nod, the Security chief pressed a button on the phone that sat next to the manager's compact computer terminal. "Send in Bannen," he ordered.

"*Hai*, Yamato-*san*," the drone's voice sounded from the speaker.

A few moments later the office door opened, and a strongly-built young man strode in. He wore a grey jumpsuit, with the Nagara logo in blue and white embroidered on the shoulders. The outfit looked familiar to Nikki, although she couldn't place it immediately.

The young man's left arm was in a cast, supported by a sling, and a white dressing covered his left eye. The skin around the dressing was puffy and inflamed, probably very painful. But if he felt the pain, he showed no sign. He stopped just inside the door, and bowed deeply to Eichiro and then Yamato. "Ujiaki Bannen reporting as ordered, sirs," he said formally.

"Stand at ease, my friend," Yamato told him. The line of the young man's body softened marginally, as if he were holding himself slightly less rigidly. "Now," the security chief went on, "you were on duty the night before last, is that correct?"

"Yes, Yamato-*san*," Bannen agreed. It was then that

 82

Nikki recognized the grey jumpsuit: it was the "off-duty" uniform of Nagara security. Bannen was a security guard, obviously one of those wounded by the raiders.

Yamato was speaking again. "You saw Miss Carlson on that night?" he asked. His tone was light, friendly.

Bannen turned his one good eye on Nikki. Even though his face remained immobile, she could feel his hostility. "Yes, Yamato-*san*," the guard repeated. "She was in the Special Projects secured lab. I don't know how she got past the security door."

"The door was unlocked," Nikki blurted. "It unlocks in an emergency."

"Yes, perhaps it does," Yamato said slowly, but his expression was one of outright disbelief. With an effort, Nikki held her tongue. Eichiro was looking at her coldly, and the guard called Bannen glared from his uninjured eye with undisguised hatred. Alienating everybody isn't going to help, she told herself.

"What was Miss Carlson doing when you saw her?" Yamato asked.

"She was facing one of the wreckers," Bannen answered at once. "He had his gun on her. I assumed he was about to shoot her."

Yamato was smiling now, the smile of a shark. "But he *didn't* shoot her, did he?"

"No," the guard replied with a brisk shake of his head. "He let her live. He turned aside and spared her life."

"Oh?" Once more, Yamato feigned surprise. "And why did he do that, I wonder? After killing anyone else who crossed his path, he spared Miss Carlson's life." He paused. With a horrible chill, Nikki realized what was coming next. "Did it appear that he spared the life of a *comrade*?" the security chief asked casually.

"Yes, Yamato-*san*," Bannen said firmly. "That is *just* how it appeared."

Nikki couldn't hold her tongue any longer. "That's not how it was!" she shouted. "I never saw them before."

"Then why did they spare your life?" Yamato's cold eyes seemed to bore into hers.

"I don't know," she answered after a moment. "I … I was a noncombatant."

"So were the scientists in the Special Projects lab," Yamato pointed out. "Yet they were killed."

Nikki couldn't resist. "So the e-mail message yesterday was a lie?"

Yamato waved that off. "Immaterial," he told her, then went back to his original point. "The wreckers had already killed noncombatants. Why leave you alive?"

"I wasn't their target."

"Oh?" Yamato's eyebrows shot up. "Interesting that you *know* with such surety what the wreckers' target was, Miss Carlson." Before she could answer, the security chief had turned to the wounded guard. "Thank you, Bannen, you may go."

The young man bowed formally. "The honor was mine, Yamato-*san*. Eichiro-*san*." He turned to leave.

As he opened the door, Yamato added, "And send in Tada, please."

"*Hai*, Yamato-*san*."

A moment later, another security guard strode into the office — this one unwounded, wearing his armored uniform, and carrying his helmet under his left arm. Although his features were different, he seemed to have come from the same mold as Bannen.

Nikki wasn't paying him much attention, however. She rounded on Yamato. "This is ridiculous!" she spat. The security chief merely shrugged.

It was Eichiro who spoke. "It may *seem* ridiculous, Miss Carlson," he said quietly. "But you will understand we have to find the truth in this matter."

"There's no *truth* here," she shot back. "This is a set-up, a kangaroo court."

"I am unfamiliar with that idiom," Eichiro told her drily, "but I can guess at its meaning from context." His heavy finger tapped the desk as he thought for a moment. "I could choose to be insulted by that, but that would serve no purpose. You are unfamiliar with our ways, Miss Carlson. This is how things are handled in Japan, and specifically within Nagara. When Yamato-*san* has had his say, you will have yours. Then I'll judge where the truth lies. Your choices are to stay, and speak your piece once Yamato-san has finished. Or you can leave, and then there will be no-one to rebut Yamato-*san*'s assertions."

Eichiro leaned forward. His eyes were calm, fixed on hers, and his manner was the epitome of sincerity. "You think our practices unfair, *neh*? They are not, and they are not meant to be. They are just different from what you are used to. Our customs have served us well for millennia, Miss Carlson. I ask that you trust to them." He smiled, a chilly expression obviously intended to be reassuring. "To quote an English aphorism, 'Truth will out.'"

Nikki hesitated. It still felt like a kangaroo court, a frame-up, no matter what Eichiro said. But she had to admit that his point about different customs was valid. The only intelligent choice was to see this matter through.

As if reading her mind, Eichiro asked, "Then you'll cooperate?"

She nodded brusquely.

"Thank you." Eichiro turned to the security chief. "You may proceed."

Yamato bowed his thanks. He faced the new security guard, standing at attention near the door. "And you are …?"

"Natsui Tada, reporting as ordered, sirs," the young man snapped.

"You may stand at ease," Yamato told him. The armored guard relaxed a little physically, but didn't lose his air of intense mental alertness. "What was your duty the night before last, Tada?"

"I was assigned to the ground floor, Yamato-*san*."

The security chief nodded. "I understand that you saw something of significance some time before one in the morning?"

"*Hai*, Yamato-*san*," Tada nodded. "I had stepped outside into the alleyway behind our building. I felt the need for some fresh air." (*You wanted a smoke, you mean*, Nikki thought.) "I recall looking at my watch. It was exactly 12:44."

"What did you see, Tada?" Yamato prompted.

"I saw two people speaking in the shadows some distance down the alleyway from me," the guard responded. "I was curious. It seemed like an unusual time and place for a meeting, so I walked toward them. I don't know if they saw me or not, but they both vanished into the shadows, one heading away from the building, one heading back toward it."

"Ah," Yamato said. "What were these two people wearing?"

"One was wearing a black jumpsuit, with a black stocking cap on his head." The guard spoke precisely and clearly. *He's rehearsed this*, Nikki thought. "It was the black-clothed man who aroused my curiosity in the first place. His outfit was not what you normally see on the streets of Marunouchi. It was he who moved away from the building."

"And the other?" asked Yamato. "What did the other wear?"

"She wore a white coat," Tada replied. "At first I didn't recognize it, but then I realized it was a lab coat, like the ones our scientists wear."

"You've seen the security camera records of the wreckers?" Tada nodded at Yamato's question. "Was

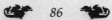 86

the man's clothing like the suits they wore?"

"Exactly, Yamato-*san*."

Yamato nodded. "Did you recognize either of the figures?" he asked quietly.

"I had never seen the man before," the guard answered carefully.

"And the woman?"

"Yes, Yamato-*san*," answered Tada. "I knew her. It was Miss Carrson." His eyes fixed on Nikki's face, burning with hatred.

Nikki bolted to her feet. "That's a *lie*!" she shouted. "When was this supposed to be? At 12:44? I was in the cafeteria on ten; I didn't meet with anyone outside." She whirled on the security guard. "Who told you to lie?" Then a thought struck her. "What did the man look like?" she asked, her voice calmer. "His face, what color was his hair, his eyes …?"

Yamato cut her off. "I'm asking the questions," he snapped.

"I demand the right to question any witness you bring against me," Nikki said flatly.

"This isn't a trial."

"It's you that's turning it into one." She turned to the division manager. "Eichiro-*san*, you said I had the right to speak."

Eichiro remained silent, motionless for a few moments. Then he nodded slowly and leaned back in his leather chair. "You may speak," he said quietly.

Nikki shot a victorious glare at Yamato, then turned to the security guard. "Answer my question," she growled, "what did the man look like? What color was his hair?"

The guard hesitated. "I couldn't see," he said slowly.

"And his eyes?"

"I couldn't see."

"Was he oriental, or was he Western? Was he a *gaijin* like me?"

Tada remained silent. His eyes shifted uncomfortably.

"You couldn't see," Nikki answered for him. "How far away were you from the people?" Again, Tada didn't speak, looking even more edgy. "*How far*?" Nikki grated.

"About forty meters," the guard said, unwillingly, as though he were admitting to a heinous crime.

"And was there fog in the alley?" Nikki asked. Tada nodded slowly. "Then how the *hell* did you recognize *me*?" she exploded. "I *wasn't* there, I never *went* outside last night. This is a set-up." She turned to glare at Yamato. The security chief looked ready to explode himself — red-faced and tight-lipped. He drew breath to yell back ...

But Eichiro cut him off. "Interesting," the division manager said quietly. "It would seem that the young man's testimony leaves some doubt. Wouldn't you agree, Yamato-*san*?" The security chief wilted under Eichiro's cold and level stare.

"*Hai*, Eichiro-*san*," he said unwillingly, "so it might seem, but ..."

Again he was cut off, this time by a soft beep from the telephone on Eichiro's desk. Eichiro face showed an instant of surprise, then he hit the intercom button on the phone. "Yes?" he snapped.

There was no answer from the phone, but instead the door swung open to admit three men. Hiroyo Suganama, the MIS director, was in the lead, with Toshikazu close behind. To Nikki's eyes, Toshikazu looked tense — determined to see something through, even though he'd rather be just about anywhere else. Suganama, on the other hand, looked cool and calm, totally unperturbed.

"My apologies for my impolite intrusion," the aged MIS director said, bowing to Eichiro. To Nikki's amusement — carefully hidden — he didn't even acknowledge Yamato's existence. "I understand that there is something of an inquest underway. Is that so?"

For a brief moment, Eichiro looked put out. Then his face assumed its familiar politely expressionless mask once more. "That is so, Suganama-*san*," he replied with a slight bow. "We were exploring the possible involvement of Miss Carlson here with the events of the other evening."

Suganama raised an eyebrow quizzically. "So? Is there evidence of such involvement?"

Eichiro shrugged slightly. "Yamato-*san* believes there may be," he said noncommittally. "I am unconvinced as yet, but it warrants scrutiny, wouldn't you agree?"

That earned Eichiro a look of hastily-covered anger from the security chief. *Interesting*, Nikki thought, *what does* that *mean?*

"Perhaps," Suganama said quietly. "But this loyal employee" — he indicated Toshikazu — "has raised the possibility that some of that evidence has been manufactured by Security Chief Yamato. I believe *that* warrants scrutiny as well."

That was too much for Yamato. His face went pale, highlighted by red spots on both cheeks. "That's a lie!" he yelled, forcefully enough to spray spittle onto the lapels of Suganama's well-tailored suit. "I manufactured *nothing* …" Then he saw the expression on Suganama's face — a look of aloof disgust that might normally be reserved for a particularly grotesque-looking worm found in his *sunomono* salad. With a Herculean effort, Yamato enforced a semblance of control. He bowed deeply from the hips. "Please pardon my inexcusable outburst, Suganama-*san*," he said through tight lips.

Suganama simply ignored him, focusing his attention solely on Eichiro. "Please, tell me what evidence the Security Chief has presented?" he asked politely.

Nigel Findley

Eichiro shrugged again casually. "Mainly circumstantial matters, Suganama-*san*," he said lightly. "Except for the last issue, which revolves around Miss Carlson's movements on the night of the raid. Just preceding the raid, in fact," he amended.

"Yes." Suganama nodded thoughtfully. "I thought that might be the case."

"Oh?" Eichiro looked surprised at that. "Why would you think that, Suganama-*san*?"

The old man's eyes were steady, meeting and holding Eichiro's gaze. "You are aware of the system that tracks the movements of those wearing corporate security badges?" he asked.

"Of course."

"The records from this system are stored in a highly secure directory on the central computer system," Suganama went on. "Certain departments and individuals — such as Security Chief Yamato and his immediate subordinates — are authorized to scan those records. For obvious reasons, no-one is permitted to modify them. If anyone had sufficient authority — we call them 'rights' — to change them, then the integrity of the entire system would be compromised."

"Of course," Eichiro agreed. "That is just how it should be."

"Then you may find it interesting that my staff detected an attempt, several hours ago, to break into that portion of the system," Suganama said coolly. "Specifically, it was an attempt to modify those records tracking the movements of Miss Carlson's badge — in other words, apparently an attempt to make it seem that she was where she was not." He paused. "That attempt was made by a programmer on the personal staff of Security Chief Yamato. The attempt was a failure," he added lightly.

Eichiro was glaring at Yamato in undisguised anger. The security chief's face was sallow, seemingly bloodless. His gaze seemed fixed on the toes of his highly-polished shoes, unable to meet Eichiro's eyes.

Suganama seemed totally unaffected by the high level of emotions in the room. He smiled mildly at Eichiro. "What portion of Miss Carlson's nightly movements did the Security Chief bring into question?"

Eichiro glanced over at Yamato, and at the security guard. Nikki noticed the young man's eyes were fixed on a spot several million miles beyond Eichiro's window, and that he was trying his best to pretend that he simply wasn't there. "Several minutes around 12:45, I believe," Eichiro said. "But I don't believe it's necessary for us to review the records."

"I respectfully insist," Suganama said firmly. "I feel it's important to set all doubts to rest." He walked around to Eichiro's side of the desk and gestured at the computer terminal. "I can display the records here."

As the old man bent over the terminal and rattled away on the keyboard, Nikki slumped back in her chair. The tight fist of tension in her belly had relaxed, leaving nausea in its wake. She looked back over her shoulder at Toshikazu.

Her friend was still standing by the door, hands by his side, eyes cast down — the perfect portrait of the respectful junior employee in the presence of his betters. But the subtle wink and the quick smile he shot her ruined the image. She sighed with relief.

Suganama and Eichiro had finished with the terminal. "I agree, Suganama-*san*," the division manager was saying, "there's little doubt Miss Carlson was with Kasigi on the tenth floor. Tada must have seen somebody else in the alley" — he glanced sharply at the young security guard — "if he saw anyone at all."

Eichiro turned to Nikki. "Miss Carlson," he began. Hastily, Nikki got to her feet. "Miss Carlson," he repeated, "I offer you heartfelt apologies for this unpleasantness, and for any dishonor you may have suffered. That was not the intention here."

Nikki nodded, not trusting herself to speak. Eichiro sounded sincerely concerned, but the anger and the shame she'd felt were still close to the surface. It wouldn't do to snarl at her boss, particularly when he was apologizing.

"This must have been stressful," Eichiro continued. "Please take the rest of the day off." He looked up at Suganama. "I wish to thank you, Suganama-*san*," he said respectfully, "for preventing a travesty of justice. I am in your debt." He sighed, suddenly looking weary. This was hard on him, too, Nikki realized. "Now, if you will forgive me, I wish to speak to Yamato and Tada in private ..."

* * *

Nikki and Toshikazu were alone in the elevator. As soon as they'd left Eichiro's office, Suganama had patted her reassuringly on the arm.

"*Domo arrigato gozaimas*, Suganama-*san*," she'd said quietly. "I am truly in your debt." He had bowed politely in response to her thanks, then he'd headed off for his office.

Now she turned to Toshikazu, her head buzzing with questions she wanted to ask. But first, "Thank you, too," she said, gently touching his arm. "I think you saved my bacon. If ..." *If you hadn't arrived, I don't know what would have happened*, is what she'd started to say, but it sounded so cliche. True, but still painfully trite. She settled for squeezing his arm. "I'm in your debt, too, my friend."

Her thanks seemed to make Toshikazu uncomfortable. He blushed slightly, and dropped his eyes. To spare his feelings, she changed the subject slightly. She asked, "What happened? How did Suganama get into the act?"

Toshikazu shrugged. "As I told you, I have a slight

connection with Suganama-*san*," he answered. "When he left the cafeteria, I followed, and I told him about the file planted in your directory. He already knew about the attempt to alter the security records, and he just put two and two together." He smiled. "And then he just took over. He stormed up to Eichiro's office and just kind of dragged me along." He shuddered in mock fear. "So I got dragged into the lion's den. Scared the hell out of me."

Nikki's return smile was half-hearted. There was something that still worried her. "What was all that about in the cafeteria?" she asked. "Why did he ignore me?"

Again, Toshikazu looked embarrassed. "Look at it from his point of view," her friend said quietly. "The grape vine was buzzing with the fact that you were connected with the wreckers. Yamato and Nagara Security were seriously interested in you — they'd put a lock on your personal directory, remember? And it was an open secret in the management ranks that Eichiro had scheduled an inquest. You were obviously under serious suspicion, and there was always the possibility you *were* guilty. So you understand he couldn't be seen to be connected to you in any way. Friendship or no, he had no choice."

Nikki's head was swimming. The elevator door opened on the sub-basement level, and they stepped out. "But *why*?" she asked again, as they walked slowly back toward the lab.

Toshikazu clicked his tongue in feigned disapproval. "*Gaijin*," he sighed, "they never understand the intricacies of corporate life. Here's the situation. Suganama is in tight with the Board of Directors. That's why he's still running his little independent empire, okay? But there are a lot of people who'd like to see him gone. His two deputies, they want his job. A couple of the division managers, because then maybe they can replace him with their own puppets." Toshikazu chuckled. "Suganama-*san* is just too independent for most people's liking.

"Anyway," he went on, sobering, "it doesn't take much to destabilize somebody's position in a corporation. Even a little whiff of scandal can do it, particularly if there are people ready to take advantage of it. If word gets around that Suganama-*san* is buddy-buddy with a wrecker ... Well, you get the picture."

Nikki shook her head again. "That's just too Machiavellian," she said.

"That's Japan," Toshikazu said with a bark of grim laughter.

Nikki had to agree. It was becoming ever more obvious that the political infighting and machinations at Nagara made the political manoeuvering of medieval Italy look straight-forward and honest by comparison.

That thought reminded her of something else. She leaned closer to Toshikazu and said quietly, "I think my apartment's bugged."

Her friend blinked. "Truly? How do you know?"

Briefly, she told him about how Yamato knew her habit of listening to the Voice of America.

Toshikazu listened in silence, his brow furrowed. "That is interesting," he mused. "I don't know whether they've actually bugged your apartment, though." He tapped her security badge with a fingernail. "Where do you hang your coat when you get home?" he asked.

"On a chair in the bedroom," she answered, then paused. "You think *that's* where the bug is? In the badge?"

"It's a possibility," he confirmed, frowning down at the badge on his own lapel. "A rather disturbing one that I'll have to keep in mind." Then his frown vanished to be replaced by a half-smile. "There's certainly enough space in the badge for some interesting circuitry, *neh*?"

"Thank God," Nikki breathed.

* * *

The corporate grapevine at Nagara was certainly efficient, Nikki had to admit. When she returned to work the next day, the manner of the other members of Group Five had changed drastically. As she walked into the lab, they actually looked up from their work and smiled at her, said *"Konichi-wa,"* politely. One of them — Bojo, usually the most taciturn — even inquired about her health. As she walked into her cubicle, she couldn't help smiling. Her colleagues were even more friendly than they'd been before the raid. *Almost like they feel bad for mistrusting me,* she thought. *But of course they can't just apologize. They'd rather have a root canal.* She noticed Toshikazu watching her from across the room, gave him a broad smile.

It's probably Toshikazu who spread the word I'm innocent, she thought as she settled down at her desk and prepared for work. *That's just the kind of thing he'd do. But he'd never admit it.* She felt a comfortable warmth in her chest — *Gratitude, it has to be,* she told herself. She should find some way of thanking him, she realized. Something that wouldn't embarrass him too much.

She felt a presence behind her, turned — unsurprised to see it was Toshikazu. "Good morning," she said.

He returned her smile. "How was your half-day off?" he asked.

"Perfect," she told him. "I went home and just *slept*." She decided not to mention the nightmares — flashes of explosions and gunfire, mixed with courtroom-like scenes where everyone she knew in Japan took turns accusing her of some heinous crime. "I feel almost human today," she concluded. "And you?"

"I've been keeping my ear to the ground," he answered tangentially. "Never let it be said that Nagara moves slowly. You know that Yamato's gone?"

Nikki blinked. "Gone?"

"Dismissed, laid off, fired, requested to tender his resignation, call it whatever you like. Or maybe he quit on his own, I don't really know."

"You're kidding."

"No joke," he confirmed. "Nobody's saying anything officially, but it's an open secret that Yamato was escorted from the premises yesterday evening, and one of his deputies is busy moving into his office."

"So why did he get the boot?" she asked, lowering her voice. "Because he tried to frame me, or because he blew it?" Toshikazu looked surprised. "Remember, 'Paranoia is a tool.'"

The young man chuckled. "'Toshikazu's First Law of Corporate Behavior' comes back to haunt me." Then his expression sobered. "Here's how I read it," he said slowly. "Eichiro's in trouble; like I said before, he's got his balls in a vice. Now, there's somebody somewhere else in the hierarchy who's got Eichiro's patronage, somebody who's 'hitched his wagon to Eichiro's star,' to use one of your absurd Western expressions." His quick smile robbed the words of any offense.

"So this somebody knows that if Eichiro falls, then *he* falls," Toshikazu continued. "How can he bolster his patron's position? By proving the 'wreckers' had inside help, that Eichiro's security arrangements *weren't* inadequate. And that's where you come in. If he's going to frame somebody, why not frame the *gaijin*? You're not quite human, so it's going to be easier to convince people that you're a traitor."

Nikki nodded slowly. "That makes sense so far," she allowed. "But how does Yamato and Corporate Security get into the act?"

Toshikazu shrugged. "Maybe it was Yamato who came up with the whole thing," he suggested. "He owed Eichiro a big one. It was Eichiro who got him the job of security chief, you know."

"I *didn't* know," Nikki admitted.

"It's true." Toshikazu paused for a moment's thought. "Or maybe it was somebody else in security, who fed information to Yamato." Another pause. "Or here's another possibility: maybe it was somebody feeding Yamato false information just so he'd get the chop …"

Nikki raised her hands in mock surrender. "That's enough," she chuckled. "This is too weird for me."

"Not weird, Carrson-*san*," Toshikazu told her in mock disapproval. "This is how civilized people handle things."

* * *

The Shinjuku district of Tokyo always had an exciting, frenetic feel to it, Nikki thought. During the day, the roads were solid streams of cars, the sidewalks and raised walkways seas of pedestrians — shoppers and business-suited *sararimen*. By night, the wide streets were still packed — now mainly by people, often drunk, seeking out the buzzing night-life the district boasted. The massive billboards, and the vast neon signs that covered many of the buildings, filled the night with light, and the glowing dots of windows high in the tallest of the office towers replaced the stars that were blocked from view by the mist.

Near the center of the district was Shinjuku station — a massive, blocky building several stories tall, that sprawled over an area of numerous city blocks. Throughout the day and evening, and late into the night, it was surrounded by an almost unbroken throng of people, coming and going on the many underground and surface train lines that met at the station. Outside one of the station's main entrances was a large square surrounded by stores — pricey jewelry stores, right the way down to cut-rate electronics emporia. Mounted on one of the buildings facing the entrance

was the massive television screen known as "Alta" —
once the largest in the world, but long since out-
stripped by a factor of three by a new Kanawa product.
Day and night, Alta ran an eclectic mix of rock videos
and strange, stylish ads.

Shinjuku by night was a district of high-tech and
lights. But it was also a district with areas that were
more traditional. In the shadow of the station itself,
and of the elevated railway lines, was a tiny neighborhood of narrow, winding streets — alleys, more like —
wending their way between small one-and two-story
buildings. Little *sake* shops, *yakitori* bars ... Walking the
badly-paved alleys, Nikki could almost imagine that
she'd travelled to another time and place. All she'd
have to do was blot from her mind the hubbub of traffic
on the main roads, and the occasional rattle and rumble
of a train passing overhead. Then she could just about
convince herself that she was in an older version of
Tokyo, dating from before the ever-increasing pace of
economic and technological change had forged the
city into the sprawling megalopolis it was today.

Nikki had come to this part of Shinjuku only once
before, in the early days of her stay in Japan. That had
been during the day. The alleyways and the small
shops and restaurants had looked dirty, sordid —
dangerous. By night, though, the feel was drastically
different — *almost magical*, she thought. There were no
street lights. The only illumination came from the
doors and windows of the restaurants, warm pools of
yellow light washing out into the alleys. Nikki knew
the dirt was still there, and she was sure that rats
watched her carefully from the darker shadows, but by
night she couldn't see anything to disturb her. The air
was filled with the aroma of cooking food — mainly
yakitori, little Japanese shish kebabs, grilling over char-
coal fires — and with the laughter of alcohol-fuelled
good fellowship from the *sake* shops.

Coming here had been Toshikazu's idea. They'd decided to leave work early — for them — at around six o'clock. Nikki couldn't remember who had first suggested having dinner together; maybe it was one of those times when two minds share a single thought without having to voice it. Regardless of how it happened, it seemed to be a foregone conclusion.

Nikki's experience with restaurants was limited. During her first weeks in Tokyo, to save money she'd concentrated on cheap coffee shops — *not* the kind of place she'd be comfortable going with a friend for dinner. And then, when she'd started work with Nagara, she'd come to eat most of her meals in the employee cafeteria, or in the establishments nearest her apartment — again, generally cheap coffee shops. So when Toshikazu had suggested he take her to his favorite restaurant, she'd willingly agreed.

The place was called the *Kirin*, named — Toshikazu said — after a mythical creature that looked something like a winged unicorn. (Nikki had heard the name before, but only as a brand of Japanese beer.) The Kirin was a tiny little *yakitori* bar, maybe a hundred meters or so from the Shinjuku Station, buried in the heart of the winding alleyways. It was obviously a family affair, run by a middle-aged man and woman who knew Toshikazu, and greeted him like a prodigal son come home at last.

The family's name was Hoho — Nikki had to struggle not to laugh when Toshikazu first introduced them. They were friendly and open, unfailingly polite but obviously fascinated that a *gaijin* would deign to enter their restaurant. Initially, they'd spoken to her slowly, in a kind of pidgin Japanese, with many broad, often comical gestures. It had taken them several minutes to realize that Nikki was virtually fluent in their language, able to carry on a normal conversation in idiomatic Japanese. Once they'd grasped that, their amazement had known no bounds. A *gaijin* who ate in *yaki* bar and who spoke their language. They'd pulled out a bottle of their best *sake*, heated it in a bowl of hot water, and poured liberally and often into Nikki's and Toshikazu's ceramic thimble-cups.

It didn't take long for the meal to become what Nikki thought of as "out of hand." The *sake* had flowed, punctuated by beer — big, artistically curved cans of Sapporo Draft. The family Hoho had joined in as well, toasting Nikki, Japanese-American relations, Nagara Corporation, the Sapporro brewery, and anything else that happened to come to mind. Throughout, they'd kept serving food — grilled *yakitori*, feather-light *tempura*, and slices of raw tuna *sashimi*. The food was excellent, one of the best meals Nikki could remember eating.

And the party had continued to grow larger. Other patrons had come into the tiny, cramped establishment, taken their seats at the bar. And the "Hoho-hosts," as Toshikazu had come to call them in English, had dragged them into the party too, introducing them to Toshikazu and to the "golden-haired *gaijin* who drinks *sake*." As it turned out, to Nikki's surprise Toshikazu had already known many of the newcomers — presumably from having met them before right here at the Kirin. He had to be a real regular here — but then she should have known that from the greeting the Hoho-hosts had given him. She shook a *sake*-fogged head. *I'm starting to lose it*.

The meal had eventually come to an end. At Toshikazu's insistence, she'd topped it off with a glass of *sho chu* — a kind of Japanese vodka that Toshikazu mixed half-and-half with warm water from a glass carafe. Her *sho chu* had a twist of lemon floating in it. Toshikazu's had a small, wrinkled, red-grey ... *something* rolling around in the bottom. "A pickled plum," he'd explained, with the overly-precise enunciation of the slightly drunk. "An acquired taste. Really, I wouldn't recommend you try it now." (Normally, that would have been incentive enough to *make* her try it. But tonight she knew she'd eaten and drunk more than she usually did — not the best time to try some new taste experience.) They finished the *sho chu*, Toshikazu instructed that the meal be put on his account — yes, he *was* a regular — and they strolled, almost staggered, into the night.

The air was cool and refreshing, clearing Nikki's head immediately. *I'm not so drunk after all*, she realized. *It's just those damn tiny* sake *cups.* Toshikazu was walking close beside her; she could feel the warmth of his shoulder through her light jacket.

There was no conscious decision. Her hand just slipped into his, seemingly of its own volition. Toshikazu didn't look at her; his expression didn't change. But his hand squeezed hers. She smiled. For the first time in several days, she felt totally relaxed and happy.

They strolled slowly through the maze of alleyways. The strange little neighborhood was deserted. The doors of all the restaurants and shops were closed, even though lights still burned in some windows. *Probably proprietors cleaning up after closing time*, Nikki thought. She glanced at her watch: just past one in the morning. She chuckled quietly.

"What is it?" Toshikazu asked.

"Another night without enough sleep," she laughed. "I think the whole world's conspiring against me."

Toshikazu smiled, squeezed her hand again. "Is loss of sleep really that bad?" he asked her softly.

The emotional intensity had just jumped a dozen notches. Nikki could feel it like static electricity around her, like the tension in the air before a thunderstorm. It wasn't unpleasant — not at all — but it was ... new. She hadn't felt this kind of tension for more than a year —

since before she left America — and she'd never expected to experience it in Japan. *Certainly not with a co-worker*, she thought.

The intensity seemed to continue growing in the silence. Suddenly she felt she had to break the tension —to establish some emotional distance from Toshikazu, if only for a few moments. *Before I get overwhelmed*, she told herself, *before things go so far we can never turn back*.

She dropped Toshikazu's hand — casually, she hoped—to brush her hair back from her face with both hands. "Whew," she breathed, "too much *sake*." From the corner of her eye she watched Toshikazu for a reaction.

There wasn't one, she was glad to see. Toshikazu's smile remained in place, maybe even grew a little broader. *As though he understands*, Nikki thought. That was good. She didn't want to offend her friend. The warmth, the bond she'd felt between them, both were still there, undiminished. It was just that the sudden intensity had diminished to a more comfortable level. *I don't want things to happen too fast*, she thought.

"Does your family work for Nagara too?" Nikki asked.

Toshikazu blinked, gave her a sidelong look. "For Nagara?" he echoed. "No, they don't. Not for Nagara."

"So how do they know Suganama-*san*?"

That surprised him. He blinked again, puzzled.

"You said he was an old friend of the family," she reminded him.

He glanced away for a moment. Then his gaze — untroubled as usual — settled back on her. "That's true," he said. His voice was steady, but there was an unfamiliar undertone to his words. "Yes," he repeated, "that's true. But they knew him from before he joined Nagara." He spoke the last sentence firmly, flatly, as if to put an end to the discussion.

Nikki fell silent — confused, a little troubled. She

had the feeling that something important had just happened, something significant. But she didn't know just *what* had happened, or why it was important. Was Toshikazu just embarrassed over talking about his family? Or was it something else? She pulled her jacket closed across her chest. The night air had suddenly felt colder.

Toshikazu seemed to respond to the chill as well. He closed his white poplin windbreaker. He glanced around at the deserted alleyways. "Perhaps we should head home," he murmured.

Nikki, too, looked around. Most of the lights were out, the alleys dark and suddenly threatening. She heard movement behind her, turned quickly — inexplicably frightened. There was nothing there, just the black shapes of the small buildings, and the amorphous piles of garbage here and there. *Just a rat*, she told herself. She drew closer to Toshikazu. He slipped an arm around her — a gesture of reassurance, not one of romance. She felt surprisingly comforted by his touch, by the firm strength of his arm across her shoulders. She shivered slightly. "Yes," she said, "let's go home."

At least there was no chance of getting lost here. The elevated rail line was clearly visible above the low buildings, dotted with red and green lights that had to be signals to trains. Just follow that track back to Shinjuku Station. She found herself looking forward to being back on wide, well-lit streets. *Maybe I'll take a taxi home*, she thought. Much more expensive than taking the subway, which was how they'd got here. But it would be quicker, and much more convenient. At the moment she didn't relish the idea of waiting on a subway platform with the usual contingent of drunk *sararimen*.

As if to underscore her thoughts, a train rumbled by overhead. The railcars were brightly lit, yellow light flooding from their windows and washing over the alleyways below. The light flickered and shifted as the train rushed past, painfully bright in comparison to the darkness around them.

And that's when she saw the figure. Just a black shape, no details visible, crouching atop a one-story building ahead of them. She stiffened in shock.

Toshikazu didn't seem to have noticed the figure. He felt Nikki's reaction, though, and turned to her with an expression of concern.

The figure *moved* — jumped down from the roof to land, silent as a cat, in the alley in front of them. The train had passed, its lights gone. In the sudden darkness, the figure was almost invisible — black against black.

Toshikazu had seen the figure too, now. He stood stock still, his eyes wide — not staring with fear, Nikki thought with a shock, just opened as wide as possible to capture all the light they could. Firmly, he pushed Nikki back, behind him. He stood poised, seemingly relaxed — *Just like the Nagara security guards*; the thought struck Nikki suddenly.

The black figure moved forward slowly, sinuously. There was something terrifying, dangerous, about the way the figure moved — like a fencer, maybe, or like a large jungle cat. Another train passed above, going in the opposite direction. Again the flickering light of the passing windows washed over the alley.

For the first time Nikki could see the figure clearly. Nikki was certain it was man, although she didn't know why. He wore unrelieved black, close-fitting clothes of light-weight material. His head and face were concealed by more black cloth. For a moment, Nikki thought he wore the same uniform as the raiders, the same velcro-pocketed jumpsuits. But no, the clothes weren't that high-tech — just a thin shirt and pants, like skin-tight pajamas. And he wasn't wearing the ski-mask the raiders had worn. A length of black cloth was swathed around his head and face, like a bandanna, concealing everything but his eyes. *A ninja* ... He couldn't be anything else.

"Holy mother of *God* ..." Nikki murmured.

She saw the ninja reach up and back, draw something that had been strapped to his back. The light of the passing train glinted on metal — a long, slightly-curved sword blade with a vicious chisel point. A *katana* — the traditional sword of Japanese samurai.

The train was past. In the sudden darkness, she felt rather than saw the ninja step forward, *katana* at the ready.

Without taking his eyes off the deadly figure, Toshikazu pushed her again, harder — shoved her farther back. "Go," he snapped at her. "Run!"

She was frozen, unable to move. Her legs were rooted to the spot, seemingly as useless to her as if they belonged to someone else. She watched in horror as Toshikazu took a step toward the ninja. He pulled the poplin windbreaker from his shoulders, wrapped it quickly around his left hand and forearm. His body looked poised, ready, like a tightly-wound spring.

"Go!" he told her again. "Get out of here."

"I can't," she moaned.

"Then we're both dead," he grated. He took another slow step forward, his cloth-wrapped left hand held out in front of him in a posture of defense. *As if it'll stop a sword*, Nikki thought.

The ninja hadn't moved. His *katana* was still ready for attack or defense, but Nikki sensed he was confused. This wasn't the way things were supposed to be working out, she thought. It must be as surprising to him as it would be for a cat who leapt upon two mice, only to find one of them challenging the attacking creature, tiny teeth bared to fight. She took a lurching step back.

Nigel Findley

The two figures — Toshikazu and the ninja — faced each other from a distance of less than ten feet, now. Both were totally motionless, like actors in a freeze-frame from a movie.

Then suddenly, blindingly fast, Toshikazu moved. He ducked his shoulders to the left as if making a break. The ninja responded, moving his sword to follow Toshikazu's shift. But Toshikazu wasn't running. His right hand flashed to the small of his back, pulled something from the waistband of his pants. Then he lashed out with his right arm, as if throwing a frisbee underhand. Something caught the dim light, a disc of metal flashing through the air.

The ninja flung himself aside — fast, but not fast enough. The metal object struck him in the left shoulder, sank into his flesh. He gasped in pain, a sharp expulsion of breath.

And Toshikazu was moving, strong legs pistoning, driving his body directly toward the swordsman. The ninja swung his *katana*, a whistling cut — hideously fast — that should have severed Toshikazu's neck.

But Toshikazu had ducked low, underneath the flashing steel, and now he was inside the arc of the deadly weapon. His shoulder slammed into the ninja's abdomen, hard enough to drive the breath from the man's lungs, to send him back two staggering steps. Still inside the sword's arc, Toshikazu brought his arms up, one clawing for the ninja's face, the other grabbing at his wounded shoulder. Simultaneously, he thrust his knee up, with all his strength and weight behind it.

Wounded and off-balance, the ninja was still almost inhumanly fast. He shifted, so that Toshikazu's knee slammed into the muscle of his thigh instead of its intended target. But he couldn't simultaneously block Toshikazu's hands. The ninja hissed, a sound of barely-controlled agony as the smaller man pummeled his wounded shoulder. Again.

"*Get out of here!*" Toshikazu screamed again in English.

Still, Nikki stood frozen. She wanted to run. To put as much distance as she could between her and the black-clad killer, to lose herself in the crowds of Shinjuku Station. But how could she leave Toshikazu?

"*Go*, Goddamn you!"

The ninja counterattacked, slamming the butt of his sword into the side of Toshikazu's head. The researcher reeled back, looked about to fall, but managed to keep his feet. He snatched something up from the alley floor. It looked to Nikki like a piece of metal pipe. *Not much defense against a katana.*

The ninja advanced slowly, sword again ready, moving back and forth in short feints. Nikki was horribly certain Toshikazu wouldn't be able to get inside that deadly arc again.

In the dim light, she saw her friend's face. Blood from a scalp wound sheeted the left side of his head. His eyes were slitted with concentration and with pain ... but he was *smiling*. A wild, feral smile, so out of keeping with his personality — or with what she knew of his personality.

"Run, Nikki!" he shouted, and there was a kind of terrible joy in his voice.

She knew what he was going to do before he moved, and she knew she couldn't watch it. As she turned to run, at last, she saw him hurl himself forward again, the pipe in his hand swinging at the ninja's head.

Metal crashed against metal — once, again. She heard a grunt of exertion behind her, a gasp of pain. She redoubled her speed, sprinting through the darkness. Then came a scream of agony, a throat-rupturing shriek.

And that shriek was her own name.

Chapter Four

It was dark in Nikki's apartment. No lights burned, and the vertical blinds covering the windows were all closed. She lay on the bed, unmoving, staring at the ceiling.

She was in a kind of shock, she knew. She felt numb — physically, mentally and emotionally. Her limbs felt leaden, or like slabs of meat that didn't really belong to her. She knew she could move them if she wanted to, but doing so would take too much effort. Her thoughts moved sluggishly, and her emotions felt packed in cotton wool. She'd been in her apartment all day, moving no more than was required for survival — to the bathroom, to the shower to wash off the sour sweat that kept seeping from her pores, only once to the kitchen for food. Outside the windows, the sound of Tokyo at night was a distant, almost subliminal hum.

She hadn't slept — hadn't wanted to sleep. She knew that her dreams would be terrible. Even awake, her mind kept replaying the events of the previous night.

She'd sprinted from the winding alleys, from the closed *sake* shops and *yakitori* bars. Running faster than she ever thought she could run, she'd bolted for the lights and the crowds of Shinjuku Station, imagining that any second she'd hear the soft cadence of running footsteps following her. Not Toshikazu, she'd known he was dead. That final, horrible scream had confirmed that. No, she'd imagined the ninja, his *katana* still wet with her friend's blood, pursuing her, closing the gap, drawing back his weapon to split her skull in two or sever her neck.

But there'd been no pursuit — and in a distant way, that had puzzled her. She'd burst from the maze of alleys into the late-night bustle of the station area. *Sararimen* — most drunk — had been everywhere, staggering alone, or walking arm-in-arm with friends and colleagues, singing Japanese drinking songs. The brilliant lights had brought tears to her eyes.

The transition had been shocking, overpowering. From the darkness and death of the alleyway to the brightness and life of the world that she considered "real," in an instant. Surrounded by normal people, she'd hesitated for a moment, looking back over her shoulder at the dark mouth of the alley. Expecting any instant to see the ninja burst forth to cut her down.

He'd never appeared. There'd been no movement in the alleyway, no black-clad figure. Had he completed his task with the death of Toshikazu? Or had the presence of others — of witnesses — saved her life, prevented him from seeing his mission through? She didn't know.

For several heartbeats, nobody had noticed her, standing there panting, soaked with the sweat of terror. But then an elderly *sarariman*, a little less drunk than the friends he walked with, had seen her and weaved his way over to her. In polite, slightly-slurred Japanese, he'd asked her what the problem was.

Even though she'd been able to understand him with no difficulty, she'd found herself unable to phrase a coherent reply. She'd stuttered in broken Japanese, mixed with English, trying to explain what had happened. But the man hadn't understood her fully. He'd understood enough, however, to know she was in some kind of trouble. Gently taking her arm, he'd led her to the station entrance, where three policemen were standing, watching the crowd.

Again, she'd tried to explain, this time with more success. The police had looked doubtful when she'd mentioned the ninja, but their expressions had grown more serious and their hands had drifted to their handguns with her description of Toshikazu's death. In simple Japanese, accompanied by hand gestures, they'd told her that they'd check it out.

Suddenly terrified of being left alone, she'd followed them as they'd walked — slowly, carefully watching all around them — into the maze of alleys. When they'd approached the scene of the fight, one of the officers had fallen back, staying with Nikki, while the others had advanced cautiously. "There is no need for you to see this," he'd said with concern in his voice.

But she couldn't just stand there, she'd found, she had to see. She'd brushed past him, following his colleagues.

By the time she'd caught up with them, they were in the stretch of alley where it had happened. They'd stood motionless, framing *something* that lay in the middle of the alley. A rounded shape that could — almost — have been a pile of garbage. Another train had passed, and in the flickering light she'd seen Toshikazu's white poplin windbreaker. And blood. Blood everywhere. With a strangled cry, she'd turned and run back into the lights of the street.

The police had been very polite, very concerned, as they'd driven her to the station and questioned her. "We apologize for the necessity," they'd repeated again and again, "but we must ask you." And then they'd had her repeat, several times, exactly what had happened, dropping in new questions each time. In some ways it had been like the interrogation after the raid on Nagara — the incessant questions, the people taking notes. But this time they'd been scrupulously polite. There'd been no indication that they thought she was in any way to blame. They'd just been trying to collect all the data they could, and making sure that they hadn't missed anything.

At first, when she'd said it was a ninja who'd attacked them, the interviewers had exchanged doubting looks. But then, some time into the process, an expert had whispered something to the officer in charge, and Nikki had overheard. Yes, the expert had said, the victim *had* been killed by a *katana* — not a common weapon among street gangs and robbers in Japan, regardless of what bad American movies showed.

Finally, hours later as dawn was touching the sky, they'd driven her home and escorted her upstairs to her apartment. With — seemingly sincere — wishes for her well-being, they'd left her alone.

And she'd stayed alone since. There was no way she could have gone in to work, not the way she was feeling. The ideas of trying to concentrate on anything, of talking to anyone, had been too overwhelming. She'd notified her department that she wouldn't be in — using electronic mail rather than the phone, so she wouldn't even have to talk to a receptionist — and then she'd just sunk into apathy.

A V/STOL buzzed by her window; she could hear it but not see it. Probably on its way to one of the landing flats atop many of the corporate headquarters downtown. She sighed, and forced herself to sit up.

Why? The question struck her again, as it had struck her repeatedly throughout the day. *Why would anyone want Toshikazu dead? And why send a ninja to do it?* She'd frequently heard rumors that some corporations hired "contract ninjas" to serve as "expediters," to perform industrial espionage, and to eliminate rivals — all "unattributably," of course. She hadn't really believed them, thinking them just sensationalistic "urban myths." But now she knew they were true; ninjas *did* exist, and they did kill people. *Why would anyone send a professional killer after Toshikazu?* she asked herself again.

And was Toshikazu the only target? That question was even more chilling. Toshikazu himself hadn't seemed to think so. "We'll both be dead," he'd told her when she'd refused to run. And then he'd given his own life to protect her. Was he right? *Why would someone want me dead?* It just didn't make any sense.

It didn't make much more sense that Toshikazu was the victim. He was just a researcher. But ...

She paused. There *had* been a couple of mysteries surrounding her friend, she had to admit. His family and his background, for one. He'd never talked about either — *except when he claimed Suganama was an "old family friend,"* she reminded herself. And then, when they left the Kirin, she'd remarked on that, and he'd acted strangely. *As if he didn't remember what he'd told me,* she thought, *as if he didn't remember his lies.*

Plus, there was the skill he'd showed when fighting the ninja. Most people would have run from a man with a sword. Toshikazu had turned to fight. *And he was* able *to fight,* she reminded herself, *that's even stranger.* With a shudder, she remembered his attack on the ninja. First he'd thrown something, some weapon he was carrying concealed — *maybe a shuriken?* — and then he'd charged, ducking under and inside the ninja's sword. That move had been his only possible option, unarmed against a trained swordsman. But he'd performed it perfectly, as though he'd been trained. Anybody else who'd tried it — somebody who'd seen it in a movie, for example — would have been cut in two.

Out of Nippon

Who the hell was Toshikazu Kasigi …?

No, she told herself firmly, shaking her head. *That's paranoia again.* There was nothing mysterious. Unusual, yes, but not mysterious. So he'd seemed to forget what he'd said about Suganama. So what? *We'd both been drinking* — a lot — *and I never saw Toshikazu drink at all before.* What was so mysterious about somebody getting a little confused, stumbling over their words, when they were a little drunk?

And his martial arts skills? A hobby, that was all. Not unusual, particularly in this part of the world — the *origin* of martial arts. Just because he'd learned to fight didn't mean that Toshikazu ever *expected* to fight. Nikki herself had taken *tai chi* at one time, but had dropped it when she couldn't make enough time in her busy schedule. She'd been interested to learn that *tai chi* — that slow, relaxing, dance-like routine — was actually based on a lethal style of unarmed combat.

She sighed, forced herself to relax. There was nothing — no individual event or fact — that she could point to and say, "That's unusual, that's not right." It was only when she took them all together that the overall *feel* was out of the ordinary. And wasn't combining ordinary parts into an *extra*ordinary whole something that paranoids did? Or neurotics, or worse? She shook her head again, pushed the thoughts from her mind.

Her computer beeped, making her jump. She smiled a little guiltily at her reaction. The beep meant that an electronic mail message had arrived. She glanced at her watch: 10:35. The only people who had her e-mail "address" were colleagues and superiors at work. Who would be working this late? Curious, she forced herself to her feet, walked over to the machine and sat down. She hit the keys to display the incoming message.

The electronic note was from someone called Sanzo Isobe. She was puzzled for a moment, not recognizing the name. Then the originating mail "address" caught her eye: Nagara Security. That made the connection. Isobe was Yamato's one-time deputy, now "Acting Security Chief" — the fellow who was busily moving his things into Yamato's office. She grimaced. Thinking about Nagara Security still left a bad taste in her mouth. But she had to admit she'd heard nothing but praise for Isobe's competence, dedication and total incorruptibility. She quickly scanned the message.

Carlson-san, it began, *first allow me to offer my sincere condolences over your loss. It was known to all that you and Kasigi-san were friends. Furthermore, accept my commiserations for the traumatic events of last night.* (Nikki had to smile at the convoluted politeness.)

You will understand, the message continued, *that Nagara Corporation is cooperating closely with the police in investigating this tragic event. We have promised the police to make our best efforts in discovering why the death of Kasigi-san was considered such a necessity as to warrant the use of a ninja. Again, you will understand that we wish to discuss with you everything that you may know about our lamented colleague. At your earliest convenience, I would like to speak with you at length. I am in your debt for your cooperation.*

Nikki sat back. *Another* interview with Nagara Security, and another five or six repetitions of what happened. *Just great.*

Of course, it was reassuring that Nagara was interested in investigating. *That's part of the deal in Japan*, she reminded herself. *You sell your soul to the corporation, and in return they take care of you, they make you feel safe.* She chuckled grimly. She couldn't think of many things more disruptive to a feeling of safety than knowing that a friend and colleague got cut down on the street by a goddamn *ninja*.

She skimmed the electronic note once more. She didn't want to talk to Isobe, or to anyone in corporate security. But it was a reasonable request. And who knew? Maybe they'd find out something the police had missed. She'd speak to Isobe when she went back to work the next morning.

* * *

"*Stay*, Nikki," Toshikazu laughed. His face was twisted in a smile of joy, almost feral in its intensity. His white poplin jacket — soaked in blood — was wrapped round his left hand. "Stay with me," he repeated. "*Die* with me." His teeth were red with blood.

Horror convulsed her stomach. She shied back from him. For the first time she saw where she was. Not the narrow alleyways of Shinjuku as she'd expected. They were in the halls of the Nagara Building's executive floors. Soft carpet was underfoot, and the walls were hung with expensive works of art, but piles of garbage filled the corners. In the shifting half-light, she saw the red eyes of a rat watching her.

"*Die* with me, Nikki," Toshikazu said again. He had something in his right hand, a gleaming disk of metal. There was a figure behind him, a figure wearing black. A figure holding a *katana*. She tried to turn, to run, but her legs were numb, paralyzed.

The figure stepped forward, reached up and removed the black cloth that covered its face. It was Yamato, smiling at her. He raised the sword, took another step toward her. She tried to cry out.

Toshikazu raised his arm to block the figure's advance. Nikki blinked. Now it was Eichiro holding the sword. He smiled coldly at her. He side-stepped Toshikazu's arm and came toward her.

There were tears rolling down Toshikazu's face now, tears of blood. He touched the gleaming disk he held to the back of Eichiro's neck. With a look of surprise, the manager crumbled to dust. Toshikazu deftly grabbed the katana from the air, before it could fall. He smiled at Nikki again with his bloody teeth.

"*Die* with me, Nikki."

Like smoke swept away by a sudden breeze, her fear was gone. She smiled at him, calmly and peacefully. "Yes," she said softly. "Yes."

Toshikazu drew the sword back. It's blade looked already wet with blood. She closed her eyes as he began his swing. The *katana* blade sang as it cut through the air ...

* * *

Nikki bolted upright in bed, gasping. Her heartbeat was a wild tattoo in her ears, her lungs and throat were on fire. *Oh, my God ...*

Instinctively, she looked around. Her bedroom was ... well, it was her bedroom. The early morning light leaking through the blinds showed nothing was displaced, nothing seemed out of the ordinary. *Of course not!* With an effort she slowed her breathing, forced the knotted muscles in her shoulders and stomach to relax. A dream ...

Of course *it was a dream*, she told herself sharply. A nightmare. She'd had enough of those over the last few nights, but this was by far the worst.

She glanced at the clock on the bedside table. Just past six in the morning. The alarm would be going off in less than an hour anyway. Why not get up now? (*That way there'll be no more dreams*, part of her mind added.) She'd have enough time to make a pot of coffee, even cook herself a real breakfast, and still be at work before eight. Her body needed more rest, she knew — her limbs still felt heavy and her muscles weak — but her mind told her she couldn't go back to sleep. *Or if I do, I'll dream again*, she knew. With a sigh, she forced herself out of bed.

* * *

The lab was a strange mixture of familiar and un-usual. In a way, it was reassuring to immerse herself again in the normal, to know that life really did go on. But the fact that a major factor was missing — Toshikazu — made it seem alien. She couldn't remember a day when Toshikazu had called in sick, when he hadn't been there to reassure her, to laugh with her. And now he'd never be there again. (*Such a facile thing to think*, she rebuked herself. But that's exactly how she felt.)

There was nothing left in the lab that belonged to Toshikazu; she checked as soon as she entered the cold room. His personal locker had been cleared out, his customary place on one of the workbenches had been rearranged so it looked as though he'd never been there. Now Bojo and Matsukara shared the space that had been his. Even the equipment had been moved so there was no hint there'd been anyone else there, ever. She could understand, intellectually, why: so there'd be nothing to remind the survivors of the tragedy, to prolong the pain. But emotionally it just didn't seem right — to sweep away all evidence of Toshikazu as though he'd never been.

Her co-workers carefully kept their heads down and their eyes averted — the polite response, avoiding any intrusion on her grief. Again, her mind under-stood it and appreciated it. But her emotions wanted more, if only a friendly good morning.

At least the interview with Acting Security Chief Isobe hadn't taken long. He'd met with her alone — no assistants barking questions at her this time — and had seemed very concerned about her feelings. His questions had all been to the point, but couched in the most polite, most gentle language possible. And at times when it seemed like her emotions would get the better of her, he'd waited patiently, eyes carefully averted, until she'd got herself back under control. Predictably, it had still been painful describing what had happened

— intensely so — but at least Isobe hadn't added to the discomfort.

When he'd asked all his questions, Isobe had quickly outlined the efforts the corporation would be going to in order to track Toshikazu's killer. Rewards ranging up to one million yen — about $10,000 — for anyone who could provide important evidence. Discreet messages sent to all the boardrooms of the city, hinting that Nagara would be deeply grateful for any help that the other major corporations could provide. Staggering amounts of money spread around the Tokyo underworld to acquire "cooperation" from those who might know how to hire freelance ninjas. Nikki was impressed.

So now she found herself back in her lab, back in her own cubicle. She felt a knot of pain in her chest. She'd had no idea it would be this difficult, returning to familiar places — places that she automatically associated with Toshikazu — and knowing that he wouldn't be there. *He's still here*, she thought as she sat down at her computer. *In a way he's still here. I can feel him.* She felt a faint tingle on the back of her neck, as though somebody were watching her. For an instant, she imagined that if she turned round, she'd see Toshikazu watching her from the entrance to her cubicle, a gentle smile on his lips. It was almost reassuring, in its own sad way. *He's not really gone*, she told herself. *As long as I remember him, he still exists.*

She powered up the computer, logged on. There was an electronic message in her in-box — a general announcement that Nagara would be holding a brief memorial service for Toshikazu Kasigi at eleven the next morning.

What about his family? she suddenly thought. They'd probably be holding their own memorial service, for relatives and close friends — something more private than an impersonal corporate event. The desire to be at such a service was overwhelming. Maybe she'd be invited — she *was* Toshikazu's close friend.

But would his parents know that? She recalled how closed-mouthed Toshikazu had been about his family and his background. Was he any less reserved about the rest of his life when he was talking to his family? The odds were good that his parents didn't even know he had a friend called Nikki Carlson. And if they didn't know she existed, how could they invite her to the service, or even tell her when and where it would take place?

Suddenly, the thought that she'd miss this last chance to say goodbye to Toshikazu, to honor his memory in her own way, became intolerable. She *couldn't* miss the memorial service, it would be a crime against her friend. Logically, she realized that she couldn't hold herself responsible for missing something that she knew nothing about. But emotionally, she felt as though missing the rite — whatever form it might take in Japan — would be a betrayal, a turning away from someone who'd meant so much to her.

So she had to get in touch with the Kasigi family. But how?

Nagara's personnel department would have to have the information she needed. She remembered the long, excruciatingly detailed forms she'd had to fill out when she joined the corporation. Parents' names — even the ubiquitous mother's maiden name — addresses and phone numbers of next of kin. If they had that on file for her, they had to have similar data for Toshikazu. She reached for the phone.

And stopped. That wasn't going to work. The personnel department was legendary for being uncommunicative. It would never divulge *any* of the information it collected on Nagara employees, not to someone low on the corporate totem pole like Nikki. From cafeteria gossip, she'd heard that even executives like MIS chief Hiroyo Suganama had to fill out complex forms — probably in triplicate — explaining just why they wanted personal data on employees. And those reasons, of course, had to make sense from a corporate — not a personal — point of view. A personal reason, like, "I want to speak to my dead friend's parents," would certainly be refused out of hand.

For a moment she considered calling direct to the Vice President of Human Resources, the head of personnel. Aburakoji — if he had a given name, she'd never heard it — an old curmudgeon of a man almost as old as Suganama-san. He was reputed to remember everything about every one of Nagara's thousands of employees. An "urban myth," of course — nobody could remember details on so many — but he just might be able to help her. If she approached him personally, explaining why it was so emotionally necessary for her to find Toshikazu's family, maybe he'd help her out as a favor.

But no. Firstly, she'd learned early on that, in Japanese corporate life, emotional needs weren't considered needs at all. If it didn't serve the corporation, a request was simply disregarded. Approaching Aburakoji on such a level would be useless. Worse. It would shame her, and — indirectly — him as well.

And secondly, she remembered how Toshikazu had described Aburakoji: "Mind like a steel trap," her friend had told her, laughing. "You have to pry it open to get anything out of it."

So that avenue was closed. What other options were there?

Why not the police? Yes, that made a lot more sense. They'd have to have found out about Toshikazu's family, if only to notify them of his death. And one of the detectives who'd interviewed her — what was his name, Yui? No, *Yuhi*, that was it — had seemed sympathetic, sharing her grief. He'd understood her emotions, and would understand her request. Maybe he'd even grant it.

Quickly, she looked up the phone number for the Shinjuku police station and placed the call.

A male voice answered at once. "*Konichi-wa*. Is this an emergency call?"

"No, it isn't," she said, then hurried on before she could be put on hold. "I need to speak to Detective Yuhi. I'm afraid I don't know his first name."

The switchboard operator hesitated. "What is this concerning?" he asked carefully. "Detective Yuhi is exceptionally busy."

"This is Nikki Carlson. I need to talk to him about the Kasigi murder." For an instant, Nikki closed her eyes. *Murder*. It was painful to even say the word.

But it had been the right thing to say. The operator's hesitation vanished. "Please hold," he told her, "I will connect you immediately."

Yuhi picked up the phone almost immediately. "Miss Carlson," he said in careful English. "How can I help you? Have you remembered something we should know?"

"No, I'm sorry," she answered, then went on to briefly explain her concerns about the memorial service. "So I would like to know how I can contact Kasigi-*san*'s family," she concluded. "Can you help me?"

She heard Yuhi sigh — a sound that she'd come to realize was one of commiseration, a sign that the hearer understood and shared the speaker's emotions. Then the detective spoke in Japanese. "So sorry, Carlson-*san*," he said — and his voice sounded as though he *were* sorry. "I am desolated to tell you that I cannot help you."

Nikki was silent for a moment. To push, would be rude. But she couldn't just back off on something this important to her. "I understand that there may be regulations," she said carefully, "but I really have to know."

If Yuhi was insulted by her insistence, his voice didn't show it. "You misunderstand me, Carlson-*san*. Yes, there *are* regulations, but I have some leeway when it comes to waiving them. I simply have no access to the information you desire. To my knowledge, nobody in the department does."

That set Nikki back for a moment. "Then how did you notify his next of kin?"

"That task was left to his corporation."

Yes, Nikki thought, *that makes a convoluted kind of sense*. The corporation, the all-knowing, bountiful corporation. The employee's home and refuge.

"But they must have claimed the body," she thought aloud. "*Did* anyone claim the body?"

Yuhi hesitated. (*More regulations*, Nikki thought.) "Yes," he answered finally. "The body was claimed."

"Who claimed it?"

"I cannot tell you that," Yuhi said slowly, "on that I have no leeway whatsoever" — a long pause — "but I *can* tell you it was not his family. And it was not his corporation." He sighed once more. "I wish I could be of more help."

Nikki was silent, a little puzzled. For an instant, she felt as though something important had just happened, but that she'd missed it. Then the feeling was gone, and nothing was left but sadness.

"*Domo arrigato gozaimas*, Yuhi-*san*," she said. "Thank you for your help." Gently, she hung up the phone, then bent forward until her forehead touched the cool desktop.

* * *

The official memorial service for Toshikazu Kasigi took place at eleven the next morning, in the large auditorium on the Nagara Building's ground floor.

Nikki was one of the first there, sitting near the back watching as the other attendees filed in. She recognized most of them — the other members of her workgroup, of course, plus others from the Genetic Research Division. Then there were some she didn't know, presumably from other divisions within Nagara. There were a few middle managers, but not many. She looked for Suganama — *maybe* he *knows how to contact the Kasigi family*, she thought — but didn't see him.

Soon there were about a hundred people there. A good turn-out, Nikki thought, and a testament to how many lives Toshikazu had touched. Perhaps unfortunately, the auditorium seated over five hundred, making the attendance look meager in comparison to the number of empty seats.

At eleven o'clock on the dot, Agatamori Eichiro — senior manager of Toshikazu's division, and thus the leader of the service — walked up onto the stage and took his place at the podium.

Nikki wasn't sure what to expect, but if she'd envisioned some kind of Shinto or Buddhist religious ceremony she was disappointed. There were no religious overtones whatsoever, no prayers or religious symbols or hymns. It was as secular as any business meeting she'd ever attended. Eichiro spoke for maybe five minutes, describing Toshikazu's achievements, his strengths, and his value to the corporation …

And that was it. He closed with a simple, "Nagara Corporation is diminished by his departure," and then he walked from the stage. With the corporate anthem playing softly in the background, people started to file out. The memorial service was over.

Nikki remained seated for a few minutes. *It just doesn't seem right*, she thought. *Toshikazu's dead, and he gets no more than a speech that's appropriate for a … a retiring employee.*

But that was the way it was in the corporations, she

admitted. Emotions meant nothing. Eichiro wouldn't have even gone to this much trouble if he hadn't known it was necessary to bolster morale. With a sigh, she climbed to her feet, and followed the other attendees out of the auditorium.

The elevator heading down to the sub-basement was full, but Bojo and Matsukara from Group Five squeezed themselves into a corner to make room for her. They accepted her thanks with polite nods, but kept their eyes averted and didn't speak to her — again, presumably not intruding on her grief.

The other occupants talked freely, however, albeit quietly. She vaguely recognized a few of them — members of her division, but assigned to other workgroups. Two of these were talking animatedly; even though they kept their voices down, their gestures and body language showed they were discussing something they considered important. Although she didn't consciously decide to eavesdrop, Nikki found her attention inadvertently focusing on their conversation.

"Eichiro-*san* is still on shaky ground," one was saying. "Kubota-*san* and the rest of the board don't trust him any more. He'll have to do something — something dramatic — if he wants to earn his credibility back."

His colleague grinned knowingly. "Perhaps he's done it already," he said quietly. "They captured the traitor, the one who helped the wreckers. Captured, then killed him."

At the word "wreckers," Nikki's concentration fully engaged.

The first man was amazed. "*Honto*?" he gasped. "Truly? He was part of Nagara?"

"Truly," the other confirmed.

"And he helped the wreckers?"

"Yes."

The first man shook his head in disbelief. "Traitors," he sighed. "How can anyone become a traitor?" He paused. "But he's dead, you say?"

"That's what I heard," the second man said. "Killed when he tried to escape from the security guards who captured him."

"It's only right," the first said virtuously. "It's what he deserved."

Nikki couldn't hold her silence any longer. "Excuse me," she said to the two men, "I couldn't help overhearing your conversation."

In corporate Japan, it was often impossible *not* to overhear someone else's conversation. But it was the height of rudeness to acknowledge it. A polite person would simply pretend they heard nothing, even going so far to deny it if anyone were crude enough to ask. The first man looked shocked at what he obviously considered Nikki's uncouth behavior. The second, though, just shrugged his shoulders and rolled his eyes, as if to say, "What else could you expect from a *gaijin*?"

Even though Nikki felt her cheeks burning, she pushed on. "The wreckers," she began, "they had inside help?"

The man who'd spoken first pointedly turned away. But his colleague at least answered her. "Yes," he told her brusquely.

"*How?*" she asked. "I mean, how do you know?"

He shrugged. "The grapevine," he said vaguely. "People talk."

"Who was he?"

He shrugged again. But this time he didn't say anything, he just turned away.

Nikki sighed. *The grapevine*, she thought. Sometimes the grapevine picked up on important news before the managers ever had a chance to learn it through normal channels. Or sometimes it was actually *used* by senior management — they'd leak some piece of information they wanted all the employees to know, without making it official.

But the grapevine was just as efficient at transmitting falsehoods — wrong conclusions, urban myths, even outright lies. Almost as often as it was right, it was hideously off the mark. Which was the case now?

Nikki thought it through as she walked slowly back to her lab. It didn't seem likely that the traitor story was true, she decided. If it were so, senior management would have made some announcement about it; Eichiro would, at least, to bolster his image.

That part of the conversation — the part discussing Eichiro — made sense to her, however. He'd still be severely shamed by the raid, and would have to do some kind of damage control ... and fast. She wondered what form it would take.

* * *

It didn't take long to find out. The next morning when she arrived at work — tired after another night of disturbing dreams — she found a message in her E-mail in-box announcing a divisional meeting. According to the electronic message, Eichiro planned to announce sweeping organizational changes in the Genetic Research Division. *Which makes sense*, Nikki thought. *Special Projects is gone, and my job is mainly to support Special Projects. What does that mean for me?*

For us, that is, she corrected quickly, looking around at the others in her workgroup. Although they weren't saying anything, she could sense their mood. The message had disturbed them ... as well it might. Even though Group Five had been busy even after the raid, their main *raison d'être* had vanished when the charges had detonated in the Special Projects labs. There was a very real chance that Eichiro-san's "sweeping organizational changes" would include disbanding Nikki's workgroup.

And what would happen to her and her people — to Omi, Ito, Toshima, Matsukara, Zakoji and Bojo? Traditionally — the way she understood it — there'd have been no doubt at all what would happen. All the members of Group Five would be reassigned within the corporation. Nobody would be let go, everybody would remain secure. The great and bountiful corporation would protect and succor its employees. Only in the case of out-and-out incompetence or misconduct would that protection be withdrawn.

That was the way it *used* to work. From what Nikki had heard from colleagues — largely from Toshikazu, she remembered — things were slowly changing. As the large corporations continued to merge — becoming *mega*corporations like Kanawa — some of the traditions of Japanese corporate life began to fall by the wayside. First among these was the life-long job security that many workers had come to depend on. A decade or so ago, if a merger made certain jobs redundant, the unnecessary workers would be kept on, kept working, until a new need for their skills arose, or until they could be retrained. Sure, it cost the corporations money to support unneeded workers, but that was part of the "social contract" between employer and employee.

No longer. Just recently, when Kanawa Corporation acquired the Magnolia Station Research Park, a well-known facility dedicated to industrial and pure science research, Kanawa management decided that many support functions like payroll would be handled through the megacorporation's central headquarters. More than fifty employees of Magnolia Station — the people who used to handle the support functions — were laid off without warning, and with only a month's salary as severance. In America, Nikki knew, the lawsuits would have flown thick and fast. But here labor laws were very different, and the terminated employees could do little but accept it fatalistically and look for another job. Some found work, but the numerous mergers had seriously depressed the job market. All too many skilled employees had to take lower-paying work — even manual labor, the kind of grunt work the Japanese used to leave to Koreans and Chinese, and was now performed by robots and other automated devices.

And some couldn't find work at all. *What happened to them?* Nikki wondered grimly. Did they join the half-starving underclass — the *burakumin* — who eked out a living in the wooded areas of Chiyoda-Ku, or lived in cardboard boxes on the normally-pristine streets of Shinjuku? Or did they commit suicide — still a socially accepted response to failure and shame?

If it turned out that Nikki lost her job, her pride would suffer the most. She was fairly confident that her skills would get her a similar position at one of Nagara's competitors. Even if nobody hired her, she had enough money salted away to support her while she arranged transit back to the United States. There was no danger whatsoever that she'd find herself among the *burakumin*.

No danger for *her*. But for the other members of her workgroup, the danger was very real. She looked at the nervous faces of her colleagues. Take Toshima, for example. He was the oldest member of Group Five, in his early fifties. A stolid worker, unimaginative and without an ounce of creativity, but reliable if he was told *exactly* — step by step and in excruciating detail — what he had to do. How likely was it that *he'd* get another job if Nagara let him go? Not very. And how likely was it that Nagara would keep him on and invest who knew how much money in retraining him? Again, not very.

Maybe they had no reason to worry, she thought after a moment. These ideas of being laid off — in her case, going home in some kind of disgrace; in her colleagues, being forced out on the street — were just fear and paranoia talking. What evidence did they have that Eichiro's "sweeping organizational changes" actually meant layoffs? *None*. Even if Eichiro *had* planned firings, wouldn't he have spoken individually to the people involved? What kind of manager would announce layoffs at a divisional meeting so the people being let go heard it there for the first time?

That made her feel a little better. But still, she was glad that the meeting was only an hour away. Nobody in her lab — or probably in the entire division — would get much done until the meeting was over.

* * *

The divisional meeting was scheduled to take place in one of the smaller lecture theaters on the fifth floor, not in the large auditorium where Toshikazu's memorial service had been held. Nikki had never been in any of those lecture halls, but she was surprised that they'd be large enough for the whole Genetic Research Division.

As she walked into the room, surrounded by a nervous knot of co-workers, she realized that size wasn't a problem. Despite what Eichiro-*san*'s e-mail had implied, this wasn't a full divisional meeting. She looked around at the people who already had their seats. Instead of the two hundred or so members of the Genetic Research Division, there were fewer than one hundred people here. She recognized most of them, even if she didn't know them by name. Most if not all were in position similar to hers — the technicians and scientists who actually worked "in the trenches." As far as she could see, there were none of the support people that made up the rest of the division — the word processors, the maintenance techs, the database clerks, etc. That was interesting, Nikki thought as she found a seat near the front. But what did it mean?

Now she had more time to look around, she spotted some people she definitely didn't recognize. They were sitting in a group right at the front, to the right of the low stage. They wore the same standard Nagara labcoats as most of the people in the room, so their appearance didn't set them apart. But there was definitely something about their body language — about the way they talked only to each other and seemed to draw back from contact with the people Nikki recognized sitting around them—that definitely segregated them from everyone else.

Without openly staring, she looked the group over. They were relatively young — ranging from Nikki's age to late thirties, she guessed — and all men (of course!). They seemed totally relaxed — unlike everyone else in the room — as if they knew what the meeting was about—which could well be the case, she admitted. And they all had a cool, calm air about them that Nikki interpreted as confidence and competence — the former arising from the latter.

Who are they? she wondered.

Before she had more time to think about it, Eichiro strode up on stage — a visual echo of Toshikazu's memorial service. "Good morning, and thank you for attending," he said brusquely.

"As you know, the heinous acts of wreckers have interrupted the work of our colleagues in this division's Special Projects lab." (Nikki had to smile grimly at that. *Getting yourself blown up tends to be an interruption.*) "Despite the delay," Eichiro continued, "Nagara considers the success of the Special Projects initiative to be vital. Senior management estimates that it would take as much as a year to bring the Special Projects research back on stream" — he paused for emphasis — "*in the form that it was.* Instead, Nagara Corporation has decided to assign additional resources to the Special

Projects initiative, and to change its focus."

Nikki heard muffled sighs of relief from around the room. "Additional resources" were the magic words that dispelled most people's fears. If this "SP initiative" needed additional resources, then nobody would be laid off.

If Eichiro had heard the reaction from his audience, he didn't acknowledge it. He went on, "The majority of the Genetic Research Division will focus its attention on bringing the original Special Projects research back on line. The remainder will dedicate their efforts to supporting a new direction of research, an entirely new and innovative approach. This new enterprise will be led by a group of highly experienced scientists transferred from Nagara's Matsushima Bay operation."

So that's who they are, Nikki thought, looking at the expressionless young men at the front of the lecture theater. She was impressed: she'd read a fair bit about the Matsushima Bay operation. Located on a manmade floating "island" off the coast of the southern island of Kyushu, it was described as the largest and the most sophisticated research facility in Japan, and praised as the originator of breakthroughs in half a dozen different fields. Nikki had to admit that the descriptions she'd read of quantum leaps in microprocessor architecture, virtual reality and X-ray cosmology could just as well have been Greek to her. But in her own areas of expertise — in microbiology and genetic engineering — she could recognize the importance of the developments coming out of Matsushima Bay. And the personnel that were assigned there — she knew them by name only, and by reputation, but there wasn't any doubt they were the finest genetic engineers in the world, or at least in Japan.

Eichiro was still speaking. With an effort, Nikki focused her attention once more on his words.

"These are the people," he was saying, "who will

spearhead the research of the Special Projects department, and who will take on a mission of great importance — one that will bring glory to the corporation.

"For reasons of security, the exact goal and the activities of this new research group will be kept secret. While this may be inconvenient, senior management trusts that you will understand why this is necessary, and abide with it."

Eichiro paused for a moment and smiled — a chilling smile, Nikki thought. "Those actually assigned to the project should have little difficulty abiding by these security provisions," he said. "This is because the actual research will not take place in either of Nagara's normal facilities. It will take place ..."

A map appeared on the rear-projection screen behind him. A map of Southeast Asia, with the islands of Japan in the top right corner. From his podium, Eichiro picked up a laser pointer. The ruby-red dot of laser light indicated an area on the eastern coast of a long island, near the Malaysian peninsula tipped by Singapore. It's Sumatra, Nikki realized with a shock.

"It will take place *here*," Eichiro said. "Once called Sumatra, many inhabitants of this island now call it *Majestic*. The research site will be located fifty miles inland, near the banks of a major river. The research outpost will be named after that river — the Inderagiri Research Facility."

More muttered reactions filled the air. The only people who didn't seem affected by this were the experts from the Matsushima Bay site. *But of course they're not affected*, Nikki thought, *they knew about this long ago*. For the rest, though, there'd be shock, and wild speculation over who'd be going.

And there was another difference between the Japanese and the American cultures. In the States, Nikki was sure, most people in this kind of situation would be eager to be sent to Sumatra, on such an important mission. They'd look on a transfer like this as exciting, as an adventure. The people who were chosen would consider themselves lucky, while the people left behind would be envious.

Not so here, Nikki knew. To all the people in this room — to anyone working for any major corporation like Nagara — Japan, and more specifically Tokyo, was the bright center of the universe. Everywhere else on the planet was a wasteland, more or less uncivilized, at the very best a pale reflection of the most sophisticated and cultured land on the face of the planet. Getting transferred away from Japan, even on an important scientific mission for their corporation, would seem like a horrible demotion, almost as bad as exile.

Eichiro was speaking again, his voice easily carrying above the mumbled conversation. "To repeat," he was saying, "the core of the outpost will be the science group from our Matsushima Bay facility. But of course they will need support: clerical staff, computer support and maintenance, and security. These groups have already been chosen, and are at this moment being notified of their great responsibility. In addition, the outpost will need technical support in order to carry out their great work. That is where the Genetic Research Division comes in."

Eichiro paused, his cold eyes scanning the faces of the audience, which had suddenly fallen silent. Nikki felt his gaze pass over her ... and pause for a moment. His thin lips twisted in a faint, chilly smile. *Is that smile meant for me?* she wondered for a moment, then squelched the thought. *Of course not. Paranoid thinking again.*

"The Inderagiri outpost will require a technical workgroup to assist the scientists with genetic analysis and immunoassays," Eichiro went on. "Nagara has selected Group Five for this task, the workgroup led by

Miss Nikki Carlson." Now there was no doubt at all. His steady eyes were fixed on Nikki's face, and his grim smile was definitely for her.

The muttered conversations broke out again, this time obviously full of relief. "Saved," most of the people would be thinking, Nikki knew. "I'm not being exiled."

She felt eyes on her — not Eichiro's; the gazes belonged to others. She looked around her.

Omi, Ito, Toshima, Matsukara, Zakoji and Bojo — the other members of her workgroup, of Group Five. They were looking at her — *staring* at her — their faces expressionless, their eyes cold. Their emotions were almost palpable — outrage, shame, sadness ... and anger. And of course, that anger was directed at her.

She could guess their thoughts. "It's the *gaijin*," they'd be telling themselves. "It was her — her shame — that caused this. So Nagara Security didn't censure her after the wreckers' raid, but maybe that was just because they didn't have enough proof. But they knew she was guilty, and now they're banishing her. And us too." It was a logical reaction, considering their background and outlook. But it was totally unfair (wasn't it?). She was innocent, she'd never done anything to harm the corporation.

Her own anger flared. Couldn't they see that this was an honor? Group Five had support the old Special Projects initiative well — so well that they'd been assigned to support this new secret venture. Didn't they realize that it would have been a subtle — or not-so-subtle — slap in the face if another group had been assigned to the new science group?

But of course they couldn't see it that way. All they knew was that they'd be going to Sumatra — a primitive, uncivilized country, in their minds — and of course they'd blame their *gaijin* workgroup leader for it. She sighed.

And how did *she* feel about it? She ran a quick inventory of her own emotions. Excitement — that was the major emotion. Excitement that she'd be part of the Inderagiri outpost, whatever its secret goal might be. She'd never been to Indonesia, to Sumatra, although when she'd first come to Asia she'd intended to visit the region if she could get the money together for a *wanderjahr*. Now she'd be going, and Nagara would be paying her for the privilege. She knew little about how what the Voice of America called the Possibility Wars had affected Indonesia, although the rumors she'd heard hinted at dark changes in the region. But still the excitement remained, albeit overlaid with faint tinges of guilt. Even though she saw this as an opportunity, she knew her colleagues considered it a punishment, a dishonor. She shrugged. Feeling guilty was stupid. She wasn't responsible for Eichiro's choice.

Eichiro. Just what did his smile mean? Did he share with the other members of Group Five the idea that this was a demotion? His eyes and his smile were certainly cold enough …

But he always looked cold, she remembered. His face just naturally fell into those lines, and any smile automatically became a sneer. Did he understand the way she'd view the transfer? Was he smiling because he knew she'd relish the challenge? Was this transfer — giving her something he knew she'd enjoy and appreciate — a form of apology for the shabby treatment she'd suffered at the hands of Iwao Yamato, the dismissed security chief … the closest to a real apology he could bring himself to offer? But of course there was no way of finding out without asking Eichiro directly, and she couldn't do that.

"I am sure that we all offer Group Five — and, of course, the Matsushima Bay scientists — our thanks for taking on this significant responsibility," Eichiro was saying in conclusion, "and wish them all possible success. This meeting is concluded."

* * *

Nikki was one of the first to leave the room. She felt a strong urge to speak to the other members of her workgroup … *But what would I say?* she asked herself. *Apologize? For something that isn't my fault? For something they should see as an honor?* No. Considering their upbringing and world view, there was no way they'd see her side of the issue. There was nothing she could do to convince them that the *gaijin* hadn't brought shame down upon them. She sighed. Yet another complexity, in a life that was already quite complex enough.

The Matsushima Bay scientists were also quick to leave the lecture theater. Again, their body language communicated that they were a tight-knit group, very distinct from the others around them.

As she was walking slowly toward the elevators, suddenly Nikki realized that she recognized one of their faces. A slender man, taller than the others, with flashes of premature grey in the hair at his temples. Where had she seen him before, and who was he?

The man, on the periphery of the Matsushima Bay group, was standing near her as they all waited for the elevator car to arrive. She studied him in her peripheral vision, overcoming the impulse to stare at him. Yes, she definitely had seen him before. But where? How? She was sure he'd never been to Nagara's Tokyo building; he'd have spent all his time in the labs and other facilities of the man-made island off Kyushu.

Then recollection came. She'd never seen him in the flesh, just in a photograph. Early in her tenure as leader of Group Five, she'd made great efforts to read all the literature published in the discipline of genetic analysis and engineering — magazines in both English and Japanese. One of these journals — the most important, but also the hardest to read — was the *Journal of the Genetic Engineering Society of Japan.* Unlike most of the other scientific publications, the *Journal* published photographs of the authors of individual papers, not just brief biographies. That's where she'd seen the man before: he was incredibly prolific, it seemed, with dozens of scholarly papers to his credit. She recalled that his photograph had appeared in almost every quarterly issue, either as co-author or sole author of a major paper. She'd noticed his face particularly, and remembered it, because he was considerably younger than most other authors, but mainly because the streaks of grey in his hair made him stand out.

What's his name? Nikki racked her brain. *Fusaaki? ... something starting with an F ....*

Funakoshi, that was it. Fusaaki Funakoshi, reputed to be one of the world's best — if not *the* best — chimeric gene splicers in the world. She remembered that he'd led a group that had succeeded in altering the genetic make-up of the tiny garden cross spider. The modifications had allowed the spider to incorporate the metal vanadium, introduced in its diet, into the silk it used to spin its webs, vastly increasing its strength. She recalled reading that the modified web had hundreds of times the tensile strength of steel of the same thickness. The paper, published several years ago, had speculated that if only a way could be found to synthesize this modified silk artificially and in great quantities, it could become an important structural material — perhaps used to make cables and hawsers a fraction of an inch thick but with a breaking strain measured in tons, or maybe as a component in high-speed aircraft or even spacecraft. Of course, Funakoshi would have seen this kind of industrialization as unimportant, a task for lesser engineers, not for pure scientists like himself. He'd almost certainly have moved on to some other project as soon as he'd succeeded with the genetic aspects of the work.

Funakoshi was staring at her, his eyes cold and hostile. Nikki felt her cheeks color. Despite her attempts not to, she must have been staring at the man.

Impulsively, she took a step closer to him. "Please accept my apologies, Funakoshi-san," she said politely. "Forgive me for staring ... but I recognized you from your picture in the Genetic Engineering Society *Journal*."

His lips curved in a faint smile — an arrogant, icy expression that reminded her of Eichiro. Even though he was an inch or so shorter than her, his manner made her feel like he was looking down on something hardly worthy of his attention.

For a moment, anger flared in her chest. *So what if I'm a gaijin and a woman? I'm still a human being*. But she repressed the emotion ruthlessly. What good would it do to show anger? His attitude — offensive as it was — was natural for him, for all too many people in this culture. They'd be working together. What good would it do her to react, and earn his enmity?

She forced her voice to remain steady, and chose the most polite form of address. "May one ask what the purpose of the Inderagiri outpost will be?"

Funakoshi's face became an expressionless mask. "One may *not*," he said flatly, his choice of words and his manner right on the verge of personal insult. She took half a step back at his rudeness, as if she'd been slapped.

The elevator doors hissed open. As a block, the Matsushima Bay scientists walked into the elevator, filling the car. There was no room for Nikki, or for the other workers standing with her. The scientists could have *made* room, but none of them bothered to move an inch.

As the doors slid shut, leaving Nikki in the hallway, she saw that Funakoshi's supercilious smile had returned.

* * *

Nikki leaned back in her chair. Taking a mouthful from the cup of tea — Earl Grey, not the traditional green Japanese brew, which she found too bitter for late-night sipping — next to her computer, she rubbed her eyes. The system that Nagara had given her for use at her apartment was light-years better than any personal computer she'd ever used in the States, but even so, late at night when she was tired, the screen still made her eyes sore if she stared at it too long. With a grunt of frustration, she logged off the public database and powered down the computer.

She'd been trying to get some kind of background on the island of Sumatra — on Indonesia in general, in fact — and on how the so-called "Possibility Wars" had affected it at all. Although she owned a decent-sized book collection, all her volumes were either fiction — mainly science fiction — or technical tomes dedicated to genetics, microbiology, biochemistry, and the other arcana of her career. Nothing in her library touched on the geography, history or culture of Southeast Asia. (Well, that wasn't quite true. She had two guidebooks for tourists visiting Japan, and a number of books in the "Learn Japanese in Some Ludicrously Short Period of Time" style. But of course none of them said a word about Sumatra.)

So she'd turned to technology, using her home computer to log onto the public databanks that had largely replaced research libraries in Japan. She'd quickly realized that searching all the many datafiles manually would take too long, so she'd written a short EXEC program to automate matters — to search through the databanks and flag any passages containing the word SUMATRA. That had sped things up somewhat, but there were still a lot of entries that she had to sort through manually.

Lots of entries, but none of them had told her what she really wanted to know. Many of them had provided basic geographic and historical background on Sumatra. It hadn't taken her too long to learn more than she'd ever really need to know about that large island.

Situated right on the Equator, Sumatra was just over a thousand miles, or about 1,600 kilometers, long, and varied in width from about 90 to 240 miles (145 to 386 kilometers. Marco Polo had visited the island in 1292, and by 1510 Portuguese traders had established commercial stations there. During the 17th Century, the Dutch moved in and took over, eventually turning Sumatra into part of the "Netherlands Indies." In 1945, the island became part of the Republic of Indonesia.

It had surprised Nikki to learn that the population at the last official census had been around 14 million people. She'd never really thought about it before, but now she realized she'd had a mental picture of Sumatra as one large, steaming jungle, largely unfit for human habitation. She shook her head in mild disgust at herself. She'd always prided herself on not being like *those* Americans — all too many of them — who never spared a thought for anything outside the United States. But here had been the kind of blatant ignorance she so despised in the "ugly Americans."

She'd skimmed through the rest of the file, looking for other false assumptions she might have about the region. The climate was just about as she'd envisioned it: temperature ranging from about 77° to 81° Fahrenheit, and fairly heavy annual rainfall. Most of the island was densely forested, with bamboo, pine, camphor, eucalyptus and teak the most common trees. The island was home to a wide range of animals — the elephant, tiger, panther, even the rhinoceros. (*The rhinoceros?* She hadn't known that.)

That was all historical data, dating back at least five years, and sometimes much longer. There were no current details, she'd found — to her disappointment

— as she'd scanned the databanks. Specifically, no information on what changes the Possibility Wars might have wrought on the area. Some files had made coy references to *Kawaru* — "the Change" — and how it had modified the ecology, culture, even the weather patterns of Indonesia. But there'd been no details. The only useful data had hinted that high technology didn't always work as expected — that, in many places, Indonesia had slipped back to a technological level that roughly matched that of the Victorian era. (There'd also been some cryptic comments implying that the *culture* of some parts of Indonesia had also come to resemble Victorian England, but she hadn't attributed much importance to those rumors.) If there *had* been a regression in technology, that probably meant the population of the island had dropped, but to what extent she couldn't even guess.

She'd flipped back to the geographical database, and keyed in the word INDERAGIRI as a search term. Quickly the screen had filled with text.

Apparently, the Inderagiri River — alternatively spelled *Indragiri*, she'd noted — was one of the island's main rivers. Like the other major rivers — the Musi, the Jambi and the Kampar — it flowed down the eastern side of the mountainous backbone of the island, the Barisan Mountains, onto a broad, gently-sloping plane. The file had pointed out that all the rivers were traditionally important for interior navigation. (Idly she'd wondered if the technological changes had made those rivers more or less important. *Probably more so*, she'd decided after a moment. *Even if you can't depend on engines any more, you can always trust the wind, or oars.*)

She took another sip of tea, staring unseeingly at the computer's blank screen. Most people, she knew, found starting off on a new venture without sufficient information frustrating or frightening. She had a tendency to view things that way sometimes. But usually all she had to do was remind herself that much of life's joy came from discovering something new. How would it be to go from day to day, always knowing everything that waited around the next corner? Safe and reassuring, maybe. But ultimately boring. The adventure of learning, the joy of discovery — those were the twin emotions that had pushed her toward a career in science, and maintained her interest in her job at Nagara.

She could view the trip to Sumatra as a threatening unknown, or as an adventure. It was entirely up to her how she thought of it. Since the choice was hers, what sense did it make to look on it as something negative? A chance to visit somewhere new, explore a new environment … *And a chance, maybe, to escape memories*, she added mentally, forcing herself to be honest.

Briskly, she stood up, carried her teacup into the bedroom, and began to pack.

Chapter Five

It should have come as no surprise to Nikki that the transfer to the Inderagiri River site wasn't anywhere near as smooth as planned. She was packed and ready to go by the date and time specified — her clothes and personal effects in suitcases, her paperwork and other necessary material from the office transferred to boxes.

But then the day of departure was postponed — once, twice and even a third time. It took much longer to package the delicate lab glassware than anyone had originally expected, and then specialists from the company that built them had to be called in to manage the shipment of the genetic analyzers. By the time everything was finally ready to go, Nikki had packed and unpacked her personal suitcase half a dozen times. The chaos of the preparations had one unexpected benefit, however: she had little time to miss Toshikazu, or to puzzle over the mystery of his death …

During the day, at least; the nights were a different story. Although they were never as bad as the nightmares of the first few nights — the visions of Toshikazu with his bloody smile, wielding a *katana* — the dreams

came every night. Usually they were replays of the
meeting with the ninja in the narrow alleyway, often
with some surrealistic elements thrown in by her subconscious. Sometimes there were witnesses to the fight
between Toshikazu and his killer — sometimes Eichiro,
sometimes security chief Yamato, sometimes the
blonde-haired leader of the raiders. Other times, the
site of the combat was different — the halls of the
Nagara Building, or Nikki's lab, or even her apartment. Whatever the details, she always awoke shaken,
unable to return to sleep until her pounding heart had
slowed.

At least the intensity of the dreams seemed to be
fading with time, she told herself. Toshikazu's death
had been traumatic; she wouldn't have been fully
human if it hadn't affected her profoundly, at a very
deep level. But she did seem to be bouncing back, if
slowly. *Maybe I'm emotionally tougher than I thought*, she
mused.

* * *

The sky was an unbroken ceiling of lead-grey clouds.
The wind gusted unpredictably, cutting through
Nikki's thin jacket, chilling her to the bone. She and the
other members of her workgroup huddled in the doubtful shelter of the elevator block atop the Nagara Building. Even in their attempts to escape the wind, the
others consciously kept a distance between them and
Nikki. She chuckled mirthlessly to herself. *They still
haven't forgiven me*, she thought. *It must be hard work to
hold a grudge that long.* Well, she didn't really expect it
to last. Once everyone arrived in Sumatra and saw it
wasn't as bad as they expected, they'd let their barriers
down again. *At least, I hope so*, she added.

The roar of powerful engines and the stuttering of
rotor blades announced the approach of a V/STOL
plane toward the building-top heliport. She set her

shoulder-bag down and watched, holding her wind-whipped hair back from her eyes with both hands.

The V/STOL was a little less than twice the size of an executive Lear jet, with large wings that swept forward — opposite to the design of most planes Nikki was familiar with. Mounted near the tips of the wings were two huge engines: turboprops, not jets, driving propellers not much smaller than the rotors of a helicopter. A couple of hundred yards away from the Nagara Building and an equal distance above the rooftop, the pitch of the motors changed. As Nikki watched in fascination, the plane slowed drastically, and the wings pivoted around their central axes. The engines and their big props moved with them, of course, tipping backward until they'd rotated through 90°. Now, instead of normal forward-facing propellers, the big turboprops were facing upward like helicopter rotors.

The sound of the motors changed again, and the heavy plane started its slow descent toward the rooftop heliport. She could see the props changing their angles, controlling the V/STOL's motion as it came on down. Fifty yards above the roof it stopped, hovering in place. Bright lights burst to life around the circular periphery of the heliport — no doubt to help the pilot better judge altitude, she thought. Even slower now, the craft restarted its descent.

As it drew closer to the roof, Nikki could see how difficult the pilot's job was. The gusts of wind that whipped at her hair and cut through her jacket would strike the plane, blowing it a couple of yards one way or another, or up or down. The pilot had to compensate, keeping the plane as steady as possible. It must take an immense amount of concentration, she thought.

The downdraft from the plane's rotors was buffeting at the spectators, adding its force to the gusting winds. Bojo, Omi and the others backed further away, pressing themselves against the concrete of the elevator block, seeking what little shelter they could find. Nikki, though, held her ground until the V/STOL's wheels had touched down.

The roar decreased as the engines throttled back to idle, and the rotors began to slow. Aft of the wings, a door opened in the fuselage. Two crewmen wearing jumpsuits in Nagara white and blue dropped to the roof, and unfolded a set of metal stairs. Then they beckoned to the passengers.

Nikki was the first one up the stairs. As soon as she was through the door and into the fuselage, the noise of the engines dropped drastically, even though the door was still open. *Great sound insulation,* she thought, *and a good thing too. This'll be a long flight.* She looked around. Inside, the plane was even bigger than it had looked from outside. There were a dozen rows of seats, two by two across a central aisle. That made for lots of legroom *and* elbow-room, she was glad to see. The layout was as spacious and comfortable as the first-class compartment of a commercial airliner.

At the back of the passenger compartment was a bulkhead with a curtain-covered doorway set in it. Presumably that led to a small galley, she thought, and to a couple of washrooms. The same arrangement was repeated at the forward end. Judging from the position of the entrance door and the length of the compartment, the forward curtained opening would lead directly into the cockpit, she figured.

As if to confirm her conclusion, the curtain was drawn back and a figure emerged into the passenger compartment. He wore the same blue-and-white jumpsuit as the crewmembers who'd deployed the ladder, but on his chest pocket was emblazoned Nagara's avian logo and a name badge reading PILOT O'NEIL. His green eyes widened as he saw Nikki, and he self-consciously reached up to brush his unruly red hair into some semblance of order. "Well, hello," he said pleasantly. "Welcome aboard."

Nikki glanced away to hide her own surprise. Not so much by the fact that the pilot of a Nagara V/STOL was a caucasian — and an American, too, judging by his accent — but by her own reaction. When she'd first come to Japan, had hung around with other Western travellers, she'd been scornfully amused by the people who said how much they relished seeing non-Oriental faces on their travels. *Latent racism*, she'd thought at the time, telling herself she'd never feel those emotions. It didn't matter what shape a person's eyes were, or what color the skin, she'd told herself — smug in the conviction she'd never feel that petty relief at seeing a familiar racial appearance. But now ...

If she was so free of racial prejudice, how come she felt such a feeling of pleasure to see Pilot O'Neil?

A slow smile spread across the man's face, and the skin around his eyes crinkled into what Nikki's mother used to call "laugh lines." *It's as if he's reading my mind*, Nikki thought.

To cover her embarrassment, she cleared her throat and brusquely stuck out a hand toward him. "Nikki Carlson, workgroup leader," she said, making her voice as businesslike as possible.

O'Neil raised an eyebrow at her manner, but his smile didn't diminish. He took her hand in a firm grip and shook. "Thomas O'Neil," he said, his voice as brisk as hers — even though the twinkle in his eyes ruined the effect. "Nagara Corporation pilot." Then he relaxed again, his voice returning to its original light, almost bantering tone. "Just make yourself comfortable, Nikki Carlson, workgroup leader. I've got some, um, *business* to attend to." Hurrying a little, he walked past her toward the rear of the compartment, working his way between Nikki's colleagues who were only now filing on board, and disappeared through the aft curtain. *Bathroom break*, Nikki thought with a chuckle.

O'Neil had left the curtain over the forward doorway open, giving her a view into the cockpit. Even without sticking her head in, she could see most of the compartment. The control panels were even more sophisticated than she'd expected. Instead of the rows and rows of dials and gauges that she'd pictured, the main elements of the panels were a number of cathode ray tubes — CRTs — like computer monitors. Some were filled with columns of alphanumeric characters, while others displayed complex graphics. Although she was sure they were easily comprehensible to a trained pilot, they meant nothing at all to Nikki. As for controls, there were two steering yokes, one for the pilot and one for the copilot. Between the two seats were a collection of levers that she took to be throttles and flap controls. Everything else seemed to be controlled directly by computer-style keypads set into the panels below the CRTs.

The left seat — obviously the pilot's station — was empty. The copilot, a sullen-faced Japanese man, sat in the right seat, muttering to himself as he punched data into a keypad. Seeming to sense Nikki's scrutiny, he turned round and shot her a nasty glare. Then he reached out and pulled the curtain shut.

Nikki shrugged. She was mildly curious, but had never been all that interested in aircraft anyway. *May as well pick a seat*, she told herself.

Her six workgroup colleagues had all settled themselves, in a tight group, in the aft half of the cabin. They were talking quietly among themselves, and their body language seemed to Nikki to indicate they were trying to isolate themselves from a reality they found unpleasant. She shrugged again. Pointedly, she selected a seat in the very first row, right behind the bulkhead separating the passenger cabin from the cockpit. She placed her carry-on bag on the aisle seat, and settled herself down next to the window. (*The legroom's usually better with bulkhead seats anyway*, she told herself.) She fastened the seatbelt loosely around her waist, and reclined the seat back to a more comfortable position. She heard the cabin door slam and latch.

"Best seat in the house."

She turned at the voice behind her. It was O'Neil, of course, a lopsided smile on his face.

She looked him over appraisingly. *Quite handsome, and he knows it*, she thought. Smooth and glib, with a good line for the ladies. She knew his type — she'd seen it often enough — and never liked it. *People like him wear a mask all the time, a facade, and you can never see the real person behind it*. She made her expression totally emotionless — *if he can wear a mask, so can I* — and stared at him coolly.

Suddenly, and to her total surprise, his self-possessed front seemed to slip. His smile faded a little, and when he spoke there was a hint of real warmth — not just banter — in his voice. "It's weird," he said. "I never thought I'd feel so happy to see another American." He shook his head, as though a little angered at himself for his honesty. His confident smile returned. "Well, I've got to get this baby airborne." He pulled back the curtain and stepped through into the cockpit. Nikki watched as he settled himself in the pilot's seat. After a quick conversation with his co-pilot — too quiet for Nikki to hear — he pushed the throttles forward a little. Outside, the roar of the engines increased as the rotors spooled up.

Nikki hesitated for moment, then moved her bag out of the way and shifted to the aisle seat. She leaned forward. "Excuse me?" she said, pitching her voice to carry over the engine noise. "Mr. O'Neil?"

O'Neil looked back over his shoulder and grinned. "Call me Tom," he suggested. "If you say 'Mr. O'Neil,' I'll think you're talking to my father."

Nikki had to chuckle. "Tom," she corrected. "Are you handling the whole transfer, Tom?"

"Not a chance," he replied. "Too many flights, too much equipment to carry. I'm handling the personnel transfers, and that's it." He hesitated. "Except for the corp big-wigs, of course. Eichiro's taking his own personal jet."

Nikki blinked. "Eichiro's going?"

"He couldn't *not* go," O'Neil stated flatly. "Whatever this thing's about, it's too important to him to handle it from a distance. He's going to be breathing down your necks every day."

Nikki frowned. The idea of having Eichiro on site made her uncomfortable. *He's one of the things I was looking forward to getting away from,* she thought. But it *did* make sense, she had to admit. If the Inderagiri River project was what she thought—an attempt to make up for the Special Projects department destroyed by the raiders, and thus a way for Eichiro to save his career—there was no way the division manager could remain in Tokyo.

"What about the Matsushima Bay team?" she asked. "When do they go?"

"You mean the scientists, right?" O'Neil laughed. "God, what a collection of overgrown egos."

"When do they go?"

"They've gone already," the pilot answered. "I flew them out to the rendezvous yesterday. All your equipment went out in a cargo plane earlier today. You guys are the last." Something beeped on the control panel. He turned to examine one of the displays, punched something into a keypad, then turned back to grin at her again. "I've got to get the wheels up, someone's getting impatient. Make yourself comfortable and enjoy the ride."

"How long's the flight?"

"Figure on about three hours."

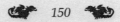

"Three hours?" Nikki was surprised. "This thing's faster than I thought."

For a moment O'Neil looked puzzled. Then she saw comprehension dawn, and his smile returned. "Where do you think we're flying to?" he asked.

"Sumatra, where else? Inderagiri River." She hesitated. "Right?"

The pilot's smile broadened. "You'll see." He slipped a pair of earphones onto his head and steadfastly refused to acknowledge any more of Nikki's questions. The engine noise increased to a crescendo, and the V/STOL rose slowly into the gusty Tokyo sky.

* * *

During the ascent, Nikki could see that O'Neil was too busy to answer any of her questions. As the plane shifted and bounced, buffeted by the gusting wind, she wondered about what he'd said. If they weren't flying to Sumatra, to the Inderagiri site — as the pilot had implied — where the hell *were* they going?

She heard the pitch of the twin motors alter, and felt a difference in the way the plane moved. *We must be switching to forward flight*, she thought, visualizing the wings pivoting, the overhead rotors becoming forward-pointing propellers. She looked out the window, hoping for a glimpse of the ground, to confirm her suspicions. But they were already in the low cloud deck; all she could see was greyness.

The motors changed pitch again, and she felt herself sinking back into her seat. Obviously the plane was either accelerating or climbing, or perhaps both.

The curtain was still open, giving her a clear view through the door into the cockpit. It was the Japanese copilot who was handling the control yoke, she saw. O'Neil was studying a map displayed on one of the larger CRTs, and punching a string of numbers into a keypad. *Navigational data*, Nikki guessed, *probably our destination.* Someone more versed in geography might have guessed something from the digits he was entering, but they could just as well have been a phone number for all they meant to Nikki.

When he'd finished entering the numbers, she saw O'Neil press a large button on the panel. A bell-like tone sounded, and a line of kanji text — too small for her to read — appeared on the central display screen. The copilot released the control yoke, leaned back in his seat and stretched. *We're on autopilot*, Nikki realized.

She leaned toward the cockpit door. "O'Neil," she called, then, "Tom."

He looked around, an irritating grin on his face. "Uh-huh?"

"Where are we going?"

He shrugged casually. "Roughly southwest."

Nikki gritted her teeth. "Where are we going?" she repeated, her voice cold.

"Okay, okay," O'Neil relented at last, "a guy's got to take his fun where he finds it. We're heading for latitude 8° north and longitude 112° east, close enough."

"Which is …?"

"Which is smack dab in the middle of the South China Sea," O'Neil answered. "About 400 miles from Borneo, the same distance from Vietnam."

"And what's there?"

"Not much," O'Neil chuckled. "A little speck of land called Spratly Island."

"Why? To refuel?"

"Uh-uh. This baby could make it to Sumatra with enough fuel left over for a jaunt to Australia for dinner."

"Then why?" Nikki pressed.

O'Neil's devil-may-care smile faded. "They didn't tell you much about Sumatra, did they?" he asked quietly.

Nikki was silent for a moment, affected by his suddenly-serious manner. "No, not much."

The pilot nodded. "I didn't think so." He glanced over at his copilot. "Iba-*san*, old pal, why don't you take over for a while? I'm going back to check on our esteemed passengers."

She saw a look of disgust cross the copilot's face, but he nodded and grunted, "Hai, O'Neir-*san*."

O'Neil slid his seat back and climbed out, careful to avoid bumping against the control yoke. He rolled his head from side to side to release tension in his neck and shoulders, then sauntered out into the passenger compartment. He indicated the seat across the aisle from Nikki. "Mind if I join you?" he asked lightly. "It's much easier to talk this way." Without waiting for her to answer, he settled himself down in the seat, stretching his long legs out into the aisle. He shot her a broad grin. "The only way to fly."

At another time, Nikki might have enjoyed his easygoing manner; now it was making her impatient. "Tell me about Sumatra," she said.

"Sumatra," the pilot began. He hesitated, reached forward and pulled the curtain closed across the doorway. Then he settled back comfortably again. "First of all, they call the area 'Orrorsh' now."

"You mean Sumatra?" She thought back to Eichiro's briefing. "I thought they called it 'Majestic,' or something like that."

"That's Sumatra itself," he explained. "Orrorsh is what they're calling the whole region: Sumatra, Malaysia, Java, Timor, Borneo, the Celebes, even parts of Thailand and the Philippines."

"So it's all one country now?" she asked.

The pilot shook his head. "Not a country," he told her firmly. "Orrorsh has nothing to do with politics or nationality. It's like ..." He paused, obviously struggling to order his thoughts. "It's a ... a place." He shrugged. "Some people call it a 'realm,' but maybe that's not the best word. Orrorsh is an area where ... where certain things happen." He shrugged again, apparently not satisfied with his explanation.

"What do you mean, 'certain things'?"

O'Neil was looking really uncomfortable, she noticed. "I'm what you'd call a shortwave junkie," he started, somewhat obliquely. "It's one of my hobbies. I've got a shortwave radio I built myself, and nights when I'm not flying I listen to shortwave broadcasts from around the world." Nikki nodded, understanding — *like me and the Voice of America.*

"It used to be I'd pick up a lot of broadcasts from Thailand, Singapore, Vietnam, even from Palembang in Sumatra," the pilot went on. "They're close to Japan so they'd come in real clear. A couple of years back, though, those stations just went off the air. Like, I'd get *nothing* from that part of the world. And that's when the stations I *could* still pick up — the ones in Manilla and a couple in Australia — started reporting weird stories. That's when they started calling the area Orrorsh.

"I'm a pilot," O'Neil said, "so I paid most attention to things that affect pilots — changes in the weather, plane crashes, that kind of thing." The man was consciously keeping his voice emotionless, but Nikki could see from his body language and expression that he was disturbed. "There were *lots* of plane crashes," he went on. "A couple of airliners went down over Orrorsh. The international airlines rearranged their flight paths to bypass the area. Research expeditions were sent in to find out what had happened. Their planes went down. The new US government in Texas sent an SR-71 Blackbird spyplane up from Kadena Air Force Base, sent it over Orrorsh at 75,000 feet for a look-see. It fell out of the sky."

Nikki felt a cold fist tighten in her stomach. There

was something highly disturbing about the dispassionate way O'Neil was describing the disasters. "Why?" she asked. "What went wrong?"

O'Neil shrugged. "Nobody really knows," he told her, "nobody outside Orrorsh. Maybe the people who still live there know — the ones who haven't fled as refugees. But they're not telling." He hesitated. "From what the shortwave stations said, the planes just stopped working. All the high technology that makes a modern plane work — computerized navigation, radar, autopilot, the hydraulics and servos that drive the control surfaces ... It all just *stopped*. From what they say, you can't trust anything more technologically advanced than ..." — he searched for an example — " ...than steamships."

Nikki shook her head. What O'Neil was saying didn't make sense. High technology worked according to the laws of physics. If it stopped working, didn't that mean that the laws of physics — the supposedly immutable laws of physics — had changed? Impossible ...

Or *seemingly* so. But wasn't this just the kind of thing the Voice of America had been reporting over the last few months? According to reliable reports, dragons cruised the skies over the British Isles. But according to the laws of physics and aerodynamics, there was no conceivable way something built like a mythical dragon could *ever* fly. *If I accept the reports that there are dragons,* Nikki thought, *doesn't that logically mean that the laws of physics have changed? And I* have *to accept them.*

Another thought struck her. "And we're flying in there?" she asked.

O'Neil chuckled. "Nagara management doesn't like to think about Orrorsh," he said, "but they're not that stupid. That's why were landing at Spratly Island. We transfer to a transport ship — a ship with its diesel turbines replaced with coal-burning boilers, they tell me — and *sail* to Sumatra. A nice pleasure cruise, they tell me."

Nikki smiled, at least partially relieved. Suddenly she realized something. "You said 'we,'" she pointed out.

O'Neil grinned broadly. "That's what I said," he agreed. "You're not getting rid of me easily, old buddy old pal. Iba-*san*, up front there, gets to fly this baby back to Tokyo. I got my transfer orders a couple of days back. I'm officially seconded to the Inderagiri Research Facility. Sounds like I'm in for the duration."

"Why?" Nikki demanded. "If planes don't work ..."

The pilot's smile faded. "Yeah, there's that. But old Eichiro-*san* wants to cover all bases. Part of the outpost's equipment is a small helicopter, stripped down for shipment. Some technicians are already there, they should have it airworthy by the time I get there. If my luck holds, the engine won't fire, or I won't be able to get the thing into the air. What really worries me is that I'll be a few thousand feet up when Orrorsh suddenly decides that helicopters ain't going to work no more." His smile returned and he chuckled. "Ah, well, that's why they pay me the big bucks. Yeah, right."

Nikki looked at the pilot with new interest. *Doesn't anything bother him for long?* she wondered. His smile was infectious, and she found herself laughing. "Maybe a little sabotage would help you out," she suggested lightly. "How about if I put some *sake* in the fuel tank?"

"No no no no," he shouted in mock horror, "that'll burn better than avgas. Now maybe soy sauce would do it, or a *yakitori* skewer in the transfer housing."

Nikki fell silent for a moment. "If nothing more sophisticated than steam power works," she wondered, "what about my equipment? Automated genetic analyzers, that kind of thing?"

"Haven't you heard?" he asked jokingly. "The cargo planes were loaded with wood-burning computers ..."

" ... And printers with steam-driven carriages," she added, laughing again, "I know."

"That sounds about right." He sighed and stretched.

"Well, I'd better get back to work. If I don't keep an eye on him, Iba's likely to make a torpedo run on the first American-flagged ship he sees." He patted her on the shoulder companionably. "See you on board ship." He shook his head in mock despair. "They've probably given me a cabin in steerage."

* * *

Nikki didn't get to see much of Spratly Island — not that there was much to see, according to O'Neil. As the V/STOL dropped below the cloud deck for its final approach, she could hear rain rattling against the fuselage like rock salt fired from a shotgun. Water streamed down the window, obscuring whatever view there might have been.

When the plane was down, she and the other passengers had to sprint across the jury-rigged airstrip, which was right on the shoreline, to a quonset hut. In the dozen or so seconds it took her, she was soaked to the skin with warm rain. The cloud cover was total — grey-black stormclouds — and lightning strobed in the sky. They had to wait in the hut for half an hour, chilling down and shivering, while the air filled with the smell of wet cloth. Then they had to brave the rain again, as they were shepherded out onto a makeshift jetty, and instructed to climb down a wet and slick ladder to the deck of a small tender. Sopping wet again, they huddled below decks as the boat pulled away from the docks. Five minutes later they were out in the downpour once more, climbing a steep, slippery stairway to the deck of the ship that would take them to Sumatra.

The ship was big, bigger than Nikki had expected: a couple of hundred feet from bow to stern, broad-beamed and low to the water. As it rode at anchor, it rocked disturbingly with the waves. *What's it going to be like when we're underway?* Nikki wondered. Already

Bojo and Matsukara from her workgroup were looking a little green around the gills, and Nikki herself — usually a good sailor — was feeling a little less than comfortable. To take her mind off her queasiness, she concentrated on unpacking some of her personal luggage, and making her cabin — a small compartment, not much larger than a single bed — as comfortable and homey as she could. She was reassured when the ship weighed anchor. Once underway, it seemed to ride much more smoothly, and her intimations of seasickness vanished.

At her first opportunity, she explored the ship. Most of it was given over to cargo holds — some refrigerated — filled almost to capacity with wooden crates bearing cryptic annotations in *kanji*. From the few designations she recognized, she guessed that much of the cargo was food, and other necessities of day-to-day life. Presumably the lab equipment — for her group and for the Matsushima Bay team — had already gone ahead on another ship.

The passenger accommodations were all in the large, blocky superstructure near the stern, while the crew cabins were directly below in the hull. There were twenty-four passengers, she was surprised to find: her workgroup — seven, including her — O'Neil and a couple of mechanics, with the remaining fourteen being Nagara security personnel. (*More than a* dozen *security guards?* she wondered. *What* is *this place we're going to?*) Each of the cabins apart from hers had two bunks, and everyone else was doubled up. *There are some benefits to being the only woman on board*, she recognized.

In response to her questions, one of the Japanese crewmembers had told her — somewhat grudgingly, she thought — the voyage to the mouth of the Inderagiri River would take about three days, at a top speed of seventeen knots. *Three days of nothing to do*, she thought.

And then we're in Orrorsh. This assignment wasn't turning out the way she'd expected.

* * *

On the second day underway, the passengers were called to a meeting on the open deck of the ship, just for'ard of the superstructure. The weather had changed overnight, and a tropical sun was beating down from a cloudless sky. For the first time, the wardrobe choices Nikki had made — mainly shorts and light cotton shirts — made some sense.

The meeting was conducted by the head of the security contingent, she was surprised to see. Arrayed behind him, like soldiers on parade, were the other security guards. The other ten passengers stood in a disorganized knot in front of him.

"We are travelling to Orrorsh," the security head started without preamble, his voice carrying easily over the low-pitched throbbing of the engines. "This brings with it certain security considerations. Your safety is our responsibility, and that of the security personnel already at the Inderagiri Research Facility." That surprised Nikki. *There's more security guards?*

"It has been decided," the man continued, "that this will be made easier if you have the ability to protect yourselves. "Therefore you will each be issued with a personal defence weapon." The group of passengers burst into confused muttering, quickly stilled as the security head went on. "The purpose of this meeting is to familiarize you with this weapon and to give you an opportunity to handle it. You will be officially issued your weapons only on arrival at the outpost."

He reached down and pulled a pistol from a holster that Nikki only now noticed on his belt. He held it above his head. "This is the Komatsu 'Viper' Personal Defense Pistol," he announced. "It is chambered exclusively for flechette rounds, with 14 rounds to a clip, and has an integral laser sighting system. You will please step forward one at a time to receive your weapon."

Nikki stared in shock. *I can't believe what I'm hearing,* she told herself. *Guns? They can't expect us to* take *them …*

But of course they do, she realized as the others moved forward to receive their weapons. *And all the good little* sararimen *go along with it without a single question.* She was surprised — and, she had to admit, a little disappointed — to see that O'Neil was near the front of the group.

He must have seen her disapproval in her expression. Separating himself from the others, he joined her at the back of the group. His smile — which she saw as maddening again, not charming — was in place. "Don't like it, huh?" he asked quietly.

"No," she snapped, "no I don't."

"Why?"

"We're scientists, not … not *cowboys,*" she almost sputtered. "I'll never be in a situation where I'll need a gun."

"You *intend* never to be in a situation where you'll need a gun," he corrected calmly. "Tell me, do you wear a life jacket when you go sailing?" Before she could respond, he asked the follow-up question: "*Why?* You don't *intend* to fall overboard, do you?"

Nikki shook her head impatiently; she'd seen the second question coming. "It's not the same at all," she stated.

He raised an eyebrow. "Isn't it?" he asked. "From the stories I've heard about Orrorsh, you carry a gun the way you'd wear a life jacket sailing in heavy seas: out of enlightened self interest."

O'Neil's smile hadn't faded, but there was something different in his eyes and in his voice that chilled Nikki to the core. *He's serious about this,* she told herself, *he's dead serious.* "What stories?" she asked, her voice hushed.

He glanced around them. For the first time, she noticed that some of the others — including a couple of the security personnel — were watching them a little suspiciously. "I'll tell you later," he said. "Let's get this out of the way."

A little cowed by the pilot's manner and his words, Nikki joined the line-up.

Eventually it was her turn. Each of the non-security passengers received the personal attention of one security guard. The man who stepped up to Nikki was short — the top of his head not even reaching the level of her eyes — but squat, and muscles bulged under his blue-and-white jumpsuit. "My name is Dei, Carrson-*san*," he said politely. "Have you ever used a pistol before?"

I've never even touched one. She didn't say it out loud, however; she just shook her head.

He held the pistol — my *pistol*, she thought uncomfortably — out toward her. "You are right-handed?" he asked. She nodded. "Then take it in your right hand, Carrson-*san*."

She looked at the pistol in his hand. It seemed to be made of black plastic, small — not too much longer than her hand — but even more deadly-seeming because of that. It wasn't the brutal, hard-edged thing she'd expected. Its swept lines were smooth, graceful even. If she could have blocked from her mind its nature and purpose, she might even have found it beautiful. She shook her head: the idea was perverse, grotesque. Slowly, unwilling to touch it but forcefully suppressing her misgivings, she took the pistol, weighed it in her hand. It wasn't as heavy as she might have thought; she guessed it weighed about two pounds. The grip was hard rubber, or some plastic that felt like rubber, ridged and grooved — *checkered*, she thought, *for a good grip, so it won't slip even if your hand's sweating.*

Dei pointed to a switch on the left side of the gun, just above the grip. "This is the safety catch, Carrson-*san*," he explained. "You can switch it on and off with your right thumb as you hold the gun. Down, like it is now, the gun is safe: it can't fire, and you can't even cock it. Up, like this" — he moved her thumb, flipped the switch up with a metallic snick — "the gun will fire. Please remember that. The most common serious mistake a gun user makes is not knowing the state of his weapon. Do you understand?"

Nikki nodded dumbly.

"Then please make your weapon safe, Carrson-*san*."

Obediently, she snapped the safety back on.

"Good," Dei said.

She looked at him. Was he patronizing her? *No*, she decided after a moment. The young man was business-like, but friendly. If he considered her a second-class citizen because she was a woman and a *gaijin*, he hid it exceptionally well. *He's just making sure I know something he considers important*, she told herself, *something he thinks might keep me alive.* She shivered.

"This" — and now Dei pointed to button, on the left side of the grip just behind the trigger guard — "is the magazine release. Please hold your left hand under the butt of the weapon" — she did so — "and press this button."

She did as she was instructed. The magazine — a metal clip a little longer than the grip of the pistol — slid free and fell into her hand.

"This, of course, contains the bullets," Dei explained. "Or not exactly bullets, in this case. As my superior said, the Viper is designed to fire what are called flechettes — bundles of tiny slivers of metal, packed tightly together. Flechette rounds are designed to be particularly effective against lightly-armored or unarmored targets." A smile, quick as a strobe light, flashed across his face. "Let us both hope you never have to check out their effectiveness personally.

"Don't worry about how the rounds go into the clip, or how to replace them," the security guard went on. "If it ever becomes necessary, one of us will give you additional clips. When a clip is empty — after you've fired fourteen rounds — press the release, let the clip fall out, and slide a replacement into the butt. Try replacing the clip now. Press it in hard until you hear it seat."

Nikki slid the metal clip back into the pistol butt, shoved hard on the base until it clicked into place.

"Remove the clip again, please, Carrson-san, and hand it to me." She did so. Dei pocketed the magazine, flashed another millisecond-long smile at her. "It pays to be safe when training beginners," he explained, a little apologetically.

"One cocks the pistol by pulling back on the slide — the upper section here," he went on. "Grip it like this" — he positioned her left hand over the top of the gun — "and pull it straight back until you hear a click. Try it now."

She pulled the way he'd instructed, but nothing happened. The slide remained firmly in place. "It won't move," she pointed out.

"And why not?" he asked.

She was silent for a moment. Then she reached up with her thumb and flipped the safety off. She gripped the slide again and pulled. This time it slid smoothly back. There was a loud metallic click. She released the slide and it snapped back into position.

Dei was grinning broadly now. "Thank you for paying attention, Carrson-*san*," he said, real warmth in his voice now. "You make my job easier. If there were a clip in place, your weapon would now be ready to fire. Please place your finger on the trigger and, um, *take up the slack*." He spoke the last phrase in strongly-accented English.

She looked at him sharply, then grinned. *He speaks English, does he? I wonder who else does around here.* As Dei had instructed, she touched the trigger, pulled it back a fraction of an inch until it reached a stop. As she did so, Dei placed a broad palm a foot or so in front of the barrel. A bright red dot appeared on his palm.

"That's the sighting laser," he told her. "Apply 450 grams of pressure to the trigger and the laser is activated. Four hundred and fifty grams is about one pound," he quickly — and needlessly — converted for her. "You must apply a pressure of almost 1800 grams — about four pounds — for the pistol to fire."

"Weapons like this are very easy to use," he went on. "Wherever the sighting dot appears, that is the center of the flechette pattern. You don't really have to aim at all, just put the dot on what you want to hit. It's simple. Now squeeze the trigger. Slowly, just steadily apply more pressure until it 'breaks.'"

Nikki did as instructed, slowly squeezing the trigger. The gun made a metallic clack noise.

"And you have just hit your target," Dei concluded. "If you ever have to actually fire it, you'll find the recoil is minimal." He smiled again. "Congratulations, Carrson-*san*, you have learned all you need to know to use your weapon safely." He took the pistol from her loose grip. "We'll keep the guns while we're aboard ship, then pass them back to you when we reach the Inderagiri River scientific outpost. Thank you for being a good student."

She thanked him quietly, feeling a little overwhelmed. *So easy,* she thought. *So easy to use something that'll kill someone.* Then, *I wish I'd had one of these in the Shinjuku alley,* she thought harshly. She turned away, horrified and disgusted at herself.

Dei laid a gentle hand on her shoulder. She turned back.

The security guard's face was serious again. "There's one last thing, Carrson-*san*," he said a little diffidently. "I know it's disturbing to think about, but it's something I feel I must tell you. If you ever have any need to use this weapon, please don't fire just one shot. That works well on television, but not well in real life. If you have to shoot someone or something, keep firing. Keep firing until your gun is empty, or until your opponent goes down and doesn't get up again. For both our sakes, remember this, please? Not doing so is the second most common serious mistake a gun user can make."

Nikki nodded dumbly. She could sense his concern. Even though the idea frightened her, again she knew he was making sure she knew something he thought might keep her alive. "*Domo arrigato gozaimas*, Dei-*san*," she mumbled, "thank you for your concern." She turned away.

O'Neil had finished with his trainer at about the same time she had, she noticed. The others — particularly Toshima — seemed to be having a hard go of it. The security guard assigned to Toshima looked like he was fuming with impatience, about ready to toss the slow-thinking fifty-year-old over the rail into the South China Sea.

O'Neil caught up with her as she entered the superstructure. "I'm going for coffee," the pilot told her. "Join me?"

They went aft to the "passenger lounge" — a small, spartan room not much larger than Nikki's cabin. Against one wall was an industrial-sized coffee urn that seemed always full of dark, bitter brew. The pilot poured himself a cup and one for Nikki. As they added cream — and in O'Neil's case, sugar too — she reminded him, "You said you'd heard stories about Orrorsh."

He nodded, but didn't say anything until they'd

settled themselves down at one of the small tables. "I talked to one of the workers on Spratly Island," he started obliquely — as he tended to do, Nikki noted. "His name was Jak-something, I didn't catch the rest of it." She nodded, recognizing that the only way to deal with O'Neil was to let him tell his stories in his own way. "He was an Indonesian, he said," he continued, "he used to work in Palembang — that's the biggest city on Sumatra." He paused for a second, apparently expecting Nikki to break in with a question. When she didn't, he smiled. "Jak-whatever was there when things began to change," he went on. "He stayed for about six months, as things steadily got worse around him. That was the time when people started calling the area Orrorsh. Finally he couldn't stand it any more, and hitched a ride on an Australian ship bound for Japan." He chuckled. "He didn't say it, but I figure he stowed away. Anyway, when he got to Japan, he got a job with Nagara as a freight handler, and they eventually shipped him to Spratly Island to help with the Inderagiri outpost transfer. That's about as close as he ever wants to get to Orrorsh, he says."

He paused, and his face grew more serious. "Jak says he left some family and friends back in Palembang. He couldn't 'arrange passage' for them. He stayed in touch, of course, as much as possible with the upheavals in technology. But now he says there's no reason to keep in touch. The last one died about a week ago."

Nikki was silent for a moment. Then she asked, "What happened?"

"He didn't want to talk about it," O'Neil said with a shrug, "not specifically. But he said — I can remember his words exactly — 'Orrorsh has become a land of horrors'. There are … *things* … in the jungle, things that kill people … or worse." He hurried on to forestall Nikki's next question. "He wouldn't say exactly what he meant by 'worse'. And now, he says, those things are moving into the cities. He implied, but he didn't say directly, that those things killed his family and his friends." He sighed. "Maybe I shouldn't pay any attention, but I can't help it. He worried me. He said 'Orrorsh is a land where nightmares become real'."

Nikki stared at the pilot, a sudden sense of sick worry writhing in her stomach. *Nightmares becoming real?* she repeated to herself, thinking of the dreams she'd had after Toshikazu's death. *What could be worse than that?* "Did he say anything else?" she asked eventually.

"Isn't that enough?" O'Neil countered bleakly.

* * *

Nikki's eyes sprung open, rolled wildly as she tried to make sense of her environment. Featureless grey ceiling above, a dull, almost-subliminal throbbing that she felt through her bones as much as heard. Faint smells in her nostrils — smoke mixed with oil. It took her several seconds — seconds of panic — before she knew where she was. *My cabin on the freighter*, she realized at last. *I'm safe ... for the moment*. She forced herself to sit upright, breathed deeply to clear the last tendrils of sleep — and the metabolic poisons of fear — from her body.

The dream had come back, as bad as it had been the first night after the ninja's attack. The major elements were the same: Toshikazu, with his bloody smile, wielding a katana to cut her in two. But the secondary details were different. This time, instead of the narrow alleys of Shinjuku, or the corridors of the Nagara building, it had taken place in the jungle: dark, fetid and claustrophobic.

And there'd been another figure involved, too: a dark, shrouded figure standing at the periphery of her vision. She hadn't been able to recognize who it was — or who it was supposed to be — but she somehow had the sense it was a male. As Toshikazu had advanced with his gleaming sword, the shadowy figure had watched. And he'd laughed — a dry, menacing sound. It had been that laugh, and the brain-numbing horror that it had caused her, that had woken her from the dream, gasping and sweating.

I guess I should be grateful, she told herself grimly. *Anybody who wakes me from one of those is a friend.* She shivered, though: no matter how she rationalized it, she couldn't accept the figure as anything but threatening.

Still breathing deeply to get her heart rate down to normal again, she checked her watch. Almost seven in the morning; almost time to get up. Even though she didn't have anything to do on shipboard, she was trying to keep to her normal schedule. They key members of the freighter's crew — the bridge officers and the "black gang" who worked in the engine room — were on round-the-clock watches, of course, so that meant the refectory on the main deck level was always open, and there was always coffee in the lounge. So she might as well go get some breakfast, she told herself.

She tried to make herself believe it was excitement that made her want to get up; after all, they'd be reaching the mouth of the Inderagiri River late this afternoon, and she might already be able to see Sumatra. But, deep down, she knew that what motivated her was fear: if she went back to sleep, mightn't the nightmares be waiting for her?

* * *

Nikki couldn't see much of Sumatra as the big freighter swung at anchor. During the night, the clouds had gathered again, and a thin mist hung over land and water. At least is wasn't raining like it had been at Spratly Island, though, she comforted herself. And even though it looked like it should be cold, the temperature actually seemed to have gone up as a result of the clouds and mist. There was no wind, and the air was heavy with moisture. She could still smell the sea, but now she could scent something else, something very different. A heavy underpinning beneath the sharp salt tang — *how do you describe an odor?* she wondered — a complex, damp smell of living things. *It must be the jungle.*

The freighter was a couple of hundred yards offshore. O'Neil had told her what he'd learned from the contacts he'd made among the crew. The Inderagiri was deep enough for the freighter — which had a shallow draught despite its apparent size — to make it a long way up-river, easily as far as the site of the outpost. (That's what everyone else had taken to calling the Inderagiri Research Facility — "the outpost" — and Nikki found herself doing the same.) So there was no technical reason for them to anchor offshore at all.

No, according to O'Neil it had been the captain's decision. For the first time, Nikki had realized that the ship wasn't officially a Nagara vessel. She should have clued in to that immediately — the logo on the freighter's funnel wasn't Nagara's blue and white crane — but the fact it was a Nagara operation, and the exclusively Japanese nationality of the crew, had blinded her to this. Instead, the vessel was of Philippine registry, operated by a Japanese shipping concern based in Manilla. Although the ship had never put in at Sumatra before, it had apparently made runs to Kampot, a port in Campuchia. *Obviously close enough to Orrorsh for the captain to have heard stories*, Nikki thought. The captain hadn't wanted to make this voyage at all, and only extensive "voluntary gifts" by Nagara — *in other words, personal bribery* — had convinced him to accept the contract. While he'd eventually agreed to sail to the mouth of the Inderagiri River, there apparently wasn't enough money in the world to convince him to sail up it. ("Smart man," O'Neil had told her with a grim chuckle, "he wants money, but he also wants to live to spend it.")

So that's why Nikki and the other passengers would be ferried the last fifty miles to the outpost in smaller vessels — "riverines," O'Neil had called them — based out of the Inderagiri facility itself. As soon as everything had been off-loaded, the captain would be reversing his course and heading for the fastness of the South China Sea at the freighter's best speed.

The first of the riverines was coming alongside, Nikki saw. She went to the rail for a better view. It was a smooth-lined boat apparently built for speed, she saw — low to the water, with an enclosed forward structure that presumably contained the wheelhouse and cabins for the crew. Painted a drab grey-green, it somehow seemed familiar, she realized with a mild shock.

It took her several moments to retrieve the memory. When it came, the recognition was disturbing. *It looks like the patrol boat from that Vietnam war movie*, Apocalypse Now.

Which only makes sense, she went on to herself after a moment. *It's built for the same kind of mission, cruising a river through the middle of the jungle. It'd be more surprising if it didn't look like that.* But, even with that rationalization, she found the connection disturbing.

The riverine approached quickly and quietly. Its engine sound was muffled, but it certainly didn't sound like the kind of steam power plant driving the freighter. *It's more high-tech than that, she recognized. What does that tell me? That the technological ... distortion ... isn't as bad as O'Neil said?* That was reassuring, at least. If it was true about the outpost as a whole, she could look forward to much the same modern standard of day-to-day life that she'd enjoyed in Tokyo. *And it means the genetic analyzers and computers should work, too.* She wondered about the helicopter that was waiting up-river for O'Neil, but put the thought aside.

Crewmen aboard the freighter threw down lines, caught and tied off by men aboard the riverine, as the small vessel came alongside. The crew aboard the riverine looked young, fit and competent, and they wore the uniforms of Nagara security. When the riverine was made fast, the freighter crew lowered the same steep gangway Nikki had used to board ship at Spratly Island.

The passengers' personal luggage had already been brought up on deck, and now the cases were passed down the gangway aboard the riverine. The other passengers themselves — except for the security guards, who'd be going on the next boat — stood in a knot near the top of the gangway. Nikki walked over to join them.

The other members of her workgroup looked decidedly uncomfortable, she noted. They didn't talk among themselves, just shifted nervously from foot to foot, their gazes alternating between the riverine below and the mist-shrouded jungle two hundred yards away. As she joined them, they turned cold eyes on Nikki, then quickly looked away. She sighed. *They still blame me for all this*, she thought.

At least O'Neil gave her a warm smile as she approached. "Ready?" he asked.

She shrugged. "Ready as I'll ever be."

They filed down the gangplank, onto the deck of the riverine. As soon as the last one was aboard, the boat's crew cast off the lines. The stern dropped a little as power was fed to the screw, and they were off. There were benches mounted along the gunwales, Nikki saw. She picked a spot for herself near the stern and sat down. O'Neil joined her.

"How long to the outpost?" she asked him.

"About ninety minutes," he answered. "Might as well enjoy the view."

The view was fascinating, Nikki thought as they

started up-river. Exotic, very different from anything she'd ever seen. Near its mouth, the Inderagiri was a wide river — at least two hundred yards, she guessed, although the mist, which seemed to be getting thicker, made it hard to judge. Its water was dark brown, almost black, presumably from mud and sediment it had picked up along the way. The jungle came right down to the river's edge, dark and thick and lush. *Just like in my nightmare*, the thought came unbidden. She shivered.

To distract herself, she tried to recall what she'd read about Sumatra before leaving Tokyo. Something about the river and the jungle just didn't seem right. Hadn't the databases said that the east side of the island, particularly around the mouth of the Inderagiri, was a coastal swamp? She didn't think she'd read anything about the jungle extending right to the sea.

What did that tell her? she wondered. She reminded herself that, in a way, this wasn't Sumatra any more; it was Orrorsh. Could that have had some effect on the jungle itself, allowing it to spread out and claim territory that had been denied it before? Certainly, she admitted, looking at the jungle, the dark, forbidding trees seemed an excellent habitat for the "things" O'Neil had talked about.

She shook her head. *Emotional foolishness*, she told herself sharply. *If reality doesn't match what I think I read, why do I question reality?*

After they'd been underway for about half an hour, they passed two more riverines and a slightly larger boat running downstream. They were going to pick up the security guards, O'Neil told her, and the cargo in the holds of the freighter. Nikki wondered about how they were going to make the transfer. *I'm just glad I don't have to worry about it*, she thought.

* * *

Her first view of the outpost came as a surprise. Eventually bored of watching the passing jungle, she'd let her mind drift and lost track of time. She'd been idly watching some big birds — too far away to recognize — circling high above the river, when O'Neil touched her on the arm. "Home sweet home," he muttered.

There was a large clearing on the left side of the river, almost two hundred yards in diameter. Not a natural clearing, she saw at once. In places there were still the massive stumps of trees that Nagara's workers had felled. (*How long did this take?* she wondered. *They can't have done all this in just two weeks.*) There was no undergrowth at all. The margin of the jungle was sharp; in a couple of steps a person would go from levelled clearing to virgin jungle.

But it was the structures in the great clearing that attracted Nikki's attention. The first thing she noticed was by far the most incongruous, totally out of keeping with her mental image of the outpost. It was a stockade fence, ten feet or more high, constructed of logs driven vertically into the ground. *Like the fence around a cavalry fort in a Western movie, for God's sake*, she thought incredulously. From her vantage point, the area enclosed by the stockade looked about a hundred yards in diameter and roughly circular. Circular, that was, apart from the area along the river bank. Where the stockade met the shoreline, the line of logs changed its angle, now leading straight out into the water fifty feet or so — presumably that's how far off-shore the river started to grow deep, she thought. The result was that the compound was open to the river for a distance of maybe thirty or forty yards.

The buildings within the compound matched the construction of the stockade fence — rough-hewn logs stacked one atop the other. The roofs were made from cut planks, slightly angled so that rain would pour off. Nikki could count eight buildings from where she was.

The largest, which looked to have two stories, was in the center, while the others — all single-floor — surrounded it. There was at least ten yards of open space between the buildings and the surrounding fence.

Nikki's heart sank. To her eyes, the entire place looked bleak, and incredibly primitive. There was nothing she could see that spoke of technology more advanced than the way she pictured the 1880s or 1890s.

No, that wasn't quite true, she realized after a moment. There were a couple of small boats tied up at two make-shift jetties extending from the bank. Smaller than the riverines, and considerably faster-looking, they were definitely contemporary technology. And there was something else near them, something that resembled a miniature hovercraft, just about big enough for two or three passengers.

As the riverine headed in toward the bank, the perspective changed. For the first time, Nikki could see something that had previously been concealed by the stockade fence. A small, sleek-lined helicopter. She nudged O'Neil and pointed.

But the pilot had already seen it, she could tell from his sour expression. "The buggers have got it waiting for me," he grumbled. "Just great."

The riverine slowed, and pulled alongside one of the wooden jetties. As security personnel on the dock tied off the lines, the riverine's crew started unloading the passengers' luggage. Carefully, Nikki and the rest stepped over the rail onto the dock, and waited for someone to tell them what to do next.

They didn't have to wait long. A senior security officer — identified by flashes on the shoulders of his uniform — strode toward them, apparently from the direction of the central building. He stopped when he reached the dock, bowed to Nikki and the rest. The angle of his bow indicated guarded respect, but certainly no deference. "Welcome to the Inderagiri Research Facility," he said brusquely. "You will please follow me to your accommodations." Without waiting for any response, he turned on his heel and strode off toward the buildings.

Exchanging a wry glance with O'Neil, Nikki shouldered her bag and followed the officer.

The ground within the compound looked soft, almost muddy, and she couldn't see any paths, either of concrete or any other material. But as she stepped off the wooden dock, she could see there *were* paths. In certain areas — like between the dock and the concentration of buildings — the earth had been chemically treated in some way. Although it looked no different from the surrounding ground, along these tracks it was dry and firm, feeling almost like concrete under her feet. *Interesting*, she thought. *High technology at work, but not in any way you'd see on casual inspection.* What did that mean? she wondered.

The security officer quickly split the group up, assigning them to different accommodation buildings — barracks, as Nikki found herself thinking of them. Toshima, Bojo and her other close colleagues were placed in one building near the center of the compound, while O'Neil and the two mechanics went to a smaller building nearer to the stockade. ("We'll talk later," O'Neil whispered to her as he headed inside.)

That left Nikki. The security officer frowned. "Your presence has posed a problem, Carrson-*san*," he grumbled. "No provisions were made for female staff when the research facility was constructed." (*He doesn't call it "the outpost,"* Nikki noted.) "When we were informed of your assignment to this project, we were forced to improvise." As he spoke, he led her back toward the center of the compound.

"This is the building set aside for your workgroup's lab, Carrson-*san*," he told her, stopping before a rectangular, one-story structure about eighty feet long and half that wide. "Originally, in addition to the lab, storage area and other facilities, it was designed with an office for the workgroup leader's use during the day. Unfortunately, since there is no other acceptable place to assign you, this office has been converted into your quarters. I regret that this means you have no office." He hesitated, then went on, "I explain this to assure you that the arrangements are intended as no dishonor to you. Do you understand?"

Nikki looked into the man's face, suddenly earnest. *The Japanese concept of "face" again*, she thought. *They want to be sure I don't think I'm losing face.* (*Except when they want me to lose face*, another part of her mind added.) "I understand," she told the officer politely. "Thank you for your concern."

The man looked relieved. *Such a contradiction*, she mused for the thousandth time. *Who but the Japanese can so well combine pig-headed, bloody-minded stubbornness with concern for all the niggling points of etiquette?*

"Allow me to show you your quarters, then, Carrson-*san*." The security officer opened the door — made of heavy, rough wood, Nikki noticed — and held it for her. She nodded her thanks and stepped inside.

And it was as if she was in another world. For a shocking instant, she thought she could well have been teleported back to the Nagara Building in Tokyo. The hallway in which she stood looked as though it had been transplanted directly from the corporate head-quarters. The same overhead strip lighting, the same light blue-grey walls and floors of the executive levels. She glanced back at the door the security man was holding open for her. The inward side of the door — the side facing her — was metal, painted the same light shade as the rest of the interior.

The security officer was smiling broadly at her confusion. "A conscious decision by the designers," he explained, answering her unspoken question. "It would seem to be advisable to conceal the nature of the research facility as much as possible." He shrugged. "Who knows? Perhaps displays of high technology would attract the … ah, the ire of this region's inhabitants."

A shadow seemed to cross the man's face as he spoke those last words. Inhabitants? Nikki wondered. *Who are they?* Or what? She considered pressing the officer for more details right then and there, but decided against it. *I'll find out soon enough,* she told herself. "Can you show me my quarters?" she asked aloud.

* * *

It wasn't hard to tell that her room had originally been intended as an office, Nikki thought. For one thing, it was small — about eight feet square, not much larger than her cabin aboard the freighter. Most of the floorspace was taken up by the bed, the metal wardrobe and the "footlocker" (as she thought of it). Adding to the cramped feeling, one corner of the small room was taken up by a table holding a sophisticated microcomputer. *So this is supposed to be my office as well,* she thought, tossing her shoulderbag onto the bed.

Curious, she sat down at the computer, powered it up and began to explore its capabilities. As well as having its own powerful processor, large hard drive and lots of on-board memory, she quickly found that it was networked to a much larger system somewhere else on the site. *The best of both worlds,* she thought, *my own computer, but access to the storage and processing horsepower of a "big iron" mainframe.*

She powered down the computer, sat back in her chair, lost in thought. *So high tech does work here, after all,* she mused. The fluorescent lighting, the silent air conditioning, and, of course — most importantly — the computer system proved that. What did that say about the rumors she'd heard, about O'Neil's tales of airplanes dropping out of the sky over Orrorsh? Where they just that — just tales and rumors? Or was there something special about the Inderagiri Research Facility — or maybe about *this part* of Orrorsh — that mitigated those weird effects?

She shrugged. Again, she was sure she'd find out soon enough.

A knock came on her door. "Yes?" she called.

A security guard stuck his head into the room — it was Dei, the young man who'd taught her how to handle a pistol. (*The other riverines must have arrived*, she realized.)

Dei grinned warmly. "*Konichi-was*, Carrson-*san*. I have been instructed to inform you there will be an informational meeting in the main refectory in" — he glanced at his watch — "in twelve minutes. The facility director requests your attendance."

She returned the young man's smile. "I'll be there, Dei-*san*," she assured him. With all the unanswered questions rattling around in her head, she wouldn't miss it for the world.

Chapter Six

Nikki walked slowly out of the large central building. The sun, a distended red ball, was half-concealed by the treetops to the west. *Due* west, she reminded herself; they were so close to the equator — about 75 miles, she thought — that sunrises and sunsets weren't offset because of latitude. *I'm in the southern hemisphere.* The thought struck her suddenly. The outpost was a little more than one degree of latitude south. *Wasn't there usually some strange ritual onboard ships when they crossed the equator? Some kind of "initiation" for people who'd never crossed the line before?* She was sure she'd read something about that.

But of course, when the freighter had hit the equator, it had already been within Orrorsh, she recalled. That explained why nobody paid any attention to strange traditions.

Her pistol, in a button-flapped holster slung on her belt, felt very strange. Not only because of the unaccustomed weight. She could imagine she *felt* the lethal nature of the weapon, an uncomfortable presence against her left hip. She let her fingertips brush the leather holster, then drew them back quickly as though she'd touched something hot. *Nikki Carlson, gunslinger*. It made her very uncomfortable to carry the pistol, but the rules of the outpost were uncompromising on that point: all personnel will be armed at all times. And the "informational meeting" had convinced her that there might actually be reason for that caution.

The main refectory was in the two-story central building — which, Nikki learned, was devoted largely to administrative functions. The refectory itself was a large room with cafeteria-style tables, quite similar to the tenth-floor staff cafeteria in the Nagara Building — but without the huge windows, of course.

In some ways, the meeting had felt much like the gathering where Eichiro had announced the Inderagiri mission. The arrogant scientists from the Matsushima Bay facility had been sitting in a solid block up front, while the other members of Nikki's workgroup had formed a similar unassailable knot. When Nikki had arrived, the only space for her had been at the very back. As she'd taken her seat, she'd spotted O'Neil sitting near the front with the mechanics and a couple of other men with oil- stained coveralls. He hadn't noticed her arrival, and she hadn't wanted to attract his attention.

Eichiro — under his new title of "facility director" — had opened the meeting precisely on time. His opening remarks had consisted largely of the "motherhood" statements Nikki had expected — glowing claims about how important the work of the Inderagiri Research Facility would be for Nagara Corporation, and how honored everyone present was to have been included in this historic undertaking. Nikki had basically tuned out the manager's meaningless words — *Semantic content zero*, she thought with amusement — while entertaining herself by watching the reactions of everyone else in the room. *If everyone here is honored,* she'd reflected with a silent chuckle, *they're certainly hiding the fact well*. It had been here that she'd finally caught O'Neil's gaze. He'd shrugged and rolled his eyes. She'd thought, *he's as interested as I am — not*.

None too soon, Eichiro had finished his preamble, and that's when he'd moved on to more important issues: security considerations. There were a number of rules that it was vital the Inderagiri Research Facility personnel must follow, he'd stated firmly, all of which were for their own protection and continued good health. Firstly, everyone must carry their "personal defense devices" — Nikki had been grimly amused by this long- winded euphemism for "guns" — at all times. Secondly, nobody but authorized security personnel would be allowed outside the stockade compound after dark. And thirdly, even during the day non-security personnel could only leave the compound in pairs or larger groups, for mutual security.

Those had been the important ones. Eichiro had gone on, in the same sententious manner, listing other "security regulations," but Nikki had tuned out as soon as she'd realized they were just common sense. *The kinds of things parents say to their kids*, she'd thought: *Don't leave the kitchen door open. Don't touch strange animals. Never point your gun at somebody else. It's all fun and games till somebody loses an eye.* She'd let her attention drift again …

Only to have it focused again when Eichiro had started talking about the dangers that existed in the area. His presentation had been much too wordy and not all that clear — *like your typical business report*, she'd thought — but the content had certainly made her sit up and take notice.

There were potentially dangerous creatures in the jungle, Eichiro had explained — panthers, tigers, plus several species of poisonous snake and venomous spiders. Most of these were as cautious about people as people were about them, the manager had stressed, so some simple — and common-sense — precautions should prevent tragedies.

But, he'd gone on, there were *other* things in the jungle as well — things that weren't as hesitant over unprovoked attacks against humans. Unnatural animals, like normal beasts somehow twisted out of true and endowed with almost-human intelligence. Creatures that seemed able to somehow change their shape. And things that the few remaining Sumatrans called zombies — *not* the magically-animated dead out of legend, Eichiro had stressed, just something that reminded superstitious natives of those monsters. (*That's what they're not, Nikki had noted, but he's not saying anything about what they are.*) These weird creatures were thought to prowl at night, the facility director had explained, and reportedly attacked solitary individuals who wandered the jungles.

"Security is everyone's responsibility," Eichiro had concluded firmly. "Our trained security forces will strive to ensure your safety, to the best of their abilities. However, without your active cooperation, they will be unable to perform their function." He'd looked around at the attentive faces one last time. "It is my honor to work with you," he finished. "I expect great results. Thank you." As Eichiro had left the room, the security personnel had come forward to lead the new arrivals out and issue them their "personal defense devices."

Nikki looked down again at the holster on her belt. This wasn't anything like what she expected when she left America.

"Well, what did you think?"

She turned. O'Neil was a few steps behind her, his perpetual asymmetrical smile in place.

"The meeting?" He nodded. "Disturbing," she admitted after a moment. "I …" She frowned. "I don't know, I'd like to hear more about the … the *things* he was talking about, the things in the jungle." She shook her head in frustration, trying to better order her thought. "My first impulse is just to write it all off as superstition, paranoia, overactive imaginations. But I can't shake the feeling that …" She hesitated again, then forced herself to go on. "I can't shake the feeling Eichiro knows more than he's telling," she finished. *I'm being melodramatic*, she told herself, *foolish*. She looked into O'Neil's eyes, searching for scorn or amusement.

But his eyes were serious, despite his smile, and even that suddenly looked a little forced. "They've already lost five men," he said quietly.

She stared at him. "What?" she asked dully.

"Five men dead or missing since they started building the outpost," he explained. "I heard that from one of the security guards."

The chill fist of fear tightened in her belly. "Industrial accidents?"

The pilot chuckled mirthlessly. "C'mon, Nikki, you know the answer to that one."

She nodded slowly. He was right: she knew. "What happened?"

"The first three just vanished," O'Neil told her, "like they'd just slipped off into the jungle. But who'd do that? And why? We're fifty miles from the ocean, hundreds of miles from any other civilization worthy of the name. Apparently the only boats on the river belong to the outpost, so they couldn't have got passage on some river-trader to bug out. Anyway, in the case of the third one they found some of his equipment later: his gun, his holster belt, and one boot. From what the guard told me, when the missing man left his boot behind, he kinda forgot to take his foot out of it first."

Nikki gaped at the pilot, momentarily speechless.

He snorted. "Amusing, huh? This happened before

they got the stockade fence up. Not surprisingly, finishing the fence got itself moved up the priority list.

"The next one went a couple of weeks later," O'Neil went on. "Now, this one was really interesting."

He seems to be enjoying this, in some kind of gruesome way, Nikki thought. *But no*, she corrected herself after a moment. *He's learned something that disturbs him, that scares him, and he's just trying to deal with his fear*. "Tell me," she prompted.

"They'd just brought in the rule about people never leaving the compound alone," he told her. "The workers building the labs, even the security guards had to patrol in pairs.

"Two guards were outside the fence at night. They heard something in the jungle — one of them later said it sounded like a human scream. They thought maybe it was one of their colleagues who'd got himself in trouble. So of course, being good little corporate security guards, they went in to find out what was going down.

"Picture this," the pilot suggested. His voice was measured, steady … Emotionless, Nikki thought. *This has really got to him.*

"Picture it," O'Neil repeated, "two guys, armed to the teeth, in the jungle, looking for whoever it was they heard scream. It's the middle of the night, pitch black, they probably can't see more than a couple of feet — if that. They've probably got their flashlights out, flashing the beam around. One of them's trying to call the security office, trying to whistle up some backup. But their radios just don't seem to work. And then suddenly their flashlights stop working, just like that. They're plunged into darkness, their night vision ruined by their own lights. For the first minute or two — it must have felt much longer to them — they're blind. They turn back, try to head back to the compound …

"And that's when it happens." O'Neil's cool, controlled delivery was enough to raise goosebumps on the back of Nikki's neck. "One of them hears a noise behind him, a noise like something large moving in the jungle, something close. In the darkness, he manages to see something right next to his partner. It looks like a snake, a big, dark snake, hanging down from a tree-branch.

"Then, before he can react, the 'snake' moves — moves like *lightning*. It lashes out, wraps itself around his partner's neck. It jerks once, hard, and he hears the dry crack as his colleague's spine snaps. The 'snake' starts dragging the limp body away.

"The survivor's stunned for a moment, frozen." O'Neil grunted. "Who wouldn't be? But he's well-trained, and he gets himself back under control fast. Gun at the ready, he runs after where the 'snake' dragged his partner.

"He finds himself in a small clearing." The pilot's grew softer. "There's his buddy's corpse, there's the snake still wrapped around its throat. And there's something else: a nest of snakes, he thinks at first. A huge, writhing mass of long, dark snakes. It looks like the snake that killed his partner is dragging the body back to its nest. Then everything changes; for the first time, he really knows what he's seeing.

"The writhing mass — it isn't a nest of snakes. It's ... *something*, something else. And the 'snakes,' of course they're not snakes at all. They're tentacles — long tentacles, a dozen of them, maybe more. And that means in the middle of the 'nest' must be the body of ... of whatever it is."

O'Neil shrugged. "The man broke," he said simply. "His control snapped, he dropped his gun, his useless radio, his failed flashlight, and he ran. It was sheer luck he headed in the direction of the compound. He ran like the devil was at his heels. He heard noises behind him, noises he didn't want to dwell on, but he made it back in one piece. And he reported everything that had gone down.

"His superiors 'debriefed' him, of course," O'Neil went on. "They had him go through his story several times, grilled him on the details, recorded it … You know how efficient the Japanese are at that sort of thing."

"I know," Nikki agreed. O'Neil heard the irony in her voice, raised an eyebrow quizzically. But she didn't feel like enlightening him. "Go on," she suggested.

The pilot nodded. "Nobody wanted to believe him," he continued. "Stories like that don't fit into the neat, orderly corporate world-view, and anything that doesn't fit is either *forced* to fit or ignored. They decided *something* had happened in the jungle, but the stuff about the 'snakes?'" O'Neil shook his head firmly. "Forget it. The man lost it, started seeing things in the shadows of the jungle. He panicked, and he left his partner behind. That was the official conclusion.

"They found the other guy the next day," O'Neil continued, "not too far outside the compound. What was left of him, anyway. He'd been … well, to put it bluntly, he'd been torn apart, and much of the body was missing, like it had been eaten. What they did find, they examined. And you know what they concluded? He'd been killed by a panther. His neck was broken, but 'obviously' that was a result of the impact of the panther's pounce. Forget the fact that the wounds in the body were obviously made by teeth several times the size of a panther's. Forget the fact that there were marks on this throat indicating he'd been garrotted by something. Forget all that, officially speaking the man had been killed by a panther. His partner might have been able to save him, but he panicked and ran."

O'Neil shrugged. "They disciplined the survivor," he said. "They might have wanted to ship him home, but they couldn't spare any personnel. So they just put him on permanent night patrol — every night, they sent him out into the jungle that killed his partner. Nice, huh?" He shook his head in amazement. "What blows me away is that he did it, he followed his orders. No way I'd have gone along. I'd have bugged out, barricaded myself in my room, shot myself in the foot … *something*. Of course, he told everybody who'd listen his side of what went down. And even if nobody completely believed him, they certainly remembered what he had to say." He smiled. "That's how I learned all this, chatting with the security guards."

"What happened to the survivor?" Nikki asked. The knot of fear still twisted in her stomach, but O'Neil's story had fascinated her. "Is he still here, or did they send him home when the new guards arrived?"

"He's dead," the pilot said flatly. "He lasted about a week, then he disappeared one night. They found what was left of him the next day. Seems the 'panther' had come back for another meal."

Nikki found she'd been holding her breath, let it out in a long, hissing exhalation. "Wow," she said simply. Then, after a moment, she asked, "Do you believe that?"

O'Neil shrugged. "There are three — no, four — possibilities," he said slowly. "One — the surviving security guard lied about the 'snakes.' Maybe he was covering up for the fact that he ran, or that he left his partner alone to get killed by a panther. It's possible. But if you're going to lie to protect yourself, why make something up that unbelievable? Particularly when there's nobody left alive to contradict you?" He shook his head. "I don't buy that.

"Two — an honest mistake." He grinned mirthlessly. "How likely is that? Mistaking a tiger for a panther in the jungle at night — *that* I can buy. But getting confused between a panther and something with a dozen tentacles … I don't buy that either.

"And three — the guy's out of his mind, either naturally or chemically: drunk or drugged. You know who straight-arrow these guys are, Nikki. How likely is that?" Again he shook his head firmly. "I don't buy it."

"You said there were four possibilities," Nikki reminded him after a moment.

"That's right," he confirmed. "Four — he was telling the truth. I don't feel comfortable with it, it's not something I can easily accept … But don't you think it's the most likely of the four?"

They walked on in silence for a few moments. Out of the corner of her eye, Nikki regarded O'Neil. *He really believes it*, she told herself. *But how can he believe it? Things like that just don't happen …*

But maybe they do in Orrorsh. The thought sprung, unbidden, from some deep and secluded part of her brain. Even though the air was warm, she felt a sudden chill.

O'Neil seemed to have sensed her discomfort, and smoothly changed the subject. He pointed to one of the outlying buildings — the one next to where Nikki's quarters were. "What's in there?" he asked casually. "I've been kinda doing an unofficial tour of the place, just scoping things out. I saw some of the workers loading equipment in there — weird-looking scientific stuff, I couldn't recognize it. So I just went over for a look-see."

He snorted. "Two security guards just appeared out of nowhere, standing between me and the door. 'High-security area,' they told me, 'authorized personnel only.' And all the while, there's one of the scientists there too, staring at me like I'm something unpleasant he'd normally see only through a microscope. What the hell's going on?"

A sudden thought struck Nikki. "What did the scientist look like?"

O'Neil shrugged. "Scrawny-looking guy. Greying hair, but still young."

She chuckled. *Funakoshi.* She knew what it was like to be on the receiving end of one of the arrogant young scientist's looks.

The pilot shot her a look. "You know him?"

"You could say that."

He looked at her quizzically again, then visibly decided not to pursue the issue. "So what's in the building?" he asked again.

"That's why we're here," she told him. "That's the main lab; that's where the main science team works."

He frowned, puzzled. "I thought you worked over there," he said, pointing to Nikki's building.

She laughed again. "That's right," she agreed, "I work over there, while the important people work over *there*." She indicated the two buildings.

"But you're workgroup leader …"

"For the support team," Nikki clarified. "We're the second squad; it's Funakoshi — the guy with the grey hair — and his crew that are the varsity."

"You mean I've wasted all this time schmoozing a second-stringer?" he demanded in mock outrage. "How the hell am I going to maintain my reputation that way?" He paused. "So what are the varsity up to?" he asked.

Nikki smiled. "If you figure it out, tell me," she suggested.

* * *

Another Goddamn nightmare. Nikki rolled over in the hard bed, breathed deeply to cleanse the adrenalin of fear from her body. She reached over to the night-table, flicked on the small reading light.

The remnants of the nightmare vanished like shadows in the light. She sat up, ran her fingers through her hair.

It wasn't too bad, she thought, *nowhere near as bad as it could be.* Already, in the few seconds since she'd woken up, the details of the dream were fading away. But she could still remember — vaguely — that it lacked the hideous, blatant features of earlier nightmares. No blood-dripping specter of Toshikazu, no direct threat to her life, nothing overtly horrifying. Instead, the terror came more subtly, like an undercurrent, implied instead of stated outright. *Like the difference between an Alfred Hitchcock movie and something by Stephen King,* she thought. Certainly, there were elements that were disturbing in and of themselves — she remembered being in the jungle, with snake-like tentacles moving through the underbrush around her — but they were almost secondary to the overall atmosphere.

Welcome to Orrorsh, she told herself wryly. *Is this what I should expect for as long as I'm here?*

She'd had enough experience with the dreams by now to know that she wouldn't be able to go back to sleep immediately. (Or, more correctly, that if she did she'd probably find herself back in the nightmare landscape from which she'd just escaped.) She needed to do something to clear her head. *Should I try and read?* she asked herself, then immediately decided against it. For one thing, the only books she'd brought with her were technical journals and research material connected with her work. Definitely not the kind of thing she needed right now. *That was dumb,* she told herself, *I should have brought some light reading. Something brainless — some lightweight adventure novels, or maybe a couple of pulp romances. Anything but texts.*

A walk. A walk and some fresh air, that was what she needed. She swung herself out of bed, padded over to the metal wardrobe, and pulled out some clothes. Even with the air conditioning, it was warm in her quarters — easily warm enough for her to be comfortable sleeping in her underwear, with only a single sheet over her. That meant it'd also be warm outside. Quickly, she threw on a light shirt and shorts, slipped her bare feet into a pair of runners.

The hallway outside her quarters was only partially lit — only every second fluorescent tube burning overhead — and she knew she was the only person in the entire lab building. That would change soon enough, she predicted. If they received the same kind of workload from Funakoshi and his prima donna scientists that the old Special Projects team had given them, they'd soon be working nights the way they had back in Tokyo. At the moment, though, everyone was still settling in. She figured things would be just as quiet over in the secure lab building as well — the only people moving over there would be the patrolling security personnel. She walked the length of the hallway and opened the door to the outside.

Warm air washed over her like a wave. She checked her watch: *Three in the morning, and it's as hot as a sunny day in Tokyo.* The door faced the stockade wall, maybe a hundred feet away, and beyond that — beyond the clear zone around the entire compound — was the jungle. The tops of the trees made an area of even darker black against the black of the sky. She looked up …

And gasped in amazement. The sky was ablaze with stars — more stars than she'd ever seen before outside of a planetarium show. Crisp, brilliant, immediate … For the first time in her life, she understood why poets and writers had sometimes described the stars of the tropics as looking like diamonds. They weren't just dots of light, like pinpricks in the canopy of the night. Here, they looked solid, like gems burning with their own strange inner light. They looked close — no more than a couple of hundred yards over her head — but when she focused her attention on the blackness between them, she felt like she was gazing into infinity. *Wonderful*, she thought in awe, *magical*.

This — just this view — makes it all worthwhile.

She took a deep breath. She could smell the jungle and the river, smell the incredible profusion of life around her — an unbelievably complex odor.

And the night was alive with sound, too. Insects whirred and clicked, creatures she had no way of identifying chittered in the darkness. In the distance, she heard the roar of a hunting cat, the death-scream of the small animal that was its prey.

I'm a long way from home, she realized, and not just in terms of distance. *I don't belong here. None of us do.*

That's when she noticed the new sound. It wasn't part of the strange, exotic music of the jungle. It was obviously man-made: the whir of an electric motor, coupled with the muted rattle of metal on metal.

She started walking in the direction of the noise, roughly south, toward the great metal gates that were — apart from the river itself — the only way into the compound. *What's going on?* she wondered.

At first, her only emotion was curiosity. But then caution began to assert itself. She hesitated for a moment. *Maybe it's something I shouldn't see ...*

And then she laughed silently to herself — at herself. *Paranoia yet again,* she chided herself. *I'm letting O'Neil's horror stories get to me.* She walked on.

There was light around the gate, she saw — light cast by two powerful arc lamps mounted on the gatehouses. She could see clearly what was going on, although she didn't at first fully understand it.

She stopped. *I can see them, but they can't see me,* she realized. Yes, the bright carbon arcs would have completely ruined their night vision. As long as she stayed in the pitch-black shadows around the buildings, she'd be invisible to them. *And maybe that's how I should keep it.* Again she laughed silently at her fear: *Stupid.* But, stupid or not, she decided not to go any further.

As she watched, the two big gates closed, and

latched with a muffled clank of metal. There were almost a dozen people just inside the gate, she could see. Most were obviously Nagara Security guards, wearing dark-blue versions of their jumpsuits. They carried rifles of some kind, and pushed up onto their foreheads were bulky goggles. (*Night vision goggles?* she wondered.) The other three people she quickly recognized as members of the Matsushima Bay science team. *Is Funakoshi with them?*

Yes, there he was, talking with a couple of the security guards. From where she was, she couldn't hear what they were discussing. For a moment she considered walking forward, making her presence known — *I've got as much right to be out at night as they have*, she told herself — but a tense feeling in her stomach persuaded her to decide against it.

There wasn't anyone else there … Yes, there was, she realized. Two other figures, dressed entirely in black. They were standing back out of the way, up against the gate itself. Only partially in the wash of light from the arc lamps, they were almost invisible. She saw Funakoshi raise his hand and gesture to them — it looked like a wave of thanks — and then the black figures really *did* vanish. One moment they were there, the next they were gone, as though they'd just dematerialized. Almost as if they were ghosts …

Dematerialized? Ghosts? Nikki snorted. *This place* is *getting to me.* Obviously they were more security guards, dressed in some kind of night camouflage. Presumably they hadn't walked out into the full brilliance of the lights because they knew what it would do to their dark-adapted eyes.

The knot of people started to break up, and for the first time she could see what had been making the electronic whirring she'd initially heard. It was a vehicle, with an open bed at the back, and a small cab — big enough for only the driver — in front. Almost like a scaled-down pickup truck, except that instead of wheels it ran on caterpillar tracks, like a tank. It was painted dark brown-green, mottled with irregular patches of black — obviously jungle camouflage of some kind. *Probably it's an ideal vehicle for the jungle*, Nikki thought.

As the people started walking way, back to their quarters, the tracked pickup cruised off as well, heading toward the equipment shed near the helipad. The motor was so quiet that as soon as it was out of her line of sight, she couldn't hear it any more.

The group had broken up; the area in front of the gate was empty. The twin arc lamps were switched off, their blue-white fading quickly to dull yellow, and then to nothingness. In the darkness, the only sound she could hear was the irregular clicking as the metal of the lamps cooled.

What did I just see? Nikki wondered. *Obviously they were out in the jungle, but why?*

And why was I afraid to let them know I saw it?

It was that question that stayed with her as she walked slowly back to her quarters.

* * *

The question was still with her in the morning, as she headed for the refectory for breakfast. She didn't know why, but she still had the uncomfortable feeling she'd seen something she shouldn't have. Logically, there was nothing to base that conclusion on — but the fact that it denied logical analysis just made the feeling stronger, almost unassailable on an emotional level.

She was still curious, of course — even more curious now than she'd been last night. *The scientists were out in the jungle at night*. That was undeniable. *But why? What were they doing, and why were they risking the dangers?* Obviously, their task had to be vitally important if Eichiro would authorize risking his oh-so-important team scientists on it.

It was just after half past eight, and the refectory was almost empty. Three security guards sat together at one table, talking quietly among themselves, while on the other side of the room sat the two mechanics who'd been aboard the freighter with Nikki, also deep in conversation. *Shop talk*, Nikki thought. What do security guards talk about? *Guns, and armor, and how to kill people?* She chuckled quietly to herself. *No, probably just sports and gossip.*

There was one other man in the refectory, sitting alone in the far corner. Funakoshi, the scientist. He'd finished his breakfast, Nikki saw, and was just finishing off a large cup of coffee. *He probably needs the caffeine to make up for the sleep he didn't get last night*, Nikki told herself.

She hesitated for a moment, then made a quick decision. Casually, she walked over to the scientist's table and sat down across from him.

"Konichi-wa, Funakoshi-san," she greeted him politely.

He glanced up, his expression cold. "Huh," he grunted.

Normally, Nikki would have reacted to his rudeness and just left him alone. But today she kept her smile in place, even broadened it. "I just wanted to tell you that I consider it an honor to be working with you," she said lightly. She giggled. "You know, I never thought I'd have the chance to meet someone as important as you."

Deep down, Nikki hated herself for what she was doing. *Briko*, the Japanese called it — the childish, giggling, almost brainless manner that so many Japanese women cultivated. Nikki had always hated *briko*; it offended her and disgusted her that women would choose to pretend that they weren't competent to make it through life without the help of men. Seeing it in others set her teeth on edge, almost like the sound of fingernails on a chalkboard. How much worse to act that way herself ...

But it seemed that Japanese men reacted well to *briko*, and the fact that her own manner was almost the direct opposite — competent and self-assured — often seemed to alienate them. If she wanted to ingratiate herself with Funakoshi — even temporarily, just long enough to find out what was going on — she had to swallow her revulsion and give them what they wanted.

She couldn't tell if it was working. Funakoshi's eyes were as cold and expressionless as always. *But at least he hasn't left*, she told herself, *or told me to leave.*

"It must be something very important you're working on here," she went on in the same manner. "Why else would they bring in someone as well-known and knowledgeable as you?"

That seemed to get through to the scientist; his hard expression softened into a self-satisfied half-smile. *Play on his vanity*, Nikki thought, *that's his weakness.*

"It must be very complex," she continued. "Do you know, I read some of your publications? Well, I tried to read them, but it was all just too confusing, much too advanced. I couldn't understand a word of it. Someone like you, you must be working on something very new, very innovative."

She almost gagged at her pretense. *I can't keep this up much longer*, she told herself.

But maybe she didn't have to, she realized. Funakoshi's smile broadened millimetrically. "Yes," he said smugly, "our work is *very* advanced. I expect a great breakthrough."

"Soon?"

He nodded. "Soon, I think," he concurred.

"And will you write a paper on it for the *Journal of the Genetic Engineering Society*?"

"Perhaps. Perhaps eventually."

That told her something, she realized — that the work

Funakoshi was doing was related to genetic engineering in some way. She could have guessed that, but it was good to confirm it. "It's interesting to come to the jungle," she went on lightly, "I've never been anywhere like this before. It's such a long way from Japan." She smiled guilelessly at the scientist. "It must be wonderful for you here: so many strange plants and animals, so many interesting samples for your work ..."

The response to her words surprised her. It was as if steel shutters slammed closed behind Funakoshi's eyes. His smile vanished, and his face was as hard as stone. He glared at her, and it was all she could do to keep her insipid smile in place.

Funakoshi stood up abruptly. "Our work is of the highest security classification," he told her sharply, "and no concern of yours. You will do well to remember that." And with that, he turned on his heel and strode away.

What did I say? Nikki asked herself, watching the scientist's receding back. *I said* something *that got to him. But what?*

She reviewed her last words in her mind. *He closed down the instant I said the word "samples,"* she realized after a moment. So what did that mean? That the "mission" — or whatever it was — last night was supposed to collect samples from the jungle? That made sense, it was logical. But then why the secrecy, and why did Funakoshi react so strongly? *How much more strongly would he have reacted if he'd known I saw him last night?* she wondered. There was something very strange going on here, maybe even stranger than she'd first thought, but she didn't have the slightest clue what it was ...

"Morning."

She jumped slightly at the voice at her shoulder. It was O'Neil. She'd been so wrapped up in her own thoughts that she hadn't seen or heard him approach.

The pilot pointed to the empty tabletop in front of her. "Having a light breakfast, I see."

"Sit down for a moment," she suggested. "I've got something to tell you."

Quickly she reviewed what she'd seen the previous night, and the details of her conversation with Funakoshi. "They're doing … *something* … in the jungle," she concluded, "something that they don't want me to know about. Don't want *us* to know about," she amended quickly. "What do you think's going on?"

O'Neil didn't answer immediately. In fact, he seemed to be concentrating on his own thoughts more than on her words, almost as if he hadn't even heard her.

She touched his arm lightly. "Earth to O'Neil," she joked, "come in O'Neil."

His eyes focused back on her. "Sorry," he said, "just thinking. What did you say?"

"I said, 'what do you think's going on?'" She hesitated, looking closer at the pilot. He was smiling as usual, but there seemed to be a kind of shadow over his face. He's *worried about something*, she recognized, *really worried*. "What's up?" she asked quietly.

His smile faded. "They're sending me up in the chopper today," he told her. "Some kind of scouting mission out over the jungle, toward the hills southwest of here. I'm to take one of the scientist with me. It's a long flight, a couple of hours each way, right at the limit of my fuel."

"Oh? What for?"

He shrugged. "I guess I don't need to know," he said wryly.

What's wrong? she asked herself. *Flying's what he's supposed to be here for.* Then she remembered their conversation aboard the V/STOL in transit from Tokyo to Spratly Island. "You're worried the helicopter's going to fail?" she asked.

His only answer was a sharp nod.

"Look around you," she suggested lightly. "There's no problem with technology. The lights work, the coffeemaker works ... hell, even the computers work, and they're more complex than your helicopter, aren't they?"

Her attempt to cheer him up hadn't worked, she saw at once. He still looked worried. "That's right," he agreed, "but that's inside the outpost, isn't it?"

"Why should that make a difference?"

He shrugged again. "I don't know, but it does." He leaned forward earnestly. "Do you feel like you're in the middle of Orrorsh here, Nikki? I don't, I feel like in ..." — he searched for words — "in a little bit of Japan. For Christ's sake, look at the walls, the floors, the lighting ... It's all just like the Nagara Building in Tokyo, isn't it?" Nikki had to nod agreement; O'Neil's words meshed perfectly with he own thoughts when she'd first entered her quarters.

"But what about outside the compound?" the pilot went on urgently. "What's on the other side of the stockade fence, Nikki? It's the jungle. It's Orrorsh. Isn't it?" Again she had to nod. "And remember the story I told you about the guards, about the tentacles? They went into the jungle, they got too far from the outpost, and what happened? Their flashlights went out, their radios stopped working. Right? I'm going a long way from the outpost ..."

In the silence, Nikki looked closely at her acquaintance — *no, my friend.* This was really getting to him, she saw, and she could understand why. Even though it made little logical sense, there was some kind of ... some kind of emotional resonance to what he said. "They're sending a scientist with you," she pointed out at last. "One of the Matsushima Bay group?"

O'Neil nodded.

"You know how important Eichiro thinks those

scientists are," she reminded him. "Do you think he's going to risk one of them if the mission might be risky?"

"No," the pilot allowed, "but Eichiro doesn't seem to pay attention to *anything* that indicates Orrorsh is different from Japan. Otherwise why would he have brought the chopper in the first place?"

A new thought struck Nikki. "Well, what about that tank thing, that pickup with tracks I saw last night?" she asked. "*It* had gone out into the jungle, and it was still working. They weren't towing it in or anything. So if that didn't fail, why would your helicopter fail?"

For the first time, O'Neil's expression lightened, and his smile returned almost as unshakable as ever. "You know what, Carrson-*san*? You're right." He reached forward, laid his hand on Nikki's and squeezed. "Thanks. I guess it's just the nightmares getting to me."

That startled Nikki a little. "Nightmares? You're having nightmares?"

"Real doozies," he confirmed.

"What are they?"

He shrugged her question off. "Typical pilot stuff," he said lightly. "Flying in a storm, lost, and running out of fuel. Coming in for a landing and the runway's been turned into a parking lot. The plane's on fire, I can't open the hatch, and I don't have a parachute anyway. Just the old fears talking."

"Do you dream anything else?" she asked. Suddenly, inexplicably, that question seemed to be of vital importance.

He smiled at her, climbing to his feet. "Why don't we discuss it over a late lunch?" he suggested. He glanced at his watch. "I've got to get going. I don't think those lab guys understand the word 'patience.' I'll see you when I get back." He turned away and headed for the door.

"O'Neil," she called after him, then, "Tom." He

glanced back. "Good luck," she told him.

He grinned, flipped her a casual salute. "Good pilots make their own luck, Carrson-*san*. See ya."

There was a knot in Nikki's stomach as she watched him leave. *Fear?* she wondered. *But that doesn't make sense, does it?* Of course not. She shook her head to clear it, ruthlessly suppressing the irrational worries that assailed her. *All I need is breakfast and some coffee,* she told herself.

But she couldn't quite make herself believe it.

* * *

The wind howled around the buildings of the compound like a live thing in torment. Even inside her workgroup's lab, Nikki could hear it. She imagined that less sturdily-built structures would be physically shaking under its impact.

The storm had hit without warning, brewing up out of a clear blue sky. She'd been outside when the first of the clouds appeared, scudding across the sky like slate-grey battleships, under the driving force of high-altitude winds. She'd watched in fascination, actually going so far as to time the process on her watch. It had taken less than five minutes from the first indication for the sky to become an unbroken ceiling of black. And then the winds had started, and the rain, whipped ferociously by the gusts.

That had been at about ten-thirty in the morning. She checked her watch: it was just before one-thirty now. According to the security guard she'd asked earlier, O'Neil's chopper had been due back on the helipad about half an hour ago. That was the flight plan, at least, and the storm had changed things drastically. The wind was blowing generally from the northeast, which meant that if the first leg of O'Neil's flight had been to the southwest, now he'd be facing a strong headwind. *And he said the flight was already at the limit of the helicopter's fuel*, she remembered. Had he taken the possibility of a headwind into account when he'd taken off?

Another gust of wind struck the building with an audible impact. Even without worrying about fuel, it had to be sheer hell up there. How well did helicopters deal with strong gusting winds?

She looked around the lab. The other members of her workgroup were busy, beginning the analysis of the first serum samples that Funakoshi and his team had sent over. The work was going to be just like it had been in Japan, she realized. Her group were given samples, with no indication of what they were or where they came from, and they had to analyze them exhaustively and "by the book." Without some clue as to what the science team was looking for, there were no shortcuts to take, or ways of making the process more efficient. *At least the automated analyzers work*, she thought, glancing over at the row of five white, refrigerator-sized machines.

She glanced at her watch again. The team wouldn't need her for a few minutes, she figured. "I'm going out for some fresh air," she told them. A couple of her colleagues looked up long enough to nod, but most didn't pay any attention whatsoever. With a last look around the lab, she went out into the hallway.

There was a major gap in her wardrobe, she'd realized early on: she hadn't brought any rain gear whatsoever. *Stupid*, she told herself, *you should have known what tropical rainstorms are like*. Fortunately for her, the outpost's supplies included raincoats—more like light ponchos, really — in Nagara's blue-and-white color-scheme with the company's origami crane logo prominent on the back. She'd snagged one of those for herself this morning, as soon as the storm had hit. Now she slung it around her shoulders and closed the fasteners down the front. She opened the door and stepped out into the storm.

Out of Nippon

The wind tugged at her poncho, lashed warm —
and slightly brackish — rain into her face. Even with
the rain gear, she knew she'd be drenched to the skin
in minutes. Although it was a useless gesture, she
raised the hood and pulled it tight about her face. She
headed toward the heliport.

Rain had already turned most of the compound to
dark, reddish mud. The reinforced paths, however,
were still firm, although wet and sometimes slippery.
She headed past the central administration building,
and reached the equipment shed.

The building gave her at least some cover, she noted
thankfully. Driven by the wind, the rain was falling at
almost a forty-five-degree angle, slanting down from
the northeast. Flattening herself against the south side
of the building, she was sheltered from the worst of the
weather, while having a great view of the helipad.

There were a couple of security guards standing around
the pad, she noticed. They had to be soaked, but if they
noticed or cared they gave no sign. One was searching the
skies to the southwest; the other glanced at his watch.
They're waiting for O'Neil, too, Nikki realized.

Almost as if the guard checking his watch had been
a cue, she heard the distant, dull *whop-whop-whop* of
rotor blades. Using her hand to screen her eyes from
the water dripping from her hair, she searched the sky.
It would be difficult to pick out the helicopter against
the dark clouds …

But there it was, closer than she'd expected judging
by the sound of its rotors, a distended black dot low
over the treetops to the southwest. It was coming in
fast: O'Neil was probably pushing the machine as hard
as he could, to get home before the wind and rain grew
any worse. Even at this distance, she could see the
helicopter lurching as the wind lashed at it. *One hell of
a rough ride*, she thought, *I'm glad I'm not aboard*.

As though summoned by the sound of the rotors,

three mechanics appeared out of the equipment shed and hurried toward the helipad. They were carrying plastic-covered wire ropes—tie-downs, Nikki guessed, to secure the helicopter against the wind as soon as it was down. With the security guards coming to their aid, they started attaching the ropes to large eyebolts set into the hard surface of the pad.

The helicopter was moving even faster than Nikki had thought. It was already over the stockade fence, slowing to a hover a hundred feet above the pad. Now Nikki could see the two figures through the bulbous, transparent canopy. She couldn't recognize them from this distance, but knew the one in the left-hand seat had to be O'Neil.

The copter was bouncing alarmingly, ten feet or even more at a time, and in totally unpredictable directions. *Can he land it?* she wondered. And then she thought, *But what else can he do?* Her stomach knotted with apprehension. The engine sound changed slightly, and the machine began to descend.

Without any warning, the howl of the wind built to a horrendous crescendo. Even in the shelter of the equipment shed, Nikki was buffeted, almost knocked from her feet. One of the mechanics, still trying to attach his tie-down, was knocked to the ground.

The effect on the chopper was even more drastic. Its engine screamed and its rotors lashed the air as O'Neil tried to hold position over the pad, but it was useless. Like a toy thrown by a petulant child, the machine was tossed backward, out over the stockade, out as far as the edge of the jungle. Another gust, even more violent than the first, struck it, tilting it so the plane of its rotors was almost vertical. The chopper dropped like a stone.

It was going to hit. There was no way O'Neil could correct in time, the chopper was going to crash in the jungle. Nikki screamed.

But O'Neil was a better pilot than she'd thought. At

the last moment, the copter responded to him. Once more upright, it slowed its precipitous drop. Its landing skids struck the treetops, but everything was under control now. The ungainly machine started to climb again.

And that's when the conceivable happened. Something — *something* — reached up out of the jungle, wrapped itself round the left landing skid. Something that could have been a thick, headless snake. The thing pulled downward ...

And the helicopter plummeted again. This time there was nothing that O'Neil — or anyone else — could have done. Rotor blades windmilling wildly, the copter disappeared into the trees. Over the noise of the wind, Nikki could hear the machine die as metal bent and ruptured. The jungle itself seemed to scream, as the rotor blades hewed at the treetrunks like giant, flashing knives, then shattered into fragments. There was silence, just for a moment. Then a fireball climbed into the sky.

The wind howled again, this time in triumph.

Chapter Seven

Nikki stood just outside the open gate of the compound, staring into the jungle. The wind had blown her poncho hood back from her head, and warm, brackish rainwater was pouring from her hair, but she didn't notice the discomfort.

The helicopter had gone down directly southwest of the outpost, she saw, twenty or so yards into the jungle. So thick were the trees and underbrush, however, that she couldn't see any sign of the wreckage. No indication that the machine had crashed and exploded, no indication that two men had died …

Except for the smoke, of course, rising like a twisted totem pole — black, thick, shot through with lurid red flames. Even the heavy downpour seemed to have no effect on the fire below. *The pyre*, she told herself.

A team of security guards and mechanics were heading for the crash site, followed by the little cat-tracked pickup she'd seen last night. The men were armed with tools — shovels, prybars, sledgehammers and the like — and the bed of the pickup was filled with fire extinguishers.

Why bother? she asked herself dumbly. Nobody could have survived the impact, let alone the explosion. O'Neil and the scientist were dead; they had to be.

Orrorsh had killed them.

She began to shudder — not from the relative cold or the damp, they had nothing to do with it. In her mind's eye she saw again the helicopter's last moments. Righting itself at the last minute, its landing skids brushing the tree top. Starting to climb away. And then the thing from below, grabbing onto the landing skid and dragging the machine down to destruction. *The wind,* she thought, *the wind helped it too. The wind blew the copter over the jungle so it could kill them.*

But no, that was ludicrous, she couldn't believe that. For a moment she felt like she was in some kind of waking nightmare. *What should I believe?* she demanded of herself. *That something in the jungle grabbed the helicopter? Or is that ludicrous, too?* It would be so easy to refuse to accept what she saw, to convince herself that she'd imagined it …

No!! she declared mentally. *No, I saw it. It was there.*

But what *was* it? What could have done that? The tentacled thing from O'Neil's story could … if she fully believed that story. *And do I?* she asked herself. She wasn't completely sure.

What else could have done it? She remembered how the treetops had been flailing, under the double assault of the wind and the powerful downdraft of the struggling copter. That had been an instant before the *thing* appeared. Could the "tentacle" have been a vine of some kind — like a liana — torn loose and blown wildly by the wind? From her perspective, it had certainly seemed that the "tentacle" purposely wrapped itself round the landing skid. *But a whip can wrap around something and it's not alive,* she reminded herself. Could that have been it, just a random event?

And what about the way the "tentacle" had seemed

to pull the copter down? How could a vine do that?

Maybe it hadn't pulled it at all. The helicopter was climbing, she remembered, probably climbing as fast as its rotor could pull it upward. What would happen when it reached the full extension of the vine? It would be like ... like riding a bike with a rope tied to the frame. Hit the end of the rope and what would happen? The rope would stretch a little, then snap back. The bike would be jerked backwards, wouldn't it? That meant the helicopter would be jerked *downward*. And it would look just like the vine dragged it down. Wouldn't it? Logically it made sense ...

But there was no way that Nikki could make herself fully believe it.

* * *

The security guards had come up to her a few minutes later. Politely — gently, almost — they'd asked her to come with them, back to the security chief's office.

And that's where she was now, sitting numbly across the desk from the security chief — Issai Hongo was the name printed in *kanji* characters on the office door's name plate. Behind Hongo stood two more senior security personnel. *Another interview with Nagara security*, she thought dully. *This is getting too familiar.*

Hongo was calm, his face expressionless, his manner completely under control. "Please tell us what you saw, Carrson-*san*," he said for the second time.

Nikki just looked at him. She felt an aching emptiness in the pit of her stomach.

The security chief sighed. "Please understand, Carrson-*san*," he said quietly, "I know that O'Neir-*san* was your friend, I sympathize with your pain. But we *must* know what happened, what it was you saw. Can you please tell us?"

Painfully, she forced herself to speak. "I saw something," she said, her voice sounding dull and lifeless in her own ears. "Something ... something reached up out of the jungle. It grabbed the helicopter, it pulled it down. That's what it looked like."

Hongo raised an eyebrow in surprise ... *Or was it surprise?* "What did you see, Carrson-*san*?"

"It ..." She stopped. Her hands were shaking, she realized. She clenched her fists in her lap, and that stopped the shaking. "It looked like a vine," she forced the words out. "It looked like a vine, but it wasn't a vine. It was ..." She searched for the right words. "It looked like a snake, or a tentacle."

The security officers exchanged glances — guarded looks, Nikki thought. Then Hongo spoke again. "You saw a vine?" he echoed. "A vine tangled with the helicopter's undercarriage, is that it?"

Nikki hesitated. *That's the logical explanation*, but ... she shook her head firmly. "I said it *looked* like a vine," she said, "but it *wasn't*. It was something else. It was a tentacle, it couldn't have been anything else. It reached up, and it dragged the helicopter down."

Hongo sighed again. "Of course that's impossible, Carrson-san," he pronounced. "It must have been a vine, neh? In the downdraft of the rotors, it was blown free and ..."

"No," Nikki cut him off forcefully. "I thought of that, but that's not the way it happened. The ... the tentacle, it *grabbed* the helicopter. It didn't move randomly, it wasn't blown by the wind. It moved purposefully."

Again the security officers behind their chief exchanged strange looks. *Something's going on here*, Nikki told herself.

Hongo shook his head slowly. "The storm was terrible," he said slowly, as though to himself. "The wind gusted, it blew the helicopter back toward the jungle. The personnel on the helipad saw that happen.

The helicopter was out of control, *neh*? Falling toward the trees? It must have been horrible to see your friend that close to death. You felt fear for him then, didn't you, Carrson-*san*?"

The remembered fear, the horror, washed over Nikki like a dark wave. Not trusting herself to speak, she just nodded.

"Any one of us would feel fear for a friend," Hongo went on gently. "That terrible fear …" He fixed Nikki with a steady gaze. "Fear plays strange games with the mind, wouldn't you agree?"

With a cold shock, Nikki realized what the security chief was saying. Hot anger flared in her chest. "I didn't imagine it, if that's what you're saying," she snapped. "I saw what I saw. I saw the tentacle."

Hongo was unmoved by her sudden emotion. "You saw a vine, Carrson-*san*," he said calmly. "It was a tragic, random accident …"

"*No!*" Nikki shouted. Then she forced herself under some semblance of control. *Emotion never convinces anybody*, she told herself. *Nobody ever believes just because they've got to.* "No," she said more calmly. "It wasn't random, I told you that." She looked into the eyes of the other security officers. Their faces were emotionless, like the faces of statues. But there was something in their eyes, something that denied their apparent disbelief.

"Didn't anybody else see anything?" she asked. "The men on the helipad …?"

Hongo shook his head. "They were closer to the stockade fence than you were, Carrson-*san*," he explained. "Their view was blocked. Nobody but you saw the helicopter actually go down."

Nikki recreated the scene in her mind, tried to judge the sight lines. *Hongo's right*, she had to admit, *they couldn't have seen anything.* "Then my … my testimony is all you've got," she stated flatly. "You've got to accept it."

In seeming sorrow, Hongo shook his head. "But we can't accept it, Carrson-*san*, can't you see? What you claim you saw is impossible. When we take your emotional condition into account, how can we? No, you were afraid for your friend — justifiably so, of course — and that warped your perception." He folded his hands on the desktop in front of him. "*Domo arrigato gozaimas*, Carrson-*san*," he said formally, "thank you for your help in this painful duty …"

Nikki shot to her feet. "*No!!*" she shouted again. "Something's out there. It killed O'Neil, just like it killed those two security guards." Again the officers exchanged their strange looks. *Maybe that got to them*, she told herself. "Aren't you going to do anything? Aren't you going to go out and look for it, whatever it was? Before it kills anyone else …"

Hongo spoke calmly but firmly, overriding her voice. "We are currently retrieving the body and the wreckage, of course," he told her. "The bodies will be treated with all due respect, and of course we'll analyze the wreckage to determine the cause of the crash. But anything else? No. Our responsibility is the safety of all the personnel on this site. If we send teams out to comb the jungle for …" He visibly changed track. "We have no choice but to keep our teams on-site," he concluded. "Doing anything else would compromise your security, Carrson-*san*, and the security of everyone else. You'll understand we can't do that. *Neh*?"

Nikki looked bleakly at Hongo. *I think I understand*, she mused, *but I don't like it. I don't like it a bit.*

* * *

The storm had cleared up as rapidly as it had appeared, Nikki noted with dull surprise. The cloud ceiling had broken, and in several places blue sky showed through. Beams of sunlight angled down to spotlight portions of the jungle and the coffee-colored river. There was still some wind, but now it was little more than a stiff breeze, not the powerful gusts that had howled through the outpost just a couple of hours before.

Just a couple of hours? Nikki checked her watch.

Yes, it was before three in the afternoon, not even two hours since she'd seen O'Neil die in the fiery crash. She shook her head in disbelief. *It seems so much longer,* she thought, *it seems like days.*

She wandered aimlessly away from the administration building. The air smelt clean, as though scrubbed by the heavy rain. *Something's missing,* she suddenly thought, then the cold emptiness in the pit of her belly returned as she realized what it was. *I can't smell the smoke,* she told herself, *I was expecting to smell the smoke.*

But of course that didn't make sense. The fire had long since burned out, quenched finally by the rain and by the extinguishers of the security team. She'd overheard from the conversation of others that the bodies — *or what's left of them,* she thought with a pang of loss — had been recovered from the wreckage, and taken to some storage area within the equipment shed. The security team had decided to leave the wrecked helicopter where it was, the people had gone on — there wasn't enough left to make the effort of salvage worthwhile.

To her dull surprise, she realized that her aimless wandering had taken her in the direction of the helipad. It was empty, of course, apart from the now-useless tie-downs still attached to the eyebolts. Will they fly in another helicopter? she wondered. And another pilot? Or have they learned a lesson, learned that Orrorsh isn't to be trifled with? She shivered and turned away.

The big gate was open.

It took a moment for the fact to penetrate her numbed mind. The gate was open, and there was nobody around it: no security guards, no mechanics. Did that mean there was a team out in the jungle after all? she wondered. Maybe Hongo had changed his mind, had decided to investigate what Nikki had seen.

But how likely is that? she asked herself. Not very, she had to conclude: the security chief had seemed adamant about discounting her report. No, it was more probable that another research group was out in the jungle, collecting ... whatever it was they were after. No doubt the security contingent would be back any time to close the gate.

But at the moment the gate was open.

She stopped in her tracks, frozen in thought. *Maybe ...*

Before she was even aware she'd made a decision, she found herself running for the gate. Running out of the compound into the cleared area outside the fence. Without stopping, she looked around her for some sign of the security personnel. *If they see me they'll stop me*, she knew. *Nobody goes out of the compound alone, that's the rule.*

There was nobody in sight, though. Slowing to a jog, she crossed the open area.

At the fringe of the jungle she stopped. *What the hell do I think I'm doing?* she asked herself. *If I'm right, that thing is out there.*

But it doesn't come out in the sunlight, another part of her mind told her. *At night, yes. In the middle of a storm, yes. But not when the sun's shining.*

She stood, torn, trying to make up her mind. *If it was out there, there's got to be some sign*, she told herself, *some evidence. Something big enough to haul down a helicopter can't move through the jungle without leaving some kind of trace*. She took another couple of steps forward, then stopped again.

Then wouldn't the security team have seen something when they were at the crash site? she reflected.

No, she answered herself immediately, *they weren't*

looking for anything like that; they were just interested in the helicopter. They wouldn't *believe that it was anything but a random accident. They wouldn't* let *themselves believe anything else.* Anger burned again deep in her chest.

And it was the anger that drove her forward, into the jungle.

Within a handful of yards, it was as if she was in another world. The canopy of foliage above was thick, so thick that it was no brighter than twilight beneath it. The heavy, complex odor of the jungle filled her nostrils and lungs, almost choking her. She could smell — could *feel* — the wild profusion of life all around her.

The jungle's alive, she thought, *everything around me's alive. Everything interrelated. Almost as if the jungle's one huge, living being, and each tree, each bird, each animal is just one cell making up the body of a larger creature.* It was a fascinating idea, but also a disturbing one. *I don't belong here,* she told herself, *I'm an invader, like ...* she searched for the right analogy. *Like a pathogen, she decided eventually, like a bacterium invading a human body.*

Did that mean that the jungle would respond to her the way the body responds to a pathogen? The thought was enough to freeze her in her tracks for a moment. Would the jungle mobilize its defenses — analogous to the body's immune system — to destroy the invader? Almost of its own volition, her hand reached down and unsnapped the flap of her pistol holster.

That action made her laugh wryly at herself. "Nikki Carlson, gunslinger," she snorted. *Damn, I'm letting my imagination run away with me.*

Certainly, the jungle was one large, interlocking ecosystem; any high school biology student knew that. But so was a lake — like the one she swam in as a child. Had the lake sent forth "antibodies" to destroy the "pathogen" invading its body? Of course not. She forced herself on.

The ground underfoot was soft — not really muddy,

as she'd expected, but more spongy than anything. It gave a little under her weight, with a faintly audible squish, but she didn't sink into it like she would into mud. She looked down. As she put a foot down, she saw her shoe sink in about half an inch, saw water squeezed out of the ground by her weight. When she lifted the foot again, the print of her shoe remained for a couple of seconds, then vanished as the ground sprung back. The water was reabsorbed as well. *That means no tracks*, she realized. *That makes it more difficult.*

The jungle wasn't alive with sounds as it was at night, but neither was it silent. She could hear water dripping, light a like rain — presumably falling from the rain-soaked upper foliage. There were the calls and songs of birds, and the background whirring of insects, but she could hear nothing large moving through the trees. That was good, she told herself: meeting up with a panther — or something worse — could ruin her whole day.

She stopped again, looking around her for some kind of landmarks to follow. She figured she couldn't have gone more than twenty yards into the jungle, and already there was no hint that the outpost clearing even existed, let alone in which direction it lay. Fortunately for her, Nikki knew she had a good sense of direction — a "bump of direction," her father had called it when she was growing up. She didn't know how it worked, but she'd come to depend on it. In a strange city, and even in the woods — *or the jungle* — she always knew what direction she was heading, and how to get back where she came from. As a result she almost never got lost.

She took a moment to orient herself. Yes, the clearing was directly behind her, she hadn't strayed off course. And that meant the crash site was ... that way. She pressed on.

I could almost enjoy this, Nikki thought a few minutes

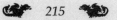

later. Even under the sheltering blanket of the foliage, it was bright enough to see, while the cover diminished the heat. The air was moist and heavy-feeling, but not uncomfortably so, and the going underfoot was relatively easy. From time to time, beams of sunlight — thin, like spears of golden brilliance — would penetrate the foliage, to lance down and pinpoint something on the ground below: a blood-red flower, a shrub of brilliant green, a fallen branch. As long as she didn't let her tension overwhelm her, Nikki found the jungle beautiful — alien, but lovely nonetheless. She checked her watch. Another two minutes or so and she'd be at the crash site …

What was that? Out of the corner of her eye, she glimpsed a flicker of movement. Suddenly chilled despite the warmth of the air, she spun around.

Nothing, just some leaves moving on a tree branch. *Probably hit by a big drop of water falling from above*, she told herself. She forced herself to relax again, breathed deeply until her heartrate had dropped back to some semblance of normal. She began to walk again, more slowly now, looking around her. *I'm getting paranoid again*, she chided herself.

But paranoia is a tool, another part of her mind recalled Toshikazu's words. For a moment, her vision blurred with unshed tears.

Crack! Loud as a rifle shot, a branch broke behind her. She spun again.

Again nothing. No movement, nothing out of the ordinary.

The sound had shaken her a lot worse than the barely-glimpsed movement. Anything could have stirred the leaves: falling water like she thought, a bird, even a slight breeze. *But branches don't just break for no reason.*

There's something out there. The realization was like ice water in her veins. *Something … the same something that pulled down the helicopter?* In suddenly growing panic, she turned slowly right the way around, her eyes — bugged wide, she knew — scanning. She couldn't see anything …

Yes. Another quick flash of movement, again in her peripheral vision. Something had moved behind the thick trunk of a tree to her right, something had ducked back into cover. She wanted to run, back to the clearing, back to the outpost. Back to safety.

But which way *was* the outpost? Her fear, and her turning around had clouded her sense of direction. *Which way?* For one of the first times in her life, she suddenly knew she was lost. She could run, but she might well head away from the outpost, deeper into the jungle.

Her breathing was fast, shallow. With a supreme effort, she slowed her breathing, forcing herself to fill her lungs with air.

The additional oxygen seemed to help. She felt her panic abating a little …

Then came another noise, close behind her. A rustle of leaves, the crack of another breaking branch. She spun again, so fast that the pistol holster thudded against her hip.

The pistol. She drew the weapon. It was cool and hard in her hands, its weight reassuring. She moved her left thumb up the grip, felt the little lever that Dei had said was the safety. She flicked it off, applied pressure to the trigger.

The sighting laser came to light, its ruby aiming dot drifting over the leaves of a thick bush a couple of yards away. That was where the sounds had come from, she knew — the bush was still moving. *There's something hiding in the bush!* What was it?

She squeezed the trigger harder, but not quite hard enough to fire the weapon. *Not yet.* It was suddenly tempting to shoot, to empty the pistol's clip into the bush.

But what if it's the security guards? she suddenly asked herself. The stockade gate had been open; didn't that mean that there might be security people in the jungle? They might have heard her moving through the undergrowth, might have thought *she* was something dangerous. Maybe they were stalking her, carefully moving close enough so they could identify her. She couldn't shoot; she could be killing one of the people who could take her back to the outpost. She removed her finger from the trigger. The spot of laser light vanished.

"Hello?" she called quietly, tentatively. "It's Nikki Carlson ..."

Something's behind me! The thought — she'd never know where it came from — struck with the impact of blow. She spun, bringing the pistol up.

There was a figure moving toward her, less than ten feet away. A human figure ...

No, a human figure made horrible, somehow twisted out of true. Its shoulders were broad, its chest sunken. Its skin was pale, the color of bleached bones, and it hung away from the *thing's* face in flaps. Beneath the skin she could see its skull. It looked like a decaying corpse.

But decaying corpses don't move. It reached out toward her with rotting hands.

She screamed in horror, brought the pistol to bear. The laser aiming spot bloomed in the center of its chest. She pulled the trigger.

Nothing happened. The gun didn't fire. *I didn't cock it,* she realized in terror.

The thing lurched forward. Nikki screamed again, turned and fled.

As if her cry had been a signal, more of the horrors burst from the undergrowth around her, reaching for her with claw-tipped fingers.

They were all around her; she was surrounded ...

No! There was a gap in the rough circle. She sprinted toward it.

A hand, as hard and cold as stone, grabbed her shoulder, its fingers sinking into her flesh. The thing spun her around.

Wailing in panic, she brought her pistol around. Not as a firearm, now, but as a club. With all her strength, she brought the barrel down on the creature's wrist, heard the dry crack of bones breaking.

The grip didn't loosen. Again she struck with the pistol, again, and again. And then the hand fell away.

They were almost on her, shambling forward like things from nightmare. But the gap was still there. She spun away from them, lowered her head and *ran*.

Sharp talons clawed her back, ripping through her light shirt and the skin beneath. The sudden flash of pain goaded her to even greater speed.

She ran, faster than she'd ever run before in her life. Dodging around trees, bursting through the undergrowth. She still had enough presence of mind to keep her knees high, to minimize the risk of tripping over something unseen on the jungle floor.

They were after her, she could hear them crashing through the vegetation behind her. *But how fast can they run?* They'd seemed like slow, shambling creatures. How could they catch her?

But of course she couldn't slow down to check, couldn't even risk a glance over her shoulder. Maybe they were quicker than they appeared, maybe they could run if they had to, run as fast as she could or even faster. She could imagine them gaining on her, reaching out with carrion-smelling hands, reaching for her back, her throat ... She forced her legs to pump even faster, ignored the burning in her lungs, the frenzied tatoo of her heart. *Run, Nikki,* she told herself, *run for your life.*

She had no idea how long the mad pursuit went on,

no clue of what direction she was running. She was aware of nothing but the branches lashing at her face, the low shrubs catching at her legs, threatening to send her flying. She might as well have been deaf; her ears were filled with the triphammer pounding of her own heart. Her lungs were on fire. Sudden pain drove into her side like a knife-thrust. But still she forced herself on.

Are they still there? Are they close? her mind babbled. *What will it feel like to die?*

The jungle lightened ahead, sunlight beaming down. A clearing. *The outpost clearing?* Somewhere, deep inside, she found the energy for one final burst of speed.

And then she was out into the clearing. Not the outpost clearing, she saw with sick horror, not even the crash site. Just a small, almost-circular natural clearing in the jungle.

There were figures ahead …

Her left foot struck something — a root? — and she was pitching forward. She struck the ground hard enough to drive the air from her lungs. For a moment she lay there, gasping into the wet ground. Her chest felt like it would burst at any moment.

Something touched her shoulder.

Galvanized, as though it was a cattle-prod that touched her, she rolled over with a shout. Even though she knew it was useless, she brought the pistol to bear. The laser dot flared in the center of a face.

Not the rotting, tattered face of one of her pursuers. This face was human, pale-skinned like her, with dark hair and a tidy, close-trimmed beard.

She looked up into the man's concerned expression. And then, without warning, the darkness took her.

Chapter Eight

Consciousness returned slowly. For an unmeasurable time, Nikki floated in a kind of dream world. She was comfortable and warm, free of pain, free of fear. She was surrounded by the muted murmur of conversation, a familiar, comforting sound. Gradually, like a diver surfacing from the black depths of the ocean, she rose toward awareness.

Nightmares, she thought muzzily. *The nightmares came back.* The dream had seemed so real, she mused, her expedition into the jungle, and the pursuit by the *things. So real ... but it's over now.* The thought was infinitely reassuring. *I'm safe. I'm awake.*

With a gentle smile, she opened her eyes.

And thought she'd been plunged back into the dream. She wasn't in her quarters in the outpost, in her own bed. She was ... somewhere else.

Still in the jungle, in a dark clearing. Instead of her own familiar ceiling, the night sky of Sumatra — *of Orrorsh* — was above her, studded with its panoply of brilliant stars. The murmur of voices — which she'd assumed was the last vestige of her nightmare — fell silent, and for the first time she heard the crackling of a fire.

"She's awake," a male voice said quietly — in English, she was surprised to realize. She rolled over toward the voice, looked around her.

She was lying on a folding camp bed of some kind, she saw, out under the sky in the middle of the clearing into which she'd plunged. (*Then it* wasn't *a dream*, she understood.) A fire was burning a dozen feet away, a small camp fire. Its flickering, ruddy light illuminated six figures sitting or squatting around it. They were looking at her, she saw, their expressions quizzical. Near her, further from the fire than her cot, were several tents — simple, canvas things supported by poles and guy-ropes.

One of the figures rose to his feet, took a step toward Nikki. She shied back a little, suddenly terrified.

The man saw her reaction and stopped. He held his hands out from his side, showing that they were empty. "I mean you no harm," he said in precise English. He smiled, his teeth gleaming in the firelight, framed by his neat beard and mustache.

Nikki recognized him. She'd last seen that face hovering over her as she lay on the jungle floor, the targeting spot of her pistol quivering on his forehead.

"May I approach you?" he asked.

Nikki hesitated, then nodded. There wasn't much she could do to stop him if he wanted to, anyway. What *could* she do? Jump up and run again, into the night-black jungle? She couldn't do that again.

The man came over to her, squatted down beside the camp bed. His smile was warm, reassuring.

He was wearing clothes that were both strange and familiar, she noted. Tan pants bloused over the top of military-looking boots, laced tight. A matching tan jacket, buttoned across his chest. Beneath the color of the jacket, she could see a white shirt and a brown tie crossed with diagonal blue lines. *A tie? In the jungle?* It took her a moment to realize why the outfit looked familiar. She'd seen men dressed this way in movies and in books. This was the way explorers had dressed at the end of the Nineteenth Century.

At first she guessed he was about forty, maybe even older. But then she realized it was just his beard that made him look that age. When she looked closer at his eyes — hazel, she thought — she revised her estimate downward. *He's probably about my age,* she judged.

"Are you well?" the man asked her, concern obvious in his voice. "You fell hard, and when you fainted I was afraid you were injured."

Nikki ran a quick inventory of the sensations her body was feeding her. Her left ankle — the one that had caught on the root or whatever it was — throbbed dully, and her legs were leaden, as if she'd run a marathon. But otherwise she didn't feel too bad. Scared, of course, and confused, but physically she was in one piece.

"I'm okay," she told him. She saw his eyebrows rise as if he didn't understand her. "I'm well," she amended.

"Good." He shifted into a more comfortable position. "My name is Peter Hollingforth," he said. "May I ask yours?" Again, his voice was precise, with an accent it took her a moment to place. *He's British*, she realized. But his accent wasn't quite like that of the few English people she'd met. It was more pronounced, almost the quintessence of Britishness.

"Nikki Carlson," she said.

His eyebrows rose again. "Nikki?" he repeated. "Would that be short for Nicola?"

"It's not short for anything. Just Nikki."

She glanced over at the other men around the fire. One of them was dressed much the same as Hollingforth. The other four, though, were wearing uniforms. Black trousers tucked into calf-high black boots. Bright scarlet jackets with stiff-looking black colors. Two rows of brass buttons down the chests caught the firelight. *Soldiers?* she wondered. *But what army still wears uniforms like that?*

"Who are you?" she asked. "I mean, what are you doing here?"

"We are a scientific expedition," Hollingforth explained, "authorized under the Victorian Majestic Charter. The leader is Professor Roderick Black. I have the honor of serving as his assistant."

That has to be the older man wearing the "explorer" clothes, Nikki thought. "And the ... the others?"

"Members of the 15th Regiment of the Gallic Legion," Hollingforth said with a touch of pride. "Sergeant MacHeath and the men of his section."

The 15th Regiment of the Gallic Legion? And the—what did he call it?—the Victorian Majestic Charter? Nikki felt as though she'd been dropped into the middle of a play — a historical costume drama — and somebody had neglected to give her the script. *Just what the hell's going on here?*

"Where are you from?" she asked.

"Well, that would be, um, something of a long story," Hollingforth said with a chuckle. "For the moment, suffice it to say that our expedition started in New London. What the natives used to call Padang," he added in explanation. "New London has been my home since I came to Majestic."

Nikki's mind stumbled over his last word. *Majestic? Oh, that's right — that's what people call Sumatra now.*

"And yourself, Miss Carlson?" he asked politely. "How might you come to be here?"

She hesitated, then thought, *What harm would it do to tell him?* "I came here from Japan," she said. "I'm an American, but I was working in Tokyo. Nagara Corporation sent me here." She could tell from the way his eyebrows rose again that something about what she'd said puzzled him. "I'm on a scientific expedition, too," she concluded.

"Are you really?" he asked in pleased surprise. "What would be your goal? May one ask?"

His convoluted choice of words was amusing, Nikki found, but his interest seemed sincere and guileless. "I don't really know, that's the strange thing," she explained. "They didn't tell me *why* we're here." She shrugged. "I'm not one of the key team, I just help out with support."

"Are you a secretary, then?"

"No," she said sharply, "I'm not a secretary. I'm a genetic analyst, and a damn good one."

Hollingforth raised his hands as if to ward her off. "My apologies," he said hastily, "I meant no insult, I assure you, Miss Carlson. If I gave offense ..."

She had to smile at his earnestness. "It's okay," she told him. *He looks like he's from turn-of-the-century England*, she thought, *he talks like it, and he thinks like it*.

"What is it that you do, then?" he inquired a little hesitantly. "May one ask?"

"One may," she answered demurely, suppressing a chuckle. "I perform genetic analysis on samples sent to me by the main science group," she explained. "I and my team break the sample down and chemically analyze it, elucidating its primary, secondary and tertiary structure." She could see from Hollingforth's expression that he hardly understood a thing she was saying. *But he's too polite to admit it*, she thought wryly. *Or maybe too embarrassed to admit his ignorance to a woman*.

"Where do they come from, these samples you analyze?" the young man asked.

"I'm not quite sure," Nikki said, "they don't tell me. I'm pretty sure they synthesize them."

Hollingforth's eyes widened. "But you say these samples are genetic material?"

"Sometimes."

"These scientists, then — they can synthesize the material of heredity?"

Nikki was surprised at the man's reaction. "Of course," she told him.

"How?"

She launched into a description of how DNA strands can be cleaved using restriction enzymes, then the fragments — in the form of plasmids — inserted into viral vectors ... But then she stopped short. Hollingforth was staring at her blankly, obviously understanding no more than if she'd suddenly broken into gibberish. "The techniques are quite complex," she concluded.

"So it would seem." Hollingforth's mouth quirked in an ironic smile. Then he shook his head again in amazement. "To synthesize the material of heredity itself," he mused. "I've heard it said that this is possible. There are some natives in New London who say that the news from the rest of the world used to discuss this, and other wonders." He shrugged. "Of course, few people save for me ever troubled to speak to the natives, and those who did never believed more than one word in five."

He glanced over his shoulder at the other men crouched around the fire. When he turned back, he kept his voice low, conspiratorial. "I would very much enjoy discussing this further with you, Miss Carlson" he told Nikki, "but I would ask you not to mention this matter in front of Professor Black. He strongly believes that such matters smack of the black arts.

"Well," he rubbed his hands together briskly, his voice returning to its normal pitch. "Our supper is almost ready. Would you care to join us, Miss Carlson?"

At the word "supper," Nikki's stomach growled. When was the last time she'd eaten? Breakfast, she recalled, at about eight-thirty. She checked her watch. That was more than fourteen hours ago. "That would be great," she told him.

"You can also meet my colleagues. May I help you up?" He rose, offered her his hand.

She swung her legs off the low camp bed, sat there for a moment evaluating how she felt. *Not bad, considering,* she decided. Her stomach felt like a fist with hunger and her left ankle still felt puffy and sore. But apart from that, she seemed healthy. She stood, declining to take Hollingforth's proffered hand.

Hollingforth led her over to the fire. "This is my mentor, Professor Roderick Black," he said, indicating the older man. "Professor Black, may I introduce Miss Nikki Carlson?"

Black looked up at her, his face creased in a frown. *What's eating him?* Nikki wondered for a moment. Then she saw the lines etched into his face, and realized that his face must naturally fall into that expression. The professor's chin was clean-shaven, but his sideburns — grey and curly — extended down his face to spread out over his cheeks in what used to be called "mutton-chops." His eyes were dark and filled with suspicion. He had to be about fifty, Nikki thought.

She extended her hand to him. "Professor Black."

He looked down at her hand in surprise. (*Aren't women supposed to shake hands?* she wondered in irritation.) With a grunt of annoyance, the man took her hand and shook once, dropping it again as quickly as he could. Then he looked away, returning to his morose inspection of the fire.

Nikki exchanged a wry glance with Hollingforth. He shrugged apologetically, as if to say, "That's just the way he is."

"And this is our Sergeant MacHeath, of the 'Glorious Fifteenth,'" Hollingforth said heartily, laying a comradely hand on the shoulder of the oldest among the soldiers. "The Sergeant is our guide and our guardian. Isn't that right, Sergeant?"

MacHeath chuckled warmly, a rumble from deep in

his broad chest. "Aye. A thankless job, but someone must keep yon babe out of trouble." If he was scandalized by Nikki's offer to shake hands with Black, he didn't show it. He extended his own hand — a hard, calloused thing with fingers as thick as sausages. She took it, expecting a bonecrushing grip. But MacHeath apparently knew his own strength — which was probably considerable, she thought — because his grip was firm but not too tight. "It's a pleasure to meet you, Miss Carlson," the soldier went on, "although we could have done so under better circumstances."

Nikki smiled down at the big man. His face was broad and large-featured, perfectly matching his muscular body. He had a thick, bushy mustache, twirled and waxed into upswept tips on both sides of his mouth. His eyes sparkled with humor in the firelight.

She found herself drawn to MacHeath ... and to Hollingforth as well, she had to admit. They were strange, totally out of place in the world that she knew. Their manners and their ideas were ... well, downright weird, but these two were open and friendly. Willing to treat her like an equal — *with occasional lapses*, Nikki reminded herself. Totally unlike Black. She glanced over at the professor, saw him sitting straight-backed, eyes averted, as if keeping himself aloof from the unseemly fraternizing going on just a couple of feet away.

Ideas shot through her mind, ideas of doing something to shock him out of his haughty reserve. Throwing her arms around his neck and planting a sloppy kiss on his nose, maybe. Doing *anything* to shock him. She chuckled to herself. She knew she'd never have the guts to do anything like that, but it was fun to think about.

She looked at the other three soldiers. "And these are ...?" she asked.

MacHeath blinked in surprise — *like he's shocked that*

anyone would care about mere soldiers, Nikki thought — but recovered quickly. "PFCs Muir, Rundle and Murphy," he said, pointing to the men in turn. They were younger than MacHeath, Nikki noted as they mumbled greetings to her, probably younger than herself.

"Please, sit down, Miss Carlson," Hollingforth suggested, indicating a folding camp stool.

As she settled herself on the canvas seat, MacHeath asked, "Will you be joining us for supper, ma'am?"

She smiled. "I think that would be wonderful," she said demurely.

*   *   *

One of the soldiers — Rundle, she thought it was — served the food. It was stew of some kind, thick and rich, that had been simmering in a large pot over the fire. Nikki ate it with relish. When Rundle shyly offered her a second helping, she accepted, and polished that off too.

She could tell the men were curious about her, but they were polite enough to hold off their questions until she'd finished eating. As soon as she set aside her bowl, though, Sergeant MacHeath began earnestly, "Not that I would pass up the honor, mind, but how did you come to … er …" He searched for words.

Nikki chuckled. "'Drop in on you'?" she suggested.

MacHeath grinned broadly. "Aye, that's it exactly. How did you come to drop in on us this afternoon, ma'am?" Hollingforth and the sergeant leaned forward to better hear her answer.

Her smile faded. Even thinking back on the creatures, on the pursuit, was enough to make her stomach knot up painfully. Briefly she outlined what had happened after she'd entered the jungle.

Hollingforth and MacHeath were silent after she'd finished, their smiles gone and their eyes troubled as they glanced at each other. It was Hollingforth who spoke first. "Zombies," he mused, almost to himself, "or perhaps even zuvembies."

"Zombies?" Nikki demanded. "As in 'the walking dead'? That's ..." She stopped. *'That's stupid,'* I was *about to say, she thought. But is it?* She remembered the decayed, tattered flesh of the creatures, the reek of rotting meat as they reached for her. *If they weren't the walking dead, what* were *they?*

Hollingforth answered her question quietly. "Yes, Miss Carlson, the walking dead." He shook his head. "I know you find it hard to believe. I did as well, when first I came to Majestic. But such is the way of Orrorsh. The dead do not always sleep quietly here." He shared a disturbed look with MacHeath. "This troubles me," he admitted. "We had hoped this area to be free of such things. The reach of the Gaunt Man grows longer than we suspected."

The Gaunt Man. The words meant nothing to Nikki, not on an intellectual level. But emotionally the phrase was evocative. She felt a chill in the pit of her stomach, a quiver of fear. *The Gaunt Man.* "Who is the Gaunt Man?" she asked in a hushed voice.

Hollingforth began to answer, but Professor Black's sharp voice cut him off. "Silence," Black snapped. "No-one will speak of *him*. The Sacellum has decreed his name will never be spoken. Mr. Hollingforth, you know that as well as I do."

Hollingforth bowed his head in embarrassment. "You're right, Professor," he said, chastened, "forgive me."

Black snorted. He fixed Nikki with a withering look before turning back to his contemplation of the fire.

Miserable old curmudgeon, Nikki thought. Quickly she stuck her tongue out at Black. The professor had his head turned away and didn't see it, but Hollingforth and MacHeath did. Both grinned, and the sergeant unsuccessfully tried to smother a laugh. Black turned at the sound. But Nikki was gazing demurely at the stars, while Hollingforth had lowered his head again in mock repentance. MacHeath covered his slip by turning his laughter into an attack of coughing. Scowling, the professor turned away again.

Nikki shifted on the camp stool, looking for a more comfortable position. The fire was warm, its light reassuring. She could feel the nighttime jungle around her, feel its life — even feel the eyes of countless small nocturnal creatures watching her. But the light of the fire surrounded her, like a charmed circle in fairy tales. Nothing could come close to the fire, she thought, could step within the circle of its light. She could almost make herself believe that this was all there was of reality, that everything outside this compass simply didn't exist: the creatures that had chased her, the Nagara security guards, the outpost itself … even her life in Tokyo. She could remember feeling strong emotions — terror when the zombies attacked her, desolation when Toshikazu and then O'Neil were killed. But right now, sitting by the fire, those emotions felt like vague memories, nothing more.

Hollingforth stirred beside her. "We must help you rejoin your expedition, Miss Carlson," he said. "They must be worried by your disappearance. Where might we find them?"

"On the river bank," she answered, "it's in a large clearing."

MacHeath nodded. "I know where it is," he said, "Rundle here spotted it yesterday. We decided to give it a wide berth."

"Oh? Why?" Nikki asked.

Hollingforth shot a quick glance at Black. "The professor has decided that any … outside interference … is to be avoided." From his expression, she could tell he didn't think much of that.

"Dinna worry yourself about that, Miss Carlson,"

MacHeath said reassuringly. "In the morning we'll see you safely back to your comrades."

She looked around her, at the black wall of the jungle around the small clearing. "Yes," she agreed quietly, "in the morning."

Hollingforth seemed to misinterpret her reaction. "Have no fear," he said firmly, "you'll be safe here. The soldiers will make sure that the fire burns brightly all night."

Something about the young man's voice made Nikki look into his eyes. He looked so earnest, obviously trying to reassure her of something he thought she'd fear. *The fire's important*, she thought with a sudden chill. *They're convinced that if it goes out, something bad's going to happen.* She glanced around again. The jungle was solid, unrelieved blackness around the clearing. *Anything could be out there* — anything.

"We usually rise with the dawn," Hollingforth explained, "to make the most of the daylight hours."

"Are you telling me it's bedtime?" she asked, amused.

"Well ..." He looked uncomfortable — *no, shy*, she thought, *he's probably blushing under that beard.* "Well, I thought perhaps you'd be tired ..."

She smiled at him, deciding not to tease him any more. "I guess I am tired," she told him. "Where do I sleep?"

He offered his arm as she rose from the camp stool. She hesitated a moment, then took it. "Good night," she told the others. "Thanks for your help."

Hollingforth led her away from the answering chorus of "good nights," stopping before one of the tents. He held the canvas flap back for her. "This is my tent," he told her.

"Ah," she said. She turned away to hide her smile. "And you'll sleep ...?" she asked casually.

This time the young man looked even more uncomfortable — embarrassed, almost mortified. She saw a flush darken his cheeks above the line of his beard. *He is blushing!*

He coughed, cleared his throat. "I ... I'll sleep with the soldiers, of course," he muttered, "I assure you I never had any other intentions, I didn't ..."

She cut him off by laying a hand on his arm. "I'm sorry," she told him, "I was just teasing you. Thank you for letting me use your tent."

"Well, I ..." he mumbled. Then he drew himself up to his full height, bowed his head formally — almost in the Japanese manner. "The pleasure is all mine, Miss Carlson. I hope you sleep well." And then he turned on his heel and strode off toward the fire.

Nikki watched his retreating back with a smile. *Nice guy*, she thought. *Definitely a nice guy, even if he is a little weird.* She chuckled quietly to herself. *He blushed when I teased him. What guy blushes anymore? It was almost as if ...*

Her brain paused on that line of thought. *It's almost as if he's an anachronism,* she mused, *like he's from an earlier time.* His shyness, his sometimes-stilted way of speaking, the way he didn't understand a lot of what she said, his comments about the natives, his amazement over her talk of genetic engineering ... And then there were the soldiers' uniforms, and the professor's condemnation of Hollingforth for talking about the Gaunt Man — *whoever he is*. When Nikki was growing up, she'd sometimes visited her uncle — a hard-line Methodist preacher in Pennsylvania — and she was sure that the crusty old man and Professor Black would find they had a lot in common.

Is that what's happening in Orrorsh? she asked herself. *Some kind of time warp or time gate, bringing people — and things — through from some past epoch?* Didn't that explain the presence of Hollingforth and the others quite nicely ...?

She snorted loudly. *Nonsense. Pure crap.* She was letting her imagination run away with her again. Time gate indeed. Shaking her head at her own foolishness, she crawled into the tent.

There was just enough room inside for a bedroll and some personal gear: changes of clothes — with two different ties, Nikki noticed — heavy walking boots, toiletries, and such like. Nothing that she could see incorporated advanced technology of any kind; there was nothing more sophisticated than a double-edge safety razor. No flashlight, no radio, no Walkman for entertainment … *who are these people?*

Quickly stripping down to her underwear, she stretched out on the bedroll, closed her eyes. Questions, stray images, wild speculations — all churned through her brain. But despite them all, the quickly sank into a fitful sleep.

* * *

Nikki woke to the smell of brewing coffee and frying bacon — *not a bad way to wake up*, she thought. Bright morning sunlight was filtering through the thin canvas of the tent.

She rolled over, stretched luxuriously. Her neck had stiffened up from her sleep on the unpadded bedroll, but it wasn't too bad. Sitting cross-legged, she rolled her head from side to side a few times to release the tension. She examined the ankle she'd injured in her flight from the zombies. It was a little puffy, indicating a slight twist, but the throbbing pain had gone. She should have little trouble walking on it, she judged. *All in all I don't feel too bad, but* — she ran her fingers through her hair — *I probably look like something the dog dragged in.* She considered rummaging through Hollingforth's toiletries to find a mirror and a comb, but decided against it. The young man's privacy was more important than her vanity. She dressed briskly, and crawled out of the tent to greet the morning.

The fire was still burning strongly, she saw. Private Rundle was frying bacon in a large iron skillet, while one of the others — Muir, she thought — was tending a large coffee pot. Sergeant MacHeath and the other soldiers were nowhere to be seen. Hollingforth and Professor Black were sitting near the fire with cups of coffee, deep in conversation. Nikki stood, stretching again. She put weight on her hurt ankle, testing it out. There was a little pain if she twisted it, but as long as she was careful it would hold her without any difficulties.

Hollingforth saw her first. With a quick apology to the suddenly sour-faced Black, he jumped to his feet and hurried over to her. "Good morning, Miss Carlson," he greeted her. "I trust you slept well?"

"I slept quite well," she replied, peripherally aware that she was picking up his manner of speech. "And you?" she inquired politely.

"I slept exceptionally well, thank you." He glanced over his shoulder at Rundle. "I think we're only a couple of minutes from breakfast. Would you join us?"

"Of course," she told him.

She was sitting next to Hollingforth, back on the camp cot she'd occupied last night, when MacHeath and his other men came into the clearing. She looked up from her plate of bacon and gave the sergeant a smile.

"Good morning, Miss Carlson," he began, "did you …?"

But the professor cut him off sharply. "Well?" he snapped. "What of the area?"

MacHeath drew himself up to his full height — almost standing at attention but not quite. *Probably the most he'll do for a civilian*, Nikki thought with some amusement. "The area is relatively clear, Professor," the sergeant stated flatly. "There are no … unusual creatures, and no obvious tracks left by same." (Black looked slightly disappointed at that, Nikki noted. *What kind of expedition are they on, anyway?*)

"We approached the stockade on the river as closely as I considered prudent," MacHeath went on. "We observed them for a while from concealment." He hesitated, glanced over at Nikki then back to Professor Black. "They have teams out in the jungle, Professor," he said. "I expect they must be searching for Miss Carlson."

Black, too, looked over at Nikki. Unlike MacHeath's, his glance contained obvious vexation. "Yes," he said drily. "That would make sense. Well, we must return her as soon as convenient. Sergeant, you and your men will take her, and ..."

"Hold it," Nikki broke in sharply. She felt anger burning in her chest over the way Black was talking about her — *about* her, not *to* her — as if she'd been a piece of luggage. "Don't I get any say in this?"

For a moment, Black looked as though he were going to explode. But then, with visible effort, he kept himself under control. "I would think you would *like* to return to your colleagues," he said.

That set Nikki back for a moment. She did, of course, but ...

"It must be understood that you will say nothing to them of having met us," Black went on.

"What? Why?" Nikki demanded.

Black's eyebrows drew together in a fierce scowl. "Because that is how I say it must be," he said fiercely. Then he turned away as if that settled the matter.

The bastard! Nikki was ready to pursue it, to follow him and tell him exactly what she thought of his attitude. But Peter Hollingforth's hand on her arm restrained her.

She spun, ready to vent her anger on anyone who was near. But then she saw his expression, earnest and concerned, embarrassed — not by her reaction, obviously, but by the actions of his superior. Her anger seeped away, as he led her back toward the tents.

"I'm so sorry," he whispered, "I know his manner is abrasive. I know better than most people." That was a telling comment, Nikki thought, incredibly communicative. *What would it be like to work for a jerk like that?* she wondered.

"He has no animosity toward you personally," Hollingforth went on softly, "he would act the same way to anyone who ... *inconvenienced* him in any way."

"Why the hell am I such an inconvenience?"

Hollingforth sighed. "To Professor Black, *anything* that fails to mesh perfectly with his plans is an inconvenience. The presence of your colleagues in the stockade, the absence of ..." — he hesitated — " ...the object of our search ..."

Nikki cut him off. "Just what are you looking for out here?" she asked.

The young man looked uncomfortable at that. "We, er, we would like to keep the nature of our expedition confidential."

Nikki crossed her arms. "You'd better tell me," she warned, "or by God I'm going to tell everyone back at the outpost everything I know about you."

"You wouldn't do that, would you?" Hollingforth asked desperately.

I wouldn't, Nikki told herself, *but you don't know that.* She didn't say a word, just stared levelly into his eyes.

Hollingforth appeared to deflate. "Alright," he sighed. "I feel uncomfortable about keeping this secret anyway." He lowered his voice another notch, glanced over his shoulder to make sure Black wasn't listening in. "I told you last night that our expedition was commissioned by the board of directors of the Victorian Majestic Charter. That is not quite the case. The Charter board authorized us to perform a survey of the unnatural creatures in the region of Solok, a town northeast of New London in the Barisan Mountains. I am shamed to say we have, er, *strayed* from our official task" — a wry smile quirked his lips — "strayed by some two hundred miles, to be precise."

"Just what are you doing?"

Hollingforth was silent for a moment. Then his hazel eyes fixed on her face, and she felt his intensity like a static shock. "If I tell you, will you keep our secret?" he asked.

She hesitated. It wasn't as if this group could have committed some terrible crime, she mused. And beyond that possibility, what business was it of anyone else's just what they did? Maybe the Victorian Majestic Charter board — *whatever the hell that is* — might care, but Nikki didn't think they'd ever be asking her any questions. She nodded her agreement to Hollingforth's conditions.

The young man looked relieved. *He's not good at keeping secrets*, Nikki recognized, *he's too honest*.

"Thank you," he said. "We are following the trail of a particular creature," he went on in a low voice, "a murderous beast whose path we crossed in the region of Solok. We have been following it ever since."

"What kind of creature?" Nikki asked.

"A shapeshifter," he explained, "a beast that can change its form. The natives refer to the creature as a 'weretiger.'"

A weretiger? Like a werewolf? Nikki shook her head with disbelief. *That's nonsense …*

But is *it?* She looked into the earnest face of Peter Hollingforth. *He believes it*, she reminded herself. *Right down to his core, he believes it. And why not?* She thought back to the previous day. She'd seen *something* — a tentacle — drag down a helicopter; she'd been pursued by things that looked like the living dead. *I'm in Orrorsh, after all*. Why can't there be weretigers? The thought was like ice-water in her veins. "Why are you following it?" she asked Hollingforth. "Why this particular creature?"

He looked away for a moment. Then, with an obvious effort, his eyes met hers again. "When we left New London on this expedition," he began, "there were eight of us. MacHeath had four privates in his section, not just three. And Professor Black had two assistants, not just me.

"His name was John Black," Hollingforth went on bleakly, "my colleague and the professor's second assistant. He was the professor's son, and my close friend.

"We were in Sokol, talking to the natives, trying to get them to trust us enough to tell us what they knew." He smiled grimly. "Well, *I* was talking to the natives, I and John. The professor wouldn't believe they knew anything worth knowing. We met a local doctor, a Dr. Ling — an elderly Chinese. He spoke better English than anyone else we met, and he was an educated man too, so we spent most of our time talking with him."

Hollingforth snorted in disgust. "We talked with Ling, we believed what he told us. And he sent us on a merry chase around the Sokol area, never finding what we were looking for. We should have suspected he was lying to us then, but we didn't.

"And then one day Dr. Ling sent a message to John, claiming that he had discovered something of great importance. The professor and I, along with Sergeant MacHeath, were busy elsewhere. If I'd been there, perhaps I would have stopped him. John, accompanied by Private Taylor, went to meet with Ling … and they never returned.

"We searched everywhere, of course," Hollingforth said slowly. "Everywhere except for where we should have searched. Since we knew nothing about the message at that time, it took us hours to consider that perhaps Ling was involved. And that was much too late."

Hollingforth's eyes were open, but Nikki knew he wasn't seeing her or the sun-drenched jungle clearing. He was seeing something horrible, some memory he'd probably never be able to escape. "We went to Dr. Ling's office," the young man continued quietly. "The *good doctor*" — the words dripped with painful irony — "was gone, of course. John and Private Taylor, thought — they were still there." He closed his eyes now, and his face looked drawn and pale in the morning sunlight. "Ling's clinic had two operating tables. Both were occupied: John was bound to one, Private Taylor to the other."

Nikki closed her eyes, too, just for a moment — not much more than a long blink. She thought she knew what was coming, but she held her tongue.

"They had both been alive when … when the *procedures* had begun." Hollingforth's voice was flat, emotionless — empty and cold, like a winter wind. "One can only hope that they didn't remain that way for long." He took a deep, calming breath before he went on. "Dr. Ling had used his surgical implements. He had …" He paused again for another deep breath. "He took their eyes first. Then he'd begun to work on their … on the rest of them. It was like a surgical dissection in a medical school, apart from all the blood, of course. We tried to find Dr. Ling, but he was gone."

Nikki shivered. She looked down at her hands. They were shaking. She clenched them into fists to stop the quivering. "Dr. Ling was the shapeshifter?" she asked. "The weretiger? How did you know?"

"We were staying in a small rooming house on the outskirts of Solok," Hollingforth answered elliptically. "Professor Black had a room on the first floor, John and I shared another. The soldiers were housed on the ground floor. That night, Dr. Ling paid us a call. I suppose he thought we would be asleep. He didn't expect the soldiers to be awake, keeping watches through the night.

"I was asleep, dreaming." Nikki saw the young man shudder. She could guess what his dreams were like. "The sound of rifle fire from below woke us. The professor and I ran downstairs.

"We saw Dr. Ling running from the front door. MacHeath and his men were firing after him. I saw several of their bullets strike him, but he seemed simply to shrug off wounds that would have felled any normal man. As he ran for the jungle, I saw him change. His body warped, twisted, until he wasn't a man any longer. He bent forward until he was running on all-fours, faster than any man could run." Hollingforth sighed. "There was no doubt as to his true nature. He was a weretiger."

There was silence between them for a moment while Nikki tried to absorb what she'd just heard. She wanted to deny what Hollingforth had said, wanted desperately to discard it all as lies, as some terrible mistake. But, looking into the young man's hazel eyes, she knew she couldn't do that. *He knows what he saw*, she had to admit, *and he's telling me the truth.* "So you followed its trail?" she asked gently.

Hollingforth nodded. "It was Professor Black who suggested it," he elaborated, "but I wanted to do the same thing myself. MacHeath took no persuading, nor his men. We all wanted to put paid to the fiend who had killed our friends and colleagues.

"Our commission from the Charter board gave us considerable freedom of action," he went on, "so there were no constraints on our movements." He hesitated. "Of course, if the board found out exactly what we intended, they would revoke our commission and call us back to New London at once. While Professor Black and I could decide to ignore their summons, MacHeath and the other soldiers would have no choice but to obey their orders."

"Why would the board do that?" Nikki asked.

"You don't know about the board, do you?" Nikki shook her head. "The purpose of the Victorian Majestic Charter, and the company that holds it, is simple," Hollingforth explained. "They intend to exploit financially the island of Majestic, and as much of the rest of Orrorsh as possible. The board of directors of the company are men of high birth, but they have the instincts of merchants, of shopkeepers." From the tone of his voice, Nikki could tell that Hollingforth considered this a dire insult. "They will commission projects that have the potential of realizing a profit, and only such projects. Honestly, I don't know what they hope to gain from our original survey, apart from possibly an estimate of the resources they would need to expand their operations. There is no way that they would countenance our pursuit; they would see it as nothing more than personal vengeance ... which, I suppose it is." He shook his head. "No, the board would call us all back to New London as soon as they knew our purpose."

Nikki nodded, more to herself than to Hollingforth. She understood the mindset of the board of directors; they and the executives of any Japanese megacorporation would quickly find they had much common ground. "Is that why Professor Black doesn't want me to tell my colleagues about you?" she asked. "He thinks they'll tell the board?"

Hollingforth shrugged. "Perhaps," he allowed. "Perhaps he considers that a possibility. More likely, though, he simply doesn't trust them not to interfere." He chuckled drily. "As you may have gathered, the professor doesn't like or trust anyone who isn't a Victorian ... and not even all of those." He hesitated, then went on diffidently, "I must admit I, too, would like to avoid any, er, outside complications. If you could see your way clear ..." He trailed off.

Nikki sighed. "I already told him I wouldn't talk about you to anyone," she told him.

"And you are a lady of your word," Hollingforth finished for her. He bowed. "Thank you, Miss Carlson. We are all very grateful."

She looked him over again. Earnest, eager … *Almost like an over-age boy scout in a tie,* she thought with some amusement. His honesty, his straightforwardness, were refreshing. She found herself liking him. "Is there anything I can do to help you?" she asked.

He started to shake his head, then paused. "Your colleagues send expeditions into the jungle, isn't that so?" he queried.

She remembered the group of scientists she'd seen returning to the compound — *was that only thirty-six hours ago?* she asked herself. "Sometimes," she told him.

"And you talk to them, I assume," Hollingforth said with growing enthusiasm. "Would it be possible, could you see your way clear to …"

It was Nikki's turn to cut him off. "If I hear anything about a weretiger," she agreed, "I'll get word to you. But how?"

Hollingforth thought that through, then a smile spread over his face. "I'll have MacHeath assign one of his men to watch the stockade during the day," he suggested. "If you have some information for us, and you can leave the compound, come to the edge of the jungle. The soldier will meet you there, take the information, and see you come to no harm. Would you do that for us?"

Nikki considered. *There are zombies out there,* she remembered, *zombies and worse. And they* do *come out during the day.*

She looked deeply into Hollingforth's eyes. She could see his pain, his remembered horror over his lost friend … and his hope. How could she refuse? *Particu-*

larly when I'll have a soldier watching over me … "I'll do it," she said quietly.

Hollingforth's smile was all the thanks she needed. "We are all grateful to you, Miss Carlson," he said formally. "If there is anything that I can do in return …"

She returned his smile. "Just see me back to the compound in one piece," she suggested.

Hollingforth beckoned to MacHeath, and the sergeant came over. "Are you ready to leave, Miss Carlson?" the soldier asked. "Professor Black said you'd be returning to your people."

She nodded. "Do you have my gun?"

MacHeath produced it from a pocket of his scarlet jacket and handed it to her. It came as a surprise to realize the pistol felt good in her hand — *like a reminder of a world I left behind,* she thought. Just looking at the precisely-machined weapon reminded her of all the other high technology she'd come to take for granted.

"I hope you don't mind, Miss Carlson," MacHeath said, "but I examined your weapon. It seems to have malfunctioned in some way. I couldn't get it to fire."

"Oh?" Nikki examined the pistol. To her untrained eye it looked undamaged. *Maybe something happened to it when I fell,* she wondered. She carefully pointed it away from the others, made sure the safety catch was on, and squeezed the trigger gently. The sighting laser flicked on, casting its ruby dot on the ground.

Hollingforth and MacHeath both gasped aloud. She turned to them, puzzled. "What's the matter?"

"The light," MacHeath said. "It never did that before. What is it?"

Quickly she explained about laser sights — what little she knew, at least.

The two men listened in unabashed fascination. "Amazing," MacHeath said in a hushed voice. "Why, *anyone* could use a weapon like this. Just think of the training time saved …"

A puzzling thought struck Nikki. "The laser didn't work when you tried it?" she asked.

The sergeant shook his head. "Neither did the mechanism," he added. "A sweet piece of engineering, to be sure, much more advanced than our Standard Cross revolvers. It took me some time to figure out how it must work." He shrugged. "Or perhaps I didn't figure it out."

Nikki frowned. Quickly she flicked the safety off like Dei had taught her, pulled back the slide. The mechanism felt smooth as silk. She snapped the safety back on. "It seems to work fine now."

MacHeath looked completely perplexed now. "As God is my witness," he said, "that's exactly what I tried to do. But the thing simply would not work for me. Ah, well," he sighed, "it's not my weapon to play around with, and you may well be needing it." He squared his shoulders and smiled down at Nikki. "Would you be ready to move out, Miss Carlson? We have a quarter-hour march to yon compound."

* * *

So the prodigal child returns home, Nikki mused the next day. *But where was the fatted calf?*

It had been almost nine in the morning when MacHeath and the other soldiers had "delivered" her to the fringe of the jungle near the stockade gate. They'd parted with warm handshakes, and then Nikki had emerged from the jungle and walked toward the gate. The security guards had seen her at once, opened the gate for her and hustled her inside.

If she'd been expecting an exuberant welcome, she was sadly disappointed. The guards had said next to nothing to her, had seemed more angry than anything else at her reappearance — *or maybe at my original disappearance*, she'd thought. Dei had been among them, and he'd given her a brief smile of welcome, but that was it. The guards had formed up into a tight knot of muscle and armor, and marched her to the central administration building.

There she'd been questioned — interrogated, almost — by Hongo, the outpost's security chief. And — surprisingly — by Eichiro himself. They'd asked her repeatedly about the creatures that had chased her, and she'd had to repeat what she remembered at least half a dozen times. Remembering her agreement with Hollingforth and Black, she'd said nothing about meeting the explorers and the soldiers. She'd outrun the zombies or whatever they were, she'd said over and over again, and had spent the night in a clearing, then had made her way back to the outpost as soon as the sun had risen.

The question that everybody had kept coming back to had been, how had she managed to escape from the zombies? The security personnel had looked at her pistol, found she hadn't fired a shot. How, they wanted to know, had she evaded the creatures when she hadn't even known enough to use her weapon? *It's almost like they're angry at me for surviving,* she'd thought at the time. She couldn't help but compare their truculent behavior with the formal politeness and concern of Peter Hollingforth.

At last everyone had been satisfied — or at least had run out of questions to ask, and they'd sent her back to her quarters to recover from her "ordeal."

And now, late the next afternoon, she was in her lab. The other members of her workgroup were ignoring her again, just like they'd done when it had been first announced that Group Five would be going to Sumatra. They answered any questions she asked, did what she told them, but their manner was uniformly sullen. *Almost as if I've shamed them again,* she thought angrily, *shamed them by coming back in one piece.*

Bojo and Toshima were tending to one of the automated analyzers, while the others were preparing more samples for analysis. The core science group — Funakoshi and his colleagues — had been busy, she noted. (In fact, according to the grapevine, they were on the verge of some kind of breakthrough.) Already they'd sent more than a dozen serum samples over to Group Five from their private lab. As Nikki had expected, they'd given the support workgroup no clues as to what the samples were, no indications of exactly what they were looking for from the analyses. That meant that Nikki and her colleagues had to perform complete, exhaustive analyses — from scratch, as it were, without being able to take any effort-saving shortcuts.

The computer terminal on her desk beeped. That meant that the results of the first analyses had been processed by the computers and were ready for examination. She keyed in the appropriate commands to bring the analysis of the first serum up on her screen as a graph.

She stared at the complex graph, trying to make sense of what she was seeing. After a few minutes, the data began to make some sense. With her finger she traced out the "landmarks," the components of the serum that would allow her to figure out what was going on. Yes, there was the lysine peak, and over here tryptophan. Those were amino acids, the chemical building blocks of proteins. That meant that the first serum — SAMPLE 1A-93-03, the file label on the top of the screen said — had to be a protein of some kind.

But *what* kind? That was obviously what the science team wanted Group Five to determine. She keyed in another command, and waited while the computer juggled the data, ordering it in another way. A completely different graph appeared on the screen.

The shape of the graph was vaguely familiar; it took only a moment to place the pattern. *This is a* human *protein*, she realized, *apparently some kind of blood protein*. She sat back in her chair. *What the hell's going on here?* she asked herself in exasperation. *Why are they sending over human proteins?* Was it some kind of test? she wondered. Were they sending over something totally mundane just to see if she and her colleagues would catch it?

But why would they waste time that way? Maybe the sample was contaminated. *That makes more sense*, she told herself. It was easy enough to accidentally nick yourself in a lab, and a drop of blood could completely contaminate and ruin a sample. The computerized analyzers were incredibly powerful, but they were rather "simple-minded." Could the machines have analyzed the contaminant — the blood of a clumsy technician — instead of the real sample? *It's possible* ... She leaned forward again to examine the graph once more. *Yes, human blood, pure and simple* ...

No, wait. What the hell is that? She traced with a fingertip an unfamiliar hump at the right-hand end of the graph. Quickly she instructed the computer to expand that segment of the plot.

Her breath whistled through her teeth as she examined the aberrant data. This wasn't a human protein — not a normal one, at least. *This structure, here ... what is it?* Again she had the computer reorder the data.

On the new plot, it was clear — there was some kind of chemical complex that just didn't belong in a human protein. *An animal protein, maybe?* No, not even that. It had characteristics that were similar to mammalian — but non-human — proteins, but it wasn't a total match. *It's like an animal, but* not *like it.* She reviewed the rest of the graph. Yes, about seventy-five percent of the protein's structure was obviously human. Twenty percent of it was just as obviously animal. That left five percent that was ... *what*?

She leaned back again, her brow wrinkled in a

frown. *It's some kind of hybrid protein,* she recognized, *something that just doesn't happen naturally.* What did that mean?

Carefully she thought it through. The mysterious five percent was marginally unstable. That meant it could change its chemical structure under certain circumstances. No functional protein, from a living creature, could have that characteristic. Which meant ...

Which meant it didn't come from a living creature, she concluded. Of course, she should have figured it out before. Funakoshi was a chimeric gene splicer, wasn't he? He'd made his mark in the scientific world by modifying the genes of experimental creatures, of splicing genes from different sources together to come up with something totally new. *A new gene that could code for a strange protein like this?* Possibly.

But where had he got the original genes to work on? Obviously one of the "genetic donors" had been human. *Which means Funakoshi's performing genetic engineering on humans, doesn't it?* There were strict laws in Japan — and in the United States, she remembered — tightly restricting genetic engineering on human tissue. The reason was safety: the risks, should anything go wrong, were just too great if the most stringent precautions weren't taken. *Is that why we came to Sumatra?* she asked herself. *To avoid Japanese law?* That made some sense. But she still had the feeling, deep in her gut, that there was more to it than that.

She'd have to keep a close watch on Funakoshi, and on everything that came out of his lab, if she wanted to understand. Working quickly, glancing around to make sure nobody saw what she was doing, she saved a copy of the analysis file in her personal directory on the computer, secured it with a password. She'd probably want to look over this later, when she had more time to think.

Chapter Nine

Nikki sat at the powerful microcomputer in her cramped quarters. Using the PAGE DOWN key, she flipped through the half-dozen analyses she'd stored in her personal directory. Her brain hurt from trying to make sense of what she was seeing. She leaned back, stretching her shoulders to release the tension, rubbed her tired eyes.

According to the time display in the upper right of the screen, it was just after five-thirty in the morning. It had been a late night — Funakoshi's group had *definitely* been busy, feeding samples to Group Five for analysis — and she hadn't made it out of the lab until well past midnight. She'd been glad to roll into her bed and fall asleep.

The nightmares had come, of course. She should have expected it, but she'd been too tired to think of it. In her dreams she'd run through the night-black jungle, waving her useless pistol, while rotting corpses gibbered and drooled as they chased her. Countless times she'd burst into the fire-lit clearing, called to Hollingforth and the soldiers for help ... only to see them smile with their decaying lips and reach for her with blood-encrusted fingernails.

At four in the morning she'd decided that she couldn't go back to sleep. She *couldn't* face what would be waiting for her. Instead, she'd padded across to the computer and called up her records of the previous day's analysis. *Might as well do something productive*, she'd told herself.

Now her head throbbed, and her shoulders and neck felt like they'd seized up like rusty metal joints. Her mouth tasted like something had died in it. What she really needed was a mug of strong coffee, she knew, but that would mean crossing the darkened compound. Much better to wait for the sun to rise in — she checked her watch again — about an hour. She glanced over at the disarranged bed. It looked so attractive … but also threatening. With a sigh, she went back to reviewing the results.

Group Five had analyzed six samples yesterday. Two of them — SAMPLE 1A-93-03 and the one that followed it — were strange hybrid proteins. The other four were …

Just weird. They were proteins too, that was undeniable. But they hadn't come from any animals or plants, insects or bacteria, that had ever lived. Certainly, they showed characteristics that were reminiscent of living creatures, but the overall structures were something totally different, totally unknown. *Just what the hell is Funakoshi building over there?* she asked herself for the hundredth time.

She sighed again. She wasn't going to make any headway now, that was for sure. Her head was too foggy with fatigue, and anyway she felt like she was trying to solve a jigsaw puzzle when she didn't have all the pieces. Carefully, she saved the file, made sure the password security was still in place. According to the strict security rules of the outpost, what she was doing was patently illegal. Any results from her analysis were to be sent — directly and electronically — to the science group in the secured lab. No copies were to be made; even any notes she or her colleagues made had to be forwarded to the scientists, or destroyed. (*Why?* she wondered. *Who do they think I might pass this stuff to? But of course that wasn't important. Strict security was as natural as breathing to Agatamori Eichiro.*)

She powered down the computer, looked over at the bed again. What to do now? She could go to the lab, but there wasn't anything constructive she could do there. If they stuck to their regular routine, the scientists wouldn't be sending over any more samples until after nine. Administrative work? That was one of the advantages about working at the outpost: there was a bare minimum of paperwork, and Nikki had cleared up the last of it before calling it a night. Read? Once again she cursed herself for not bringing any light reading. She certainly didn't feel like wading through a text book.

She rose, stretched her back until she heard the vertebrae popping. *I wonder what Peter's doing*, she found herself thinking. *Probably up and about, getting ready for another day of searching for the weretiger.* Unbidden, the image of Hollingforth formed in her mind. *He's so friendly*, she thought, *not outgoing, but that's just his background. And he's doing something he really believes in, something he considers important. He'll stick with it, even if there's a chance it'll kill him.*

And what about me? she asked herself. *Do I believe in what I'm doing? Do I care about it?* A few months ago, the answer would have been "yes." *But now?*

She shook her head. *What do I think I'm going to do?* she asked herself harshly. *Run away from the outpost, go join Hollingforth and Black in the jungle?* She laughed wryly. I need some coffee.

Unfocused fears nagged at her as she strode out of

the building into the compound, but she ruthlessly forced them from her mind. The sky was still black overhead, but the stars were fading and to the east the first pink wash of dawn had begun to light the sky. The air was pleasantly cool, but she knew that wouldn't last. *It's going to be another hot one.* She turned right and headed for the administration building.

The men were no more than ten yards away as she turned the corner of the support lab building. She and the others saw each other at the same moment, and stopped in their tracks.

There were four security guards accompanying three scientists, Funakoshi among them. All were wearing the dark blue jumpsuits she'd seen a few nights ago. One of the younger scientists was carrying something gingerly — an elliptical steel container, about two feet long and half that wide.

The security guards moved first. One swung something up, pointing it at Nikki — *a gun?* she thought in panic. But then the beam of a powerful flashlight caught her full in the face, dazzling her.

"Stop!" the security guard snapped. "What are you doing here?"

Nikki shielded her eyes with a hand. "It's me," she shouted hurriedly, "Nikki Carlson."

The security guard lowered his beam so it shone on the ground at Nikki's feet. He and another of his armed colleagues came forward, accompanied by Funakoshi. At a harsh command from the silver-haired man, the other scientists and security guards headed off for the secured lab at a fast walk.

Flanked by the guards, Funakoshi stopped a couple of yards in front of Nikki. The flashlight had ruined what night vision she had, and the light in the sky wasn't bright enough for her to see his expression. But his voice made it obvious he wasn't happy.

"What are you doing here?" he barked, echoing the

words of the security guard. "Where do you think you're going?"

Her fright at the sudden encounter was quickly turning to anger at Funakoshi's rudeness. "If it's any of your business," she snapped back, "I'm going to get some coffee. I'm free to go anywhere I want. I'm not a goddamn prisoner."

Funakoshi stared at her emotionlessly, untouched by her anger. And that only made her madder. "I want my coffee," she growled. She turned to walk around them.

"Stop!" Funakoshi glared at her, his eyes narrowing with thought. "You spoke to me at breakfast the other day," he said. "You asked me about my work, and now you're out here observing us." Nikki started to object, but something about the man's expression stopped her. "You seem very curious, Carrson," he mused, his omission of the honorific "-*san*" making her name sound like an insult. "Curiosity is bad for security. What other security provisions have you broken, I wonder? And why?"

With that, he turned on his heel. Still flanked by the two guards, he strode off toward his lab building, leaving Nikki fuming in his wake.

* * *

The summons — there was no other word for it — came several hours later. Nikki was in the lab, working beside Omi, the most technically skilled of her people, struggling to get a recalcitrant analyzer back on-line. She hadn't seen the security guard come in, noticing him only when he spoke.

"Carrson-*san*," he said formally, with a slight bow. "Eichiro-*san* requests your presence."

Nikki looked up in surprise, brushing a lock of hair out of her eyes. "I'm busy," she said shortly. "This should take about an hour. After that …"

"*Now*, Carrson-*san*," the guard cut her off. "Eichiro-

san requests your presence immediately." Although his choice of words denoted a polite request, the hard edge to his voice made it an order.

Nikki felt herself flushing, felt the eyes of her colleagues on her. *Another shame*, she knew they'd be thinking. Emotions warred inside her ... and anger won out.

But she knew it would do no good yelling at the guard — which was what she wanted to do, of course. He was just delivering a message, and shooting the messenger — or even shouting at him — wasn't practical. She settled for shooting him a hard glare, which of course left him totally unfazed.

She glanced over at Omi. "Can you handle this yourself?" she asked.

The technician nodded, but didn't even deign to speak to her.

She wiped her hands on her labcoat and glared at the guard again. "Take me to Eichiro-san," she ordered. She could feel the eyes of the others on her again as she followed the guard's broad back out of the lab.

* * *

Eichiro's office in the outpost was almost exactly the same size as the one he'd had in the Kanawa Building, Nikki saw as she stepped through the door. The carpeting was the same light blue-grey, and even the furniture looked exactly the way she remembered it. *Maybe he had it brought with him*, she thought. The only difference was that Eichiro's Tokyo office had a window with a view of the Imperial Palace. Here there was no window. In its place, on the wall behind the manager's large desk, was a large painting — an abstract that inexplicably made Nikki think of oppression and hopelessness. *Or is that just my mood?* she wondered.

Eichiro himself looked just the way he had in Tokyo. He wore the same dark suit of conservative cut, a white shirt, and a brightly-patterned "power" tie. A suit and tie were totally inappropriate for a site in a tropical jungle, but there was something about the man's aura the man seemed to exude that made Nikki — in her shorts and light blouse — feel like she was the one out of place.

The manager was reading something when the security guard ushered Nikki in — a file of some kind. (*My personnel dossier?* Nikki wondered.) After a moment, he looked up, marking his place with a thick finger banded with a heavy gold ring. "Carrson-*san*," he said with a millimetric bow. "Thank you for your promptness." There was no hint of irony in his voice, Nikki noted with mild surprise. "Please, sit down." He indicated one of the comfortable visitor chairs.

She did, keeping her eyes on him.

"If you'll allow me a moment …" Without waiting for her response, he returned to his examination of the file open in front of him. After maybe a dozen seconds, he grunted to himself in satisfaction, pulled a gold pen from his inside pocket and initialled the bottom of the page he'd been reading. Then he closed the file and slipped it into the top drawer of his desk. "My apologies," he said, "but the requirements of this job are sometimes heavy."

Nikki looked at him, puzzled. There was something … *strange* … about Eichiro. The other times she'd met him he'd been hard, cold, emotionless as a machine or a jungle predator. But now he seemed … Friendly? Open? *Human*? At some deep level, that disturbed her.

"What can I do for you, Eichiro-*san*?" she asked politely.

He sighed, a strange sound coming from someone as apparently imperturbable. "One of my responsibilities is managing some very valuable personnel," he began slowly. "Personnel of great potential, but sometimes a little … shall we say, lacking in maturity and personal stability? Sometimes these personnel get an idea and cling to it, even though there's no evidence that they're right. My duty is to work through such ideas with them, solve the problem — whether real or imagined — and allow them to return their attention to what they should be doing. Do you understand, Carrson-*san*?"

Nikki nodded. She thought she knew what was coming.

She was right. "I'm referring to Funakoshi-*san*, of course." The tone of Eichiro's voice implied this was an uncomfortable admission. "He has … well, he has got it into his head that you are a security risk, Carrson-*san*. He has taken unrelated incidents, and in his mind has found relations between them." The manager gestured airily with his hand. "A conversation over breakfast where you questioned him about his work. The fact that you were — he claims — spying on his movements this morning." He grunted. "He even tied it in with your disappearance from the outpost the other day and your miraculous escape from the creatures in the jungle. All foolishness, of course, but I have to set his mind at rest by investigating. You understand, Carrson-*san*?"

There's definitely *something wrong here*. Eichiro was talking openly and honestly, obviously trying to set her at her ease. From anyone else, she'd have welcomed it as a thawing of icy reserve, an indication that the "iceman" was actually human after all, with emotions just like anyone else. But from Eichiro? Something just didn't seem right, didn't jibe. What was it? His words *did* make sense, she could understand what he was talking about. And the way he was acting implied he was as uncomfortable as she was.

Acting! Was that it? In the lengthening silence, she stared at Eichiro. *Is he acting?* she asked herself. *Is this all a masterful performance?*

"Do you understand the necessity, Carrson-san?"

Eichiro asked again.

"Uh, yes," she stammered. "Yes, I understand."

"Then I must ask the question," he said, a tinge of sadness—Or feigned sadness—in his voice. "Has there been any other occasion when you have tried to penetrate the security of Funakoshi-*san*'s lab? Have you spied on him and his colleagues, tried to eavesdrop on their conversations? You understand that I ask these questions not to shame you, but merely because my responsibility requires it." He fell silent, his black eyes steady on her.

Nikki looked into those eyes, looking for some hint of the emotion in his voice and in his manner. There was nothing. The eyes were as cold and hard as ever, devoid of the slightest trace of humanity. It felt as though those eyes were looking deep into her, examining her soul and weighing it in some balance.

Tension knotted her belly. Should she tell him that this morning wasn't the first time she'd seen one of Funakoshi's nocturnal jaunts? *No.* For some reason, she couldn't bring herself to admit it. Even though it had been totally innocent, completely accidental, something inside her knew that Eichiro wouldn't believe that. *And then what would happen?*

"Never," she said levelly, holding his gaze with hers. "I didn't do anything to compromise the security of the project."

For a few more seconds, Eichiro stared silently into her eyes. Then he nodded sharply, as if he'd got what he wanted. "Thank you for your time, then, Carrson-*san*," he said briskly. "You may return to your duties."

She stood and turned to go. As she opened the door, she glanced back. Those black, soulless eyes seemed to glint with sharp understanding.

* * *

Why didn't I tell him? Nikki asked herself again as she walked into the refectory for lunch. *I saw something*

*I shouldn't have seen, but so what? It was an accident. And
I don't know what the hell it was anyway!*

What did I think he'd do if I told him? she thought
disgustedly. The worst he could have done was give
her a dressing down, orders to keep her curiosity
under control in the future. Nothing more. Fire her?
Send her back to Tokyo in disgrace? Not likely, considering the inconvenience of finding someone to replace
her. No, she concluded, her decision not to tell him was
just paranoia, pure and simple. *Again.* She took her
tray, selected a salad and two sticks of *yakitori*, then
chose a seat at a table near the door.

Lunch was lonely. There was nobody there she
really wanted to talk to — or, perhaps more importantly, who'd want to talk to her. She needed somebody to bounce ideas off, to talk to about what she'd
learned. O'Neil would have been good — for all his
cynical humor, he was a smart man, and he'd have
understood. Toshikazu would have been even better,
of course — it had been he who'd helped her through
the bad times in Tokyo right after the raid on Nagara.
But both were gone. *It's been a rough month for friends*,
she thought sadly. Nikki had never really had to deal
with death before, the loss of someone close. Certainly
people she knew had died; nobody could get to her age
without knowing someone who died. A boy she'd
known in high school had killed himself when he'd
driven his car into a brick wall, and a classmate from
university had died from leukemia. But neither had
been close friends. Death had always been something
that happened to other people — a distant event that
did nothing more than brush the periphery of her life.

No longer. She'd lost the closest friend she'd ever
had, and then someone who had the potential for
becoming a very close friend.

I understand how Peter must feel, she realized. She
knew what his grief must be like. *And Professor Black —*

how much worse must it be for him? He lost his son … No wonder he was withdrawn, rude, hostile. Although she still couldn't bring herself to like the man, she found she could empathize with him. *To understand all is to forgive all? Maybe.*

Her thoughts turned back to Peter. He might be someone she could talk to about what was going on. She knew he wouldn't understand the details of what she'd learned — as a self-styled "scientist," his understanding of biology and biochemistry seemed incredibly limited. And she was positive he couldn't comprehend her misgivings, her fears about what Eichiro was up to. He was simply too honest and straightforward for that. (*And what does that say about me?* she asked herself.)

Nevertheless, it would be good to talk to *someone.* Even if he couldn't understand the details and the complexities, she knew that Peter Hollingforth would be supportive. And that's just what she needed at the moment. Maybe she should sneak out of the outpost, meet up with the soldier who'd be watching from the jungle fringe, and go see Peter …

Annoyed at herself, she shook her head. *That's dumb, Nikki,* she told herself. *Risking the ire of Eichiro and the rest, just because you're too weak to handle it on your own?* If she had something important to tell him — if she'd found out something about the weretiger — then maybe. But now it just didn't make sense.

She looked up as she heard a familiar voice. A group of security guards had entered the refectory, seating themselves at a table nearby. Dei was among them. As before, he flashed her a quick smile, then went back to his conversation. *At least there's somebody here who doesn't hate me,* she thought. She shook her head again at her emotional reaction, and returned her concentration to her lunch.

Even though she wasn't actively listening, she

couldn't help but overhear the guards' conversation. "I didn't see it, I told you," one of the men was saying. "It was Uramatsu in Section Three. He saw it, and so did some other men in his section."

"*Honto*?" Dei asked. "Truly? Then why wasn't anything said?"

"They were ordered not to speak of it," the first man said.

"So you're breaking regulations telling us about it?" another guard put in. "Thank you so much for including us in your infraction."

"When was this?" Dei queried.

"After the helicopter crash," the first guard replied. "Section Three was sent out to recover the bodies, remember? That's when he saw it."

"That's when he *imagined* it," another voice corrected. "Come on, you expect us to believe Uramatsu saw some kind of half-man half-beast?"

The words jolted Nikki like an electric shock. She snapped her head round to stare at the security guards. Sensing her eyes on them, they fell silent. All but Dei stared at her challengingly.

"*Sumimasen*," she said hesitantly, "excuse me, but what was that? What did you see?"

The guard who'd spoken first looked at her scornfully. "Your question is out of place," he began. "Security regulations prohibit ..."

But Dei laid a restraining hand on his arm, shot him a look that Nikki translated as "She's okay."

The man's opposition subsided. He was young, Nikki saw, like most of the security personnel, and probably enjoyed the opportunity to be the center of attention. "It wasn't me, Carrson-*san*, it was Uramatsu."

Nikki nodded in understanding. "But what was it he saw?" she pressed.

The man blinked in reaction to her urgency. "I don't quite know, Carrson-*san*," he said. "What he *said* he saw was a human-like figure covered with fur. When it spotted him, it dropped down onto all-fours and ran away like a beast."

One of the other guards snorted. "Nonsense, of course."

Nikki nodded slowly. "Nonsense," she agreed quietly. But deep inside she knew otherwise.

* * *

The conversation stayed with her as she returned to her quarters after lunch. *Half-man half-beast.* She remembered the security guard's words as she sat down at the computer. *Sounds like a weretiger, doesn't it?* Now the question was, what to do with the information?

Peter and his colleagues would probably want to know that the *thing* was still in the area — or, at least, that it had been a couple of days ago. That was the kind of information they needed. But how to get it to them? As she'd returned to her building from the refectory, she'd seen the gate of the compound had been open. That probably meant security teams were out in the jungle, searching for the zombies that had threatened her. The gate had been open, sure, but there'd been two very tense-looking guards standing by it, weapons at the ready. How could she get past them? She'd have to give that some thought.

She powered up her computer and keyed in the command to retrieve the analyses stored in her personal directory. The computer hummed for a few seconds, the screen remaining blank. Then the first graph appeared on the screen.

She leaned forward, staring at the machine in puzzlement. Usually computer response was a lot faster than that. When she'd been viewing the records earlier this morning, it had taken the system less than a second to flash the first graph on the screen. Why was it slower now?

She thought it through. It had to mean that somebody else was using the system — or multiple people — doing something that required a lot of processing overhead. No matter how fast the central mainframe was, if the demands on its processing power got too much the overall system response would degrade. What could be using so much computing power?

Breaking the security on my personal files? The thought struck her with an almost physical impact. Suddenly feeling cold, she remembered the events back in Tokyo, when her personal directory there had been locked, and then when the strange file — STORM.LET — had appeared in the directory listing. Was somebody accessing her personal files again?

She shook her head. *That's paranoia talking again*, she reprimanded herself. *Why would they bother?* It just didn't make sense.

But, nevertheless, it *did* seem a pointless risk to keep the files around any longer. She'd studied them for so long, so intently, that she was sure she could draw them accurately by hand if she ever had to. If somebody ever did bother to check her directory — Eichiro, for example, at the urging of Funakoshi — the fact that she had the files would only cast more suspicion on her. *Just what I need.*

Working quickly, she commanded the computer to erase the files. When they were gone, just to make sure, she removed the entire directory. That way, she thought, if anybody looks, they might find out that some files used to exist, but there would be no way to discover exactly what they were — even what they were named.

With that out of the way, she felt a little better. *But would anybody ever have bothered looking?* she asked herself. *Why would the computer services people ever make the effort?*

The answer was obvious: yes, they would have made the effort ... if they were ordered to. The personnel of Nagara were very conscientious when it came to following orders, even if those orders made little sense.

An idea that had been nagging at the edge of her mind suddenly became clear. She sat back, staring into nothingness, while she thought it through. Yes, she decided after a moment, *it had a good chance of working*. She powered down the computer and left the room — checking that her pistol still hung at her hip as she did so.

*   *   *

The stockade gate was still open, she saw, but the security men guarding it didn't seem to be there. Maybe she wouldn't have to try the ploy she'd devised after all. She straightened her back, put energy and determination into her step as she strode toward the gate. *People are less likely to question you if you look like you know what you're doing*, she told herself.

She was only a couple of yards from the gate when the security guard appeared. *He must have been standing around the corner*, Nikki realized. The man raised his hand in the international gesture for "Stop."

Nikki didn't slow her pace, she just strode up to him. She forced her face into an expression of intensity and concern. "*There* you are," she said briskly before he could speak. "I thought maybe you were shirking your duty."

The guard's eyes opened wide. Shirking duty was one of the worst crimes in the canon of Japanese sins, she knew. "No, Carrson-*san*," he said quickly, "I was attending to my duties. I'd just stepped away for a moment, I could still see the gate, and …"

She cut him off with a sharp gesture. "It doesn't matter. You're here now. Eichiro-*san* and Hongo-*san* want to see you, right now, in Eichiro-*san*'s office."

"*Honto*?" he asked in surprise. "Why?"

She pumped as much scorn as she could into her voice. "It wasn't my place to ask," she said haughtily — with the unstated implication, "It isn't yours either."

Her words struck home, she could see it in his eyes. He drew himself up to attention. "*Hai*, Carrson-*san*," he barked, "yes, of course." He hesitated. "What about the gate, though? The gate must be watched ..."

"Do you think Eichiro-*san* would not have thought of that?"

"Then another guard is coming to take my duty?" He bowed sharply. "Then I will go, Carrson-*san*." And then he turned on his heel and headed for the administration building at double-time.

Nikki watched him go, a smile creeping onto her face. *Blind obedience to authority*, she thought, *or even supposed authority. It's useful sometimes*. She turned and strode out through the gate, keeping her pace steady and determined. She looked around her as she walked. There were no other security guards in view. *Good*.

And what will happen when he finds out Eichiro doesn't want him? she thought. She shrugged. *Well, I never said outright that Eichiro had told me directly — personally — to pass the word*. When it came down to it, she could always claim that one of the other security guards had told her to pass the message. *Which one? So sorry, Eichiro-san, I don't know. You realize that all Japanese look alike to Westerners*. (She smiled. A cliche with little truth to it, but cliches are sometimes convenient to hide behind.) And why didn't she ask why the guard was supposed to leave the gate? *But one doesn't question orders, Eichiro-san, isn't that right?*

She knew they wouldn't believe her, but there wasn't any proof — *hard* proof — that she was lying. So what did it really matter? And again, what could they do to her? Ship her back to Tokyo? The information she had to pass to Peter was important. She was aware that she was letting her emotions — her desire to help Peter, her need to talk to *someone* — get in the way of her logic. But she had to admit it didn't really matter at the moment.

She reached the edge of the clearing without seeing anyone and, she figured, without anyone spotting her. If someone *had* seen her, they'd definitely have stopped her, or at least yelled after her. She ducked into the cover of the jungle, walked a few more yards forward until she couldn't see the clearing behind her. Then she stopped, quickly checked that the flap on her holster was unsnapped and the pistol ready to draw. She looked around her.

In the bright sunlight, the jungle was beautiful — still alien, but beautiful nonetheless. Memories of the zombies — *or zuvembies, or whatever the hell they were* — filled her mind, and she felt the short hairs at the nape of her neck stir.

But I'm relatively safe here, she told herself. *I'm close enough to the clearing to make a run for it. There's a soldier out here somewhere — he must have seen me leave the outpost — ready to protect me. And I've got this.* She rested her hand on the ridged butt of the automatic pistol. *This time I know to cock it if anything happens.* She checked her watch. *I'll give him five minutes*, she decided. *If he doesn't show up by then, I'll go back.*

She heard the soldier before she saw him — cautious movement through the underbrush. She drew the pistol, snapped off the safety and drew back on the slide the way Dei had shown her. Then she put the safety catch back on, carefully held the barrel pointing at the ground. *Just in case it* isn't *the soldier*.

But it was. She saw a flash of scarlet through the undergrowth, then the soldier was next to her. It was Muir, a large bolt-action rifle held casually before him. The weapon had a lethal-looking bayonet — a long knife with a razor-edged blade — mounted below the barrel, extending a good eighteen inches beyond the muzzle. Polished steel flashed in the beams of sunlight filtering through the foliage above.

The young man smiled at her, showing crooked

teeth. "Good afternoon, Miss Carlson," he whispered. "Would you like to come with me, ma'am?"

"That would be fine, thank you," she said primly, smiling in return. She slipped the pistol back into her holster, and followed the soldier as he started off toward the expedition's camp.

They followed a narrow path through the lush undergrowth, barely wider than Nikki's shoulders. Throughout the journey, she kept looking around her, for anything that looked out of the ordinary. Muir was keeping a careful lookout too, she noticed. *Another two minutes to the camp*, she figured ...

There was no warning, no warning whatsoever. One moment she and Muir were alone, the only things larger than small birds that were moving in the jungle. Then she saw a flash of movement ahead.

Almost magically, a black-clad figure appeared in the path ahead of them. A familiar figure — Nikki had seen one very much like it before. Her thoughts churned in panic and confusion. She looked around wildly, surprised that she wasn't in the narrow alleyways of Shinjuku.

That was where she'd see this figure, or one like it, before. The ninja who'd killed Toshikazu ...

Ahead of her, Muir reared back in shock. But then his military training took over. He swung his gun down from port-arms, brought the barrel to bear and pulled the trigger. The rifle crashed, its report muffled by the heavy growth around them.

With almost unnatural speed, the ninja spun aside, dodging off the soldier's line of fire. Instead of slamming full into his chest, the bullet merely plucked at the shoulder of his black garb. In the same movement, the ninja drew his *katana* from the sheath on his back and leaped forward.

Muir was trying to jack another round into the rifle, but he didn't have time. The katana flashed toward his neck. At the last instant, Muir brought his rifle up, parrying the sword with the gun's barrel. Steel clashed against steel. Muir countered instantly, quick as a cat, thrusting the lethal bayonet toward his opponent's belly.

Even quicker, the ninja threw himself aside, the bayonet missing his flesh by inches. The long sword whistled as he wheeled it around his head, directing another cut at the soldier. Again, Muir barely blocked the blow — the razor-sharp blade chunking deep into the rifle's wooden stock.

"*Run*, Miss Carlson," the soldier yelled.

It was an echo from her memories, from her nightmares. For a few racing heartbeats she stood frozen.

The sword was still imbedded in the rifle butt. Muir twisted hard, trying to break the blade, or at least disarm his enemy. But somehow the ninja managed to free his weapon. Before he could dance back out of range, however, the soldier brought the bayonet around, slashing it into a black-clad thigh. The ninja gasped with pain.

As if the sound had been a magical spell, Nikki found herself able to move again. But what should she do? *Run*? That was the logical move, but it would be too much like a replay of the events in Shinjuku. She couldn't leave someone else to his death, defending her at the cost of his own life. She pulled her pistol, snapped off the safety, and stepped off the path into the underbrush. She levelled the gun, squeezing the trigger to turn on the sighting laser.

It wasn't easy to get a shot. Ninja and soldier were moving too fast, as if in some lethal dance. Cut and parry, thrust and counter, riposte and block. A lightning-fast slash had got through Muir's guard. He'd managed to duck — otherwise the flashing blade would have cloven his head in two like a melon — but he was bleeding from a scalp cut, blood masking the left side of his face. The red aiming dot drifted over the two figures as Nikki waited for a clean opening.

She didn't have to wait long. Muir again brought his rifle up to parry a cut, but at the last moment the ninja flexed his wrists, deflecting the angle of the blade's travel. Instead of striking the poised rifle, it slashed into Muir's forearm, cutting cleanly through bone and muscle. The young soldier howled, staring in horror at the stump of his arm, gouting jets of bright blood. Then the ninja's return cut took his head from his shoulders. The decapitated body crumpled ...

Which gave Nikki the opening she needed — *but at such cost*. The laser spot steadied on the ninja's chest. She pulled the trigger.

The ninja must have seen the laser out of the corner of his eye, understood what it meant. Just as Nikki squeezed the trigger and the small gun boomed, he tried to spin aside again.

Not fast enough. The gun kicked in Nikki's hand, harder than she'd expected. The report was deafening. But the shot went true.

Or almost true. The ninja's movement was enough to take him partially off-line, enough so that Nikki shot didn't slam into his heart. Instead, the flechettes — dozens of tiny metal slivers — tore into his right shoulder. In horror, Nikki saw the shoulder seem to explode into a cloud of blood and tissue. Agony wrenched a guttural cry from the man's throat. The katana fell from suddenly nerveless fingers, and he lurched backward from the impact of the round.

But somehow he managed to lash his left arm around. Something flew from his hand, something that flashed metal-bright in the sunlight. Nikki threw herself aside — just in time — as a sharp-bladed throwing-star parted the air next to her ear and thudded into the bole of a tree behind her. She squawked in horror turned and ran.

He should be dead! The thought pounded in her head as she fled through the jungle. *I shot him in the chest, he should be dead.*

But only once, another part of her brain pointed out. What was it Dei had said? *If you have to shoot someone or something, keep firing. Keep firing until your gun is empty, or until your opponent goes down and doesn't get up again.*

She heard movement in the undergrowth behind her. Running footsteps.

No!! she screamed silently. *He can't be after me, he can't!*

But he was, she knew. Somehow the wounded ninja had found the strength to pursue her, despite the horrible wound in his shoulder. Sobbing in terror, she forced herself to run on.

The crashing in the bushes behind her was getting closer. Even wounded, he could run faster than she could. She desperately wanted to turn, to shoot him again, to empty the clip of flechette rounds into him. But, judging from the sound, if she stopped — even if she slowed down — he'd be on her before she could do anything. *And will shooting him again do any good anyway?* the thought yammered in her brain. *One shot would have killed any normal man.*

Where the hell was she? Which direction was she running? Unlike the first time, her panic hadn't obliterated her sense of direction. She knew she was running toward the clearing where Hollingforth and the others had their camp. She couldn't be more than a few dozen yards away. If she could keep ahead of the ninja for just a few more seconds … She ignored the pounding in her chest, forced herself to run harder.

Without warning she burst into the clearing. The sudden sunlight, no longer attenuated by the foliage, dazzled her. Peter and a couple of the others were there, she saw. But they were too far away to help her. She knew the ninja was right behind her, ready to slice her in two. Nobody could save her.

Nobody but me. The thought was sharp and clear. She turned, still running, brought her pistol up. Her momentum carried her over backward, but as she fell she saw the laser dot on the ninja's stomach, less than two yards away. The *katana*, held in only one hand now, was raised for the killing stroke. She pulled the trigger, saw the flechettes shred the ninja's abdomen.

Simultaneously a rifle boomed behind her. With a solid *whock* noise, the ninja's head burst like a watermelon struck by a sledgehammer. She crashed to the ground, the air driven from her lungs by the impact, while the headless body crumpled bonelessly a couple of feet away. The *katana* blade flashed in the sunlight as it fell.

Temporarily winded, she rolled over, looked back at the others. Hollingforth and Black were standing stock-still, their mouths open in surprise and horror. As she watched, MacHeath lowered his rifle from his shoulder. His expression was calm, controlled — professional.

Suddenly overcome with reaction to the terror and the flight, Nikki wretched uncontrollably. She felt a calming hand on her shoulder, but couldn't look up — couldn't move at all — until the spasms in her belly had stopped. Finally she was able to climb to her feet, wiping her mouth with the back of her hand, then wiping off the dark bile on her shorts.

Hollingforth and MacHeath were beside her, concern on their faces. It was Peter whose hand was still resting, comfortingly, on her shoulder. Black stood a few paces away. He was as horrified by events as the others were, she could tell.

It was Peter who spoke first, his voice hushed with shock. "Miss Carlson — Nikki — what happened?"

She took a deep breath to clear her mind. MacHeath handed her a water bottle. She took a mouthful, swished it around in her mouth to clear away the taste of vomit, then spat it on the ground. Another mouthful. This time she swallowed. Then she handed the bottle back to the sergeant with a smile of thanks.

"What happened?" Peter asked again.

Briefly Nikki described what had happened — her meeting with Muir, the appearance of the black-clad swordsman, the fight in the jungle.

MacHeath's face clouded as she described the death of the young soldier. "Muir was good with the bayonet, he was," he pronounced sadly, "one of the best I ever trained. He would have made a fine sergeant someday." He smiled down at Nikki, his expression suddenly fatherly. "You handled yourself well, Miss Carlson. Excellently well. Your shot would have put paid to him without my interference. I should have conserved my ammunition."

The sergeant stepped forward and prodded the bloody figure with his toe. "And just what *is* this ... this *gentleman* anyway?"

"A ninja," Nikki said shortly. "A trained killer."

MacHeath raised his eyebrows. "A ninja? That's Nipponese, isn't it?" He bent down and picked up the blood-wet *katana*, carefully tested its edge. "Bloody fine piece of steel," he said admiringly. "And he knew how to use it, I warrant?"

Nikki nodded.

"But what the bloody hell is he doing here?" Hollingforth almost exploded. "And why was he chasing you?"

"To kill me," Nikki said tiredly.

"But *why*?"

To kill me. The words echoed in her brain. *To kill me.* She'd seen a ninja twice: once here, and once in Shinjuku. In Tokyo, she hadn't known where the killer had come from, or whether he was after her or Toshikazu. Here, though? There was no doubt. She had to be the target.

Did that mean she'd been the real target the first time as well?

And where had this ninja come from? Ninjas were Japanese — "Nipponese," as MacHeath had said. The only Japanese in the area were at the outpost. *But Eichiro didn't bring ninjas with him ...*

But of course he did. She remembered the dark-clad figures standing in the shadows the night she'd seen the first science expedition returning to the outpost from the jungle. She remembered the way they'd just faded into the darkness when they were dismissed, almost as if they'd never really existed. What could they have been other than ninjas?

So Nagara had sent ninjas after her, not once but twice. Why?

Her mind went back to the first time, that night near the Kirin yaki bar. What could have motivated an attempt on her life? What had been happening at Nagara then?

It was easy enough to remember. The raid by the "wreckers," the suspicion of inside help. Eichiro had been in serious trouble, she recalled, the security precautions he'd been in charge of had failed completely. The only way he could get off the hook, if only to some degree, was by proving the raiders had inside help. (Nikki remembered Toshikazu had figured that one out.)

Okay, so that explained the attempt at framing her — the bogus computer file, and the kangaroo court in Eichiro's office. But what good would killing her do?

Unless the plan was to have me killed, then concoct more evidence when I wasn't around to refute it. That made a ghastly kind of sense. But then why didn't he finish the job? Why had the ninja not come after her once he'd killed Toshikazu? Taking the present ninja — the one who lay dead at her feet — as a sample, the man in Tokyo should have had little trouble running her down. So why?

Maybe because Toshikazu's death would do the job, she realized. Evidence could be faked up incriminating Toshikazu as the traitor as easily as to frame her. Maybe the ninja's orders were to eliminate one of them. Either one would do — although Nikki figured she was still the target of choice because, as a *gaijin*, she'd be easier for people to distrust.

Again, that hung together. But the question remained: why, then, didn't Eichiro follow through with his plan and implicate Toshikazu?

Or maybe he did. From out of nowhere, she remembered a conversation between two technicians she'd overheard in the elevator right after Toshikazu's funeral. The grapevine had claimed that the traitor — the Nagara employee who'd helped the "wreckers" — had been captured, but shot while attempting to escape. Nobody knew who the traitor was … nobody outside the executive offices, at least. Wasn't it possible that Eichiro had put together false evidence incriminating Toshikazu — who was now dead — and shown it to Kubota and the other senior executives? With Toshikazu himself not able to defend his name, and nobody else in the organization aware of who the "traitor" was, there'd be no-one to refute Eichiro's claims.

Maybe that was why Eichiro had come out of everything so well — relatively speaking, of course. He'd had to scramble to make up for the loss of the original Special Projects lab — hence the Inderagiri Research Facility — but at least he hadn't been fired in shame, which would be the usual penalty for a screw-up the magnitude of the "wreckers'" raid.

Quickly she ran it all through one last time in her mind. Yes, that tied up all loose ends. Of course there was no proof, but this would never be discussed in a court of law, she knew that.

Suddenly she felt cold, a combination of rage and

fear welling up inside her. Up to that moment, her review of the facts had been entirely intellectual — like a kind of logic puzzle. But now the emotional reality of her conclusions struck home. *Eichiro killed Toshikazu,* she told herself. *He killed my* friend, *and he tried to kill* me. She balled her fists, feeling her knuckles like knobs of hard ivory under the skin.

Abruptly she realized the two men were staring at her quizzically. In the back of her mind was the knowledge that Hollingforth had asked her a question, but she couldn't remember what it was.

"I'm sorry," she told him, "what was that again?"

"I asked 'why,'" Hollingforth repeated. "Why did the ninja want to kill you, and who sent him?"

"My employer sent him," she said, surprised at the lack of emotion in her tone. "Agatamori Eichiro. He wants to see me dead."

"Another Nipponese?" MacHeath queried. Nikki answered with a nod.

"But *why*?" There was real anguish in Peter Hollingforth's voice.

He probably can't understand how anyone can betray any kind of trust, Nikki told herself. She started to answer, but MacHeath spoke first. His voice was quiet, but seemed as impossible to ignore as a rifle-shot. "You know aye too much," he suggested, "isn't that it, ma'am?"

She looked at him. *Perceptive man,* she thought, *more perceptive than he looks.*

Because that was what it had to be, of course. She'd stirred up Eichiro's pet scientist by asking him questions and by showing up, by accident, at the wrong place. She'd seen the late-night expedition returning; Eichiro didn't know the details of that, but Nikki was convinced he'd known she was lying when she said she'd seen nothing else out of the ordinary. And then she'd kept copies of the serum analyses on her personal computer — Nikki knew that Eichiro, or his security drones, had found them. Finally, she'd tricked a gullible security guard at the gate, and vanished into the jungle.

Where did Eichiro think she'd be going with what she knew? She couldn't even guess. But, judging from her limited experience with corporate Japan, his first conclusion would be that she was selling out to some enemy of Nagara. She snorted. *You think I know a lot more than I actually do*, she thought. *I haven't got the first clue what's really going on at the outpost.*

She realized that MacHeath was still waiting for an answer to his question. "Yes, Sergeant MacHeath," she told him, "I know too much. I know too much to live," she added bitterly, "and I don't know anything at all."

* * *

There was no way she could return to the outpost, that was for sure. Nikki lay on her back in the camp clearing, staring up at the infinity of sky above her, as it faded to the royal blue of early evening.

At first she'd wondered just how Eichiro was planning to cover up her murder — or her disappearance — if the ninja had managed to succeed. It didn't take her long to figure it out, though. All he'd have to do would be leak the word that — despite her lucky escape the last time — Carrson-*san* had wandered off into the jungle. The obvious conclusion would be that, this time, Carrson-*san* hadn't been so lucky ... particularly if a security sweep happened upon bloodstained scraps of her clothing, looking like they'd been shredded by fangs or claws. Oh yes, it would be entirely too easy for Eichiro to cover up her elimination.

Just like he covered up Toshikazu's. She ground her teeth in anger. He'd done it differently, but he'd got away scott-free with that murder too.

Eichiro killed my friend, she told herself again, *and he tried to kill me*. His decision to come down here had led indirectly to O'Neil's death — *so doesn't that mean Eichiro killed him too?* And then, of course, there was Private Muir, the soldier who'd lost his life trying to protect Nikki. Eichiro had a lot to answer for. *And he's* going *to answer for it*, she swore to herself, *every last bit of it*.

But how? There was nothing she could do directly. She couldn't burst into the camp, charge into his office and empty her pistol into his chest. Even if it was physically possible, there was no way she could bring herself to do it. *That'd make me no better than him*, she recognized.

Still, she wanted to hurt him — hurt him badly. She had no legal recourse, she knew — even though seeing him humiliated in court would be apt punishment. She had no proof — no proof whatsoever — that he'd done anything illegal. So what did that leave?

Over to her right she could hear the sounds of MacHeath and the two surviving soldiers preparing supper. Hollingforth and Black were in quiet conversation, discussing how they could use Nikki's information — that the weretiger had apparently been spotted by the outpost's security — to their advantage.

How would Peter handle this? she asked herself. *How would he see Eichiro punished?*

She chuckled to herself as the obvious answer came to mind. *He'd challenge Eichiro to a duel, that's what he'd do*, she reflected. *Pistols at dawn, and that kind of thing.*

And Eichiro would just whistle up a ninja to cut Peter in two. Her smile faded. *No*, she considered, *Peter wasn't the duelling type. He'd just decide Eichiro was a "merchant," a "shopkeeper," and write him off.* She closed her eyes, tried to shut out the disturbing thoughts.

Then, suddenly, her eyes snapped open again. *Eichiro's a merchant.* The thought reverberated around her brain. *And how do you hurt a merchant?*

A grim smile spread over her face. She'd have to give this serious thought.

* * *

The jungle was dark, and alive with noise — the whirring of insects, the rustle of small animals moving through the bush, the occasional growl of a predator and the death-squeal of prey. Nikki moved through the undergrowth as quietly as she could. Her pistol was in her hand, cocked, and safety off. Her finger was on the trigger, but not pressing hard enough to activate the sighting laser. Her eyes, well-adapted to the night by this time, scanned all around her.

This is nerve-wracking, she thought. Every time she'd been alone in the jungle — or not even alone — something terrible had happened. This time, though, she was ready — or as ready as she could be. This time she had a real goal, a mission. This time she felt like the hunter, not the hunted.

Part of her mind jabbered, *This is stupid. This is suicidal.* But the more rational part of her was calm, knowing that this was the most logical thing she could do — the only way she could ever strike back at Eichiro.

When Hollingforth and the others had called it a night, she'd gone to her tent too, but she hadn't slept. Constantly checking her watch, she'd waited an hour and a half, until some time after one in the morning. That should give Peter and Black time to fall into a deep sleep. Certainly, she knew that MacHeath and the other soldiers were keeping watch. But she'd observed their movements from behind the flap of the tent. She knew their routine, had been able to see when they were facing away from her. When the time was right, she'd pulled the tent flap back and raced across the open space into the jungle. Nobody had spotted her.

And now she was heading for the outpost.

How do I hurt Eichiro? she asked herself again, this time with a grim smile. The answer was simple as soon as she posed the question in the right way. *How do you hurt a merchant?*

She had to find out what it was that Eichiro was up to, the real purpose of the outpost. Obviously, that purpose was important — important enough to kill to protect — and one that Eichiro wanted to keep secret. Once she knew that secret, she could spread it across the newspapers of the world, pass it on to all the corporations in competition with Nagara. That would destroy the market advantage that Nagara had to be looking for. It would cost Nagara money, and it would cost Eichiro his job. *And* that's *how you hurt a merchant*, she told herself.

When the idea had first come to her, she'd desperately wanted to bounce it off someone, work through the ramifications, and pick out any weaknesses that she might have missed. She would have liked to talk it over with Peter …

But that wouldn't have been a wise choice, she'd recognized at once. Peter, with his ethical code — which she thought of as Victorian — would have refused to allow her to do what she had to. Even if she'd persuaded him that it was necessary, he'd have insisted that he go along — how could he let a woman go alone into danger? She smiled. His protectiveness was charming, in its way, although it was totally misplaced. Peter wasn't scientist enough to understand what he'd see inside the outpost. He didn't know how things worked, how the security guards operated and thought. If he'd accompanied her, he'd have made some mistake — "blown" the mission, to use a phrase from the spy novels she'd read as a child — and got them both killed. Or — almost worse — he'd have got *himself* killed, and then Nikki would have to face losing another friend. And this time it would be worse than before: she'd know that she'd directly caused his death. No, that just wasn't acceptable.

It took her over twenty-five minutes to reach the outpost clearing. Now she crouched at the margin of the jungle, examining the stockade in the moonlight. The gate was closed. That was unfortunate, and she could have hoped otherwise, but she hadn't really expected a stroke of luck. And she hadn't depended on it in her planning. She moved back into the jungle, out of sight of any security guards near the fence.

Moving like a wraith in the night, she made her way clockwise around the roughly circular clearing. Throughout the journey she stayed near the fringe of the jungle — close enough that she could see if anyone left the stockade, but enough under cover that she was confident nobody could see her. Even though most of her focus was on the outpost, she didn't forget to keep a close eye on the jungle around her. She remembered the attempted ambush by the zombies. She wouldn't let that happen again.

At one point she was sure she heard stealthy movement through the undergrowth—the rustling of leaves, the occasional crack of a breaking branch. But it sounded like it was some distance away. She crouched motionless, silent, listening. The sounds were still there. Yes, certainly *something* was moving through the jungle. But it wasn't near her, and if anything seemed to be getting further away. She shrugged, and moved on.

It took her another ten minutes to reach the river. She was at the furthest western extension of the compound. From her position in the periphery of the jungle, she could see the stockade fence where it extended out from the river bank, out into the water. Maybe fifty feet out, the fence ended. *How deep is the water at that point?* Nikki wondered. Almost certainly over her head.

So she'd have to swim for it. Well, that's what she'd

expected. That was why she'd come to this side of the clearing when her objective — the secured science lab — was on the other side of the outpost. If she'd come in from the other side, she'd have had to swim against the current. This way she could let it carry her, saving a lot of energy.

The swim was expected. But that didn't mean she relished the idea. In the moonlight the water of the Inderagiri River looked black and oily, roiled slightly by the current. What lurked beneath that opaque, concealing surface? Aquatic analogues of the monsters prowling the jungle? No, there couldn't be anything totally out-of-hand like that, otherwise the builders would never have left the outpost open to the riverbank.

At least, the river wouldn't contain anything that would threaten people on shore, then. But what about swimmers? Even something totally mundane — like pirhanas, for example, or their Sumatran cousins — would ruin her night.

She let the second thoughts flow through her mind for a few moments, then ruthlessly crushed them. She hadn't come this far to turn back now. She'd known the risks, and they were ones she could accept — when she compared them with the potential gains, at least. Quietly, she crept to the river's edge and stepped in.

The warmth of the water came as a surprise. Intellectually she knew that water retained its heat longer than the land, absorbing it and giving it up more slowly. That was why areas near large bodies of water had more moderate climates than inland areas. That was intellectually. Emotionally, though, a river at night *should* be cold.

The ground sloped off gently as she walked slowly into the river. When she was waist-deep, she squatted down so that only her head was above water — that and the hand holding her pistol. She could feel the current tugging at her — nowhere near strongly enough to pull her from her feet or put her at any risk. But it certainly was there. Making sure that she didn't splash or leave too much of a wake, she waded deeper.

By the time she was thirty feet out from shore, the water would have only come up to her chest if she'd stood up. A few feet later, so suddenly that her head almost went under, the river bottom just dropped away from under her feet. She kicked her legs, treading water to stay afloat. It was difficult when she had to concentrate on keeping her gun hand clear of the river. Maybe she should clench the gun in her teeth, like a movie pirate? She chuckled at the image — *Nikki Carlson, scourge of the Barbary Coast*. If she had to, she'd do it. At the moment it didn't seem necessary.

As soon as her feet left the bottom, it looked to her that the river bank, and the stockade fence, had started to move slowly upstream, to the west. The opposite was actually the case, of course: with nothing to hold herself in place, the current had a hold of her and was carrying her to the east, downstream. She couldn't feel herself move, but that was because the water that surrounded her was moving downstream at exactly the same speed. By watching the bank drifting by, she tried to judge that speed — a couple of miles an hours, she guessed, a little less than a walking pace. Kicking, and paddling with her free arm, she increased her distance from the bank.

The extended end of the stockade fence passed her by — or she passed by *it* — almost close enough to reach out and touch it. As soon as she was past, she began kicking and paddling again — much more cautiously now, since noise was a major risk — to bring herself back to shore. After a few feet, the bank seemed to slow its stately glide by as the current slackened. *I have to be in the shelter of the fence*, she realized. Without the current to worry about, she could be even more careful about keeping totally silent.

From this angle, she could see quite a bit of the

compound. There were no lights, and to her relief the whole region seemed empty.

No, that wasn't quite true. There was movement, over toward the building that contained Funakoshi's lab. Two security guards — she could see them better as they moved out of the building's shadow into the moonlight. They carried rifles of some kind — much smaller than those carried by MacHeath and his men, but even more lethal-seeming for that. Their faces looked bulbous, bloated ... *Night-vision goggles*, Nikki realized with a sudden chill. *I knew they had them; I spotted them when I saw Funakoshi's first expedition coming back. But I just plain forgot about them*. That was a serious risk. She'd been depending on the night to shield her from view. But with night-vision goggles — if they worked as well as they did in the movies — these guards could see as well as if it had been full daylight.

As she watched, one of the guards glanced out over the river. She could almost feel his gaze, scanning like a spotlight beam, across the water. She wanted to duck underwater, but feared any movement would make her even more noticeable to the security men. The guard's gaze passed over her — stopped and scanned back. He stopped walking.

He sees me. No, she corrected at once, *he sees* something; *he isn't sure what it is*.

She saw the guard speak to his colleague, but the distance was too great for her to hear the words. They started walking slowly toward the riverbank. One had his rifle at the ready, its barrel pointing in Nikki's direction. *They're coming for me*, she realized with a spasm of fear, *they're coming to kill me*.

What the hell was she to do? Turn and swim off, hope they wouldn't fire after her? She felt her gun as a reassuring weight in her hand. Kill them before they can kill me? No, she couldn't even think about that.

None of this was the security guards' fault; they were just following Eichiro's orders. She couldn't make them suffer — make them die — for his crimes.

No, if they came close to her, or looked like they were about to shoot, she'd identify herself, give herself up. Concoct some story about how she came to be drifting down the Inderagiri River at two in the morning. She'd tell everyone she could about the ninja attack, tell them that Eichiro was trying to kill her.

But that wouldn't work, would it? Eichiro would just have her declared insane — her claims would certainly sound unbalanced to any loyal Nagara employee — and then have her quietly eliminated later. There had to be another answer. But what? The guards drew closer.

What was that? A sudden rip of sound, a brutal, flat drumming from the direction of the gate. The guards heard it at the same moment, spinning around, instantly forgetting about whatever it was they'd seen in the river. Nikki saw them exchange quick looks, then jog of in the direction of the commotion.

Lucky escape, Nikki told herself. The adrenalin of fear was still coursing through her body, making her shudder. *They're gone, but they'll probably be back.* Luck had given her this opportunity, but she had to take advantage of it. More quickly, now that there was no-one around to see her, she swam into the shallows, then waded out onto the bank.

Her sodden clothes clung to her, dripping. *I must look like an escapee from a wet T-shirt contest*, she thought wryly. Even though the night was warm, she knew her wet clothing would make her chill down really fast. If she didn't want to get numbed by cold, and maybe pick up a good case of pneumonia, she had to hurry. In squelching shoes, she jogged toward Funakoshi's lab building.

The sound came again, the same harsh drumming.

This time she recognized it: it had to be a machine-gun or submachine-gun firing on full automatic. (She'd never seen or heard one fire, of course — except for on TV or in the movies, and that didn't count — but what else could it be?) Other weapons joined it, and now she could hear cries of fear of pain, merged with screams that couldn't have come from human throats. *What the hell's going on? It sounds like a war.* Her curiosity was almost overpowering — she wanted to find out what was happening — but she forced herself to stay in control. *No!* she told herself sharply. *I'm here for a reason, not as a spectator.*

She reached the secure lab building, flattened herself against a wall around the corner from the main door. Cautiously, she peeked around the corner …

And was heartily glad she'd done so. A security guard — a *nervous* security guard, his weapon at the ready, and looking entirely too edgy for safety — was standing in front of the door. Nikki pulled her head back before he could spot her. Her heart pounded in her chest, and it was all she could do to keep herself from panting with tension. When she was sure she had herself under better control, she peered around the corner again.

She needn't have worried, she saw immediately. The guard wasn't looking her way. She'd approached from the river side; he was looking in diametrically the opposite direction, toward where the sounds of battle rang out. *He doesn't want to be here,* Nikki realized. *He wants to be in it, whatever it is.*

That was all very well, but how was she going to get past him? She thought about it for a few moments.

The problem was solved for her. The guard raised his had to his ear, to the radio headsets all security personnel wore on duty. "*Uramatsu desu,*" he snapped into the microphone, identifying himself ("This is Uramatsu"). He listened for a moment, then nodded sharply as if the person on the radio could see him. "*Hai*, Hongo-*san*. Immediately."

The guard turned, pounded on the door behind him. When it opened, he gabbled something so fast that Nikki couldn't catch it. Then, weapon at the ready, he ran toward the distant gate. Two more security guards, these two carrying only pistols, burst from the door and followed.

Nikki watched until they'd disappeared. She smiled grimly. Whatever was going on, it had drawn away the security guards. *Or some of them, at least,* she amended quickly. There still could be some on duty inside.

Looking around to make sure she wasn't being observed, she ran to the door. The guards had left it open a crack. She paused, listening for a moment. But there was no way she could hear anything over the sound of gunfire. *Only one way to find out if there's anyone there,* she told herself. Gently she opened the door.

There was no-one there; the hallway before her was empty. She stepped in, blinking her eyes rapidly. As with her building, at night only half of the overhead lights were on. But even that level of illumination was painful after more than an hour of nothing but moonlight. She wiped tears from her eyes as she pulled the door closed behind her.

This building seemed to have much the same layout as the one containing her lab and her quarters — which made sense. Why use more than one floorplan for buildings that served essentially the same function? That meant the lab itself would be ... that way.

Nikki turned right, followed the hallway to its end. Yes, the door was familiar: the same heavy steel thing that closed off Group Five's lab. (*Steel?* she wondered for the hundredth time. *Why steel?* She shrugged. It didn't really matter.) She paused, listening again. But, as before, she didn't hear anything. Cautiously she pulled the door open.

Fluorescent light washed out, painting an oblique parallelogram of dead white on the floor at her feet. Out of sight behind the door, Nikki waited for a reaction. Nothing happened — no gasp of surprise or alarm, no "Who's that?" no approaching footsteps. There were sounds from inside the lab — faint rustling noises and others harder to place or describe — but she had no idea what might be causing them. She waited another couple of seconds, then opened the door the rest of the way. She stepped through ...

And thought she'd walked into a nightmare.

The floorplan of this building *wasn't* exactly the same as Group Five's building. Instead of one large lab, this are of the building was divided up into several rooms. The space Nikki was facing was relatively small, obviously used as a specimen room, a storage area for experimental animals. In the far wall was another door, presumably leading to other labs. Small cages lined the walls, larger ones rested on tabletops, while the largest of all — a cubic metal lattice eight feet on a side — held pride of place in the center of the floor.

Nikki had seen specimen rooms before. Some — particularly those at primate labs, where the labs contained all-too-human rhesus and spider monkeys — could look like chambers of horrors, particularly late at night. She was used to that, prepared for the ambience of a specimen room.

For a *normal* specimen room. Not for something like this.

At first glance, the cages around the walls appeared to contain small rats or large mice. But they *weren't* rats or mice, Nikki knew that at once. The shape of the bodies, the color of the fur, the size and configuration of the skull ... All were dead wrong, as was the silent, steady — *intelligent* — way the ugly creatures were watching her. She could feel the small creatures' hatred, their hunger.

In another cage, something that could have been a rabid spider monkey — except from the wings which sprouted impossibly from its shoulders — hissed evilly through overlarge teeth and reached for her with a claw-tipped hand. In yet another an ovoid container of stainless steel — like a metal egg — lay open, while a disembodied hand crawled, spider-like, around the cage floor. From everywhere in the room, eyes — cold, malevolent, and all too aware — were fixed on her.

But, even despite the other horrors that surrounded her, it was the central cage that caught and held her attention. It was occupied, like all the others. A single creature crouched on its straw-covered floor, watching Nikki calmly from bright green eyes.

At first Nikki thought it was a tiger: its orange fur, streaked with black, were unmistakable. *But no*, she realized in numb horror, *it* isn't *a tiger*. Its body, its head, even its posture were all subtly *wrong*. The fact that it looked *close* to a tiger made it even more a disturbing sight.

A tiger … Oh, holy mother of God …

Before the thought was fully formed, the creature in the cage began to change. Its forelimbs shortened, its hind legs stretched. Its spine, chest and pelvis shifted, the bones and muscles moving sickeningly under the tawny pelt. And even *that* changed, the short fur vanishing as though absorbed by the skin. In a handful of seconds, the beast was gone, to be replaced by …

By a man. A short, slender man squatted calmly on the floor of the cage. Naked, his skin with a yellowish tinge. His eyes almond-shaped, flashing bright green under their lids. A middle-aged Chinese man, balding, with an expression of unshakable calm on his face.

"Dr. Ling …" Nikki gasped.

"Yes," the man said quietly. "Are you to be my next patient, *hmm*?"

Chapter Ten

Her mouth working silently, Nikki took a step back from the horrors that faced her.

"Dr. Ling" — the weretiger — watched her with what appeared to be benign interest. "Yes," he mused, "such a pretty child, so young, so pure …" Then another expression — more speculative — spread over his face. "Yet there is more to you than that, child. You have power. Power you have not yet learned to use …"

She took a second step backward. Another. She bumped into something yielding behind her. She spun with a gasp.

It was Funakoshi. His eyes were flashing, almost insane, she thought. In her shocked state, she found herself waiting for him to change form into some beast — perhaps a wolf, or a dog. She backed away from him, bumped into a table. The cage on it rattled as the disembodied hand flung itself at the bars, trying to get to her.

"You?" Funakoshi snarled. "You should be dead."

Well, that settles any doubts I had. Impossibly, some part of Nikki's mind remained calm, almost dispassionate.

Funakoshi turned, yelled over his shoulder, "Security!"

Within a couple of seconds, two guards — breathless from running — appeared, flanking Funakoshi. At first Nikki thought they'd responded to the scientist's summons. *But no*, she quickly saw, *it's something else*. Both of the guards were terrified, not just tired, and one was wounded: blood dripped from a gash in his cheek onto his jumpsuit.

"Restrain her," Funakoshi ordered haughtily, pointing at Nikki.

But the guards didn't spare her more than the briefest glance. "*Sumimasen*, Funakoshi-*san*," the lead guard said, with a bow. "I'm sorry, but your safety is our only concern at the moment."

Funakoshi glared at him scornfully. "You will follow my order," he snapped.

The guard bowed again. "I beg forgiveness, Funakoshi-san, but we are following our orders, issued directly by Eichiro-san himself. Your safety is more important than anything else." (*Even your lives*. Nikki's mind filled in the unspoken phrase.)

The guard looked nervously over his shoulder. "The attackers will be here soon," he told the scientist. "We must take you out of here to a place of safety. We can use the rear door."

"Leave here?" From the outrage in Funakoshi's voice, the guard might as well have suggested he eat his own child. "*Never*! The work here" — his gesture included everything, from the staring rats-but-not-rats to the weretiger in his cage — "is of vital importance. It must be protected. I will not leave here."

Both guards' faces went totally expressionless, cold and hard as stone. "We will do our duty," the older guard said ironically.

As he started to turn away, Nikki grabbed the guard's arm. "What's happening?" she asked. "What attackers?"

It was the younger guard who answered, seemingly relieved to talk to someone who wasn't being stubborn. "We don't know what they are, Carrson-*san*," he blurted. "*Monsters*. Things with wings and no faces, bodies with the flesh rotting off them, things with faces all over them ..."

"They came over the fence near the gate," the senior guard said, addressing both Nikki and Funakoshi, "and *through* the gate itself. We destroyed many, but they just kept coming." Nikki saw him suppress a shudder. "We've been cut off from the main force, Funakoshi-*san* — the four of use here, plus maybe three more outside. Their orders are to fight a withdrawing action, falling back to this building. We have no choice but to hold out here" — he shot a fierce look at Funakoshi — "until the remainder of the force relieves us."

Nikki looked at the guards, noticing that neither of them wore radio headsets, although they both carried pistols. She also saw that the younger one had no shoes on, and his superior's jumpsuit wasn't properly zipped up. They looked like they'd just got out of bed — which was probably the truth. "Does the rest of the force know we're here?" she asked.

The senior guard's bleak look was answer enough. The guard turned to the scientist. "*Sumimasen*, Funakoshi-*san*," he started. His voice was scrupulously polite, although Nikki could sense the effort that was costing him. "*Sumimasen*, so sorry, but you must reconsider. You are more valuable to Nagara than any specimens, any data. If you survive, you can replicate whatever was lost. If you die, the data is useless, because you are no longer around to analyze it, *neh*?"

Nikki had to admire the man's diplomacy. His argument was solidly logical, but also gave Funakoshi's ego a healthy stroke.

But it didn't affect the scientist at all. "*No*," Funakoshi snapped. "You will defend the contents of the labs, to the death if that's what it takes."

Both security guards bowed. "*Hai*, Funakoshi-*san*," they chorused.

Submachine-gun fire rattled — close, just outside the building. A scream of torment that could never have come from a human throat made Nikki jump.

"Well, it seems as though my friends will soon be paying you a visit." Everybody turned at the soft voice behind them.

The weretiger — "Dr. Ling" — was watching them with detached amusement. "Your torment at their hands won't be as longlasting as mine at *your* hands, I should think," the creature went on to Funakoshi. "But it will be more intense."

Funakoshi strode to the cage. "Help me," he ordered, "tell me how I can defeat the ... the things outside."

"Dr. Ling" just smiled.

"You helped me before," Funakoshi barked. "Help me now."

"I never helped you," the creature contradicted sharply. "You *took* from me. You took my blood, you took my genes for your experiments. You asked me questions, and I answered them when I saw fit. But help you?" The weretiger laughed, a chilling sound.

The gunfire was closer, but still muffled by the building's outer door. And then suddenly the noises were louder, sharper, more immediate. Nikki knew somebody — hopefully one of the security guards — had opened the door.

"Funakoshi-*san*," the senior guard said urgently, "we must leave. I cannot allow you to be killed."

"Then protect me," the scientist shouted. "Discharge your duty. But we are not abandoning this lab."

The two guards bowed again, quickly checked that

their pistols were ready for action. Nikki saw the weretiger smile mildly, shaking his head in ... In what? *Disappointment? Amusement? What would amuse a weretiger?* She shivered.

Her pistol was still in her hand. For an instant, the temptation was almost overwhelming to bring it up and empty the clip into the gently smiling creature in the cage. *Why not?* she asked herself. *It killed John Black, didn't it, and the soldier? Tortured them to death. Why shouldn't I kill it?* Her hand tightened on the grip, and she started to raise the pistol.

Then lowered it again. She knew she couldn't shoot the caged creature — not in cold blood, and *particularly* when it looked like a harmless old man. (Of course, her mind knew that was just a guise, but her emotions reacted differently.) How would she feel, watching the flechette rounds shredding "Dr. Ling's" flesh? How would she feel about herself afterward?

Not that the weretiger didn't deserve death. And not that she'd hesitate to shoot it if it were free and attacking her or anyone else. But gunning it down as it was helpless — executing it, making herself into judge, jury and executioner ... That she couldn't do. A creature of Orrorsh might think it natural, but not her.

She felt "Dr. Ling's" green eyes on her. His smile broadened slightly, as though he could read her decision — her weakness, she knew the creature would call it — in her face. She turned away.

Another rip of submachine-gun fire echoed through the lab, followed by a very human shriek of terminal agony. The door to the lab opened, and a third security guard — bloodstained, his jumpsuit torn, but his submachine-gun at the ready — staggered in. He spun and triggered a short burst of fire into the hallway. "They're coming," he gasped, "they're right behind me." Nikki had seen the man before, she knew, but it took a moment to place him. *That's right, the one on duty outside this building. Uramatsu, his name was.* He looked quite different now. His short hair was matted with blood, and his pale face was streaked with it. His left eye was a gory mess. *He must be in agony*, Nikki thought. But he wasn't letting that get in the way of his duty.

"What about the others?" the senior guard snapped.

Uramatsu shook his head. "Gone," he said simply. He triggered another burst out the door at something Nikki couldn't see. She heard the bullets thudding into something, heard a bellow of pain and rage. "Get out the back way," he said. "I can hold the corridor for long enough." The man's simple heroism was enough to bring tears to Nikki's eyes.

But the senior guard shook his head. "Unacceptable," he stated flatly, favoring Funakoshi with a withering look. "We make a stand here."

Uramatsu looked about to argue, but then his face became expressionless and he bowed. "*Hai.* We make our stand here." He positioned himself in the doorway, steadying himself against the frame. The other two guards dropped into combat crouches, their guns trained out into the hallway.

"What do we face?" the senior guard asked. "I don't see anything …"

Uramatsu started to answer.

And then all hell broke loose. The two crouching men opened fire with their pistols, while Uramatsu squeezed off short, controlled bursts from his weapon. Nikki backed away from the chaos in the doorway, deeper into the lab. She could hear "Dr. Ling" chuckling quietly.

The senior guard was the first to die. A red tentacle, dripping with slime, lashed into view, driving with hideous force into the man's chest. Blood sprayed. The guard screamed, a terrible gurgling wail, and then was silent. Nikki turned away, her gorge rising in her throat.

I have to get out of here.

Funakoshi was backing away from the doorway, horror graven on his face. He bumped into a table, almost overturning a cage. The cage's occupant squealed, a high-pitched giggle. He took another step back, toward the center of the room.

Nikki grabbed his arm. "Come on," she urged, pointing to the door in the far wall, "we can get out of here."

But Funakoshi shook her off. "*Iie*," he shrieked, "No!" And then to the guards, "Kill them, kill them all!" He turned his fevered eyes back on Nikki. "Why do you want me to leave? So *you* can take credit for all I've accomplished? Is that it?"

She looked into his eyes in horror, knowing that Funakoshi was insane. Had he been unstable to begin with, or was it just the work he was doing — and the fact he was doing it in Orrorsh — that had driven him over the edge? She'd never know. She turned away, ran to the door in the rear of the lab. One last time she looked over her shoulder.

Uramatsu and the other remaining guard died together. A mass of black-furred, scurrying creatures flooded through the door. The rats-but-not-rats leaped on the men, their fangs and claws tearing at them. As they fed, the dozens of creatures screamed in exaltation.

She heard a choking gurgle, turned to the center of the room.

Funakoshi was dying, too. He'd backed further away from the door, until he'd bumped into the weretiger's cage. Now he had his back to the bars, struggling to free himself from "Dr. Ling's" fingers, which were sunk in the scientist's throat. Funakoshi's eyes were rolling wildly, his face already turning a dark, mottled purple. His heels drummed against the floor and against the cage, as the slightly-built Ling effortlessly lifted him clear of the ground. Ling was smiling, cooing to victim as he died, "So nice, so nice, yes ..." Nikki turned, gagging, and burst through the door.

Another lab. She didn't see anything but the door opposite her. She ran to it, wrenched it open. A hallway and another door, and then she was outside.

The compound flashed with intermittent lights — flashlight beams, the muzzle flashes of guns, occasional bursts of flame. Shapes moved in the darkness, most human but some most definitely not. Twisted shadows ran and gamboled in the moonlight. It looked like a scene right out of hell.

Nikki ducked around the corner of the building, flattened herself against the wall. She couldn't see the chaos any more — the battle seemed to be concentrated around the gate and the helipad — but she could still hear it. The stuttering of automatic weapons, the sharp crack of pistols were punctuated by screams of pain or rage. Again, some of the screams were human, but many weren't.

Her heart was hammering in her chest and in her ears, her breathing fast and shallow. She was overwhelmed, totally and completely — too much had happened too quickly, too many shocks to her mind, too much horror for her to witness. "*Stop*!!" she wanted to scream. Escape — *any* kind of escape ... that's what she wanted. She needed to withdraw, hide, anything to get it over. Even death would be an escape ...

No! She forced herself to breathe deeply, slowly, flushing the poisons of fear from her body. Her heart was still racing, but at least now it wasn't the triphammer beat she could feel in her head. She had to get out of here — *that* was the escape she needed. The gate was out. So that left the river. She ducked back around the corner in a painful crouching run.

A figure loomed up out of the darkness ahead of her:

a pale figure, small, unarmed. She stopped dead in her tracks. It was "Dr. Ling," running toward the tumult at the main gate, hideously — inhumanly — fast. "Perhaps we'll meet again, Miss," he said softly, without breaking stride and without his voice betraying any exhaustion. "I should like that." And then he was past and gone, vanished into the darkness. Belatedly, Nikki brought her pistol up, but the lancing beam of the laser found no target.

He's loose. The thought filled her with cold horror. *The weretiger's loose. None of us are safe.* Than another thought struck, and she grinned in wry amusement. *And* this *is safe?* she asked herself.

There was fighting on the river bank as well — small knots of security guards hunting down and eliminating intruders, or groups of intruders hunting guards. It looked to Nikki's inexperienced eye that the Nagara forces had regained the upper hand, but there were still a frightening number of horrors loose in the compound.

Nikki was still in the shelter of a building — her building, she realized with irony — maybe ten yards from the water's edge. She started across the open space …

"Carrson-*san*! Help me!" Nikki spun as the voice rang out behind her.

It was Dei, the guard who'd taught her how to use her pistol. He had his back against a building a dozen yards away. Unarmed, his right arm — or the tattered remnant that was all that was left of it — hung uselessly by his side. In front of him, ten feet away and approaching slowly, was a walking corpse, its rotting flesh hanging in shreds from its bones. It reached for Dei with clawed hands.

"Help me!" the man screamed again.

Nikki brought her gun up, steadied it in both hands, and touched the trigger. The laser aiming dot bloomed on the back of the zombie. She squeezed the trigger, fought the recoil as the gun boomed. Brought it back on line, and shot again. Again. Again and again, until the gun clicked empty.

The flechettes flayed the flesh from the creature's back, deflecting from bones with a thin buzzing whine. The destruction the shots caused was sickening.

But it didn't stop the creature's advance. Even as Nikki's rounds were tearing it apart, it reached out toward Dei, plunged its chisel-like claws into his throat. Twisted and pulled. The guard's final cry was cut off. His body collapsed in a bloody heap.

Slowly, the creature turned to face Nikki, began to advance. She thought she heard it chuckle.

Nikki screamed, turned and ran. When she hit the water she kept running as long as she could, then hurled herself forward in a surface dive. She took three strong strokes, with the current, letting the river carry her away from the horrors behind her.

* * *

Nikki was exhausted. The aftereffects of terror had drained all the energy from her body. Her wet clothes, clinging to her body, were cold, steadily leeching away even more of her stamina. It was all she could do to keep walking, keep pushing her way through the jungle. It would be so tempting to just lie down, close her eyes if only for a moment. But no, she knew, there were still threats in the jungle. To sleep — here, undefended — would be to die.

The river had carried her more than a hundred yards downstream from the outpost before she'd been able to make it back to the bank. But that was all to the good, she figured. The outpost was still a battlezone. Who knew if the horrors were bringing in reinforcements?

She'd dragged herself from the water, resting for a moment on the bank before forcing herself to her feet and moving on. There was no safety for her anywhere in the jungle, not out here alone. She'd fired all the rounds in her pistol, and besides she'd dropped the weapon when she'd run into the river. She had no way of protecting herself — *as if even the pistol would do it*, she thought grimly. The only place she'd be safe was in Peter Hollingforth's camp, with the remaining three soldiers to protect her. (*And will I be safe even there?* She crushed the unbidden thought.)

On the way out, it had taken her more than twenty minutes to get from the camp clearing to the outpost. The way back would take her considerably longer, she knew. For one thing, the current had taken her some distance east of the stockade; for another, she'd decided to take a wide detour around the area of the outpost. It would take her almost an hour to reach safety, she figured — an hour in which all the horrors of Orrorsh could try to kill her, and she had no way of stopping them.

But what choice did she have? She pressed on.

* * *

Nikki checked her watch. Almost forty minutes since she'd emerged from the river. By her original estimate, that meant she was maybe twenty minutes from the camp and safety.

But how accurate is that estimate? she asked herself. Her "bump of direction" told her she was headed the right way. But as for distance and speed, she could only guess.

She found a narrow path, one that led in approximately the right direction. That would let her move faster, knock some time off the trip.

She'd been surprised — pleasantly so, but surprised nonetheless — to have seen or heard no signs of anything threatening in the jungle. No sounds, no cries, no movement, nothing. (Of course, her imagination had worked overtime to *manufacture* such threats where none existed — the night breeze through the foliage was stealthy movement, a deep patch of shadow was a tentacled creature ready to grab her, that kind of thing. She could almost laugh about it, except that the fear she felt from false alarms was very real, even though the cause might not be. The narrow path curved, entered a tiny clearing.

There were people ahead. Almost a dozen, dressed in dark clothing, carrying weapons. They saw Nikki at the same moment she spotted them. The one in the lead brought his weapon up.

With a cry of alarm, Nikki hurled herself aside. The figure's weapon spat. Something plucked at the sleeve of her wet shirt. Bullets stitched the bole of a tree behind her.

She struck the ground hard, but rolled with the impact, coming back up onto her feet. She ran, expecting any moment to feel the numbing impact of bullets into her back, expecting shots to tear her life from her.

But nothing struck her. The sound of her own passage through the jungle filled her ears; there was no way she could hear any pursuit. Her lungs felt like they were about to burst. She couldn't run any further.

Trying to mute her gasping she stopped, ducking behind the thick bole of a tree. She listened, trying to pick up sounds of pursuit.

Nothing. She could hear nothing but the night-sounds of the jungle. But did that mean the gunmen weren't after her, or only that they were experts at moving silently? She kept her back against the tree trunk, remained motionless while she listened, and counted seconds.

One hundred and eighteen seconds, one hundred and nineteen, one hundred and twenty ... Two minutes, and still no sound or sign of pursuit. No matter how carefully the gunmen were moving, surely they'd have passed her by now ... She craned around the bole of the tree for a quick look.

Nobody was there. She could see no movement, no suspicious shapes. Of course, her pursuers could be skilled woodsmen, sneaking up on her, or just waiting for her to expose herself. She flattened herself against the tree trunk, counted to one hundred and twenty again, then a third time. Still no movement.

They've gone, she told herself. *They weren't looking for me, they were doing something else. They just met me by accident. So why would they bother chasing me?* Logically, that reasoning made sense. But, she had to admit, she was steadily losing her faith in logic. *Logically, Orrorsh can't exist, and none of this can be happening. So much for logic.*

Cautiously, she stepped out from behind her tree. To her wry amusement, she realized she was tensing her muscles — *as if that would stop a bullet.*

But nobody shot her, nothing moved in the darkness around her. Who were they? she asked herself. In the suddenness of the encounter she'd seen no details — just the dark figures themselves and the weapons in their hands. Then there'd come the muzzle flash, and she was running for her life. *Nagara security, out on a search-and-destroy mission?* She didn't think so, although she wasn't quite sure why not. Apparently, her subconscious had noticed something but wasn't deigning to tell her conscious mind about it. Oh well, it didn't matter, did it? They were going their way, she was going hers.

Wishing for eyes in the back of her head — and jumping at even the slightest sound — she resumed her original course.

* * *

It was almost dawn by the time she reached the camp clearing. In the growing light, she could see that Hollingforth, Black and the soldiers were up and around. She stepped into the clearing.

MacHeath saw her first, had his rifle half-way to his shoulder before he recognized her. Then they were all running toward her — even Professor Black.

Peter pulled to a stop a few feet short of her. She could see the relief in his face, but also the indecision — should he hug her, or would that be presumptuous? She made the decision for him. Laughing wildly with the release of tension, the realization that she was safe, she flung her arms around his neck, buried her face in his beard. It took him a couple of seconds to reciprocate, but then his arms tightened around her back hard enough to almost squeeze the air from her.

Then, firmly, he pushed her away, held her at arm's length. His face was flushed, working with mixed emotions. "Where the bloody hell did you go?" he demanded. "What kind of bloody fool stunt was that?"

If it hadn't been apparent from his face, the fact that he was swearing in front of a woman — *to* a woman — told Nikki how seriously he was taking this. Even through her relief, she felt remorse for the pain she'd caused him. She lowered her eyes. "There was something I had to do," she said quietly.

"What?" This from MacHeath. He was a little more under control than Hollingforth, but he was disturbed too.

"I had to go back to the outpost."

"Why?" Peter wanted to know.

Briefly she outlined her logic about finding the outpost's secret, about using it to discredit Eichiro and destroy his career. "It's important," she stressed. "He killed two of my friends — one directly, one indirectly. And he tried to kill me." She paused. Through the relief, the horror of the night seeped back into her heart. "And there's more," she said quietly.

The bleak timbre of her voice struck them, she could see it. "What happened?" MacHeath asked in hushed tones.

She told them about her approach to the stockade, about taking to the river to avoid the fence. She painted a verbal picture of the specimen room, its cages full of small creatures, hideous and evil. "And *it* was there, too," she went on, her eyes flicking back and forth between Peter and Black, "the thing you're after. Dr. Ling. The weretiger."

Black's eyes sprung wide open. "What?" he shouted. "At the outpost?"

"It's not there any more," she admitted, "it escaped." She shivered. "It's free in the jungle. Somewhere."

"But why?" Hollingforth wanted to know. "They had it captive. Why?"

"Why not destroy it?" Black added.

"I don't know. They were collecting monsters as specimens, but I don't know …" Nikki's voice trailed off. *Specimens*? she thought. *No*, experimental subjects! What had "Dr. Ling" said to Funakoshi? *"You took my blood, you took my genes for your experiments,"* wasn't that it? She remembered the strange sera that had come to Group Five from Funakoshi's lab. Sera that showed characteristics of both human and animal proteins, similar to both but matching neither, strangely mutable. Sera she'd assumed had come from gene-splicing experiments.

Why couldn't those samples have come directly from the veins of the weretiger?

"They were experimenting on it," she told the waiting men. "They were taking samples of its blood. They were analyzing its genetic material …"

"Black arts!" the professor thundered. "Profane practices!"

To her surprise, Nikki found she had to agree. Normally she was firmly opposed to people who resisted scientific research and progress on religious grounds. *Stop something if it's dangerous, but not because some musty book says it's Something Man Was Not Meant to Know.* Genetic research was neither good nor evil, in and of itself. Like anything to do with technology, it was only the way that people used it that made it good or evil. *And this* is *evil,* she told herself.

"What were they trying to do?" Hollingforth asked.

She shook her head. "I don't know. They never told me before, I doubt they'd tell me now."

"Whatever it was, it was evil," Black pronounced. Again, Nikki couldn't argue with him.

"You said the weretiger escaped," Peter reminded her. "How?"

She explained about the raid on the outpost by the mixed force of monsters. "I don't know if they were coming specifically to free it," she concluded, "or whether that was just a sideline."

MacHeath nodded. He still was obviously a deeply troubled man, but he looked as though his mind had been set at ease on one matter. "That explains a lot," he said. "I had the watch at about two o'clock — that must have been after you'd snuck away, Miss Carlson" — he shot her a pointed look; she felt herself blush, and lowered her eyes — "and the jungle just came alive. You know the normal night sounds, I warrant?" She nodded. "One minute those were all the sounds there were. The next, well ... I've never heard such a howling and a crying in my life. It sounded like an army was on the move, but such an army as I've never known before, and never *want* to know.

"I thought they were coming for us, whatever they were," the sergeant went on. "I woke the others, and that's when we found you were missing." His steely eyes were steady on her face, his expression and voice emotionless. He was dressing her down, Nikki knew, but in such a way that she couldn't take umbrage. She wouldn't have anyway — she knew she deserved it.

"Our first assumption was that the things had taken

you," MacHeath continued. "I had to almost physically restrain Mr. Hollingforth here to stop him from going after you. The only thing that really held any of us back was that we didn't know where you might have gone — or been taken — or what direction to look."

She felt her blush deepening. "I'm sorry," she mumbled.

"Going off alone was asinine," Black pronounced.

"In enemy territory it *was* tactically unwise," MacHeath added judiciously.

"Why did you do it, Nikki?" Peter's eyes were troubled. "Why? You could have been killed."

She couldn't meet his gaze. "I had to do it. I told you why."

"Why didn't you tell me?" From his voice she could tell that has his real question, the issue that was really troubling him. "I could have come with you, protected you …"

She shrugged, unable to voice the real answer. *Don't push*, she urged him silently, *don't make me say something that'll hurt you.*

MacHeath let her off the hook — either by chance, or because he was a lot more sensitive than his demeanor indicated, she wasn't sure. "Be that as it may," he said brusquely, "what about the assault on the stockade? They managed to free the beast, but apart from that how did they fare?"

"They killed a lot of people, I think," Nikki responded eagerly, glad to get off an uncomfortable subject. "Mainly security guards, I'd guess. When I escaped the fighting was still going on, but I think the outpost people were winning."

"What about the people who were doing the work?" Hollingforth asked.

"One of the key scientists was killed. From the way he talked, the program might have been his idea."

"Then it was right and it was meet that he met his

fate," the professor said piously.

"It was Ling who killed him," Nikki pointed out, and that shut him up.

"Can they continue the work?" Peter pressed.

Nikki thought about that for a moment. Funakoshi had been the only one of the scientists she'd known by name, and apparently one of the guiding forces behind the project. But the entire Matsushima Bay research team had a reputation for brilliance. Even with Funakoshi gone, the outpost wouldn't suffer for lack of brainpower. And, of course, Eichiro was still there to drive things along.

"They can continue," she announced bleakly.

That silenced them all for a while.

Eventually Peter spoke. "Nikki ..." Then he corrected himself, "Miss Carlson ..."

"Nikki," she told him firmly.

"Nikki," he agreed with a smile. "Would you agree that the project in the outpost must be stopped?"

She didn't have to think about that one at all. "*Yes.*"

Hollingforth nodded, exchanged glances with the other men. "We are all agreed, then," he said. "There are some men in the area who share the same goal. Sergeant MacHeath met them several hours ago. Their camp is nearby. I think we should meet with them. You can provide them with important information, perhaps, and we can help them in whatever ways we can. Will you do that?"

She thought it through for a moment, then shrugged. *Why not?* Anybody who wanted to rain on Eichiro's parade — whoever they were and whatever their motives — was okay with her. "Let's do it," she said firmly.

* * *

It took just a few minutes for the men to get ready to travel. Nikki took the opportunity to duck into a tent and change her wet clothes for shirt and trousers that Hollingforth had loaned her. The shirt didn't fit badly around her chest, although the sleeves were massively too long and the lower hem was half-way down her thighs. The trousers were a disaster. Even with the legs rolled up and the waist cinched in using the belt from her shorts, the only thing that could be said about them was that they concealed her legs from casual view. *Which is probably a major issue for Professor Black,* she thought with amusement. She wished there was something she could do with her hair — more from a standpoint of comfort than vanity, she told herself — but she didn't have too many options. She found a broken bootlace on Peter's camp cot, used that to tie her wet hair back from her face.

By the time she emerged from the tent, Hollingforth, Black and the soldiers were ready. The men glanced her way as she appeared, then carefully looked away. *Great,* she told herself, *I must look even more of a treat than I thought.* "I'm ready, gentlemen," she told them.

MacHeath took the lead. Black and Hollingforth, with Nikki between them, followed, while the two surviving privates took up the rear. The soldiers all had their rifles held at the ready, bayonets mounted and rounds in the chambers.

They were heading roughly southeast, Nikki noticed. "Where are we going?" she asked.

"The men we go to meet have a camp a mile or so from here," MacHeath told her. "We should be there in less than half an hour."

The soldiers and the explorers seemed to have little doubt that meeting with the strangers was the right thing to do. Nikki couldn't bring herself to feel so confident. "Who are they?"

"Soldiers, most of them," the sergeant answered without taking his eyes from the jungle around him. He chuckled. "They didn't say so, but one military man can usually spot another. The others?" He thought for a moment. "I must say I don't know exactly what to make of them. They're not military, not a member of any army I've ever imagined. But they're trained as well as any soldier I know, and they definitely consider the outpost to be their enemy."

Not a member of any army I've ever imagined. That had a slightly ominous ring to it, Nikki thought. "They're human?" she asked hesitantly.

MacHeath chuckled again, then cut it off. "Sorry I laughed, Miss Carlson," he apologized, "considering what you saw at the outpost that is aye too appropriate a question. But set your mind at rest; they're as human as you and I. I trust them, ma'am," he went on earnestly. "I know I have no right to offer anyone's trust but my own, but I give that willingly. I think you'll do the same when you meet them. Wouldn't you say so, Mr. Hollingforth?"

Peter nodded, smiled reassuringly at Nikki. "I'm no military man and I know little of soldiers — except for our brave colleagues here, of course — but I pride myself on being a good judge of character."

"And you like them?" she pressed.

Peter hesitated. "Like them?" he mused. "I don't know as I'd say that. Their manners are strange. And anyway, liking and friendship can only come with time. But I did trust them."

"You should have something in common with them, Miss Carlson," MacHeath added. "Their weapons are much like yours, much more complicated than our trusty Westons." He slapped his rifle with a grin of real affection on his face.

Nikki had to smile. Her doubts had lessened, although they hadn't totally vanished. *We'll see,* she told herself. *Don't borrow trouble.*

The journey took longer than the half hour MacHeath had estimated. It didn't seem that the men were lost.

Nikki's bump of direction told her that the sergeant was leading them along as straight a course as it was possible to follow in the heavy jungle. The frequent detours they made were to bypass knots of under-brush that would have been impenetrable without machetes, not through any doubts as to their direction. The sergeant was setting a good, steady pace, but Nikki had the impression that he could have gone faster if he'd wanted. Maybe he was moderating his pace for her, she thought with a flash of anger — she never liked thinking she was being patronized. But then she saw the dark stains that were growing under Black's arms, and the line of sweat down the back of his tan jacket. *MacHeath's taking it easy on him,* she realized with a wry smile. The professor was doing his best not to slow them down — and of course he was too proud, too much into keeping a "stiff upper lip" to complain — but he was obviously not in as good shape as the younger men.

The sun was rising higher, and the relative cool of the early morning was giving way to the fetid heat of day in the jungle. Nikki knew she was in good shape, and her muscles still felt fresh and full of energy — even after the exertions of the night. But the heat sapped energy, and she could feel her own sweat seeping into the clothes Hollingforth had loaned her.

She was glad when they reached a small clearing and MacHeath announced, "We're here."

The clearing was even smaller than the one where the explorers had set up camp, and this one was almost completely filled with tents. Not the simplistic canvas tents Hollingforth and his colleagues used. These were modern dome tents, free-standing, made of light-colored artificial fabric that she guessed was something like gortex.

There was no movement. Apart from the tents, the clearing was empty. She took a breath to remark on that to MacHeath …

And that's when the men emerged from the jungle on the other side of the clearing.

She *knew* them, she realized with a horrid shock. In the light of day she could see their clothes were dark jungle fatigues, mottled with green and brown. The submachine-guns in their hands were familiar, too — she'd been on the wrong end of one not too long ago.

The man in the lead raised his weapon, centering its barrel on Nikki's chest. In the shade of his campaign hat she saw his dark eyes narrow in recognition. With a sharp metallic *snick* he flipped the safety catch off his gun. "I *told* you I didn't get her," he announced.

Chapter Eleven

It's them! The thought struck Nikki with an almost painful impact. The dozen or so men across the clearing were the ones she'd met in the jungle on the way back from the outpost — the ones who had shot at her. And now they were ready to finish the job. She looked around wildly at her friends.

MacHeath and the other soldiers had lowered their weapons, thinking they were with friends. She remembered how fast the sergeant had reacted, putting a bullet into the head of the ninja, but she knew there was no way he could respond fast enough to save her life if the hard-eyed man decided to trigger his submachine-gun. *I'm dead*, the thought rang in her head.

"Sergei, no." Another man emerged from the fringe of the jungle, joining his comrades across the clearing.

For a moment, Nikki thought her sanity was going. *Orrorsh has finally done it*, she told herself, *it's driven me mad*. It was like a horrible kind of *deja vu*. She thought, just for an instant, that she was back in the sub-basement lab at the Nagara Building. She'd heard the

311

same words then, when the leader of the raiders stopped one of his gunmen from killing her.

And it was the same man who'd spoken. There was no blood matting his short blond hair now, but she recognized the hard, finely-chiseled face, the steel-grey eyes, even the snap of command in his voice. And Sergei himself ... *It's the same men. It's the raiders.*

Unwillingly, the one called Sergei lowered his weapon. The blond leader slapped him on the back as he strode into the clearing. With a muttered comment in a language Nikki didn't recognize, Sergei turned aside.

The leader strode forward, stopped a couple of yards short of Nikki and her party. He smiled. *He's handsome*, she realized, *when he doesn't look so intense.* The realization that she was going to live started to relieve the knot of tension in her belly.

"Professor Black, Mr. Hollingforth," he said formally. To MacHeath and the soldiers he just shot a comradely smile, one warrior to another. He turned his gaze on Nikki, and his smile broadened. "And you must be Ms. Carlson. Ian spoke about you at length." He inclined his head to MacHeath (*Ian* MacHeath. Nikki committed the name to memory. Nobody else had bothered to tell it to her.)

"I'm sorry our two previous meetings have been, um" — he hesitated — "a tad unsociable, Ms. Carlson. But Sergei sometimes is a little overquick to react, if you know what I mean." *So he recognizes me*, Nikki realized. *He remembers me from Nagara.*

"Who *are* you?" she asked slowly.

"Leftenant Dick Beames of the Royal Australian Armed Forces, 3rd Paras, at your service." For the first time Nikki noticed the accent, the broadening of the vowels, and the clipping of some syllables. He gestured at the rest of the group, who were going about their personal business in the clearing, paying no attention to Nikki and the others. "These are my comrades. We call ourselves the Tiger Team."

"Australian?" She inspected the other men. Four of them were light-skinned like Beames, apparently European (or Australian). But the others were darker-skinned, obviously Oriental. Not Japanese or Chinese. *Indonesian, maybe?*

"Just me," he said with a disarming smile, "my mates say one fellow from Oz is quite enough. We've got a Pommie, a Yank, one guy who's a real Heinz 57. And there's Sergei, of course — he comes from whatever the USSR is calling itself at the moment."

"Then you're not army?" Nikki pressed.

Beames shook his head. "Officially I'm on detached duty," he explained. "We're ... Well, we call ourselves Storm Knights." He saw Nikki's puzzled expression and asked, "You know about the Possibility Wars, of course?"

She shrugged. "I've been in Japan the past few years," she revealed. "You don't get much international news there."

"I reckon," Beames agreed wryly.

"I've heard something about it," she went on. "It's like ... It's like reality's changing, right?"

"Other realities are invading," he corrected, "that's what it is. Storm Knights are the people trying to stop it."

"What about the others?" Nikki indicated the darker-skinned men around the campsite.

"*They're* army," Beames answered. "Thai infantrymen, from the armory in Bangkok. The Thai government is interested in what's going on in Orrorsh — for slightly different reasons from us — so there were no worries getting a little extra help."

One of the other caucasians was wandering over toward them. His face made him look about Nikki's age, maybe a couple of years older, although his dark hair was prematurely streaked with grey. He had dark

Nigel Findley

brown eyes set in a tanned, open-looking face. His smile was easy, relaxed.

"Here comes our Heinzer," Beames announced. "Ry, this is Ms. Nikki Carlson, a friend of our Victorian mates. Ms. Carlson, he's Ryan Davis. Tell her your background, Ry."

Davis shrugged. "Born in Trinidad, grew up in Texas, England, Saudi Arabia, Nigeria; pick a place, I've been there." He chuckled.

Nikki found herself drawn to his easy smile. "Army brat?" she speculated.

"Oil brat," he corrected. "At one time or another my father got shipped to just about anywhere with an oil patch, and I went along with him." He had a trace of an accent, almost impossible to place. *New Zealand? Or South Africa?* Nikki mused. *Or maybe just a mixture of lots of accents.* She found herself smiling back at him.

Until she saw what he was doing, then her smile faded. As he spoke to her, he was slipping lethal-looking bullets into a long submachine-gun magazine — casually, without even looking, as if it was something he did every day. *And maybe it is.* The sight was so out of keeping with the man's relaxed manner that it snapped her back to reality.

"You blew up the lab at Nagara," Nikki said to Beames. "You killed the scientists and the guards. *Why?*"

The Australian's smile faded, and he nodded. "Okay, business. Look, Ms. Carlson, why don't you come over here and sit down? We've got a lot of things to discuss."

* * *

They sat or crouched in a rough circle in the middle of the clearing. Hollingforth and Black sat on either side of Nikki, while the other Europeans had settled themselves nearer to Beames. Ryan Davis was there, along with the Britisher called Norman Leeds, and a tough-looking, laconic Texan Beames had introduced as Dusty Rhodes. Sergei was present too, sitting a yard or so back from the others, as though uncomfortable to have people too close. His dark eyes flicked constantly around him, as though he didn't trust Orrorsh not to materialize some kind of threat at any moment. All the others were unarmed, but Sergei cradled his submachine-gun in his lap. Watching him, Nikki almost expected him to caress it. The others — the Thai soldiers, and MacHeath and his men — were elsewhere, talking quietly in small groups, or cleaning and servicing their weapons.

"Okay," Beames said to start the informal conference. "Ms. Carlson, you asked about the Nagara operation." He paused for a moment, apparently getting his thoughts in order.

"You said you know something about the Possibility Wars," the Australian began. "Then you know that the Earth — the whole universe, really — is being invaded. Other universes — we call them cosms — have become linked with ours. The links are Maelstrom Bridges, gateways between our reality — our cosm — and others. The other cosms are very different from ours. They have different physical laws; technology that works on Core Earth won't work there, or things that work there won't work here. In some, magic works. In others — like the one that's linked to Orrorsh — some of the inhabitants are monsters, although not all. Mr. Hollingforth and Professor Black know that all too well, right, gentlemen?"

Peter and the professor nodded soberly. Nikki found herself staring at her friends as though seeing them for the first time. Was Beames hinting that Peter and the others — *he'd called them Victorians*, she remembered — were from that other reality, that other cosm? How could that be? Wouldn't Peter have told her?

But he *had* hinted at it, hadn't he? When she'd asked

him where he'd come from, he'd said it was a long story.

And didn't that explain a lot of things? Their Eighteenth Century beliefs and manners? Their clothing, and the scarlet uniforms worn by MacHeath and his soldiers? The bolt-action rifles — *with* bayonets, *for Christ's sake* — and the fact that MacHeath had found her pistol so unusual?

Beames was still talking. "The areas where the cosms are linked to Core Earth, we call them *realms*. There's the Cyberpapacy in France, the Living Land in North America, Aysle in Britain, and the Nile Empire in Africa. And, of course, Orrorsh. There are Storm Knights all over the world, all trying to stop the realms from spreading, and trying to destroy them — often working from within."

"But what about Japan?" Nikki asked. "You attacked the Nagara Building in Tokyo. Japan's not a realm, is it?"

The Australian was silent for a moment. "We don't know," he said eventually. "There are hints" — he shrugged — "but not much more than that. All we know is that some of the Japanese megacorporations — particularly Kanawa, but some of the others too — are supplying weapons and other equipment to the realms we *do* know about. Those realms then use the weapons to fight the Storm Knights." His voice became cold, almost harsh. "We're fighting for our planet, and our cosm, Ms. Carlson. We're trying to drive out the invaders. And the Japanese megacorps are opposing us — directly or indirectly, it doesn't much matter, does it? That seems an awful lot like treason to me, betraying Core Earth to its enemies."

Nikki struggled to digest that. "Nagara too?" she asked in a hushed voice.

"Parts of it, certainly," the Britisher Leeds answered. "The corporation has a facility at Matsushima Bay, and we know that's involved. And the Special Projects lab in Tokyo."

"That's why we hit it," Dusty Rhodes explained. "They were into genetic engineering, you know? We got word they were ... building, I guess ... They were building some new kinds of critters, real nasty animals with human intelligence. Or they were trying to when we paid them a visit."

"The Special Projects lab had a contract with Malraux," Beames went on, "the Anti-Pope himself. The Inquisition wanted guard animals and trackers to help them hunt down and destroy the Storm Knights in France. The contract was so lucrative that Nagara was glad to oblige." He smiled grimly. "We figured we'd set the project back at least a couple of years. I don't know how many lives we saved in the long run, but it was worth it."

Nikki nodded slowly. *That makes an ugly kind of sense,* she realized. The samples she'd been analyzing in her lab in Tokyo, the weird DNA and the proteins sent in from the sealed P3 containment lab next door ... Couldn't they have been part of a project to genetically engineer animals? Of course they could. In fact, she and Toshikazu had speculated on that themselves at the time.

She shuddered. *I was part of that, and I didn't even know it.* "You had proof?" she asked hesitantly.

"Everything we needed," Dusty Rhodes told her with a firm nod, "all documented and backed up. Hell, you think we'd just waltz in there and mess up the place if we weren't sure? I mean, *real* sure?"

She scanned the eyes of the men — the "Storm Knights," as they called themselves. There was no doubt, just absolute, unshakable certainty. *No,* she thought, *you wouldn't have done it if you hadn't been sure.*

"It came as a complete surprise when we found out that Nagara was sending a 'scientific mission' to

Sumatra — to Majestic," Beames corrected, glancing at the Victorians. "We didn't know what they were up to, we didn't have enough information to tell. But we expected the worst. The project was initiated by the same cobber who did the original Special Projects program — Agatamori Eichiro." He glanced at Nikki. "You know him?"

She nodded. "Yes," she said simply, "I know him."

"And the scientists came from the Matsushima Bay project," the Australian continued. "That didn't look good right there. And security was tight ..."

"Tighter than a rat's ass," Rhodes expanded.

" ...Which told us it was something Nagara thought was very important." Beames shrugged. "We had to find out what they were doing, and that's why we're here."

"You're going to blow up the outpost too?" Nikki asked.

Lt. Beames hesitated. Nikki could see him trying to decide how much to tell her. Then his expression cleared as he made up his mind. "If that's what it takes," he told her honestly. "It depends what they're doing there, and what the consequences are going to be. You understand that, don't you?" He looked at her almost imploringly.

This isn't some mad bomber, Nikki realized, *some wrecker*. Beames had a conscience. She could see he didn't like what he had to do, but recognized that he wouldn't let his own feelings get in the way of something he thought was necessary. *And it* will *be necessary, won't it?* she asked herself, remembering what she'd seen in Funakoshi's lab. She shuddered. "Yes," she told the Storm Knights. "Yes, I understand."

Beames leaned forward intently. "Sergeant MacHeath told us you worked at the outpost, Ms. Carlson," he said quietly. "Maybe you can tell us what we need to know. Just what the hell *are* they doing there?"

Nikki took a deep breath to steady her nerves. "You're not going to like it." As concisely as she could, but without leaving out any detail that might be important, she told the Storm Knights what she knew about the outpost. The alien, mutable proteins she and her workgroup had been tasked to analyze. What she knew about Fusaaki Funakoshi's background in genetic engineering. The horrible contents of the specimen room. And finally, her own conclusions about where the serum samples had come from. "I don't know why they're doing it," she finished, "but I know they *are* doing it."

The Storm Knights were silent when she'd concluded. She could feel their tension, see their horror and disgust in the looks they were exchanging. Beames, Rhodes, Davis and Leeds kept their reactions under tight control, but Sergei was muttering in Russian under his breath. She could see his knuckles standing out, white as ivory, as he gripped his submachine-gun.

"It makes sense," Beames said at last. His voice was emotionless, as though he were trying to suppress his feelings, preventing them from interfering with his analysis of the situation. "It makes a lot of sense. We destroy their project in Tokyo, the one designed to build animals for the Cyberpapacy from scratch. There's no way they can replicate their work, and complete the project, in time to meet their contract. So they decide to take a short cut. Why build an intelligent monster — that's what they were trying to do — from the ground up? Why not start with something that already exists, and make the necessary modifications on that?

"So they come to Orrorsh and they capture monsters," he went on levelly. "They probably started with the little ones, like those rats you told us about, just to get the techniques down. Then thy go out and net the big specimen." He shook his head in revulsion. "Jesus, a weretiger. A shapechanger. Intelligent as a man, and bloody downright lethal. If they could do it, they'd want to keep the intelligence, the physical abilities — and of course the shapeshifting, though I don't know if that's possible. Tweak its mentality and outlook a little so that it's tractable, trainable …

"And what have you got? " he asked rhetorically. "The ultimate tracker, the ultimate assassin for the Inquisition — or anyone else who can pay the price. It's smart enough to follow a group of Storm Knights, track them … maybe even infiltrate their group, pretending to be an ally. Then when their guard's down, it changes into a bloody tiger and rips them apart."

Nikki found herself shivering. The scenario was hideous. It sounded like something out of a bad horror novel; if she hadn't seen the weretiger herself, she never would have believed it.

But she *had* seen it, hadn't she? She'd seen it in tiger form in its cage, seen it change its shape to become the quiet, innocuous-looking "Dr. Ling." Seen it strangle the life out of Fusaaki Funakoshi.

She could feel the tension, the hatred, in both Black and Hollingforth. *They know — personally — how lethal the creature is,* she recognized. *It fooled them, then it killed their friends — Black's son. They want it dead.*

And so do I. She had to admit it.

"You're going after the outpost, aren't you?" she asked quietly.

"We have to, don't you see?" Beames' voice was urgent, earnest. "We have to stop this. The weretiger escaped, but they can capture another one … or maybe something even worse. You understand that, don't you?"

Nikki nodded slowly. *The thing is, I really do understand.* "Yes," she said softly. "But I've got colleagues there," she added more forcefully. "They're just like I was, they don't know what they're involved in. They're just technicians. You can't hurt them."

"No worries. We don't hurt non-combatants." The Australian smiled. "You know that personally, right?"

You *might not*, Nikki thought; she glanced over at Sergei. *But what about him?* She sighed. The leftenant was right, she told herself. The Storm Knights *have* to close down the outpost. *The security guards will fight — that's their job — and the Knights will probably have to kill some of them.* That worried her, deep down inside. The Nagara security guards weren't any more involved in the project than Nikki, Bojo, Toshima and the others in Group Five. They'd be just doing their job ... and they might get killed for it. That wasn't right.

She could feel Beames' grey eyes on her — steady, almost as though they were looking into her soul. "We'll try to minimize casualties all the way around," he said reassuringly. "The purpose is to close down the project, not to kill people."

"They have ninjas there," Nikki said suddenly, remembering she hadn't mentioned the black-clad wraiths before.

The Storm Knights exchanged glances. "That makes it tougher," Dusty Rhodes allowed. "Those bad boys are quick as greased lightning."

"Nikki killed one who was chasing her," Hollingforth said. "There are enough of you to handle them."

Beames and the other Knights looked at Nikki appraisingly. She could see new respect in their eyes — even in the hard, dark eyes of Sergei. *That's what you understand best, isn't it,* Nikki thought, *killing people?* She shivered. There was something incredibly disturbing about the Russian. He seemed more like a soulless killer than a real human being. *What happened in your past to make you that way?* she wondered. *Or have you just been living with violence so long that you don't know anything else?* She found that idea chilling, and unutterably sad.

Nigel Findley

"Okay." Beames nodded firmly, more to himself than to the others, Nikki thought. "We'll go in tonight."

The Storm Knights' expressions were grim, businesslike. Now that the decision had been made, their friendly manner had evaporated. They looked like soldiers, preparing for an assault. *They* know *they might be killed*, Nikki realized, *but that doesn't matter. This is something they know has to be done.* Only Sergei was smiling, a thin, tight expression on his pale face. He was looking forward to it.

Hollingforth glanced over at the professor, then back to Beames. His expression was fixed, determined. "We want to come along with you," he said quietly. "MacHeath and his men will come too."

Beames raised an eyebrow. "Why?" he asked. "This isn't your fight."

It was Professor Black who answered. "Yes it is." From his expression, Nikki could tell that he was associating the work of the outpost with the weretiger who'd killed his son.

The Australian was silent for a moment, then he nodded. "You're in," he agreed. "The more the merrier." He turned to Nikki. "Thanks for the information, Ms. Carlson."

I'm being left out, she realized, *they're thinking of leaving me behind.* "I'm coming too." The words were out of her mouth before she was even aware she'd made the decision.

The Storm Knights regarded her silently for a moment. "Why?" Norman Leeds asked.

She looked over at Sergei, saw the way he was stroking his weapon. She could imagine him triggering the lethal little submachine-gun, the bullets ripping the life from Toshima, or Matsukara, or Bojo. *My colleagues.* Certainly they were closed-minded, stolid, unimaginative. Certainly they resented her. But they didn't know what the outpost represented. They were innocents, just like her. They didn't deserve death. *Maybe if I come along I can protect them.*

And then there was Eichiro, of course. Agatamori Eichiro—the man who'd killed Toshikazu, and caused the deaths of her other friends. Who'd almost had her killed as well. Could she just wait in the clearing while the Storm Knights dealt with him? *No.*

"It's my fight, too," she said quietly.

Beames looked at her steadily for a long moment. Then he smiled. "Okay," he agreed. He looked around at the others. "That's it then, gents. We move out one hour after sunset."

Chapter Twelve

They moved through the darkness of the jungle in an extended column. MacHeath and a trio of the Thai soldiers were fifty yards ahead, out of sight of the others, scouting the terrain before them. Lt. Beames led the main group, with Sergei beside him. Nikki walked directly behind them, Peter Hollingforth at her side, while the others followed behind.

Nikki's fingers brushed the butt of the heavy pistol that weighed down the holster on her hip — a Walther P.88, Ry Davis had called it. It was larger than the Viper she'd lost, and heavier, too. Instead of flechettes, it was loaded with standard 9mm rounds. Under the barrel, strapped on like an afterthought, was a small cylinder that was the weapon's laser sight. Beames had been a little hesitant about arming her at all, but Sergeant MacHeath had told the Australian how well she'd handled the encounter with the ninja — exaggerating her calmness quite a lot, Nikki thought — and the lieutenant had eventually agreed. Now the touch of the cool grip and the solid mass of the weapon was reassuring.

How much I've changed, she mused. *Packing a gun, going on a commando mission … How can I ever go back to my old life?*

Of course, if things went bad tonight, it was quite possible she'd never have the chance. There was a good possibility that her life would end here, in the jungles of Orrorsh.

Surprisingly, the thought didn't hold much fear. Now that they were underway, there was little time for personal fear. All that mattered was the mission. *We have to destroy the outpost*, she knew, *it's important*. Indirectly, the outpost was a threat to everyone, to the whole fabric of life in the world — and, if the Storm Knights were to be fully believed, in the entire "cosm" of "Core" Earth. What did one life, more or less, really matter compared to that? For the first time, she could really comprehend — not just intellectually accept — the Storm Knights' dedication.

Beames dropped back, letting Sergei take the lead alone. He walked in silence beside Nikki and Peter for a few minutes. Then he asked, "There's high technology working in the outpost, isn't that right?"

She nodded, describing the automated genetic analyzers, the powerful personal computer in her quarters. "The individual computers are hooked up to a central system, too," she explained. "I assume it's a mainframe."

"That'll be where they're storing all their data, right?" She nodded in answer to the Australian's question. "And where would that be?"

She thought about that for a moment. She'd never seen the mainframe computer, or heard anyone talk about it. But, the more she thought about it, the more she realized that it was the heart of the outpost. All of the important data coming from the labs would be concentrated there, stored on massive hard disks and backed up regularly onto tape for safety. *Where would you find the heart of the outpost?*

With the question phrased that way, the answer was obvious. "It'll be in the administration building," Nikki told the lieutenant. "That's where Eichiro's quarters and his office are. I think he'd want to be near the mainframe, just so he can keep a close eye on everything."

"Makes sense," Beames allowed. He walked in silence for another couple of minutes. Nikki could almost feel his mind working.

"Something that's been bothering me," the Australian said at last. "All that high tech … It shouldn't work in Orrorsh."

Nikki thought back to her conversations with O'Neil. The pilot had said much the same thing. There was something about the realm that was inimical to advanced technology. She reached out and tapped the sleek submachine-gun Beames carried at port-arms. *"That* works," she pointed out.

"That's different."

"Why?" she wanted to know.

The lieutenant was silent for a moment, ordering his thoughts. "Some people are able to change reality," he explained, "for a short time, in very localized areas. These people are able to set up what we call a 'reality bubble' around themselves. Within that bubble, the axioms operate the way they do in the person's home cosm. What that means is things work the way they should for that person, the way they'd work at home." He paused. "I'm from Melbourne, way down south. Orrorsh has never spread that far — thank God, and let's hope it stays that way. My 'home cosm' is Core Earth, which means all the technology you're used to works with no worries. Inside a reality bubble, that means that my equipment works just the way it's supposed to, no matter where I am — whether I'm in another realm or not."

"You can create a ... a reality bubble?" She struggled with the concept.

He nodded. "We call the ability being 'Possibility-rated.' That's what sets Storm Knights apart from 'ords.'"

Nikki looked down at the pistol on her hip. *I was able to fire the Viper*, she thought, and it was modern technology. *What did that mean?*

Beames was still talking. "Computers shouldn't work in Orrorsh. If they do, it means either that the computers themselves are 'talismans' — that means they carry their own reality with them — and somebody at the outpost is Possibility-rated and has the ability to 'charge' them." He frowned. "But the power needed to build a talisman ..." He shook his head. The idea obviously worried him. "It's not something any of us can do."

"You think Eichiro can?" Nikki wondered.

"Maybe." Beams frowned, "Eichiro might have the ability to 'make' a talisman — more likely, there's a group of 'stormers' — Possibility-rated bad guys — who help him, and he's their leader."

She looked at his face, his fixed expression. Nikki thought of the Matsushima Bay scientists. It is Eichiro. Tension was a twisting, acid knot in her stomach.

* * *

They crouched in the underbrush on the edge of the clearing. The stockade gate was closed — *of course!* — bathed in the harsh light of carbon arc lamps mounted on the top of the fence. In the brilliant wash of light, Nikki could see five security guards, bulky weapons — *machine guns?* — in their hands. They looked tense and alert, ready for anything.

Which only made sense, of course. It was less than twenty-four hours after the assault by monsters, the escape of the weretiger. They had to be worried about a renewed assault, this time maybe by a larger force.

She'd suggested to Beames that it might be better to wait a couple of days, until their level of readiness had decreased. But the lieutenant had shaken his head. "They lost people last night," he'd pointed out, "and you can bet your life Eichiro will be bringing more guards in to replace his losses. Maybe *lots* more, to beef up their security even more. We've got to hit them before reinforcements arrive. It's unfortunate they're on alert, but we don't have much choice." Nikki had been forced to agree.

A black figure, more sensed than seen, moved in the shadows outside the illumination of the arc lights, flitting silently along the outside of the fence. "Ninja," Nikki pointed out.

But the Storm Knights had already seen the gliding figure. Sergei had his weapon to his shoulder, sighting down the barrel, finger tense on the trigger. Waiting for Beames to give the word to open fire. But the lieutenant laid his hand on the Russian's shoulder, whispered something to him too quietly for Nikki to hear. Reluctantly, Sergei lowered his gun.

Leeds chuckled softly beside Nikki. "Our *stilyagin* is always a little overeager," he whispered.

"How are we going to do this?" Hollingforth asked, looking worriedly at the gate. "I don't think a frontal assault's a good idea."

Beames grinned. "Good observation," he whispered wryly. He thought for a moment. "Okay, three teams. I'll lead team one. Norman, Ry, you're with me. Sergeant MacHeath too. We'll take two of the Thais, and head west. We'll go in by the river." The Storm Knights he named nodded agreement.

"Dusty, you lead team two. Take Sergei, Hollingforth, Black and Ms. Carlson, plus the two Victorian soldiers. Head east, you'll go in by the river too." He grinned at Nikki. "Sorry about that, Ms.

Carlson, but you're going to get wet again.

"And Sergeant Songgram" — he inclined his head to one of the Thais — "you're going to be our diversion." The Thai officer nodded acceptance. "Give us fifteen minutes to get into position, then blow the hell out of the gate. Stay under cover, I don't want anyone killed. But do everything you can to make them think it's a major assault." He looked around. "Does everyone understand their assignments?" Nods, and a chorus of muttered agreements confirmed everyone was ready.

The Australian smiled. "Okay, you know the drill," he reminded everyone. "No non-combattant casualties, but I want you all back in one piece. Find the mainframe computer, blow it to shrapnel. Torch the labs. Then get the hell out. Make your own way back, we meet at the camp. Everyone got that?" He didn't need to wait for an answer; the expressions on the men's faces were enough. He slapped Dusty Rhodes on the shoulder. "Okay, team two, move out. Team one, on me. Fifteen minutes, Sergeant," he reiterated to Songgram. "Let's get it done."

* * *

Dusty Rhodes had the lead. Despite his size, the burly Texan moved like a wraith through the jungle. The underbrush seemed to part before him, of its own free will, and close behind him without a sound. The others tried to emulate him, but there was no way they could match his skill. Sergei moved well, too, but he seemed almost clumsy in comparison to Rhodes. As for Nikki herself, no matter how hard she tried to remain silent, the noise of her passing sounded — in her own ears, at least — like a rhinoceros crashing through the brush.

They kept a relatively fast pace, and it took only ten minutes for them to reach the margin of the clearing on the river bank, to the east of the outpost. They crouched in the underbrush while Rhodes scrutinized the stockade fence and the river.

"How deep's the water out at the end of the fence there?" he asked Nikki.

She shrugged. "I don't know exactly. Too deep for me to wade."

"Kinda what I figured. Guess we're going swimming." His face split in a rebel smile, his teeth white in contrast to his tanned skin. "Lock and load, boys and girls," he ordered. "It's almost party time. When the crap hits the fan, we move *fast*."

Around Nikki, the members of team two gave their weapons one last check. Rundle and Murphy worked the bolts on their rifles, sliding rounds into the chambers, then made sure the bayonets were properly mounted. Hollingforth and Black held large, brutal-looking revolvers — held them uncomfortably, as though they weren't familiar with such things. (*Gentlemen probably don't use guns*, she thought with grim amusement. *Except for hunting, of course.*)

Nikki pulled out her own pistol, glad that the mechanism worked the same way as the Viper. She pulled back the slide, cocking the pistol, the way Dei had taught her.

Dei. She remembered his pleading cries for help, her flechette rounds flaying the rotting flesh from the back of the zombie — with no real effect. The horrible sounds as the creature tore out the security guard's throat. *At least there'll be no monsters tonight*, she reassured herself, *just ninjas and security guards. Bad enough ... but if I have to shoot — and I hope it never comes to that — at least bullets are going to stop them.*

She checked her watch. Songgram and the other soldiers should be starting their diversion any moment.

As if looking at her watch had been the cue, the night was split with the sounds of automatic weapons fire.

For a few seconds, the only reports were the thin, ripping bursts from the submachine-guns wielded by the Thais. Then came a volley of deeper-throated, stuttering blasts — obviously the guns carried by the Nagara guards. It sounded to Nikki as though a full-fledged war had broken out.

Dusty Rhodes was on his feet, already heading for the river. "Mount up," he ordered.

Nikki and the others waded out into the water. For the third time in two nights, she felt the muddy water soaking through her clothing. She held the Walther pistol high, making sure it stayed dry.

The water seemed shallower on this side of the outpost. She'd almost reached the end of the stockade fence before the mud underfoot shelved away and she had to swim. She rolled over on her back, which made it easier to keep the pistol above water, and started to kick.

Rhodes, Sergei and the two Victorian explorers had little trouble making headway. With their heavy rifles, Rundle and Murphy were having a harder go of it — *I hope they ditched their boots*, she thought — but they struggled gamely on.

The current plucked at her baggy clothing. For a few moments she thought she wasn't making any headway at all against the river flow. But she needn't have worried. It took less than a minute for them all to get past the extension of the fence. She changed direction, kicking hard for the bank, trying to get into shallower water before the current drove her back against the stockade. Her feet touched bottom, and she quickly stood up. Staying close together in a tight knot, team two waded toward the bank.

There was no-one to see them as they came ashore, no guards to blow them apart with assault rifles, no ninjas to cut them in two with *katanas*. Nobody moved in the area of the compound they could see. The heavy gunfire still rang out from the direction of the gate as

Songgram and his men continued their diversion.

Then, suddenly, there came the ripping of a submachine-gun from the west, along the river bank. She turned to see if she could spot something, but the building against which Dei had died blocked her view of any muzzle flashes. Even without seeing, though, she knew what it had to mean: team one — the group led by Beames — had met opposition.

Rhodes obviously recognized the significance as quickly as she had. "Double time," he ordered quietly. Then he and Sergei took off in a fast, crouching run, past the building containing Funakoshi's lab, toward the large administration building. The remainder of team two followed, guns at the ready.

Team two was no more than ten yards from the administration building when the rear door flew open and a squad of armored security guards burst out, carrying assault rifles. Both groups saw each other at the same instant. Sergei fired first, his long burst cutting three guards down in their tracks. Then, simultaneously, Rhodes and the Nagara guards opened fire. Two more guards were down before Nikki could even react. A burst of fire stitched Murphy from crotch to throat, and he went down without a sound. Rundle's big rifle boomed, and another guard dropped with a guttural cry.

Something whip-cracked past Nikki's ear, and she shrieked. She brought the Walther up, squeezed the trigger. The heavy pistol boomed, the recoil brutalizing her hand and wrist. She hadn't taken time to aim — the shot had just been an instinctive response — and she didn't know where the bullet had gone. She tried to drag the big gun down, back onto line.

But there was nothing left to shoot at. Precise bursts from the two Storm Knights' submachine-guns had put the remaining guards down.

There was more shooting from the west side of the

compound. Beames and his team had hit heavy resistance, Nikki realized. They'd probably be too busy protecting themselves to do much about the administration building. But the rear door was still standing open. There was nothing between team two and their objective.

They sprinted for the lighted doorway. Sergei was the first one through …

And the next one to die. A brilliant red beam, about as thick as a pencil, flicked into existence for an moment from a source Nikki couldn't see, struck the young Russian full in the chest. With an explosion of bloody steam, Sergei's torso burst as the water in his body flashed instantaneously into vapor. He fell without a sound, undeniably and messily dead.

The others flung themselves back from the doorway — Rhodes only after he'd sent a quick burst of fire into the building. The beam blinked on again, for a split second looking as solid as a glowing plastic rod, probing harmlessly out into the night. This time Nikki heard the weapon's report, an electronic *zip* sound.

Crouching low, Rhodes ducked around the doorframe, triggered a longer burst. The carbon dioxide laser beam — that's what it had to be, Nikki realized — lanced out again, passing a foot above his head. A second later, Rundle too craned around the frame, ready to send a heavy rifle slug at the enemy Nikki hadn't even seen yet.

The Victorian trooper wasn't as lucky as Rhodes. The laser flashed, missing him but striking his rifle. The cartridge in the chamber detonated, blowing the rifle breech apart a hand's-breadth away from the soldier's face. He staggered back, screaming, his face torn by fragments of metal.

"Get out of the way!" Rhodes yelled. A little needlessly: Nikki, Peter and Black were flattened against the outside walls of the building on either side of the doorway. Nikki's heart was pounding, and there was the sharp, copper taste of fear in her mouth.

"Damn it to hell," the Texan muttered almost musingly. "Enough of the goddamn subtlety." He pulled something from a pocket of his camouflage jacket — a small sphere not much larger than a golf ball. *A hand grenade*, Nikki realized with a shock. He pulled the ring at the top, let the small lever it restrained spring away. He counted quietly to himself — a pause that seemed like forever to Nikki. Then he rolled it through the doorway into the hall.

He'd timed it perfectly. The ruby beam flicked out again, missing him by inches as he flattened himself against the outside wall. Simultaneously, the grenade detonated. Splinters whizzed through the air out of the door, and the pressure pulse made Nikki feel as though someone had slapped cupped hands over both her ears. Almost before the shrapnel had stopped flying, he spun around the frame, crouched in the doorway, emptying his submachine-gun in one long burst.

No laser beam licked out to blow him apart. Quickly tugging out his empty magazine and slamming a replacement into place, he signalled for them to follow as he darted in the door.

There were only three left to follow him. Rundle wasn't dead — he was on the ground moaning, clutching his bleeding face — but he was in no condition to take any further part in the night's work. Nikki looked back at him, sympathetic pain knotting her stomach. She wanted to help him, but there wasn't much they could do now. This had to be a quick hit-and- run operation if they wanted to survive it — Beames had made that clear during the trek to the outpost — and Rhodes needed support. "We'll be back for you," she told the wounded soldier quietly. Then she followed Black and Hollingforth in through the door.

The grenade had made one unholy mess of the

corridor. An interior door to the right, about ten feet down the hallway, was hanging on one hinge, and fragments had punched holes in the walls.

It had made an even worse mess of the man who'd been wielding the laser gun, she saw. Her stomach did a queasy flip-flop, and she tasted bile. He was wearing heavy armor of some kind — segmented plates of what looked like metal, with some kind of compact mechanisms at the joints — but it hadn't helped him much. The grenade had detonated right at his feet, and the combination of shrapnel and overpressure had almost literally torn him apart.

Rhodes was prodding the gory remains with the toe of his combat boot. "RKD armor," he said obscurely, "heavy duty crap.

"Watch the hallway," he ordered, bending to examine the laser weapon. The guard had dropped the business end — a deceptively small gun that somewhat resembled the Storm Knights' submachine-guns — but the power pack to which a cable connected the projector was still on the dead man's back. "Busted," the Texas pronounced. "Shoot, coulda used that bad boy."

He stood back up. "Okay, Ms. Nikki, you're our guide. Which way to the computer room?"

Nikki looked around her. She'd never been in this part of the administration building before, didn't know where the mainframe computer might be. But of course none of the others would know either; they'd never even been inside the outpost before. And that made finding their goal her responsibility, didn't it?

She thought for a moment. "Probably in the middle of the building," she said, pointing down the hallway. It was about twenty-five feet long, ending at a grey metal door. "That looks promising."

Rhodes nodded. "Sounds good to me. I'll take point. You three watch my back." He hesitated. "And check your targets, team one might be coming in here too."

That adds some complexity, doesn't it? Nikki realized as the Texan moved off down the corridor. *Damn it, I'm not cut out for this.* Hollingforth and Black followed him immediately — brutal revolvers still held tentatively — leaving her to bring up the rear. She walked past the door to her right, blown almost off its hinges.

Movement. A muffled sound, a minuscule movement of the air.

Beside her!

She tried to spin, tried to bring her Walther up.

But something smashed down with crushing impact on her right wrist, sending bolts of pain up her arm into her shoulder. She felt bones crack. The pistol fell from suddenly nerveless fingers. Something — hard as a bar of iron — locked across her throat, cutting off her cry of pain and dragging her brutally backward.

Dusty Rhodes heard — or sensed — something. He turned — seemingly in slow motion, as Nikki's time sense suddenly kicked into overdrive — whipping his submachine-gun around.

Too late. Something boomed next to Nikki's ear — a double report, a brutal *ba-bam*, almost more felt than heard. A double muzzle plume flared, scorching her right cheek and lashing it with unburned powder.

The two bullets caught the Storm Knight in the forehead, exploding out the back of his head. The sheer impact knocked him over backward, his death spasm emptying his weapon into the ceiling.

Peter and Black turned — *much* too late. Nikki expected to see them blown apart the same way as the laconic Texan, expected to follow them into oblivion a second later.

But there were no further gunshots. Something hot — a painful, burning circle — pressed against Nikki's right temple. It took her an instant to realize it was a gun muzzle, still hot from the passage of the two bullets.

Nikki's ears were ringing painfully, and she was slightly dizzy from the concussion of the double gunshot. The bar — or whatever it was — was still across her throat, making breathing difficult. And her right wrist arm, from the broken wrist right the way up to her shoulder, felt like it was on fire. She tried to turn her head, tried to see who — or what — was holding her.

"Don't move, Carrson-*san*," a familiar voice hissed in Japanese. *Eichiro!* she realized with a sinking feeling in her stomach. To reinforce the words, the gun muzzle ground painfully into her temple. She gasped, her eyes blurring with tears. "And don't *you* move, either," the voice added in English.

Peter and the professor were standing ten feet away from her, their pistols levelled ineffectually at Eichiro behind her. They couldn't shoot — they knew it, she knew it and Eichiro knew it — without hitting her. She saw Peter's face twist in an uncharacteristic snarl as the full realization of his helplessness hit him. They couldn't do anything to help her..

But maybe *she* could. She shifted a little in Eichiro's grip, pressing back a little against him, trying to sense exactly where his body was positioned. If she could figure that out, maybe a quick elbow to the groin would settle the matter …

"I said *don't move*, Carrson-*san*," Eichiro grated. He viciously jerked on her throat, so hard she felt her trachea was about to rupture. Ruthlessly he dragged her backward, forcing her to walk backward. The slightest hesitation was rewarded by a tightening of the agonizing grip. He pulled her back, through the drunkenly hanging door, out of the hallway, into a small anteroom. Then through another door into a much larger room.

The air was suddenly cold against her wet skin. She knew where she was without even having to look — the air-conditioned computer room. *Of course*, she told herself, *why put the computer room in the middle of a building? If it's near the outside you don't have to run the air ducts so far to vent them to the outside.* If she could have drawn enough breath, she would have sobbed. I should have known that. If she had known it, Eichiro wouldn't have got her, and Rhodes wouldn't have died. She wrenched against his grip.

It was totally useless. With a hissing chuckle, Eichiro just tightened his grip, cutting off her air altogether. The world swam before her eyes, tiny points of light drifted around the periphery of her vision. Then he released the pressure incrementally, just enough to let her breathe again. She dragged air gratefully into her lungs, each breath feeling like torture as it passed through her brutalized throat.

As her vision cleared, Nikki could see that Peter and Black had followed them into the computer room. They were still about the same distance away, still with their guns aimed, ready ... and useless. She saw Peter move slightly to his left — probably trying to flank Eichiro — but the manager took another step back, dragging Nikki with him, until his back was safely planted against one of the big tape drive cabinets.

"This is what you were coming for, wasn't it, barbarians?" Eichiro almost cooed, in English again. "The computer room? Well, now you've found it. How unfortunate it will never help you." He chuckled again, then suddenly he spat, "Drop your guns. Now."

Neither of the men moved. Peter's expression made him look like a biblical conception of an avenging angel, and Black's face was twisted with pure hatred.

"I'll kill her if you don't."

"If you harm her, we will certainly kill you." Peter Hollingforth stated it unemotionally, as absolutely and unequivocally as he'd state a physical law. "Count on it." His eyes looked cold, almost as soulless as Sergei's had been.

"I won't hurt her if you drop your guns," Eichiro offered, trying — and failing — to keep his voice reasonable. "If you drop your guns, I'll let you all go." He gave a short bark of laughter. "Do you think your lives matter to me? All that matters is the success of this station."

To her surprise, Nikki realized that half of Eichiro's statement was the absolute truth. *Success is all that matters, isn't it?* she asked herself. *That's the nature of life in "new Japan."* But as to the rest of his statement?

"He's lying," she shouted. She gasped with pain as he wrenched on her throat, but she wouldn't be silenced. "Drop your guns and he'll kill us all," she croaked.

"Decide!" snapped Eichiro. "Stand there long enough and my guards will get here. And *they'll* kill you, make no mistake about it. They'll probably want to execute Carrson-*san* too, as a traitor to Nagara, and what possible incentive would I have to stop them?" From her peripheral vision, she saw him smile — the heartless smile of a shark. "The only chance you have for survival is to trust me. Drop your guns."

For a long moment, nobody moved. Then first Hollingforth, followed by Black, lowered their revolvers. The two heavy pieces of ordnance thudded to the floor.

"*Nooo!*" Nikki screamed, but her howl of anguish was drowned out by Eichiro's maniacal laughter.

The hot circle of his gun barrel was gone from her temple as he brought the weapon to bear on Peter.

The gun was gone …

She tried to lash back, hurt Eichiro, break his bones. Kill him. But she had no strength left. Half-choked, her head was swimming. Physically he was much more powerful than she was. There was nothing she could do, just watch while he killed her friends. Two *more* of her friends.

No!! This isn't right, her mind raged. *This isn't the way the world should be. Monsters, ninjas, laser guns, corporate killers. This isn't the way the world* is! Everything around her — everything she'd known for the past few years — was some kind of perversion of the real world. The world seen in some horrible, dark, distorting mirror, like something in a corrupt funhouse. *This isn't RIGHT!!* she screamed mentally. Outrage, anger, hatred — they all raged in her chest.

And then there was something else there, too, alloyed with the burning emotions. A new heat — emotional heat, but also *physical* heat — that flared inside her. She gasped at the onslaught of the new sensation, felt it lash through her body like an electric charge.

Images of home, of her childhood, struck her with the impact of a speeding bullet train. Her friends, her family … That was the way it was before the Possibility Wars. That was the way it still was in the places Beames had called "Core Earth." That was the way it *should* be.

Not like this.

This is wrong.

WRONG!!

A sudden muscle spasm ripped a scream from her torn throat. Tore her away from Eichiro's grip. She spun to face him.

Her vision was blurred — inexplicably. It was if a mist was building around her and Eichiro, *between* them. A mist that pulsed and throbbed with power, flickering around the periphery with electrical discharges that shimmered like heat lightning.

I'm dying, she told herself. *Eichiro must have cut off oxygen to her brain for too long. I'm hallucinating.*

But no. Out of the corner of her eye, she saw Peter and the professor reeling back, hands raised to shield their faces from the energy lashing through the computer room. *Then it's real?*

Eichiro's face was frozen in a rictus of horror. He

muttered a Japanese phrase she'd never heard before and couldn't directly translate — *something about a maelstrom?* His massive pistol fell from nerveless fingers.

She tried to back away from him, but found herself frozen. It wasn't as if her limbs were simply immobilized. Her brain was sending out the correct nerve impulses, and seemed to be receiving the appropriate feedback from the muscles. According to her physical sensations, she should have been backpedalling as fast as her legs could carry her, back and out of the computer room, away from … *whatever it was* that was manifesting itself between herself and Eichiro.

That's the way it felt. But she could clearly see that she wasn't moving. Her body was as rigid as a statue. *Which do I believe?* she asked herself. *My body or my mind? Or are they both lying to me?*

The mist was getting thicker, still pulsating with some impossible, internal energy. The sheets of heat lightning were brighter, more frequent, illuminating the computer room like photographer's strobes. *What in the name of God is happening?*

And then, in a silent concussion, reality fragmented around her.

* * *

The words hit her from nowhere — she's never heard them before, but she knows they're right. She knows they mean the same thing as Eichiro's phrase, the one she didn't understand.

Reality Storm.

The world flickers and shifts in her view. The walls, floor and ceiling of the computer room warp and twist — or at least they seem to. Is it just an effect of the distorting fog? Or is it something else?

Wind howls around her, plucking at her clothing, whipping her hair wildly. Everything seems to be happening in slow motion. She can see and sense the motion of each discrete hair, as though time is passing at a fraction of its normal rate. She sees Eichiro open his mouth to scream. The sound, when it comes, is low-pitched, horrible — something not quite human.

The heat lightning strobes so brightly that she screws her eyes shut against its actinic brilliance. But, impossibly, she can still see clearly, even though her eyelids are closed.

The mist surrounding her and Eichiro thickens, until it becomes opaque. They are contained in a small bubble of clear air, beyond which there is ...

Nothing.

That's what it feels like to her. This region, this bubble, is all that exists, all that ever existed. Beyond its grey periphery is Nothing — non-existence, Chaos, the Void. How could she ever have believed that there was ever any more to existence? America, Japan, Sumatra, Orrorsh ... Meaningless creations of her brain. This is the whole universe, just her and Eichiro.

She hears a sound — originating from nowhere, from everywhere. The slow, deep tolling of a great iron bell. The sound surrounds her, penetrates her, its vibrations quivering through her bones, through every cell and fiber of her being. With each stroke of the bell, the grey nothingness surrounding them seems to darken momentarily, then return to its original level. And with each continued stroke, the darkening effect becomes magnified. Soon, each time the bell sounds, there is a moment of blackness, of blindness.

What is the sound? she asks herself. The answer takes a fraction of a second — or a millennium — to emerge. It's my own heart.

She feels the fluctuations of light and darkness, feels them right down to her core. She is linked to them somehow. The sensation intensifies. With each moment of darkness, she ceases to exist; when the light returns, she is recreated anew. But is the recreation perfect? She thinks not — with each turn of the cycle, there is a change, so subtle that she cannot identify it.

The wind intensifies around her, its ululating wail synchronized with the light-dark creation-dissolution cycle. For a moment she wonders whether Peter and Black managed to escape the Reality Storm. But then she remembers that they don't exist, they never existed.

For an instant she has forgotten Eichiro. Now she feels his presence, pressing down on her, wrenching at the fabric of her existence. She screams silently as something tears within her — not something physical, it's much more complex than that. She feels as though part of herself — part of her individuality, part of what makes her Nikki Carlson — has been wrested from her. With the psychic pain comes fear — overwhelming terror. If he can tear away something of her very existence, why can't he take all of it? What would be left? A soulless husk, a drone, going through its daily existence without any thought about the big picture. Images of the milling crowds of Tokyo fill her mind, a multitude of sararimen, of lemmings …

No! I will *never* become like that!

With all her energy, she lashes out at Eichiro, driving her outrage, her hatred into him in punishing psychic waves. You'll never break me, you perversion! She sees her foe reel backward, as though struck by a shotgun blast. For an instant she thinks he will be driven into the greyness that surrounds their pocket universe. But at the last instant he recovers.

He is at her again, she feels his taint as he rips at her sanity, at her grasp on reality. But with an intense effort she fights back.

She has him on the defensive now, she realizes. He tries to erect a barrier before her, anything to protect himself from her onslaught, but it is futile. Driven by the rage that burns in her core, she is unstoppable. She tears at him, peeling away layer after layer of his existence.

Images fill her mind once more. More hordes of faceless wageslaves, soulless, hopeless. Squalid tenements in a city that sprawls from horizon to horizon, millions of people *packed into each square mile. For an instant she thinks this is Tokyo. But no, it's somewhere else — somewhere that can't exist, shouldn't exist, but does. No!*

She rips deeper into the corruption that is Agatamori Eichiro. She senses his paranoia, his ruthless drive. They soil her psyche as she claws deeper. It is like ripping layers from an onion, except that each layer is like armor. There seems to be no end to them — below each layer is nothing but another layer ...

And then, suddenly, she is at the core. The armor is gone, the protection is gone. Naked, exposed, the truth that is Eichiro lies before her. *Pathetic,* she thinks for a moment. But then the anger returns, and she lashes out one final time.

She sees Eichiro's physical body lurch backward again. This time there is nothing he can do to stop himself, and he plummets into the greyness.

And again reality fragments.

It is like a nightmare, a nightmare that never ends, as the Reality Storm — the Maelstrom — tears at her.

She is a child again, sitting on the back porch of her parents' house. The sun is warm on her skin, the sweet smell of new-mown grass in her nostrils. A bird on the apple tree bursts into song.

Shift.

The river current tugs at her clothing. A smell of vegetable decay fills her nostrils. Her body shivers, not with cold, but with anticipation of the upcoming assault. Keeping her gun clear of the water she swims on.

Shift.

The air is crisp, and the dry snow crunches under her skis. The Rocky Mountains rear around her. Shift.

O'Neil smiles at her as they lean against the deck rail of the freighter.

Shift.

With a jolt, the plane sets down at Narita Airport. Excitement tingles in her breast. Japan at last!

Shift.

Toshikazu smiles at her, his teeth red with blood. "Die with me, Nikki!"

Shift. Fresh-baked bread. Shift. Gunfire, screams.

Shift. An arm around her waist, a warm presence beside her.

Shift. Sergei's empty eyes. Shift. Toshikazu's smile. Shift. O'Neil's laugh. Shift. Shift. Shift.

Nothing.

* * *

She was ... *somewhere*. A room, its walls lined with electronic devices. The air was cold on her skin. *Where am I? Who am I?* For an instant, she couldn't decide whether she was Nikki Carlson or Agatamori Eichiro.

"Nikki?" A tentative voice from behind her.

Reality flooded back. She was in the computer room of the outpost. She looked around for the grey fog that had enveloped her, some remnant of the Reality Storm that had almost consumed her. But there was nothing.

Peter Hollingforth was at the door, staring at her in undisguised concern. "Nikki?" he asked again.

"I'm alright," she told him, a quaver in her voice. "I'm alright." She turned back to look at Eichiro.

The man was on the floor, slumped against one of the large computer tape drives. Physically, he looked unchanged. But to some other sense — something beyond the physical — the change was undeniable.

He looked up at Nikki, and she saw the change in his eyes, in his face. The harsh, cunning gleam was gone from those eyes, the stubborn set of the jaw subtly changed. For the first time, when she looked at him Nikki saw not a ruthless senior executive of a megacorporation, but a young man, not yet out of his thirties, little more than a decade her senior. Eichiro looked around him, blinked uncomprehendingly.

"Eichiro-*san*?" she asked quietly.

He looked up at her again. "*Hai*?" he responded.

"Yes?" She could see him struggling with his memory. "*Sumimasen*. Excuse me, but …"

"It's alright," she told him quietly. She turned away from the man who was — yet, in another way, *wasn't* — Agatamori Eichiro, and smiled at Peter. "It's alright," she said again.

She walked to the door, while around her the computers began to shut down.

Epilogue

The flames from the burning lab buildings were rising into the sky, reflecting a shifting red light from the low-hanging clouds. *Burn!* Nikki thought fiercely, looking back over her shoulder as she led the remnants of team two through the jungle. *Burn, all of it, right down to the ground, so there's nothing left. Nothing at all.*

The outpost was doomed, there was no doubt about it. The fires set by the other Storm Knights would definitely spread, until everything was consumed, and there was nothing anybody could do about it. Even as Nikki led Peter, Black, and the wounded Rundle back into the jungle, the surviving security guards were herding the scientists, technicians and others onto the riverines.

Where will they go? she found herself wondering. *Can they call for help, or won't the radios work any more? Will they ever make it back to Japan?* She didn't know, and found she was just too tired to care.

What about Eichiro? She could imagine the security guards politely ushering the transformed young man aboard one of the riverines, with formal protocol that he wouldn't understand why he deserved. The image was both amusing and a little pathetic.

* * *

They reached the camp about dawn. The surviving Storm Knights and the Thai soldiers were already there when what was left of team two staggered into the clearing.

Losses had been heavy, Nikki saw. Of the dozen Thai regulars, only half had survived. From team one, Norman Leeds was dead, and both Ryan Davis and Sergeant MacHeath were seriously wounded. And then, of course, there were the casualties from team two: Dusty Rhodes, Sergei and Murphy all dead, and Rundle almost blinded. *A heavy price to pay*, Nikki thought. *Was it worth it?*

It was to the surviving Storm Knights. There was no celebration — too many friends had been lost for that — but there was an air of grim satisfaction, of an important job well done.

They think we've won, Nikki mused. *Maybe we have, in a way*. With the outpost gone, and Eichiro broken, the Special Projects initiative had suffered an incredible — possible insurmountable — setback. The contract between Nagara and Jean Malraux would go unfulfilled.

But Nagara still exists, she realizes, *all the other megacorporations still exist. There'll be more contracts, and more deaths, more Storm Knights doing what they can to turn things around.* In the grand scheme of things, this wasn't any more a victory than the capture of a pawn early in a game of chess. *The game goes on, and nobody knows until it's over who's won and who's lost.*

The surviving Storm Knights and the Thais gave themselves only a couple of hours' rest before they started striking camp. When they were almost ready to move on, Lt. Dick Beames came over to talk to Nikki and Peter.

"Where are you heading now, Leftenant?" she asked him.

He smiled tiredly. "To the coast," he said, "then south to where we left our boats. Over to Singapore, then north and out of Orrorsh. Then another mission, I'm afraid." He chuckled. "No rest for the wicked." He paused. "And you? You know that you're both more than welcome to accompany us. We'll get you to Bangkok — that's right on the edge of Orrorsh, so you can depend on the technology — and from there you can catch a plane to anywhere in the world. How about it?"

It was Peter who spoke first. "I thank you for your offer," he said formally. "I have to admit to a real curiosity about the rest of this world. But we have a task to perform, Professor Black and I. Just like you do, Leftenant. We can no more turn aside from that than you can from *your* duties."

The soldier nodded in understanding.

Hollingforth turned to Nikki. "And your plans, Miss Carlson?"

She looked into his eyes. There was a question there that he couldn't bring himself to ask. "I'm sorry," she said, answering that unspoken question. "This isn't my world. I belong elsewhere."

Peter kept his expression carefully schooled, but still she could sense his sadness. She felt it too — he was an honorable man, a true friend, and somebody with the potential to become, with time, more than a friend. *But he has his mission,* she told herself, *and it's not mine.*

But what is *my mission?*

She turned back to Beames. "After Bangkok, where are you going?"

He grinned wryly. "Back to Japan, I'm afraid. We've heard rumors of great advances by one of Kanawa's weapons labs. It's something we've got to check out."

Back to Japan. Back to that bleak, depressing, paranoid culture …

Yes, but for the purpose of striking a blow against those that control it. That makes it all different, doesn't it?

"And what about you, Ms. Carlson?" the Australian asked.

What about *me?* Return to the States? Go back to school? Use what she'd learned in Japan at some research lab? A normal life — a normal life at last, back in the safety of her own country …

How could she do that, knowing what she knew now? Knowing of the Storm Knights, struggling — and dying — to protect people who didn't even comprehend their existence? *No.*

She looked up into Beames' face with a smile. "Is there room for another on your team?" she asked.

DON'T MISS THESE OTHER GREAT

PRODUCTS!

Adventures and Supplements

☐ Full Moon Draw $12.00
☐ Pixaud's Practical Grimoire $15.00
☐ Kanawa Personal Weapons $13.00
☐ Kanawa Heavy Weapons $13.00
☐ Kanawa Land Vehicles $15.00
☐ Operation: Hard Sell $12.00
☐ The Land Below $15.00
☐ Crucible of Pain $12.00
☐ Creatures of Aysle $18.00
☐ Creatures of Orrorsh $18.00
☐ Cylent Scream $12.00
☐ The Storm Knights' Guide to the Possibility Wars $15.00
☐ The Temple of Rec Stalek $12.00
☐ City of Demons $12.00
☐ Central Valley Gate $12.00
☐ Infiniverse Update, Vol. 1 ....$18.00
☐ Los Angeles Citybook $18.00
☐ When Axioms Collide $12.00
☐ Ravagons $15.00

**If you can't find the game product you want
at your local hobby shop or book store,
use the coupon below.**

- -

West End Games
RR3 Box 2345, Honesdale, PA 18431

Please send me the items I have checked.

I am enclosing $_____

(please add $3.00* to cover postage and handling for the
first item and $1.25 for each additional item).

Send check or money order — no cash or C.O.D.'s please.

Name:_____

Address:_____

City:_____

State:_____Zip:_____Tel:(____)_____

*For deliveries to Canada, add US $5.00 for the first item ordered and US $2.50
for each additional item.
Allow 4-6 weeks for delivery.